REA

Master
— of —
Disaster

a tale of manifestation, mayhem & magic

Master
— of —
Disaster

Jan Longwell-Smiley

for the evolving human spirit

HAMPTON ROADS
PUBLISHING COMPANY, INC.

Cover design by Grace Pedalino
Cover art by Patrick Cardiff

For information write:
Hampton Roads Publishing Company, Inc.
134 Burgess Lane
Charlottesville, VA 22902

Or call: 804-296-2772
FAX: 804-296-5096
e-mail: hrpc@hrpub.com
Web site: http://www.hrpub.com

If you are unable to order this book from your local
bookseller, you may order directly from the publisher.
Quantity discounts for organizations are available.
Call 1-800-766-8009, toll-free.

Library of Congress Catalog Card Number: 98-71587

ISBN 1-57174-105-4

10 9 8 7 6 5 4 3 2 1

Printed on acid-free paper in Canada

Dedication

To Tom, whose support made this book possible. You thrashed your way through the twists and turns of the metaphysical maze with me, a quest that took us from sleepless nights and supernatural sights to magical rites and astral flights. A great husband then, and still a great friend, thanks for bringing home the bacon (soy, of course!), and giving me the freedom to write this book.

Table of Contents

Chapter One

Of Backward Drivers
& She-Demons
from Hell

This time the car didn't just appear out of nowhere; this time he saw it coming straight at him, in reverse. He swerved to the far side of the dirt road, trying to avoid a collision, honking his horn hysterically. The car swerved, too, as though homing in on his intentions. In a last-ditch effort to avoid the inevitable, he threw his car into reverse, but the momentum of the other vehicle put him at a disadvantage. He braced himself . . .

"Jeez, buddy, I didn't see ya! Where the hell did you come from, anyway?"

How many times had he heard those words before? Rubbing the knot on his head, he tried to focus on the face that was peering through his window. Then he turned on his wipers to clear away the antifreeze spewing on the windshield, attempting to gauge the damage done this time around. Totaled again.

The backward driver headed for a nearby farmhouse to call the police, leaving him alone to ponder his plight. What was the tally now? Eight? Nine? He'd lost count. But once again, it wasn't his fault. Andrew Morgan, master-of-manifestation-in-training, was a victim of a universe gone mad.

He gripped the steering wheel tightly and shouted to the empty road: "I hate the Universe; I hate my life! Why does everything always get so screwed up when I'm doing everything right?" Thinking about the job he was supposed to start the next day, he banged his head on the wheel again and winced in pain. "Why isn't it working for me? I just wish I could understand it all . . ."

"Are you sure about that, Morgan?"

Andrew spun around, looking for the person behind the voice. "Huh?" The car was empty himself. "Oh shit, now I'm hearing things . . ."

"Not things, silly—thoughts. But then again, thoughts are things."

"Now wait just a minute . . . who are you? Where are you?" His questions were met with silence. "Great, now I'm talking to myself!"

"Exactly! Maybe you're a faster learner than I thought—"

The voice was suddenly interrupted. "Hey, buddy, you all right?"

Andrew jumped at the sound of the backward driver. "Yeah, I'm fine . . . except maybe for this bump on my head." He peered in the rear-view mirror just to double-check the truth of his words. His handsome face was still in one piece—just a small gash on his brow, half hidden by his tousled, sandy-brown hair.

But even with such a minor injury, Andrew had a hard time keeping his attention trained on filling out the police report. It wasn't every day that he heard voices out of nowhere. Finally sloughing it off as some sort of temporary aftershock from hitting his head, he concentrated on making arrangements to have his car towed away, and hitched a ride back to his apartment. He had thought about calling Amy, his latest girlfriend, for a ride, but she had dumped him the week before for a paving contractor with a Porsche. The only reason he had been on this particular dirt road in the middle of God-knows-where in the first place was to spy on her at her new boyfriend's country home.

Fiddling with his keys in the dark, he ducked behind a bush to avoid running into his landlord whom he spotted making his way across the courtyard. Sure enough, the old geezer was headed straight for his place. Andrew had run out of excuses. Just four months ago he'd used his patented I-wrecked-my-car-but-the-insurance-money-will-be-here-any-day excuse. Actually, it had taken a full month for the insurance check to arrive, which had pushed the landlord's patience and good will to the limit. He wouldn't buy the same story again, even though history was repeating itself.

After making sure the coast was clear, Andrew slipped silently into his apartment. He resisted turning on the lights that would betray his presence, and instead collapsed on the threadbare couch, not even bothering to remove his shoes. As he lay there in the dark, he stared at a spot of moonlight that was skipping across the rotating blades of the ceiling fan. The same moon, he thought, that had cast its light upon Amy's beautiful face six months before, singling her out from all the other girls at the beach party, as though to say, "There she is, the girl of your dreams, the one you've been waiting for."

How could it be, Andrew wondered, that Amy had deserted him just when he needed her most? And for another guy, one with—of all things—an exact replica of his dream car! He knew Amy was mad at him for not getting his act together and find-ing—or should he say, keeping?—a real job. Didn't she understand that anyone could dig a ditch or wait tables, but that he was destined to do great things? The right opportunity just hadn't found its way into his life yet, but he knew it would. After all, he was only twenty-six; he still had time.

In some respects, as far as he was concerned, he was actually ahead of almost everyone else, for Andrew was a serious student of manifestation—the art and practice of mentally drawing objects and events into one's reality that weren't there before. He knew full well that if any changes were to come about in his life, they first had to occur in the realm of thought and imagination. So, each day he religiously practiced his techniques of creative visualization to make his life better. He was a man obsessed.

Andrew bought any and every book on the subject of manifes-tation he came across, especially those that taught him how to create money. He'd just as soon go without eating as chance missing one piece of the prosperity puzzle. He believed, as many of the books insisted, that those who chose to rely on working for a living as their only means of drawing wealth and abundance into their lives would be stuck going that route. There were other options in life besides "work"; simpler, easier ways to make a buck; nine-to-fiving it just didn't cut it with him. Although, Andrew admitted to himself, he often had to cave in and take some menial job, just to survive until he mastered the art of manifestation.

Dollar signs swirling in his head, he closed his eyes to the dingy apartment and drifted off, escaping into his favorite place, into the world of dreams, where sometimes—if he was lucky—his desires manifested themselves. ". . . Though from what I've observed, it usually takes you a while to catch on." Jolted by the continuation of the voice he had heard earlier in his head, his eyes sprang open. There were his windshield wipers, methodically working to wipe away the now-dried antifreeze. Andrew sat up and blinked, trying to sort out his conjured images from the ones before his eyes. The dirt road was gone, and was replaced by a setting of wrecked and rusting cars. Where on Earth was he? Junkyard Heaven?

He grabbed his head and groaned. Was the bump on his brow making him hallucinate, or was he having some sort of cosmic experience? Hearing a tap-tap-tapping right behind him, he craned around and saw a pair of purple high-topped sneakers beating out a rhythm to a silent tune against the rear side window. Attached to the shoes were two long legs, clad in torn, faded blue jeans, disappearing beyond his field of vision.

Mouth agape, Andrew warily stretched himself higher to get a better view of the occupant of his back seat, and then quickly surmised that cosmic experience was definitely out. The woman he saw certainly wasn't what he would expect to find in the Angelic Realms.

"This car gave its life to teach you a lesson—may its soul rest in pieces, if you'll pardon the pun!"

"Who the hell are you, and what are you doing in my car?"

"Well, from the look on your face, it's obvious I'm not the girl of your dreams, so maybe I'm your worst nightmare come true." She sat up, unlit cigarette dangling from her red painted mouth, and leaned over the seat to push in the cigarette lighter. "And for your information, Morgan, this isn't your car anymore. You killed it, remember?"

Tearing his eyes from the emerald stud imbedded in the side of her nose, Andrew demanded indignantly: "Whatdaya mean, I killed it? It wasn't my fault! That jerk hit me; I had nothing to do with it. Besides, how can you kill a car? And the name's 'Andrew,' if you don't mind." As angry as this strange young woman made him feel, he couldn't help but admire the long, silky copper hair that temporarily hid her pretty face from view. Her face that somehow seemed so familiar . . .

Lighting her cigarette and blowing the smoke in his direction, she said, "Well, let me ask you this, Morgan: What were you thinking about right before that 'jerk' smashed into you? What little mind games were you playing with yourself, Mr. Manifestor?"

"I don't know what you're talking about. You're nuts!"

"*I'm* nuts? Anyone who spends days on end fantasizing about Porsches and not expecting his grand-old-lady-of-a-Pontiac to take offense is nuts. And what about the five hundred dollars you've been trying to manifest to pay your bills? Where did you expect that to come from? The ethers? Outer space? God, maybe? Well, you manifested it all right; five hundred dollars is just about what you'll get in a week or two when that 'jerk's' insurance company pays you off." Leaning back, she calmly puffed on her cigarette, and blew smoke rings at the windshield.

Andrew could feel his face turn red with embarrassment. How did this woman know his thoughts? He raised himself up to glare at her over the seat. "I didn't visualize my car getting wrecked. I didn't say, 'Oh great Universe, wreck my car please so I can pay my bills.' I didn't ask for that! I just asked for enough money to keep the eviction notice off my door. Besides, I did it just like all

13

the books say. You know, hold an image of the thing you want in your mind, put some feeling into it, believe it'll happen, and eventually it's yours! The more you do it, the sooner it comes."

"Yeah, sometimes in reverse; right, Morgan?" Chuckling sarcastically, she magically changed the next two smoke rings into dollar signs. "There are a few things your books fail to mention; obscure, basic little principles that can't be omitted, for they are the essential ingredients needed to create real, lasting magic in your space and time system. For instance:

"Space-Time Principle Number 20:

Everything comes from somewhere.
Everything you need already exists in
physical reality in some form."

She settled back in the seat cross-legged, wriggling around to get comfortable, and continued: "All energy connected with your system flows through what you could call an 'energy exchange' that everyone pulls from and adds to. Every needed or desired object is derived from other materials, either fashioned by Earth itself, or composed by man from resources taken from Earth. Each man-made object exists only because of the synthesis created from the energy of Earth's raw materials and the energy man generates through his creative activity as he works with them. Co-creation!"

Andrew listened dumbfounded, as this offbeat stranger rattled off concepts that were completely unfamiliar to him. Was he hallucinating her?

"Each person has the innate urge to seek his own greatest fulfillment, and when this is done properly, it adds to this exchange in such a way that individual fulfillment graces and benefits all other consciousness. Since everything is energy, when a transference takes place it can be pretty abstract, not necessarily tit-for-tat. What one person puts out may be returned by someone else entirely. But, if a person doesn't add to this energy exchange yet constantly pulls from it, then an imbalance eventually develops. The abuse of this basic give-and-take process causes a disturbance deep within the exchange, which will then send out signals to the person that something is out of kilter. Warning lights will flash and crisis after crisis may occur to bring to his attention the need to establish balance."

"Sounds to me like you're trying to restrict where my manifestations are going to come from!" Andrew said defiantly. "I have unlimited energy at my disposal, and I'm not confined to just the physical dimension with only physical elements to play with. I have to believe that the Universe takes care of all my desires. There are no limitations! That's what all the books say." Caught between his irritation at her words and his annoyance with the persistent screeching of the windshield wipers, he fiddled impatiently with the controls, trying futilely to make them stop.

"You live in a physical reality, Morgan, and there are limitations, but none that you didn't agree to accept upon entering it. Be careful of that word 'limitation,' though. Your species elected to narrow its focus and concentrate it into specific areas of experience so it could see what its thoughts and feelings could produce in a world of space and time. Space and time in themselves are limitations through one perspective, and yet they offer freedoms that are impossible to experience without them. You desire freedoms that are mine in my reality, but in doing so, you're eliminating the purpose for entering physical reality in the first place! To other forms of consciousness—even yours if you saw the larger picture—my reality could be considered a limitation. Unlike you, from where I am now, I can't appreciate the exquisite feeling of soul-in-flesh, as it luxuriates in its creaturehood, surprising itself day by day with the mysterious elements of physical existence. But these are limitations that I accept. If I want to change them, I have to change realities. Who knows, Morgan," she said, leaning over the seat again to push in the cigarette lighter, "maybe next time around we'll reverse roles!" Then, placing her hand against the windshield, she stopped the obstinate wipers dead in their tracks.

"Is this a ghost I'm talking to, or what?" Andrew asked himself, completely bewildered.

"But we're getting off the subject; we're talking about your reality, not mine. Back to co-creation: There was once a time, very long ago, when man understood the natural give-and-take relationship that existed between himself and all the other species and elements that shared his world. It was a time when man acknowledged the energy exchange and consciously cooperated with it. He observed the natural world around him and learned things from it. Nature was man's greatest teacher, and also his mirror; and he took the time, once in a while, to dance in the rain and play in the puddles, looking at the reflection he cast back to himself. Sadly, those days have all but been forgotten."

She seemed to drift off, lost in her own words and smoke rings for a moment, but then snapped back to continue voicing her thoughts: "If you want to fully understand and master this thing you call manifestation, Morgan, if you want to make magic happen in your reality, you have to regain your inherent understanding of the interrelatedness of all things and of your connection to the whole. Then you'll recognize the truth behind the principle, Everything comes from somewhere. Every atom and molecule that groups together to form an object eventually returns to the earth, there to be recycled into yet another physical form. Ashes to ashes, dust to dust. Wrecked Pontiac to rust, to scrap metal, to steel, to . . . who knows what? Maybe a brand new Porsche someday. Reality recycled!"

Andrew rolled his eyes impatiently. "Great philosophy, but I don't happen to have a lifetime to wait around for a recycled car. It's easier just to create one with my thoughts."

"You didn't hear a word I said, did you?" She shook her head sadly. "If everyone demands a free Porsche but doesn't want to give anything along the line in return, what happens to the poor sucker who spends eight hours a day in a factory making them? What happens to the guy who works in a foundry to make the steel out of the original ore; or, for that matter, what about the fella stuck in a hole all day mining that ore? What? Screw them? They ain't enlightened or they wouldn't be laboring their lives away? Remember, there wouldn't be any cars at all if it weren't for all those 'unenlightened' workers." She patted the car seat appreciatively.

Andrew swatted one of her smoke rings out of the air in irritation and squirmed uncomfortably. "Yeah, but maybe those poor suckers like busting their butts; maybe they're deriving something from their experiences that I don't need. Besides, they wouldn't be in that position in the first place if their beliefs were right."

"Likewise, if your beliefs were 'right,' Morgan, you wouldn't be talking to a 'ghost' in the remnants of your only means of transportation while your body is asleep in an apartment where you can't even turn on the lights for fear that the landlord will know you're home."

Relief swept through Andrew as her words made him realize that he was dreaming. And with that recognition, he instantly returned to the safety and security of his familiar flesh in space and time, leaving the diabolical dream creature behind.

◆　◆　◆

"Whew, what a nightmare!" Andrew mumbled to himself as he got up and risked giving himself away by illuminating the kitchen with the opening of the refrigerator door, hoping to find something to quiet his growling stomach. But he quickly closed it again in disgust—empty as usual. Rummaging around in the dark, he located a few stale crackers and stuffed them down, just to kill the hunger pangs. His television was in the pawn shop—it had paid his last electric bill; an ironic sacrifice, he now thought, since it was the one thing he used electricity for to any degree. His lights now threatened to advertise his whereabouts to his landlord like a glaring neon sign.

Andrew picked up his phone, surprised to still hear a dial tone. Amy hung up before he finished uttering his first three words. Slamming the receiver down in kind, he felt his face flush with humiliation. Why couldn't he just accept the fact that he had been dumped and get on with his life? But then, hadn't Lana, his psychic friend, done an astrological chart comparison on Amy and him and predicted that this girl would stick with him for better or for worse? Hadn't Lana's findings shown they were twin souls throughout eternity? Maybe Amy would eventually come to her senses and see the light. He just needed to get his life together first, that was all. Deciding to put his love life on the back burner, he impulsively called Lana to talk to her about the incident with his car. Maybe she would have some answers for him.

"Lana? It's Andrew. I've gotta talk to you. I need your advice."

Lana had just finished giving her class on chakra balancing, and so had a few minutes to talk. He told her about his car accident and the backward driver—a story that had become all too familiar to her by now—give or take a detail or two. Not giving her time to respond, he went on to describe his dream experience and the voice he had heard in his head right after the accident.

"Jesus, Lana, she was a real she-demon straight from Hell! Why on Earth did I create such a creature in my dreams?"

Lana prided herself on her expertise as a dream interpreter, among other things. She had taken Andrew under her wing a couple of years before, figuring he needed the answers only she, in her infinite wisdom, could provide. He was impressed with her many years of experience in the field of psychic phenomena and her endless credentials, therefore he felt secure in consulting her in most matters. Besides, for some reason, she never charged him as she did everyone else.

"Well, Andy, there's always the possibility that she wasn't just a dream creation; it would all depend on what plane of existence you happened to have found yourself on. From the way you've described her, however, and seeing as how she first made her presence known to you as a voice in your head before you went to sleep, I would surmise that she's a lower-astral entity of some sort, trying to drain your psychic energies. I've had such encounters myself many times, my dear. All true light-workers are challenged in this manner eventually. It's the ultimate test! I've told you—and you need to start listening to me now—that you must begin working with the White Light of Spirit."

As she spoke, Andrew could picture her clearly, repositioning the pins in her neatly coifed, jet-black hair, resisting any facial expression for fear of creating new wrinkles.

"So when and if I see this thing again, you're telling me I should imagine surrounding it with light?"

"No, no, no! That would only serve to strengthen its powers. You have to surround yourself with the light, and tell the entity to be gone! Nothing can penetrate the White Light of Spirit."

"Okay, I'll do it. But I still don't understand why my car got wrecked when I was doing everything right!"

He could still see her in his mind's eye, as she shook her head—gently, so as to not disturb her hair—and smiled her knowing wisp of a smile.

"But don't you see, Andy? The entity in your dream told you a bunch of lies, trying to rob you of your powers of manifestation. Look upon the loss of your car as a blessing, a sure sign that the new car you were visualizing is on its way. It's always darkest just before the dawn!"

"But . . ." Andrew sighed in confusion, "I don't know what to do now! Without a car I can't even start my new job tomorrow. But I guess that isn't a big deal since it was a stupid job, anyway. I'll just have to hang on until the insurance money comes, like last time." His long face lifted briefly, but then immediately fell again. "But it'll all have to go to bills in the end, and I'll still be on foot."

Her voice rose a pitch or two in irritation. "Andy, how many times do I have to tell you not to limit where your good is going to come from? Remember, the Universe moves in mysterious ways. Losing this job is no different from all the other jobs you've lost, except now you're improving; you didn't have to waste time starting it to realize that you're not here to do as the masses do. You're here to rise above the herd, to show others there's a better way. You don't have to work to create abundance; abundance is all around you. You just have to open yourself up to it. 'Consider the lilies, how they grow: they toil not, they—' "

She cut herself off with the abrupt announcement that her nine o'clock appointment had arrived, leaving Andrew to face his problems alone in the dark once again.

Chapter Two

The White Light Meets a Lady of the Night

"C'mon, I know you're in there, Morgan!"

Andrew awakened with a start, cringing at the sound of his landlord's voice. There it was again: every time someone addressed him by his last name, it meant trouble. Jumping up, he saw the determined old man peering through the cracked blinds at him. There was no escape. He couldn't even say the check was in the mail—although ironically, in a manner of speaking it was. He would have rather been anywhere—even the Realm of the She-Demon—than where he was right now.

Assuming his well-rehearsed, I'm-too-cute-to-be-mad-at expression, he answered the door. But before he could open his mouth, the landlord screamed in his face, "Four hundred dollars, Morgan, right now, or I slap this on your door!" He waved an eviction notice wildly in the air. "I've got a waiting list of people as long as your list of excuses. They're willing to pay me, on time and everything, and not talk me out of the security deposit like you did, you good-for-nothin' son of a bitch!"

"Look, Mr. Briggs, I know you won't believe this, but—"

"You're goddamn right I won't believe it!" Purple-faced, Briggs pushed Andrew roughly out of the way and stuck the notice on the door, true to his word." I want you outta here within twenty-four hours; you got it?" He stormed off, as Andrew closed and locked the door behind him.

What was he to do? No car, no place to go, ten bucks in his pocket, and his insurance check not due for days. And this time Briggs meant business. He tried to get a grip on himself. He had to manifest something fast; he had to create his own salvation. Calming himself as best he could, he assumed the lotus position that he had learned in one of Lana's meditation classes and began to visualize. First, the mental image: a new apartment, much nicer than this one, with an easy-going landlord; lots of food in the fridge—thick, juicy sirloin steaks; a sexy blue-eyed blonde reclining on the plush new couch; a big-screen TV, complete with VCR; stereo system from floor to ceiling; five thousand dollars cash in his pocket—big bills, of course; and last but not least, a shiny new red Porsche sitting in his personal parking space, visible through the large picture window.

Second, lots of emotion: Andrew knew that intense emotion breathed life into his images, helping to fill them out and bring them into space and time. Persistent pretending in any area would eventually actualize physical versions of whatever he visualized.

Third, keep the faith: No matter what his senses told him to the contrary as time went on, he had to keep the image of his desires in the forefront of his mind and maintain the feeling that they were already a reality. Expectation created objects and events. The more he expected, the sooner they would come.

He swore he could feel it starting to work, as he drifted deeper and deeper into an altered state, disassociating himself from the unpleasant atmosphere surrounding him. Andrew wasn't sure how long he had been under before his concentration was interrupted by a frantic knocking on the door. Untwining his legs and unplugging himself from the Universe, he got up to answer it. He was still vibrating from head to toe and a little disoriented as he opened the door to see Maggie, a girl he had befriended at the apartment complex swimming pool the month before. Tears in her big blue eyes, she asked if she could come in, and without waiting for an answer, swept past him and plopped down on the couch.

"I have a big favor to ask of you, Andy," she said, pulling him down on the couch next to her.

"Anything, Maggie, you name it!" He was always a sucker for tears, especially when there was a pretty face behind them.

"You got a beer?" she asked shakily.

"No. I'm afraid I don't have much of anything to offer you right now; I've been too busy to go shopping." Andrew guiltily looked away from her questioning eyes. "So what is it you need, Maggie?"

"Well, I don't want you to think I'm trying to come on to you or anything, so it kinda makes it hard for me to ask you this. . . ." Maggie looked helplessly into his eyes for a brief moment, before casting her gaze downward and wiping away a solitary tear. "But then, I could tell the minute I met you that you were *soooo* understanding and would accept me no matter what."

"Why? What's there to accept?"

Maggie jutted out her delicate chin and stated bravely, "I'm a call girl."

It took Andrew a couple of seconds to make his mouth work. "Okay, I can deal with that," he said finally, trying not to let his expression betray his shock. "But what does that have to do with me?"

"I don't know if you remember Rick; you probably saw me with him a couple of times at the pool. Anyway, that's who I live with, or I guess I should say 'lived' with, until last night."

"Something happen between you? You two have a fight?"

"No, no, you got it all wrong! Rick was just my driver, my protector if I ever needed him. But late last night he packed up his things and left town in a hurry to keep from getting busted. I got scared and split, too—I got my stuff and got out of there real fast. And it's a good thing I did, because the neighbors said the cops showed up and ripped everything apart looking for drugs. I guess it's a horrible mess over there."

23

"Does this mean you're out of business? Was he your . . . uh . . . pimp, too?" Andrew squirmed uncomfortably at the sound of the word.

"I don't need a pimp," Maggie said, sticking out her lower lip and tossing her blonde head indignantly. "I'm self-employed."

"I didn't mean to offend you . . . it's just that I don't know very much about your line of work."

"That's okay, I know you're a sweetie." The pout instantly left her face, and she nuzzled his neck affectionately. "That's why I immediately thought of you in my time of desperation."

"Let me guess . . . you need a place to crash."

"And a new driver—just temporarily, of course, until I can figure out where to go from here."

"You want me to drive for you? I don't get it."

"It's simple. You just let me stay here, allow my clients to call me on your phone, and drive me to my appointments."

"But I only have the one bed—"

"Now don't go getting the wrong idea!" Maggie interjected. "I don't want to put you out. I don't mind sleeping on the couch."

Reluctant to tell her the truth, Andrew stared at the floor and cracked his knuckles nervously. "Look, Maggie, I'd really love to help you out, but I wrecked my car yesterday."

"That's no problem; I wouldn't expect to use your car. We'll use mine."

Realizing he was backed into a corner, he swallowed his dwindling pride and confessed, "Well, I'm afraid there's one other little problem: old man Briggs is evicting me tomorrow morning. Didn't you see the notice on the door?"

"Oh, is that what that was? Well, that's no big deal either. Here, how much do you owe him?" She pulled a wad of bills out of her purse and started unfolding them right in front of his face.

Andrew's eyes bugged as he stuttered: "Four hundred dollars . . . just to catch up from last month. Another four hundred is due in a week."

"Well, no sense getting ahead of ourselves. A week's more than enough time to come up with the rest." She peeled off four one-hundred-dollar bills and stuffed them in his hand.

"I can't let you pay my rent; that wouldn't be right!" Andrew made himself say the words, even though it hurt.

"Oh c'mon, Andy, you're the one doing me the favor. And you're gonna make big bucks working with me; just consider this an advance. So, do we have a deal?"

"Well, it sure seems to be a quick solution to both of our problems, but I don't understand why you need me. Why not get your own apartment and drive yourself?"

Maggie looked up at him with her liquid azure eyes and whispered softly, "I just don't feel safe without a big, strong man nearby."

Andrew blushed and resisted puffing out his chest. "Well . . . I guess if it's just temporary. Oh what the hell, why not?"

"Good!" Maggie kissed him on the cheek and jumped up, heading for the kitchen. "So, what's for lunch, partner?" Opening the refrigerator door, she frowned at the bare shelves and said, "First thing I have to do is go shopping."

Grabbing her purse on the way out the door, Maggie yelled back over her shoulder, "You like steak?"

Andrew stared at the closed door in a daze for a full minute before sitting down and trying to assimilate everything that had happened to him since he woke up. He was amazed at how quickly his immediate problems were soon to be solved: rent paid, food in the fridge, and a way to make a little money for the time being. He didn't really feel any guilt at the thought of being involved with a prostitute; after all, prostitution was a victimless crime. Besides, he was desperate.

He worked up the courage to walk across the courtyard and hunt down Mr. Briggs. At the sight of the four hundred dollars cash, the landlord mellowed a bit and stuffed the money quickly into his wallet. "Remember, Morgan, you owe another four hundred in less than a week—no more excuses!"

Andrew assured him that he would have the rent on time from now on, and returned to his apartment just in time to see Maggie staggering under two large bags of groceries.

"There's more stuff to carry," she said breathlessly, setting the bags down on the kitchen table before disappearing into the bedroom. She re-emerged two minutes later with her swimsuit on and flounced out the door. Andrew spent the next half-hour putting away groceries and lugging in Maggie's extensive wardrobe of slinky outfits.

They spent the rest of the day lounging around the pool, as Maggie spelled out his job description, preparing him for his first night in her employ. He was to wait patiently in her car as she visited her clients. It would be dark, so he wouldn't even be able to pass the time reading. He decided he could make good use of the time meditating and visualizing.

By nine o'clock they were on the road, heading for her appointment. She only had one client that evening, but informed Andrew it would be at least two hours before she would return. "Watch the building for a few minutes after I enter it," she said. "I'll blink a light off and on to let you know which apartment I'm in in case something happens."

As she walked up the sidewalk toward the swanky townhouse, heels clicking, Andrew tried not to think of what she meant by "in case something happens." He kept his eyes glued on the building until he saw the flickering light, and then stretched out in the front seat to plug himself back into the Universe.

Drifting off again into the imaginary realm where all his fondest desires materialized before his eyes, Andrew pretended the car he was lying in was really his Porsche. He imagined the smell of the new upholstery and the feel of the rich leather seats. In his mind, he was in his Porsche.

He slipped deeper into the fantasy, totally blocking out rock-bed reality. But after a while, a slight, irritating sound began disturbing his altered state. Opening one eye, he searched out the distraction, afraid to move too much for fear of breaking the illusion he had so perfectly created. There was someone rapping softly on the driver's-side window. Sighing in frustration, he sat up and rolled down the window, assuming it was Maggie.

"Hey, good lookin', wanna have a good time?"

Rubbing his eyes in disbelief, he peered directly into the face of the she-demon from Hell. "Oh shit! Not you again!"

Andrew looked around him frantically. With relief he confirmed he really was in his dream car, but the uptown neighborhood of Maggie's rendezvous had vanished. In its stead was a dingy, littered avenue lined with dilapidated buildings. He could hear an irritating buzzing coming from the ancient neon sign hanging precariously above the old hotel across the street.

"S'matter, honey? In a bad mood tonight? C'mon home with me and I'll make you feel allll better!" She threw her hip out seductively, almost ripping her tight red mini-skirt. Her long copper hair was molded into wild ringlets that danced up and down crazily in unison with her undulating hips, and was topped off with a scarlet rhinestone-studded beret. The high-topped sneakers she had worn in the junkyard were replaced by silver high heels, her long legs now sporting black fishnet stockings with crooked seams.

Still trying to determine how he had crossed paths again with the she-demon, he was struck speechless. Leaning in his window, she grinned at him provocatively, waiting for his reaction.

Andrew's mind raced. What had Lana said about the White Light of Spirit? Frantically, he pieced together her instructions. In his mind he conjured up the brightest, whitest burst of light he could muster and enveloped himself in it. Proudly, and with some astonishment at his accomplishment, he surveyed the protective light-shield he had created, feeling confident that he was now safe from her evil clutches. He grinned back at her through the open car window, taunting her with his new-found power, and waited for her image to dissolve into nothingness. He could still see her clearly as though through distorted glass. She was shaking her head and laughing. He glared back, miffed: the least she could do was take him seriously.

"Oh lighten up, Morgan," she said, her voice muffled by the translucent barrier. Then, removing the hat pin from her beret, she struck the classic fencer's pose. "*Touché!*" she hollered, and jabbed the pin straight into Andrew's bubble of light.

With a loud "pop!" his light creation exploded all around him, blinding him temporarily like a camera flash.

Andrew blinked his eyes, and in a rush of pent-up, unleashed fury, flung the car door open and lunged out. "I've about had it with you!" he yelled, backing her up against the damp, graffiti-covered wall. "Just who do you think you are, anyway?"

Seemingly unperturbed by his aggressive action, she cocked her head to think a second before answering. "I am, you are, and we be."

"Now what the hell does that mean . . . 'We be?'" Meeting her steady gaze, Andrew became vividly aware of his body vibrating from his uncharacteristic display of anger.

"Simple words, dear Morgan, to help you understand who I am and the nature of our relationship. Maybe you'll figure it out as we go along." She slipped nimbly by him and walked to the curb.

"You're no relation to me! I refuse to accept that."

Swiveling around to face him, she rocked back and forth on the broken pavement. "Oh, you prefer a 'she-demon from Hell,' maybe?"

At this moment she sure looked the part, he thought: her swaying figure framed by the flickering neon light; flaming hair blowing crazily in the wind; red dress clinging to her body.

"Look, 'We-Be,' or whatever your name is, why don't you just leave me alone? I didn't ask for any of this!"

"Are you sure about that?" she said, raising her painted eyebrows sarcastically. "I seem to remember hearing a fella who looked just like you sitting on a dirt road in the middle of nowhere in a car he had just killed, screaming at the Universe all about how he hated it and wished he could understand it all. Sound familiar, Morgan?"

Recalling clearly the S.O.S. he had sent out into the cosmos the day before, Andrew tried to bury his fists in his eye sockets, completely mortified. As much as he hated to admit it, he was obviously responsible for bringing this We-Be creature into his reality. He had sure goofed up somehow! His mind thrashed around, looking for another possible explanation. Could it be that the bump on his head hadn't been so minor after all? Maybe he was brain damaged or something. . . .

"You prefer bruised brain cells to admitting the reality of my existence?" she asked, reading his mind. "You sure know how to hurt a lady!"

"Lady?" Andrew blurted out. "Hardly!"

"Oh yeah, that reminds me, I wanted to get your honest opinion on my get-up. Am I dressed right for the occasion? Do I fit the theme of the day, or did I overdo it?"

"I wasn't talking about your clothes, I was referring to your demonic streak," Andrew added a little too quickly, trying to divert her train of thought away from his new line of business.

We-Be laughed and said mischievously: "You don't really think I'm a she-demon, do you? But I can be if you want me to be. . . ." She threw her outstretched arms theatrically toward the night sky.

"No, no, no! I get the idea!" Andrew instinctively backed toward his open car door, stopping only because she lowered her arms and changed the subject.

"So, it looks like you manifested your way out of your predicament—steaks and everything!"

Breathing a sigh of relief over her abrupt change of subject, he reflected on her observation. He hadn't really thought about it that way, but the realization suddenly dawned on him. "You're right! I did manifest steaks, didn't I?"

"And a sexy blue-eyed blonde, too; don't forget that!" We-Be said, batting her eyelashes.

"Wait a minute . . . I don't feel romantic toward Maggie! How could I feel that way about a prostitute?"

"Oh? And what's wrong with being a prostitute?"

"C'mon, a streetwalker isn't exactly what I had in mind. I can't respect someone who makes her money that way!"

29

"Ahh, but you'll take her money to keep yourself off the street. What's the difference between you and her? She sells her body, you sell your self-respect—which you don't have enough of to spare in the first place. How do you expect to manifest anyone 'respectable' into your life if you don't respect yourself? If you gaze deeply enough into Maggie's big baby-blues, you may see your own reflection."

"Oh, so you're calling me a prostitute, too, huh? That doesn't make any sense."

"Sure it does—figuratively speaking. When someone doesn't use his talents and abilities in a constructive way, he's prostituting himself. At least Maggie's applying her talents, as she sees them. You, however, ignore any talents you have, undermine any constructive opportunities that come your way, and try to materialize all your desires out of thin air."

Andrew shot back at her, "Don't try to tell me again that I can't wish something into existence—form it out of the ethers!"

"Well, you can certainly wish for things and get them, Morgan, but remember: Everything comes from somewhere. You can't constantly attempt to get something for nothing and not expect it to eventually catch up to you. You claim to be a manifestor, but what you're actually trying to do is 'materialize,' which is something else entirely. Don't forget, everything that's physically possible to desire already exists in your reality. It's simply a matter of magical redistribution!" She clicked her heels on the pavement and snapped her fingers.

"One of the underlying objectives when entering physical reality—whether mankind remembers it or not—is to learn the magic of the give-and-take process. By trying to 'materialize,' you're only concentrating on the taking aspects of this process. If you could simply materialize your way through life, then what would be the point of being physical in the first place? The challenge is to work with what you have at your disposal."

"Sure, sure," Andrew said sarcastically. "I have so much at my disposal. Without Maggie, I'd be out on the street."

"Without Maggie, you'd be staring your self-created problems square in the face and learning how to deal with them head on. How do you expect to deal with any new elements in your life if you can't even work with what you already have?

"*Space-Time Principle Number 34:*

When you appreciate what you have, it grows.
Accept what you have for now
and work from there."

"So I suppose I should have walked away from Maggie's offer—my manifestation—and settled for living on the street? Only a fool would do that." Andrew shook his head in mock disgust.

"No, Morgan, a fool is someone who demands that everything be handed to him on a silver platter, rather than trying to figure out how he got into his predicament in the first place. You've developed a pattern in which you continually back yourself into a corner and then are forced to accept any solution that makes itself known. If you don't open up avenues for creativity by putting forth your physical energy in some manner, and instead, insist on having a one-way, I-me-mine perspective, then all you'll ever receive are the dregs of the Universe. Your much-desired manifestations can only follow the patterns you've already established, the grooves you've already cut. You'll get your manifestations all right, or at least part of them; but when you don't give the Universe any creative elbow room it has to squeeze your manifestations into your reality as best it can, which usually distorts them into caricatures of your true desires. You were trying to manifest money while at the same time hating your car. Well, your car is out of your hair now, and the insurance money ought to be in your mail box within a week or two. The Universe did the best it could with the limited elements you provided."

While talking, We-Be had slowly made her way over to his dream-Porsche and now lifted herself up to sit on the hood.

Andrew pulled her roughly back onto the pavement and then, with his shirt tail, wiped the smudges off the shiny, candy-apple red paint job.

"Sounds like you're telling me I have to impress the Universe by getting a job before it'll bestow its blessings upon me. I'm not a victim; I shouldn't have to take just any job that comes along."

"Maybe not just any job, Morgan, but at least some job; one that you stick with long enough so that you're in a position where opportunity can find you. If your ideas about work are such that they seem to bring you only unfulfilling job situations, then perhaps you should accept where you are for now while working on changing the ideas that limit you. The ideal manifestation is one in which you combine your mental and physical energies. You want the perfect job right now, or nothing at all! And since nothing is perfect, you do nothing! Think about it, Morgan: if a job were perfect, what would it need you for? What would the challenge be?"

Andrew hated these kinds of lectures, and fought to not feel the guilt connected to the chord she was trying to strike in him. "If you ask me, you're really hung up on the old Puritan work ethic," he spat at her. "Guess you expect me to happily do as the masses do and accept a lifetime of drudgery, working by the sweat of my brow."

Placing her purse on the sidewalk, We-Be sat down on it in a very unladylike fashion, and, pulling off her shoes, wriggled her painted toes and rubbed her arches.

" Space-Time Principle Number 35:

Accept everything as it is for now,
but not necessarily as your lot in life."

Andrew's facial muscles tightened with obstinacy. "If I do that then I'm admitting I'm a helpless victim of circumstance. The Universe is my benefactor, and I can have anything I want. It delights in sharing its endless supply with its offspring."

"Jesus, Morgan, you're playing the game that the Universe is a parent, a parent who gives the child anything it wants without expecting anything in return, even respect and responsibility for those things. It's time to grow up and face the fact that there is no parent-Universe, in those terms. You're equal partners with everything—a co-creator, a part of a cooperative whole—in which every participant should give and take equally, according to each one's talents and abilities. The more you become aware of your part in this mass creation, the less you'll have a need to make things happen, for then your desires will be clearly recognized by the whole and become part of the overall give-and-take structure."

"Whatever happened to 'I and the Father are one,' 'Ask and you shall receive,' or 'Knock and it shall be opened to you'? Those are some pretty age-old wisdoms, you know." Andrew gave her his best try-to-get-yourself-out-of-this-one look.

"All right, Morgan, we'll play your little the-Universe-is-my-parent game for a while. What happens to the child who is given everything his little heart desires?"

"I'd say that kid is one hell of a little manifestor!" Smirking, Andrew buffed the top of his Porsche with his sleeve.

"Quit being a smart-ass; this is important. Any responsible parent knows that if he or she constantly gives in to the demands of the child, that child will find it very difficult later to accept responsibility, to respect and appreciate his possessions, or to develop any real sense of accomplishment. Even with older kids, this can be seen clearly. For instance, the sixteen-year-old who is handed the keys to a brand new car rarely appreciates that car to the extent that his friend, who mowed lawns for three years to save the money to buy a much lesser car, does. If some parents are intelligent enough to recognize the wisdom behind this concept, then wouldn't you expect your great 'Universal Parent' to be that much wiser?"

Andrew clenched his teeth in irritation, but didn't interrupt her.

"If you want to know my personal opinion, your basic problem stems from a lack of self-esteem due to the absence of a sense of accomplishment. That sense of accomplishment has never been developed because you've never done anything to earn your own self-respect! The two go hand in hand. You have a tendency to place most of your energy into trying to manipulate the world around you, rather than looking into the reasons why you get yourself into your predicaments in the first place. When you do this, it's like putting deodorant on B.O. You can't just wish away the stink. You have to clean up your act first, which means changing your ideas about yourself. And that, Morgan, calls for action, not just 'wishing for'!"

Andrew watched her as she stood up in stocking-feet, lit a cigarette, and leaned against the wall, as though to take a brief break from her lecture. "Figures," he thought to himself, "that the first nonphysical being I encounter would end up appearing as a hooker who expounds on body odor."

"It's your lack of self-respect and the circle game you create of depending on others for your answers and salvation that I'm trying to get you to look at here. You need to begin feeling that same sense of accomplishment that the teenager mowing the lawns has—that's the area you need to direct your energies toward."

Trying not to let his anger get the best of him, Andrew leaned over the car and punctuated his retort with a pointed finger: "No, I need to direct my energies toward what I want now—right now—because that's where my power lies—in the present moment. That kind of persistence and concentration takes work, and all the real work is done in the mind."

"Yes and no," We-Be said. "Think about it: you're using your mind and now-power to try to create objects and events rather than to try to discover the underlying reasons for your lack of those things in the first place. Manifesting 'things' won't heal your life. They'll simply distract you from your real problems temporarily. Your normal way of dealing with problems, Morgan, is evidently the problem itself."

Andrew watched her, his expression tight and sullen, as she paced back and forth on the cracked pavement, puffing away fiercely on her cigarette. As far as he was concerned, the worst problem he had was We-Be herself; and he had no idea at all how to deal with her and make her disappear forever from his mind.

"And as far as your Father-in-Heaven belief goes, it's one of the major stumbling blocks in your understanding of these principles. It creates a separation between you and the cooperative whole that actually impedes the manifestation process. If you think about it, 'I and the Father are one' is really a contradictory statement, for the words 'Father' and 'I' automatically imply a separative state of being—not to mention a hierarchical relationship—which obviously negates the state of oneness."

Across the street on the front of an old brick building, a large, rusty antique clock started chiming the hour of midnight.

"Well, gotta go," We-Be said, flipping her cigarette into the gutter and slipping back into her shoes. "Your latest manifestation will be joining you in a minute. Wouldn't do to have her see you with another woman!" She leaned over to straighten the black seams running up the back of her legs.

"Wait a minute! How do I get out of here?"

"Why don't you ask the White Light of Spirit?"

Andrew jumped in front of her to keep her from leaving. "Are you making fun of me? Are you saying the White Light doesn't work?"

"Anything works if you believe it will, Morgan—even a white light. Except on me, of course; you wished for me first, remember? You don't need protection from me, but you may from Lana. Why not try it on her? Or may I suggest a garlic necklace instead? How 'bout a wooden stake?" She winked at him playfully, her expression showing more than a trace of sarcasm. And with that, she walked off briskly—disappearing into the fog that was settling, as though to soften the harshness of the sleazy city street.

Slowly climbing back into his Porsche, Andrew squinted at the spot in the fog into which she had vanished. He leaned his head back against the soft leather seat and closed his eyes, an electric-like buzz coursing through his body. This latest bizarre encounter with the etheric mystery woman had undeniably exhilarated him in a way he had never felt before. For a minute he could still hear her heels clicking against the pavement as they faded away, leaving only the barely discernible street noise and the echoed sounds of two cats screaming in their animal ecstasy. Eyes still closed, he rolled up the car window and locked the door against the night strangeness. His mind was a jumbled assortment of concepts he had never heard before. As he attempted to organize them, Andrew thought he could hear the click-click of her heels again in the distance. Were his ears playing tricks on him? No, the sound was definitely getting louder, closer. He couldn't possibly deal with any more We-Be weirdness tonight. Relief swept through him as he remembered he had locked the car door, and he kept his eyes closed, feigning sleep. Still, the impatient tapping at the window startled him, making him jump. It was insistent, and he finally groaned and rolled down the window, just a crack.

"Christ, Andy, lemme in; it's freezing out here!"

Maggie stood there in her flimsy dress, hugging herself to keep warm, her blonde hair whipping in the cold night breeze. He had forgotten all about this girl who had hired him; and for the briefest second, Andrew felt a pang of disappointment at the realization that it was her. He reached over and opened the passenger door, and she slid in quickly, cuddling up to him to warm herself. The combined smell of the bourbon on her breath and men's aftershave assaulted his nostrils as she whispered in his ear, "Not bad for a couple of hours work, huh, partner?" Giggling, she fanned him with two crisp one-hundred-dollar bills as he started her Chevy and pulled out of the parking lot to head for home.

Chapter Three

Toyota Highs
&
Tequila Blues

"God, it sure feels good to have my TV back, Maggie," Andrew said, flicking through the stations with the remote control to locate his favorite wrestling program. Maggie had bailed his television out the day before and paid his phone bill, as partial payment for his first six-day stint as her chauffeur. So far she hadn't given him any real cash since his original four-hundred-dollar advance, but she had assured him he had at least made enough to pay the rent, due the next day. It seemed as though his life was starting to come together.

Maggie smiled an indulgent-mommy smile and continued to buff her nails, humming some top-ten hit off-key. She drained the last of her beer, set the empty can on the floor next to at least a half-dozen others, and got up to get another.

Andrew stared at the aluminum trash pile collecting on his carpet and fought back the agitation created by his natural inclination to neatness. Setting the remote down, he started picking up the cans and empty pizza boxes from the night before.

"I'll get that stuff later, just leave it," Maggie said, as she settled back down on the couch with a fresh beer. Andrew just nodded and continued to straighten up the living room. He reminded himself he would be out on the street if it weren't for this messy, inconsiderate woman.

She picked up the control and switched the channel. "Oooh, I just love this show; I used to watch it all the time!" She sprawled out on the couch, immediately engrossed in the soap opera.

Andrew bit the side of his lip and made himself keep his voice steady and pleasant: "I think I'll go check the mail." Eyes glued to the screen, Maggie was oblivious to him as he walked out the door.

He was finding it harder and harder to ignore Maggie's bad habits and constant demands; the incredible messes she could make in just a short time; her wet Frederick's-of-Hollywood underwear draped all over his bathroom; her insistence that he should never answer his own phone; the way she ordered him around in public. As he headed for the mail box, he tried to concentrate on the positive side of the situation. He was getting ahead again, wasn't he? He just had to learn to take the good with the bad for now, and eventually find a way to break from Maggie. Once he was on his feet, "something" would come along; he just had to get serious again about his manifesting.

Andrew rarely bothered to check his mail. No friends ever wrote him, and the only things he ever received were bills or junk mail. But he knew that sometime in the next week or two he would get the insurance settlement for his wrecked Pontiac, and, therefore, had checked his box religiously for the last three days. Fiddling with his key, he tried to imagine the official-looking envelope in his mailbox while attempting to ignore the skeptical thought in the back of his mind that told him it was too soon to expect it.

"Allll right!" Andrew shouted jubilantly, as he pulled out a single official-looking envelope. He did a little dance in celebration of manifesting a miracle-come-early, and then, with shaking hands, ripped the letter open. Breathing a sigh of relief at the sight of the $501.23 check, he hugged it to his chest. He already knew what he was going to spend it on; he had a plan of action all laid out.

Racing back to the apartment, he burst through the door waving the check in the air. With a start, Maggie looked up briefly before resuming her normal expression of boredom. She clicked the TV volume up a notch and blew on her freshly painted fingernails. "C'mon, Maggie, I need you to drive me someplace!" Grabbing her arm he pulled her up, as she protested, trying to protect her nails. Andrew handed her her purse and dragged her out the door.

◆ ◆ ◆

"Just forty-three thousand miles, huh?" Screwing up his forehead, Andrew looked under the hood for a second time and fiddled with a wire, trying to look like he knew what he was doing.

"You drove 'er, you tell me; is this a sweet little baby or what? I'm practically givin' it away at this price. Just replaced the air conditioner compressor last week, and the two front tires are brand new!"

Andrew walked around the car one more time, trying to ignore the slight dent in the rear quarter panel and Maggie's impatient tugging at his sleeve. Wiping the sweat from her brow, she finally gave up; and, leaning against a pickup truck, stared blankly up at the large weather-worn sign: "Wally's World O' Wheels—Buy Here, Pay Here! No Credit? No Problem!"

"And to tell ya the truth, I was askin' seven hundred down, but seein' as how you only got five hundred, and with your little lady bein' such a looker n' all . . ." Grinning lecherously, he eyed Maggie up and down as she smiled at him sarcastically and then turned away.

"Tell ya what . . . you give me five hundred right now and you can drive 'er off the lot today!"

The smug look on Andrew's face showed that he felt pleased with himself for getting the guy to lower the down payment. He realized, of course, that this meant the weekly payments would be higher, but then, he knew he was on his way to creating great prosperity in his life—no sweat. The car—a five-year-old Toyota—wasn't by any means his dream car, but it was in nice shape and a lot better than walking or depending on Maggie to haul him everywhere. "You've got a deal, mister," Andrew said, and followed the salesman into the office to sign the papers.

Maggie trailed behind, looking like a wilting flower. "Can I leave now?" she asked in a petulant little voice.

Preoccupied with the business at hand, Andrew waved her off and she peeled out, in a hurry to catch the last remaining rays of sun at the pool.

After the papers were signed, Wally himself walked Andrew out to his new car. "Well, son, you got yourself a fine little machine here. Take care of her and she'll take care of you. Just remember, miss one payment and she's back on my lot!"

Andrew nodded responsibly and drove off, amazed at how everything was falling into place. It may not have been his Porsche, but he felt like he was gaining ground—at least this car was the right color!

By the time Andrew got back to the apartment, it was too late to join Maggie at the pool. He busied himself washing dishes and straightening up, enjoying the short time alone in his own apartment—so rare these days. Maggie returned in a sour mood—pouting, he supposed, because he had dragged her along on his car-buying venture—and headed straight toward the bathroom to take a shower.

As if on cue, the phone rang just as she had finished. Andrew could hear bits and pieces of her conversation; evidently her engagement for the evening had canceled. Banging the phone down angrily, Maggie stormed back into the living room.

"The hell with it; I needed a night off anyway. Let's go have some fun!"

"Can we afford to go out? Remember, we have to pay the rent tomorrow."

"Jesus, you're always worrying! Look, here's the rent money." Grabbing her purse, Maggie pulled out four hundred dollars. She walked over to the bookshelf and dramatically stuck the money in-between the pages of his newest book, *Making Money with Your Mind*. "There, now you can forget about the stupid rent and we can go out and have a good time."

It had been a while since Andrew had really been out on the town. That had been one of the things that had upset Amy so: he had rarely made enough money to pay his bills, much less made any extra to spend on her. Whenever they had gone out, it was usually "Dutch," and toward the end Amy had ended up paying his way, too.

Andrew was feeling more secure than he had in quite some time. Rent money on time, a decent car, and a night on the town. Still, his male ego would have felt more secure if he could have paid for their evening out, but he was down to the $1.23 in change left over from his insurance check after paying for his Toyota. Since Maggie had already declared that the evening was on her, he insisted they take his car to balance things out.

"So, where to?" Andrew asked, opening the car door for her.

"Oysters! I want oysters! How about that new place over by the pier?" Maggie swigged from the fifth of tequila she had brought with her, and then stashed it under her seat.

◆   ◆   ◆

Andrew nursed his third beer; he was already starting to feel a slight buzz, though Maggie was way ahead of him. Dinner had been great, although watching Maggie slurp down the slimy, raw oysters had almost made him lose his appetite. The place was crowded and noisy, obviously a real hot spot. Peering through the draped fishnets and layers of cigarette smoke, Andrew could just make Maggie out, at the juke box, moving her body suggestively to the music.

Sure enough, some guy had moved in on her. Was her night off going to turn into an evening's work after all? Andrew watched in curiosity as Maggie pulled back from the man, artfully stepping aside as he grabbed for her. She headed back toward their table at an almost-run, with the guy following right behind. A perplexed frown began to appear on Andrew's face. Was she playing some sort of silly hard-to-get act?

Frantically, she wedged herself in-between Andrew and the wall behind his chair, causing him to spill his beer. As she dug her fingernails into his shoulders, it began to occur to Andrew that this wasn't a typical barroom flirtation he was witnessing; the guy on Maggie's tail looked as though he were furious with her, his face inflamed and fists curled.

"Make him go away, Andy!" Maggie's eyes were wide with fear, her suntan faded to a sickly white.

"You stay outta this!" the guy raged, making another grab for Maggie. Andrew was suddenly aware of how big this troublemaker was, which was magnified by the fact that Andrew was still sitting down, pinned in by Maggie's body behind him.

"Now wait a second—" Andrew's words were cut off by the fist that slammed into his mouth. Knocked sideways out of his chair, he landed in a heap with Maggie, the chair, his beer, and her empty oyster shells. Shaking his head to try to see straight, he managed to get up before the brute could get around the table.

On guard and mad himself now, Andrew squared off and yelled: "Wait just a goddamn minute! What the hell's going on?"

"That bitch stole my wallet last year; I'd know her anywhere! A week's pay—gone! All for a stupid whore who wasn't worth twenty bucks!"

Andrew looked at Maggie, who glared back defensively. "He's crazy, Andy! I didn't steal his wallet! Make him go away!"

Once again the guy lunged for Maggie, this time catching her by the hair. She screamed hysterically, desperately clutching the air between herself and Andrew. Andrew reacted instinctively and grabbed the man's hand to keep it from pulling her hair out by the roots. Shoving the table out of the way with his one free hand, he punched the antagonist, first in the stomach and then in the nose, sending him reeling into the next table, a strand of blonde hair still clutched between his fingers.

Shocked at his own strength, Andrew stared at his clenched fist and then at his adversary's bloody face. People gathered around, and Andrew could hear Maggie's frenzied cries behind him: "Kill him, Andy; beat the shit out of him!"

Someone was helping the troublemaker to his feet. He didn't look as though he would be up for another round for at least another minute or two. Fumbling with Maggie's purse, Andrew pulled out thirty dollars and tossed it onto the table. Then, grabbing her by the arm, he dragged her out of the place, as she struggled against him.

"Coward! Chickenshit! How could you let that jerk off so easy? Didn't you hear him call me a whore? A stupid whore?" Maggie's arms flailed against Andrew's chest as he stuffed her into the back seat of the car.

"Shut up," Andrew said coldly, as he slid behind the steering wheel and peeled out of the parking lot.

"What do you think I pay you for, anyway? You're supposed to protect me! You shoulda killed the son of a bitch!"

Andrew could feel his stomach churn, as the vision of the man's smashed nose flashed before his eyes, offending his up-till-now, basically gentle nature. He had never physically hurt another person before in his life. Trying hard to ignore Maggie's drunken insults, he kept his eyes glued to the road.

"He called me a stupid whore! I'm not stupid, you are!"

Reaching his limit, Andrew snarled at her: "Yeah, but you're a whore, aren't you? Who is he, a john you ripped off?"

Maggie slapped his face from behind, catching him in the same spot that took the blow a few minutes earlier. "I'm not a whore! And I don't have to steal anymore; I'm good at what I do. If I took his wallet, it was because he was a real psycho and deserved it!"

Wiping away the trickling blood from the corner of his mouth with the back of his hand, Andrew wondered how he could have ever gotten mixed up with such a trashy little bitch. He had to get her out of his life—fast. His life was basically on the mend now, and he couldn't face even another night on the job with Maggie. She had obviously brought the evening's incident upon herself with her sleazy lifestyle and obvious dishonesty. Guilt swept through him as he realized that he had allowed himself to take sides in a drama seemingly not of his making.

Pulling up to his apartment, Andrew climbed out of the car and opened the passenger door for Maggie. She stumbled ahead of him into the apartment and collapsed on the couch. Dropping her purse at her feet, Andrew turned on his heels to leave. As he reached the door, he wavered for just a second to look back at her sprawled-out figure. Her dress was hiked up almost to her waist, exposing her scanty underpants and the runs in her nylons; mascara and red lipstick were smeared all over her face—all in all a grotesque picture. Not hiding the disgust he felt, he said, "I'm going back out for some fresh air," and shut the door firmly behind him.

Andrew drove straight for the beach, to the spot he had discovered with Amy. He wanted to listen to the surf, remember Amy, and feel sorry for himself for a while. Pulling out the half-empty fifth of tequila that Maggie had stashed under his seat earlier, he dragged himself toward the dunes and plopped down to do some serious drinking.

Chapter Four

The Significance of Being a Shellfish, or Periwinkle Philosophy

He woke up to the "clang-clang" of a distant buoy. Somewhere, off in the fog-laden night sky, a lone sea gull screeched. He sat up, head still reeling, and strained his eyes toward the horizon. Dawn was still far off; a full moon dominated the heavens, casting an eerie glow on the cresting waves. Struggling to his feet, Andrew tripped over the empty tequila bottle as he staggered to the water's edge; then, squatting down, he scooped up some water in his hands to soothe his injured mouth.

"Why can't my life just be simple?" he thought. As though reflecting his question, his attention was caught by a bunch of wriggling little shelled creatures, as they worked their way in and out of the wet sand under his feet, looking for all the world like they enjoyed their uncomplicated existence. Absorbed in their seemingly trivial activity, he wondered out loud, "Why on Earth would any consciousness want to be a periwinkle, anyway?"

"Because it feels good, silly!"

Andrew was too drunk to be startled, though he hadn't been haunted by the street-walking she-demon for almost a week. Planting a smirk on his face, he turned around nonchalantly, proud of his ability to take her sudden appearance in stride this time. Slowly, though, the smirk faded and he stood there awestruck.

Gone was her garish attire, gone was the cheap hooker persona. She was dressed in a long, flowing white gown, her brilliant hair fanning out softly in the sea breeze. All about her was a magical, luminescent glow, as she hovered three or four inches above the sand. The whole setting looked like some old Renaissance painting he had once seen in a book.

Andrew rubbed his eyes and stepped back, speechless. Then, forcing himself to remember the bizarre personality that resided underneath this new impressive image, he took a deep breath and said sarcastically, "Looks like you're about ready to sprout wings!"

"Don't need wings; that's a misconception. I'd have to be physical to need wings."

We-Be settled gracefully on the ground and leaned down to study the little creatures, picking up her thought where she left off: "You see, Morgan, being a—what did you call it, a periwinkle? Yeah, being a periwinkle is a purely sensual experience. The water flows in and out of its shell and over its tiny body continuously. Just imagine being stroked nonstop, from birth to death, gently caressed and massaged by the actual medium in which you live. All its needs are met by the forces of nature as it leads its simple life. Sounds like Heaven on Earth, huh?"

Her words made Andrew realize how sore and aching his whole body was becoming from the scuffle with Maggie's ex-john. "Yeah, I could go for a nice rubdown myself right now." Looking down at the periwinkles, he now saw them through a new perspective, suddenly envious of them and their simplistic lifestyle.

"You wouldn't need a rubdown or be in the mess you're in if you just tried to get with the rhythm."

Moaning, Andrew walked back a few steps and sat down in the drier sand. He could tell he was in for another long kooky lecture, and he was too groggy to fight it.

"What does dancing have to do with anything?"

We-Be smiled angelically and floated a foot or so higher. "Every consciousness, be it periwinkle or man, is innately in touch with the eternal dance of the Universe. Every consciousness is provided with all its needs when it's in rhythm with the Universe and aware of its place in the scheme of things. Give and take; remember, Morgan? A periwinkle naturally gives and takes, without even having to think about it, because its got rhythm. You may not be able to perceive what the periwinkle's position is in this rhythmical extravaganza; it probably doesn't either. It doesn't have to. It is its nature just to be . . . a dancing periwinkle by the sea." We-Be giggled and added, "Ooh, I just made a rhyme!" and settled down in the sand next to Andrew, looking very pleased with herself.

He couldn't help but grin a little. She caught it out of the corner of her eye and said, "Hey, I think I like you better when you're drunk!"

Andrew laughed and leaned back to get a better look at her. She was pretty cute, he had to admit, though redheads had always scared the hell out of him. She seemed softer tonight in her angelic guise, but he surely wouldn't buy this image. Still, she appeared less like a demon from Hell and more like a real woman, drunk hallucination or not.

"Well sure, being a dancing partner with the Universe is easy for a periwinkle; it doesn't have to worry about anything except whether or not the ocean will still be there in the morning when it wakes up, or if some little kid is going to come along and squish it. All my needs should be met, too, and that's what this manifestation stuff is all about. I want to be able to just lie back and enjoy the good life without all the hassles."

We-Be's face suddenly became more serious and she sat up straighter. "There's a marked difference between you and the periwinkle, Morgan. It realizes it's a part of nature and accepts nature's terms. Its consciousness knew full well upon entering physical reality that it wouldn't experience free will as a periwinkle. You, however, have choices because you do have free will."

She looked at Andrew sideways, as though measuring him carefully. "One of those choices could be to rely strictly on nature for your sustenance, just like the periwinkle, operating fully within nature's framework and on its terms—if that's really what you want. You could have all your needs met, too; it all depends on how you define 'needs.' If you should decide to go this route, I can lay out a game plan for you."

We-Be fixed her direct, sea-green eyes on Andrew as she waited for a response. Getting none, she continued: "Simply go off into the woods, leaving all the comforts of modern technology behind, to find your natural place in the scheme of things. No guns allowed, by the way—they ain't natural! The worst problem I see with this approach is the bears. They have everything that you'll want. You'll have to fight them for the berries and figure out a way to get them out of their caves. That's nature's way: survival of the fittest, or the smartest, or the biggest, as the case may be. That's the way it is when you throw yourself fully into nature's arms, divorcing yourself from any trace of civilization. And I need to warn you that it can get pretty damn cold out there at times, and a bear's natural coat is much nicer than yours—but remember, no guns allowed!"

Rolling his eyes, Andrew said, "Don't you think you're carrying this 'roughing it' bit to the extreme? Who says there's anything wrong with technology?"

"Well, if you want nature to provide for you, she has to be able to find you!" We-Be tapped her lips with her index finger, trying to hide a mischievous smile. "But okay, we'll allow a little technology into your choices. Your other alternative, then, is to return to the same woods in a self-sufficient yet well-prepared manner, accompanied by tools, know-how, and lots and lots of seeds. You'll have to build your own cabin, plant your own garden, carry your own water, and chop your own wood. I'll even grant you a gun this time around—but no electricity allowed, unless you can generate it yourself. Sounds like a lot of work, huh, Morgan?" We-Be said, the irony obvious in her tone. "Sunup to sundown, helping nature provide your needs."

Andrew patiently emptied the sand out of his shoes, trying to act unruffled. "Let me guess, you're trying to convince me that I shouldn't have any desires or expect any luxuries in life, right?

That I should be content with simply having my basic needs met and be happy with just the bare essentials? Well I don't buy it. Man doesn't live by bread alone, you know!"

"The key word here is 'needs,' Morgan. And I never said there's anything wrong with having desires. One of the reasons you chose to enter space and time was to enjoy yourself, after all! But whether you want to live in a technological society or in a more natural habitat, you have to play by the rules. And at the risk of repeating myself: Everything comes from somewhere; technological things from technology, natural things from nature. So, you can follow the way of the periwinkle, if you want to, and have all your needs met; just don't expect Mother Nature to plop a Porsche at your feet!

"Space-Time Principle Number 21:

Porsches don't grow on trees."

Andrew threw his hands up in frustration. "That's no Space-Time Principle!"

"I know that, silly! I made it up, just for you. Where's your sense of humor?" Pulling her knees up, she peered over them at him with laughing eyes.

Andrew let out his breath in exasperation and threw himself backward into the sand.

"Morgan, you need to realize that man stepped outside the framework of nature by choice; and as his technologies progressed, he became more and more reliant on them and less and less in tune with the natural order of things. He established a new set of rules, based solely on his technological needs and desires." As if on cue, a low-flying jet screamed overhead, cutting a path across the disk of the moon setting on the horizon.

"How can nature provide man with all his needs when his needs are outside its framework and in a different context entirely? Porsches don't grow on trees, unless you look at it figuratively, as in the myth of Adam and Eve. Not so mythical really; their biting into the apple symbolizes man's conscious decision at one point in history to step outside the instinctual framework of the other animals and develop free will. He acquired new appetites that the 'garden' couldn't satisfy. He didn't get thrown out of the garden or fall from grace, so much as he willfully chose to enter a new dimension of experience. He sought knowledge and the ability to develop that knowledge without limitation or outside interference, and in doing so, set himself apart from the rest of Earthly consciousness. He strove to be a god in his own right. Unfortunately, he left behind his deep, mystical connection to nature and began to forget his innate sense of rhythm, his real god powers."

Andrew had been silent and still for more than a few minutes, and We-Be reached over to touch him to make sure he was still awake and paying attention. He jumped at her touch and sat up again, conscious, but yawning.

"I'm not boring you, am I?" she asked.

"No, no," Andrew assured her, his voice betraying the genuine interest he was developing in what she had been saying. He had never thought of the creation story in quite this way before. He had visions in his mind of Adam and Eve leaving the Garden of Eden—driving off in matching his-and-her Porsches, discussing their destination on cellular phones.

But catching himself starting to sound agreeable, he added, "Woman left the Garden, too; don't just blame the man."

We-Be, her eyes still smiling, spoke slowly to Andrew, as if explaining something to a small child. "We say 'bird,' not 'boy-bird' or 'girl-bird.' We say 'cat,' not 'girl-cat' or 'boy-cat.' We say . . ."

"Okay, okay, okay, I got it," Andrew interrupted.

"Well, I can say 'he or she,' 'him or her,' 'his or her,' but it will really complicate things and slow me down, and I'd like to get back to the topic under discussion," We-Be said.

"Fine, fine, say 'man' for girl and boy humans, just get on with it." Andrew sat up, propped his elbows on his knees and leaned his chin in his hands. He looked as if he might nap right there. "What is the topic under discussion?"

"Technology and nature. Taking the laws of nature into a technological society and demanding they work there isn't the thing to do, nor is using Mother Earth merely as a source of raw materials—which your species seems so hell bent on doing these days. Your industries take her pure resources and convert them into different substances entirely—synthetic products that are needed to fuel the hungry technological beast. The wastes created by this ravenous beast are then returned to the body of Earth, as though trying to convert her into a cesspool." We-Be's face grew sad.

"What your species needs to learn is how to recapture its natural sense of rhythm and use it to revamp its technological way of life. Hopefully this is the next step in the evolution of man, one in which he once again becomes aware of his connection to the whole. He will realize that he is a co-creator with nature, not its master, and that he is not here to dominate the other species but to act as their caretaker through his properly applied technological abilities. He will no longer see nature as an unpredictable adversary, but rather as an intriguing, spontaneous expression of being. He will wed his human intellect with his god intuition. Give and take, Morgan, once again."

Falling silent, We-Be narrowed her eyes and concentrated on a sea gull landing at the edge of the water a few feet from them. The bird began pulling at something shiny, trying to claim it as its prize. Suddenly the gull started struggling and fell over on its side, screeching. We-Be cursed softly under her breath, and, springing to her feet, ran quickly to the feathered creature's rescue. Andrew couldn't make out what she was doing as she leaned over the bird, gently cooing to it. Then, standing up again, she tossed it into the starry sky and stood, as still and elegant as a Greek-goddess statue, watching it fly away.

Stern-faced, she rejoined Andrew and sat down, carrying the shiny something in her hand. "Gotta knife?" she asked. Andrew patted his pant's pockets and shook his head "no." Shrugging her shoulders, she handed the object to him and picked up a jagged piece of shell lying next to her. He turned the flimsy object over in his hands and recognized it immediately: a plastic loop six-pack holder for canned drinks. We-Be took it back from him and sliced through each loop with the shell before stuffing the remnants in a fold of her garment.

Shaking her head sorrowfully, she continued: "When you can comprehend all this, and really feel it, you won't need to ask why any consciousness would want to be a periwinkle. You'll simply understand, like it does. What you and the rest of mankind need to do is rekindle that god-part of yourselves that realizes the significance of being a shellfish."

"But I already am God!" Andrew whooped, jumping up and stretching his arms wide as though to embrace the entire expanse of the ocean. "I'm God, you're God, we're all God! I have the power to work miracles, the power to move mountains; all I have to do is believe that I do!"

"For God's sake, Morgan, powers come to the wise, so wise up! You're trying to plug into the Universe with a cheap two-dollar extension cord. You need to develop the qualities befitting a god before presuming to have authority over anything besides yourself. You're a god with a little 'g,' or a part of God with a capital 'G.' All the little g's make up the big G, see?" We-Be giggled again at her accidental play on words.

"And I guess the big G's a bearded old man, sitting in the clouds somewhere, passing judgment on all us little-g mortals, huh?" Andrew sat down regally, mimicking his version of a Sunday school God.

"No, but it sure sounded like you thought that the other day when you were treating the Universe like a great big parent in the sky, trying to wheedle it into giving you your heart's desires. Now you're telling me that you are God! You better figure out who's God and who isn't before attempting to relocate any mountains."

"Just who do you think you are, anyway? You act like you think *you're* God!" Andrew said, pursing his lips tightly.

We-Be's expression was strained as though trying to remain composed over his outburst. "Titles are meaningless, Morgan, until they're earned. You have to fill the job, that's the important thing. What does the title 'God' mean to begin with? The intricacies of God are beyond the bounds of human comprehension—beyond my comprehension; kinda like one of your periwinkle friends trying to understand the incredible breadth and living complexity of the entire ocean. Anyone who has ever claimed to have received a so-called glimpse of God has taken his experience and compartmentalized it and limited it by the mere act of titling it God. Some have even gone so far as to build entire religions around it. But, without exception, what they experienced was god, with a little g—the incredible glory of themselves. It's a paradox, to be sure, that there are no real separations between all the little gods, and yet there is constant individuation. Separation within unity—what a concept!"

We-Be sifted sand through her fingers, studying it intensely, as though each granule held its own mysterious, individual secret. Then, patting it gently, she smoothed it back into the ground between them.

" Space-Time Principle Number 204:

It can be safely said that
'We are all one,' but to say 'I am all'
is a gross misunderstanding."

"Most humans aren't even vaguely aware of their little-god state, let alone their connection to the whole. This shows in every walk of life; for if they understood, even just a little, who they really were and what their relationship was to everything around them—not just to a few select other humans—there would be no divisions between religions or countries, no starving children, no polluted waters, no war, no sea gulls getting caught in plastic death-traps. When you see someone working to bring the world together in peace and harmony, then you see a person who comes close to comprehending his own godliness, who is ready to discover his own powers, for the powers come to the wise."

"I have no business trying to fix other people's lives for them when I have problems of my own." Andrew felt uncomfortable with the bent the conversation was taking.

"But, Morgan, can't you understand that the first step in dealing with your problems is recognizing your connection to the whole? This recognition will magically lead you to the powers that you're looking for. You'll begin seeing your problems differently, and dealing with them differently. And the powers, when given their own magical freedom, will lead you to a deeper understanding of your true desires, thereby eliminating many of your difficulties. For the powers were designed to help you comprehend the interconnectedness of all things, and in the process, paradoxically enough, to help you develop a stronger sense of your individuality. But they can only work with you when you provide a space for them. And they certainly don't like to be abused or misused, for they are the stuff God is made of."

"This is too much to comprehend right now," Andrew groaned. "I'm trashed." He rubbed his eyes to try to keep them open, wishing now that she would just go away so he could crash, right there on the beach. "I need to deal with my immediate problems in a few hours; I can't handle thinking about the plight of the whole world. Why not leave me with a few final words of wisdom and let me get some sleep?"

We-Be crooked her pretty head and thought for a moment. Then, getting up and brushing the sand off her backside, she enunciated each word of her answer slowly but firmly: "Get . . . a . . . job!" And with that statement her image blinked into a tiny firefly-like point of light that shot straight up into the sky to blend into the backdrop of scattered stars.

Andrew rubbed his eyes again, thrown off balance by her quick disappearing act. "The hell with you! 'Get a job?' What kind of cosmic wisdom is that?"

But the beach was now empty of anyone but himself, and no answer to his question came. Too tired to make the drive home, he stood up to take off his jacket to use as a pillow, still cussing We-Be out loud.

"And don't forget to pick up that tequila bottle before you leave, Mr. God-with-a-little-g-in-training!"

"Aaahhh!" Andrew shrieked, and jumped back instinctively as We-Be's voice thundered from out of nowhere. As exhausted as he was, it took him fifteen minutes to drift off to sleep, as he kept expecting his personal she-demon without wings to return to torment him.

Chapter Five

Psychic Sympathy

Andrew awoke to the piercing cry of a sea gull not three feet from his head, the sun beating red hot against his eyelids. He must have kept his guard up unconsciously while asleep, for at first he thought the noisy bird was We-Be, back to terrorize him. But then, that had all been a dream, hadn't it? Wasn't that all she ever really was—part of his own subconscious? He still wasn't sure; there was the possibility that Lana had been right, and his dream creature was some sort of lower-astral entity. But, as much as Andrew hated to admit it, he was beginning to feel an affinity for this woman who haunted him. Could Lana, the great dream expert, have been wrong? She had, after all, been wrong about Amy's undying love for him. Surely, We-Be must just be a dream! But even so, her strange, eccentric philosophy must hold some sort of validity. He knew that serial-style dreams were rare and shouldn't be ignored. Laughing at his thought, he winced at the sharp pain that stabbed him in the lip. Ignore We-Be? Impossible!

Actually, Andrew preferred the weird dream reality to the physical nightmare he was presently caught in the middle of. He wished the whole restaurant scene of the night before had only been part of his dream, but his swollen lip attested to the full reality of the situation. And now it was time to go home and face his latest manifestation gone awry.

Whimpering, he half crawled, half walked up the dunes to his car. His temples were pounding in rhythm to the surf, either from the fist fight of the night before or the half-bottle of tequila he had downed, or maybe both. The sun bounced off the sand, directly into his bloodshot eyes, as though purposely trying to compound his agony. Making his way toward the red blur that he knew was his car, he tripped and fell over something, almost landing flat on his face. Spitting sand out of his mouth, he looked at the tequila bottle lying at his feet that he had littered the beach with the night before. We-Be's last words echoing in his head, he snatched the bottle up and dragged himself to his car to head for home, a hot shower, and three aspirin.

◆　◆　◆

103? Yep, that was the number on the half-open door. He walked into his apartment cautiously, a bad feeling in the pit of his already-churning stomach. Looking around, his eyes froze, locking onto the empty spot where his TV used to be. He had been robbed.

"Maggie! Where the hell are you?"

In a mad panic, he ran through the apartment looking for her, while at the same time checking to see what else had been stolen. Nothing else seemed to be missing, except Maggie . . . and all her belongings.

"That bitch!" Andrew shouted to the naked wire hangers on her side of the closet as he tore them down and, with a vengeance, bent and twisted them into a deformed metal tangle. His anger spent, he sank to the floor and sat there motionless with his eyes closed. Her stale perfume hung in the air, gagging him, reminding him of how much he had really resented her presence. "Good. She's gone," he told himself, "out of my life forever. So what if she ripped off my TV? Big deal. That's a small enough price to pay to get rid of her."

Still sprawled on the floor, Andrew tried to muster up enough energy to take a shower by peeling off his sand-caked clothes. Struggling to his feet, he headed for the bathroom, trying to run all the positive aspects of the situation through his mind. "After all," he reminded himself, "I did get a car out of the deal and another month's rent money . . ."

The silent words hung perilously in his head: "Rent money!" Andrew's mind went numb, and for a minute he couldn't remember how to breathe. Shaking visibly, he walked slowly into the living room, eyes frozen on his bookshelf.

"She couldn't have . . ." he whispered hoarsely, as he reached a trembling hand up for the book in which Maggie had hidden the rent money. Closing his eyes, he pulled it down and held it tightly against his chest for a moment, trying to remember an affirmation—any affirmation—to make the four hundred dollars still be there. His mind was blank.

Taking a deep breath, Andrew fanned the book open, trying hard to see the money fall out on the floor. Nothing. He tried again, holding the book open with both hands—still no money.

"Must be the wrong book," he rationalized desperately, as he grabbed another one off the shelf and tore through the pages.

Sobbing, he frantically searched through volume after volume of manifestation manuals, flinging across the room each one that failed to yield the cash. Then he raged through the place, kicking Maggie's latest collection of empty beer cans around, until he collapsed on the couch in exhaustion. Looking down he remembered he was naked, his body streaked with sweat, running in rivulets through the powdery sand still clinging to his skin. Andrew had never in his entire life felt as miserable as he did at this moment.

Something jabbed his bare thigh, and pulling it out from under him, he saw the words *Making Money with Your Mind*. All his anger surged through him, directed at the book—the book that was supposed to contain the four hundred dollars—as he jumped to his feet, reared back, and hurled it through the air. The sound of splintering glass came a split second later, followed by his door crashing open into the wall.

"What the hell's going on here?" Looming in the doorway was Mr. Briggs.

Andrew stood mute and still, his mouth gaping open idiotically. Briggs also seemed speechless for several seconds, as his eyes took in the sight before him. Beer cans and books and slivers of glass littered the place, the furniture thrown askew. His tenant stood before him, stark naked and sweaty, hair standing on end, eyes red and puffy. His nostrils were assaulted by the smell of stale beer. Morgan was definitely "on something" or drunk out of his mind, Briggs decided, for he didn't even make a move to try to cover his nakedness.

Briggs finally broke the silence. "I said, what the hell's going on here?"

Andrew shook himself out of his stupor, trying to make his head work. "I've been robbed; they took my TV and—"

"Lemme guess . . . your rent money, right, Morgan?"

"That's right! I—"

"Robbed my ass! You've wrecked the place! Who's gonna pay the damages, huh? You? Ha! You didn't even pay your damage deposit. I oughta call the police and have you thrown in jail; that's what I oughta do. So if you're smart, you'll be outta here in one hour! Got it?"

Andrew felt completely humiliated. He was too off balance to even try to plead his case, so he nodded his head, unable to look his landlord in the eye, and offered no fight at all. He stood there, immobile, stripped of all dignity for what seemed like hours, until he finally realized Briggs had gone, leaving the door wide open. Curious neighbors stood back at a distance, cautiously trying to peer inside.

A part of Andrew's mind was screaming at him, "Hurry! Hurry!" but it was all he could to do drag himself to the bedroom and throw on some clothes. All he wanted in the world right now was a shower, but he couldn't risk taking the time. He had to pack fast and get out in an hour, for he had no doubt that Briggs really would call the police.

Luckily, all the furniture had come with the apartment. Andrew's main possessions were his books, which he had to make himself pick up, for at that moment he felt deeply resentful of them, as if they were to blame for all his misfortunes.

"Well, at least I don't have to clean up this dump before I leave," Andrew muttered as he slammed the door behind him and walked to his car, last pile of books in hand. He had no idea what he was going to do, but instinctively headed for Lana's house. It was a starting point, anyway. He could at least take a shower there, get some psychic sympathy, and stash his books temporarily in her basement—or so he assumed.

Rubbing the stubble on his face, he peered in the rear-view mirror at himself, gasping at the image that looked back at him. His normally healthy complexion looked like paste. Black circles ringed bloodshot eyes that were almost swollen shut, making it difficult for him to see straight. "Coffee . . . I need coffee," he croaked weakly to his reflection.

Pulling into a convenience store, Andrew emptied his pockets and stared at his last dollar, trying to decide whether he really wanted to spend it on a cup of coffee. If he didn't buy it here, he wouldn't get it at Lana's. "Caffeine kills," he could remember her insisting. The most he could hope for from her was a cup of herb tea—not even real tea. She had a strange, exotic tea for every occasion and every ailment. He could never tell one from the other; they all tasted like oriental perfume to him. With the memory becoming vivid to his taste buds, he bought an extra-large cup of the forbidden brew and gulped it down as he continued heading in the direction of Lana's house.

Andrew never failed to be impressed by the hulking mansion in which Lana lived, all by herself, with the exception of Sia and Mia, her two Siamese cats. It brought to mind the Gothic horror flicks that Hollywood became infatuated with from time to time. Lana had even been approached once by some movie producer who wanted to use her house in his film. But when she found out the title of the film was *House of Satan*, she refused to cooperate. She was afraid of the type of vibrations that would linger in her surroundings long after the cast and crew had departed. Besides, she hadn't recognized any of the actors' names.

Lana greeted him at the door with her regal trace of a smile and all-knowing eyes. "I knew you were coming to see me today," she said. "My guides are never wrong!" She wrapped her arms around him, bestowing her customary hello hug on him.

Andrew winced, remembering her guides' insight into Amy's and his relationship. "Soul mates," they had declared, "destined to be together forever and always, without question." But then, maybe it would still work out with Amy one day. . . .

Lana glided down the long foyer, her flowing silk gown sweeping the tile floor behind her. Andrew trailed after her, enthralled as usual with the assorted wall hangings: Peruvian artifacts, brightly colored mandalas, replicas of ancient Aztec warrior masks, Native American dream catchers, even a ceiling-high, gold-gilded plaster casting of the zodiac. The musty smell of the aging mansion intermingled with the aroma of the ever-burning incense: African Violet, Andrew guessed.

Entering Lana's sitting room, he suppressed the urge to open the heavy maroon drapes to let in some light. It was a good thing Lana didn't have any house plants, he thought, for they would surely die a horrible death in this dark tomb she created around herself. But the atmosphere fit her well: Lana had always reminded him of a never-aging, rather benign vampire who had lived in the same house for centuries. He suspected she shunned the light for fear of exposing her finely-sculpted face to the sun, an act which she insisted was detrimental to the skin. Andrew often wondered how old she actually was, but intuitively knew better than to ask. As far as he knew, Lana never left her own environment, never used the Rolls-Royce parked in the garage out back. But people flocked to her from far and wide, seeking her great occult wisdoms.

"You look terrible, Andy dear," she said, touching his bruised lip gently. Andrew figured he must be near death if she could make out his condition in such poor light.

"I feel terrible, if you want to know the truth. You wouldn't believe the mess I'm in this time."

"Oh yes I would," Lana's eyes shined with mystical all-know-ingness. "My guides told me you were in trouble, just yesterday, and I verified the information by pulling your birth chart from my files and doing an update on your planetary transits."

Andrew's eyes glistened with intrigue. She had done his astro-logical chart as a favor a few months before, and with the exception of the predicted importance of Amy in his life, everything had seemed to be pretty accurate. He sat down gingerly on the grand Victorian sofa, hoping he wouldn't damage it with sweat and sand, and waited in anticipation as Lana searched through her papers. Then, finding what she was after, she settled in next to him.

"But first, Andy dear, tell me exactly what has happened since the last time we spoke. It'll help me interpret my findings cor-rectly."

On the verge of tears, Andrew commenced to tell her the whole story of Maggie: the fight with her ex-john, the missing rent money, and his unsympathetic landlord. Eyes gleaming, Lana let out little exclamations of triumph every now and again, as she matched in her mind the planetary configurations to Andrew's recent dilemmas.

Finally running out of words, Andrew's whole body went limp with the relief of telling someone his tale of woe. Lana, on the other hand, appeared exhilarated, almost unable to contain her-self.

"Well, it's not hard to see why you got into that fight, since Mars just happened to be in exact opposition to your Sun yester-day. And with transitting Saturn squaring your natal Venus, it's no wonder that when that girl left your apartment she took your televi-sion set and the rent money with her. Saturn-Venus contacts always cause problems with money, possessions, and the opposite sex."

Thoroughly spent emotionally and transfixed by Lana's authoritative voice relentlessly spelling out his fate, Andrew almost jumped out of his skin when her cat leaped onto his lap. Was it Sia or Mia? He could never tell the two apart. He stroked the big Siamese, as it purred and nuzzled against him affectionately.

"Your sudden need to relocate is easy enough to understand, since Uranus is currently in your fourth house," Lana said, scooping up the other cat who was crying jealously for equal attention. "Uranus is notorious for causing sudden upsets and, in the fourth house, often brings about unexpected moves. And of course you're confused, poor dear; transiting Neptune is sitting right on top of your Saturn. This configuration represents 'The Dark Night of the Soul,' a great testing period that's full of horrible trials and tribulations."

She leaned back dramatically, sighing in sympathy before continuing: "You simply have to be strong and try to weather the storm. Remember, your potential for enlightenment in any given lifetime is in direct proportion to the amount of suffering you've endured. Suffering is good for the soul, for eventually, after you've suffered enough, you'll learn how to manifest your way out of it and into the abundance you deserve."

Lana's eyes bore right through him, as though reading his very soul with the help of her charts. "Let's see what else I can find," she said, pulling out an ephemeris from a large lacquered Chinese box where she stashed all the more mysterious tools of her trade. She flipped through the pages, stopping here and there to close her eyes and psychically assimilate the data. Finally, closing the book, she glanced back at his birth chart and shook her head sadly. "There's a solar eclipse coming up in a couple of weeks, I'm sorry to say, and it's going to be in almost exact conjunction with your twelfth house retrograde Pluto." Lana leaned over and tapped the chart with one exceptionally long, well-manicured fingernail, indicating the sore spot in question. "I'm afraid it's going to get worse before it gets better, Andy, so be prepared! You may even be tempted to take your own life during this period, for Pluto is the Lord of Death. I've seen it happen before."

Andrew didn't need her to warn him about suicide, for after hearing what the stars had in store for him, he was already wishing he were dead. But, at least now he knew that there was a cosmic reason behind all his bad luck; he didn't have to feel responsible for it. It was truly incredible how astrology could be so right on! He didn't know whether to laugh or cry, and was too tired and burned out to do either.

Deep in thought, Andrew could hear the numerous clocks through the house chiming the hour. Lana collected old clocks and was obsessed with their synchronization. Getting up, she released Sia—or was it Mia?—and leaned over to pat Andrew gently on the back. "I have an appointment now, dear, and two more after that. You entertain yourself for a while, okay? And remember, don't touch anything!" Then, smoothing her hair, she lifted her chin a notch higher in the air and swept regally out of the room, cats on her heels, closing the big oak doors behind her.

Andrew sat stiffly on the uncomfortable sofa, rerunning through his frazzled brain everything Lana had told him. He hadn't even remembered to ask her if he could take a shower, and was afraid to push his luck by snooping around the big old house looking for a bathroom other than the one open to her clientele. Besides, he'd probably get lost wandering through the great maze of a mansion, never to be found again.

There was no way he could just sit there in his exhausted agony. His eyes fell on the huge pillows scattered around the room, and, getting shakily to his feet, he gathered them up and made himself a bed against the window wall. He was sure Lana wouldn't be pleased with him crashing on her exotic, oriental pillows, but right now he was too tired to care.

Chapter Six

The Medium of Magic

Andrew snuggled in, grateful to be able to relax for the first time in hours. Sleep settled softly down upon him, ready to carry him off and release him temporarily from his woes.

"Wham!" He sat straight up, startled out of his blissful state by the noise right behind his head. Wincing in pain, he twisted around to see what had so rudely awakened him. A large, timeworn volume of *Anacalypsis*—a rare collection of esoterica—lay inches from where his head had been. At one time Lana had told him how priceless the book was, how long it had taken her to get her hands on a copy of it. He lay back down, trying not to wonder how or why the book had fallen, and closed his eyes. But Andrew found himself fidgeting; he knew he had to get up and return the book to its shelf, for Lana would have a tizzy if she saw it out of its proper place. Struggling to his feet, book in hand, he strained his eyes in the sunless room, trying to locate an obvious gap in the endless miles of occult literature. There it was—a large rectangular hole, just above eye level. It took all his waning strength to lift the mammoth metaphysical masterpiece above his head and aim it at its spot. Stumbling a little, he put his weight against the shelf and thrust the book back where it belonged.

Suddenly the room seemed to spin, and Andrew grabbed hold of the shelf to keep from falling. The floor vibrated and creaked under his feet, and he realized with amazement that the room was indeed spinning, or at least the part of it that contained him. Stupefied, he watched Lana's parlor disappear from sight, to be replaced by a damp stone corridor, curving gradually down toward a faint light. Andrew stood motionless for a few seconds, trying to comprehend where he was. Distant sounds of rock 'n' roll music echoed faintly from the same general direction as the light, and gathering his courage, he warily tiptoed toward it. As tired as he was, he still decided to have a peek at what this secret passageway contained, before figuring out a way to get back to where he was supposed to be.

Fighting his way through the draping cobwebs, Andrew homed in on the music and light. He could make out the lyrics to the song now; it was some classic sixties tune from before his time. Listening to it, he couldn't help but think how incongruous it was with the spooky setting of this catacomb-like place, or, for that matter, the entire dwelling itself. He hesitated briefly, and then made himself round the corner to spy on Lana or whoever it was playing the music.

"You? What are you doing here?" He blurted the words out without thinking, in his surprise to see We-Be in Lana's secret domain.

"Christ, Morgan, you scared the hell out of me! I really wasn't expecting you this soon." Reaching over to the CD player, she quickly pushed a button, cutting off Jim Morrison in mid-song. "Sorry, wrong atmosphere!"

Andrew tried to remain calm. "I said, what are you doing here?"

"It's your dream, Morgan, you tell me! If you want, I can leave; there are other things I could be doing besides trying to help you pull your life together, you know." She looked at him with an expression that was a mixture of hurt and indignation.

Andrew studied her closely in the dim candlelight. She was dressed in classic Gypsy attire, hair pulled back and covered with a purple bandana tied sideways. Jewelry dripped from her neck and both arms; large loop earrings dangled from her ears. As she moved, he could hear little bells tinkling from underneath her voluminous skirts. "No, that's okay—stay. Who knows? I may need you to help me find my way out of this place!" He knew he was developing a soft spot for this crazy dream creature, and a part of him was actually glad to see her, though he didn't know why.

"It's just that I thought I was awake," he said. "It all seems so real!"

"Oh, so you don't think dreams are real, huh? Boy, have you got a lot to learn! And what makes you so sure you're dreaming, anyway?" We-Be fiddled with the stereo and started another CD, what Andrew supposed was authentic Gypsy music.

"You just told me I was dreaming!"

"And do you always believe everything you hear?"

Ignoring her needling, he moved in closer, taking in everything, trying to assure himself that this was indeed a dream setting. The room was draped in filmy silken material, in every hue imaginable, and was empty except for a small wooden table, two chairs, and a high-tech stereo system—not unlike the one Andrew fantasized about regularly. In the center of the table sat a candle and a crystal ball; to the left of it was what appeared to be a deck of Tarot cards.

"So, a lot's happened since I saw you last; wanna talk about it?" We-Be pulled out a chair and sat down at the table, resting her chin on her hands.

"Why are you dressed like that? I liked your last get-up better."

"Oh, I dunno . . . figured I'd get back to the old theme-of-the-day approach! Go ahead, ask me something! I shall gaze deeply into my crystal ball . . ." She fluttered her ring-covered fingers theatrically over the glass orb.

Pulling out the other chair, Andrew sat down across from her. "I'm not sure I can handle any more insights into my future right now; thanks anyway." He had a dangerously fragile look about him, like a porcelain cup teetering precariously on the edge of a table.

"Future? Who said anything about predicting your future? No one can do that, not even you, though you're the one who forms your future with your thoughts and ideas, just as surely as if you had formed it with your own two hands. I was going to talk to you about your now, for it's in your now that you form your tomorrow. Course, in a sense your tomorrow forms your now, too, but let's not get ahead of ourselves here."

"Sure, sure, I create my own reality, right? That's what I've been trying to tell you the whole time and you keep arguing with me. But I'm beginning to think it's all just a bunch of nonsense, anyway. I try and try to manifest good things into my life, and what do I get? A hooker who steals from me and gets my face smashed in; kicked out on the street by an insensitive landlord; and let's not forget that everything I own in the world is sitting in the trunk of a car that's probably going to end up getting repossessed!"

"Whew! Talk about predicting a lousy future! What kind of manifestation is that?"

"It's not a manifestation. I don't ever wish for horrible things to happen to me; they just do. And when the good things I wish for do manifest themselves, they don't seem to last very long."

We-Be cleared her throat and gazed into the crystal ball, cupping her hands around it. The ball seemed to cloud up momentarily, and then a luminescent blue light began to strobe from under her hands, casting an eerie glow on her face.

"What are—"

"Shhh!" We-Be interrupted. "I think I'm getting something . . . ah, yes here we go. . .

> " Space-Time Principle Number 30:
>
> If you look at most negative aspects in your life closely, you'll realize that you didn't wish for them . . . you worried for them."

The strobing light dimmed somewhat, and We-Be took her eyes off her principle-producing prop to look at Andrew intently. "I've noticed, Morgan, that whenever you try to manifest something you want, you do it with the belief that you won't get it naturally.

The mere practice of ritualizing manifestation says that you don't trust the magic of your own being. Magic doesn't like to be tamed, for it is its nature to be a wild thing. If you insist on making magic behave, you break its spirit, and it's no longer freewheeling or spontaneous. A true magic-maker doesn't try to manipulate magic but allows it to flow through him, unimpeded by any ultimatums. Manifestation, you see, is manipulated magic."

"Hold on a second! Are you telling me again that manifestation is wrong, that all the studying I've done on the subject has just been a waste of time? I won't believe that for a minute!" Perturbed, Andrew pushed himself away from the table and stared into the blackness that hid the ceiling.

"Did I say that manifestation is wrong? I don't recall saying that. It can work, and it doesn't always have to backfire in your face, either. But it's so much easier to just let the magic flow through you, to let it surprise you at every turn. And there's no reason to worry about whether unfettered magic is your friend, for magic likes to please you. It simply listens to your thoughts and responds. When your mind is in a state of constant turmoil, it sends out conflicting messages, confusing the magic and making it impossible for the magic to determine what you really want. You therefore end up getting what you concentrate on and believe in the strongest, for the magic assumes that you must want what you concentrate on. It can't figure out how to discriminate between your wish-thoughts and your worry-thoughts. So if you're going to worry about something, worry about what your own thoughts are telling the magic."

Her face registered an affected expression of surprise and she pointed dramatically at the crystal ball.

"Space-Time Principle Number 31:

A worry is the result of a wish that didn't believe in itself."

Andrew continued to stare upward and drummed his fingers on his leg as though trying to show his mounting irritation with her words.

"And, if you continually try to maneuver magic or force it to go where you think you want it to go, then you may be selling yourself short, depriving yourself of things you've never even dreamed of. You may get what you think you want, only to realize that you didn't really want it after all; your life is full of examples of this. If you just flow with things, however, you'll know when something wants to be in your life—when it should be in your life—and when you're trying to force it to go against the grain."

"Oh yeah? Well just exactly how am I supposed to tell when something should be in my life and when I'm trying to force it to happen? I don't like guessing games."

"It doesn't involve guesswork, Morgan; actually it's quite easy. There's even a simple formula you can follow to help you figure out the difference: If what you want doesn't slip smoothly into your life after putting a reasonable amount of energy into it, then back off from it temporarily to get a better perspective. Put some distance between it and yourself so that you can see beyond it. You may come to realize that maybe it just wasn't for you, that perhaps there was something better waiting around the corner that the magic was trying to give you all along."

Just a trace of a smirk touched We-Be's lips as she glanced into the crystal ball and then leaned her chair back, gracefully easing her bare feet up on the table.

"Space-Time Principle Number 72:

Magic works best when
you get out of your own way."

Andrew leaned back in his chair, too, almost tipping over on the uneven floor. "What do you mean 'get out of my own way'? Why do I even exist in the first place if I have to get out of my

70

own way?" Sinking down into his chair, he stuck his lower lip out petulantly, like a little boy. "What am I supposed to do, just sit back and allow this big-deal magic to do whatever it wants to me? What about my individuality? What about my own imagination? Aren't I allowed to imagine what I want?"

"Morgan, you're not listening to me!" We-Be put her feet down and leaned over the table in exasperation, sticking her face inches from Andrew's. You are the magic! And of course you're allowed to use your imagination. But you need to realize that it's not what you purposely concentrate on for five or ten minutes at a time that creates your reality, so much as all the countless, seemingly insignificant thoughts that flit through your head throughout the course of your day. These unexamined, uncontrolled thoughts, after a period of time, coalesce and end up concentrating your experience along certain lines. They create patterns, patterns that can't be changed or ignored simply by occasionally visualizing desired objects and events." Andrew pushed himself farther back from the table in agitation, bumping his chair into the wall behind him.

Seemingly unperturbed by his attitude, We-Be settled back into her seat and gently caressed the glass globe. The light emanating from it once again intensified, wave patterns flowing across its surface and forming luminescent letters that she then read aloud to Andrew.

"Space-Time Principle Number 16:

It isn't that you get what you concentrate on so much as you end up where your energies are concentrated."

We-Be lifted her feet back up and crossed her ankles nonchalantly, contemplating Andrew over her painted toenails. "Or, if you want to get scientific about it: energy follows the path of least resistance; same difference.

"You may be able to manifest things into your life even though your negative patterns have gone unchecked, but don't be surprised if your manifestations carry along with them many of the elements of the patterns you ignore, elements that end up undermining your desired creations. Your situation with Maggie was evidence of this. You got out of your predicament all right, but look at the new problems you created! Those five or ten minutes you spend visualizing just can't create enough of a disruption in the deep patterns you constantly, unknowingly follow in your mind to make much difference. You're trying to imagine objects and events and bring them into your life on top of those that have already been created by the thoughts you never consciously examine. You have to become more aware of your thoughts—the constant stream of images that bounce around in your conscious mind—for until you are aware of them you can't change them."

We-Be paused and closed her eyes as though searching through her mind for her next words. "Imagine, Morgan, that you have a garden and it's full of weeds . . ."

"Oh no, not the old weeds-in-the-garden analogy!" Andrew rolled his eyes and sighed. "Getting kinda unoriginal aren't you?"

"Shut up! It's a good analogy, and I bet you've never heard it put this way before. Listen and you may learn something for once." She glared at him and bounced one foot up and down in annoyance.

"What are you going to do if I don't . . . put a Gypsy curse on me?"

We-Be continued, pretending not to hear him: "These weeds represent the undesirable thoughts and patterns you've created up to this point. Let's pretend that you plant a beautiful exotic flower right in the middle of this garden of weeds. Every time you water and fertilize the flower, the weeds benefit as well. They strengthen and become more firmly rooted. As the flower grows, the weeds do also; and in time, the weeds will either choke the flower out of existence or intertwine themselves around it so thickly that it becomes hidden from your view. If you cut the weeds back a little, here and there, to give the flower more room to grow, it helps; but it doesn't really solve the problem, for if you forget to tend the garden for even a short while, the weeds sprout back up and overtake the flower again. They have to be pulled out by the roots."

We-Be looked at him closely to see if he was following her analogy. "Likewise, you can delay getting to the root of your problems, discovering the real beliefs behind your experience. You can bitch and moan about your lot in life and the 'weeds' that choke your desires into nonexistence. Or you can try to hold them at bay by conjuring up a flurry of positive affirmations. But you can't pretend the weeds out of your garden by putting a pretty flower right in the middle of it. And you can't pretend away the self-destructive patterns that you've created within yourself by trying to manifest beautiful blondes and stereos stacked to the ceiling—or Porsches, for that matter."

"Sure I can! My imagination creates everything I experience. If I don't like what I'm experiencing, all I have to do is change the picture in my mind." Andrew thumped his forehead dramatically.

"Oh, but what pictures do you play through your mind the majority of the time?"

"Huh? What do you mean?"

"I'm not talking about the pictures you play in your mind when you plug yourself in to the Universe with your two-dollar extension cord for five minutes, three times a day, Morgan. I'm talking about the images that are formed in your head continuously by your everyday thoughts and emotions, the ones you consider irrelevant and try to ignore—the weeds in your garden. They're not fun to pull, that's a fact; weeding can seem like a pretty big chore."

The candlelight flickered wildly, casting shadows on her face, with only her green eyes standing out clearly, looking strangely catlike.

Andrew struggled to look away from the hypnotic pull of her eyes, trying not to feel spooked. "Look, Little Miss Know-It-All, anyone knows you use your imagination to change the patterns in your mind. You have to imagine things to be different before they can become different. When I visualize, I use my imagination to make my life right!" He could feel his face becoming purple with rage at this impudent pseudo-Gypsy who was so rudely challenging his philosophy.

"No, Morgan, you use your imagination to project all the things that could go wrong, or to remember all the things that have gone wrong . . . the majority of the time, that is. And your psyche is very democratic: majority rules!"

"Those five or ten minutes, three times a day that I spend visualizing produce a lot of energy, and I'm sure that that overrides any negativity I may unconsciously put out at other times throughout the day."

"Not 'unconsciously put out,' Morgan," We-Be said, shaking her head. "Quite consciously, but not necessarily recognized. You delegate things to the so-called unconscious that you refuse to be conscious of—pure and simple. When you boost your energy levels for those five or ten minutes, do you really think the energy dwindles back down afterwards? It doesn't. It not only goes into whatever you're trying to create, it lingers to boost your other thoughts and emotions throughout the day. For your magical energy isn't biased; if you think something long and hard enough, the energy instinctively cooperates with the thought and attaches itself to it, thereby drawing a physical version of it to you. Again, energy follows the path of least resistance. Don't forget, when you fertilize the flower, you fertilize the weeds as well, because they share the same soil, just as your thoughts—good and bad—share the same mind."

"Jesus, now I'm a victim of my own energy! I might as well not even do anything, except try not to think all day." Andrew pulled at his face in frustration.

"Don't be ridiculous. There's nothing wrong with thinking about what you desire; but in addition to this, you need to put some of your energy into becoming more aware of the constant barrage of thoughts that fly automatically through your head during the day, some of which may actually be undermining your desires. Stop yourself, every time you think about it; catch hold of one of your thoughts and study it." She motioned with her hands, as though she was grabbing a flying object out of the air around her head.

"Try to trace it back to the belief behind it, by association. Work backward as far as you can go. Do this often; make a habit of it. Isolate a single thought and look at it closely. Challenge it, if you want. Understand, there is no way to become totally aware of every thought you have as you have them—not even the majority of them. They roll and tumble endlessly through your mind at amazing speeds, taking twists and turns and creating offshoots that are impossible to predict.

"When you become familiar with the types of thoughts you have and eventually the beliefs behind them, you'll discover that you like some of the beliefs you find and decide to cultivate them, while determining that others have long outlived their purpose and have to go. Some may be easy to spot and remove; others may be harder to extract—just as some weeds' roots grow deeper than others and stubbornly cling to the soil. But you can't pull weeds if you don't open your eyes to see them, or choose to ignore them when you do."

Scowling, We-Be leaned forward and fiddled with the deck of cards in front of her. "If you want to be the master of manifestation you're striving to be, Morgan, then you need to start opening your eyes wider and broadening your focus to see the bigger picture."

"I don't need this!" Andrew jumped up, feeling his tired legs turn to rubber beneath him. Wobbling, he braced himself on the table and stretched his cramping muscles. "You contradict every-thing I believe in, everything I've learned from all my books."

"Yeah, all the books sitting in the trunk of the car you just prophesied losing!"

"Oh, c'mon, I was only being a little overdramatic when I said that. I don't really believe I'm going to lose it."

"Oh yes you do." Her voice lilted in an annoying know-it-all manner. "In fact, if you're interested, I can tell you exactly how many times you've thought about or imagined losing it versus how many times you've thought about ways to keep it."

"Get serious! You don't know that!"

"Wanna bet? I'll tell you." We-Be stood up defiantly and threw her shoulders back, hands on her hips. "Since you bought your car, not even twenty-four hours ago, you've put out exactly forty-nine worry-thoughts about having it repossessed, or wrecking it, or having it break down. In that same time period, you've wish-thought exactly zero times about having the car paid off and in perfect running condition. You've also spent no time at all wish-thinking about ways to generate a regular income to make your regular weekly car payment."

"I haven't had time to wish-think about anything!"

"No, but you sure made the time to worry-think, huh?"

"You know what? I think I'm beginning to not like you again. I don't want to be here anymore. I want to wake up now and—"

"And water your weeds some more while you whine and cry to Lana? Aw . . . poor little master. Master of Disaster! He wants to run back to the great and powerful Lana, all-knowing mistress of the stars, and receive absolution from his planetary sins! But, gee, I don't know, Mr. Manifestor, a solar eclipse conjuncting your twelfth house retrograde Pluto doesn't sound very hopeful to me! Maybe you ought to just kill yourself now and get it over with!" She plopped back down in her chair, hand to her head in the classic "woe is me" pose.

"Now I know I don't like you! And what gives you the right to come down on astrology like that?"

"I'm not coming down on astrology *per se*, I'm coming down on Lana. What gives her the right to plot out the course of your magic in advance for you?"

"She's just telling me what's already there. . . ."

"If you form your own reality, Morgan, then you don't need someone to draw up a chart for you to show you where you've already been, where you are now, or where you're going to end up! The mere fact that you're letting her tell you what supposedly lies in your future tells me you don't really believe you're the creator of your own experience. You tell yourself you are when it's easy or desirable, but when the going gets a little rough, you disclaim all responsibility and start looking to others for excuses and answers."

She was being hard on him and she knew it, so in an attempt to control her mounting frustration with Andrew, she picked up the Tarot cards, shuffled them, and fanned them out in front of her. "Pick a card, any card!"

"Forget it. I don't want to hear what your dumb cards have to say!" Andrew withdrew from her a step or two.

"Okay, I'll pick one for you. Let's see . . ." We-Be closed her eyes and ran her jewel-laden hands over the cards, humming softly to herself, as though tuning in to the cosmos. Then, in a flash, one hand snatched a card and displayed it face up for him to see. It wasn't a typical Tarot card, after all. There was no actual picture on it, no mystical symbols; but instead, writing of some sort. Andrew moved imperceptibly closer, trying to hide his curiosity.

"Oh, this is a good one. Wanna read what it says?"

"No thanks. You picked it, you read it."

She picked up the card and read it aloud, trying not to smile.

"*Space-Time Principle Number 92:*

If you want to be told everything, there are plenty of people who will tell you what they know. But then you will see through their eyes instead of learning to see through your own."

We-Be winked at Andrew, and when he didn't respond, she made a face and crossed her eyes. He was still mad, but begrudgingly sat back down and stared stone-faced across at her.

"Look, Morgan, I've been a little rough on you today; guess I can be a real sarcastic bitch when I get riled. It's just that I want you to free yourself from all the crap and gain some clarity. Don't be mad at me, okay?" She grinned winningly at him, showing her dimples, as she waited for his response.

Andrew sat motionless for a few seconds, melting inside from her words of apology and her irresistible smile that he somehow felt he had known forever. "Well, okay. I guess even she-demons from Hell can have their off days. Maybe Mars is opposing your Sun today, or something!"

They both laughed, clearing the tension in the air. We-Be leaned over the table and reached for Andrew's hand. Affectionately, she squeezed it and then got up to change the CD that had quit playing sometime in the middle of their argument. Her back to him, she said: "You know, Morgan, it really is useless to ask other people about where your magic is going, because the only magic they can really know about is their own."

She peered around to make sure her continuation of the subject wasn't upsetting him again. He seemed to be completely engrossed in the crystal ball, as he squinted hard, trying to look into its depths, and showed no reaction to her words at all.

As We-Be rejoined him at the table, she continued: "Magic is personalized and cut to fit, tailor-made to your best interests. Using other people's interpretations or perspectives is like wearing their cast-off clothes instead of creating your own tastes in fashion. Your mere existence is proof of your own magic. What is it that grew you from an embryo to an adult? What keeps you breathing without your even having to think about it? What assures you that when you begin to speak a sentence you'll be able to finish it with just the right words, so that it ends up making sense? Magic, of course! And if you can't trust your own magic, then how can you trust someone else's? Is his or her existence more valid than yours?"

Andrew remained silent, contemplating what she had just said. He had to admit to himself that her use of the word "magic" intrigued him.

"Your beliefs are like spells that you have cast upon yourself, Morgan. You are transfixed and mesmerized by the constant thought-incantations your beliefs murmur in your head every moment of your life. The spells that you don't like can't be broken by simply muttering an occasional 'abracadabra,' for you're completely enchanted by the illusions that your beliefs cast. And it does no good to say that an illusion isn't real, because when you're part of an illusion, it is very, very real. The illusion is as real as you are; for to say that any creation of yours is simply an illusion—that it is not real—is to say that you're an illusion and not real, too. Everything in your reality is an extension of you, formed by your thoughts. And thoughts not only form things, they are things!" We-Be looked very satisfied with her dissertation, and gathering up the cards, straightened them into a neat pile.

"But don't think I'm trying to tell you that you're stuck forever in the illusion-reality you've already created. Spells don't have to be permanent. For every spell cast, there's a counterspell; and only you can break your own spells. The spells that aren't fun anymore can be broken by simply eavesdropping here and there on the thought-incantations you recite silently in your mind, and by watching the images they conjure up. Those images may seem illusory, but they form your reality; and then your reality, in turn, reinforces the images. So where does an illusion begin and reality end? When you find yourself in the dream environment—supposedly an unreal reality—are you not still very real to yourself? And wouldn't your normal reality seem unreal—dreamlike—from that stance?" Picking the top card from the deck, she flipped it over for Andrew to see.

" Space-Time Principle Number 80:

Reality is where you find yourself—always.

"I may be an illusion to you—just a dream creature—but then, you may be an illusion to me; it's all a matter of perspective. But we are both real to ourselves in our own distinct reality-systems. And right now, you and I meet on a magical bridge that spans our two separate yet overlapping realities, blending the two to create a special reality composed of our joint energies. From this experience, we can both learn from one another and become more than we were."

"Are you saying you're learning something from me? What on Earth could you possibly learn from me?"

"More about myself."

"Huh?"

"What you are today, I was yesterday, and what I am today, you will be tomorrow. But you will express what I am differently from the way I am expressing it right now, just as I expressed what you are today differently when I was you. Of course, all of this is really happening at the same time anyway and it's all us."

"Whaaat???"

"Never mind. Wait till 'tomorrow' and then you'll understand and can explain it to yourself like I did."

"This is nuts. You sound like a Zen Buddhist or something."

"No, not anymore. That was a long time ago."

"Okay, I give up. Can I wake up now . . . please?"

Andrew leaned over and firmly put a hand over the deck of cards as though to stop her from pulling out another principle.

"Sure, if you want to; I can't keep you here. You're gonna have to in a minute anyway, because Lana will be real pissed if she finds you sprawled out on her expensive imported pillows. Her third customer has been thoroughly analyzed, energized, and exorcised and is forking over his usual hundred bucks, even as we speak. Jesus! She has more clients than Maggie does!"

Andrew got up and made his way to the wall nearest his exit out. He collapsed against it, but immediately pulled away when his hand touched something slimy. "Look, you've got me completely confused, and as much as I don't want to hurt your feelings, I don't think I'm ready to give up on my own ideas yet. I just need to stick it out and stop getting sidetracked. The only way out of this mess I'm in is to manifest my way out, as far as I can see. I've got a car payment due in a week, you know, and I've got to find a place to stay. I'd really like to humor you and your weird philosophy, but I think it's time for some heavy-duty manifesting instead."

He held his hand awkwardly out to the side, trying not to get the gooey gunk on his clothes. We-Be stood up and walked over to Andrew. Removing her bandana, she politely handed it to him before answering, "Okay, have it your way, Morgan, but don't expect me to bite my tongue and not say 'I told you so!' "

Andrew wiped his hands on the bandana, glad it was too dark to see what he had unwittingly touched. Walking back to the table, he laid the bandana next to the crystal ball. "Now that's a prediction if I ever heard one! I form my own reality, remember?"

"Touché! You sure do! Just keep that in mind when you rejoin the great sage, seer, and soothsayer Lana in her metaphysical mausoleum!"

Once again, the room started spinning crazily, and darkness enveloped him. He could feel the pillows twisted into lumps under his back and hear his own ragged snoring. But, even as Lana's sitting room slipped back into his reality, he could hear We-Be's voice trailing after him, connecting their two realities with a last jab of her cynical humor: "Have you ever noticed she doesn't have a single mirror in the whole damn place?"

Chapter Seven

Missing Mirrors
&
Last-Minute Miracles

Evidently We-Be had an uncanny sense of timing, for Andrew had no sooner put the last pillow in its proper place than Lana swooped back into the room, cats chasing her skirts.

"Well, that's done, and I'm totally exhausted, my psychic energies zapped for the day. How about some tea?"

Andrew would have killed for another cup of coffee, but was grateful at this point for anything to wet his parched throat. He followed her into the kitchen and watched as she put the kettle on the stove. This was his favorite room in Lana's house: the white plaster walls, oak cabinets, and brick floor lent a certain cheeriness to the otherwise dreary surroundings. She laid out some cheese and crackers and fruit, and Andrew helped himself, trying not to look as starved as he really was.

"So, what are your plans, dear?"

"God, Lana, I don't know. I'm so tired of feeling desperate all the time. I always seem to be caught up in these ridiculous dramas, feeling like an outsider, like life's going on just fine all around me but without me. It's the same thing, year after year." Andrew stuffed the last cracker in his mouth and stared longingly at the plate that was as empty as he felt his life was.

Getting up to silence the whistling kettle, Lana busied herself making the tea. "You simply need to get hold of your emotions,

Andy, and learn how to embrace the feeling of being rich and successful. Can't you do that?" She set a china cup full of steaming tea down in front of him. "Here, this'll calm you down; it's good for the nerves. You really do need to learn how to relax, you know."

Andrew sipped at the brew, scorching his tongue. He leaned back, trying to figure out how to relax in the torturous, high-backed wooden chair, and, staring blankly into his tea, contemplated how to really make himself feel something he had never felt before: rich.

Lana sat down and cleared her throat, signifying the beginning of a serious conversation. "Look at me, Andy."

Andrew looked up, his expression betraying his discomfort under the fix of her penetrating gaze.

"What if I were to give you a million dollars right now? How would that make you feel?"

"Like a million bucks, I guess!" Andrew laughed out loud.

"I'm being serious, Andy." His face turned red as she glared at him, and his laughter died in mid-stream as she repeated, "Tell me, how would you feel?"

Not giving him time to respond, she continued: "What I'm trying to get you to see is that the only way out of your situation is to get hold of the feeling of being very wealthy and to maintain that feeling throughout the day, ignoring everything else. And until you can accomplish this, I'm afraid you're going to continue creating a miserable life for yourself. There is no other way."

"But I thought that because of what the planets are doing to me, it wouldn't matter anyway!"

"Oh no, dear, that isn't necessarily so! A true master can transcend his karmic obligations to the Universe."

"But—"

"There are no 'buts' about it! You know what you have to do. You've known it for a long time now. You know the methods, and if you really wanted to get out of your predicament you'd be applying them. Evidently you want to be miserable and poor, or you'd be doing something about it. And I'm not talking about just getting a job, either. A job isn't the solution to your problems. Actually, it's a sin against your spirit to work at a job that your heart isn't in. You never see me working, do you? Anything I do, I do because I enjoy it, not because I need the money." Lana leaned back in her chair and scanned her surroundings proudly, comfortable in her strong sense of superiority.

"Then why do you charge so much for your services?" Andrew asked. "Why not do it for free, just for the satisfaction of knowing you're helping someone?"

Lana sucked in her cheeks in irritation. "If I were to simply give my talents away, they wouldn't be fully appreciated. In order for my clients to see the value in what I have to offer, they have to pay me good money. Surely you know that if you get something for nothing it means nothing!"

"But what about people who don't have any money? What if they need your help?"

"Well, obviously they need my help if they don't have any money!"

"But . . . how can they afford to get your help in the first place?"

"If straightening out their lives is important enough to them, believe me, Andy, they'll find a way to come up with the money."

Andrew blinked in confusion, his mind struggling to make sense out of what she was saying. "So you don't really need the money you make from your sessions?"

"Of course not. I don't have to do anything to maintain my level of prosperity. I never suffer from any lack whatsoever."

"Easy for you to say, Lana," Andrew said, a little braver than usual. "I've got to start from scratch."

"Where do you think I started from? That's the challenge! Everything starts from scratch; this whole universe started from scratch. It started from nothing more than an image in God's mind. If God can do it, you can do it, for remember, you are God!"

"With a little 'g'," Andrew mumbled under his breath.

"What was that?"

"Nothing, nothing, I was just thinking out loud," Andrew said, not wanting to openly question Lana's authority.

"You need to program your dreams for wealth and abundance, too—which you've obviously been neglecting. Start carrying the feeling of being rich into the dream state, for that adds energy to your images and helps actualize them." Lana got up to pour them more tea.

"And speaking of dreams, whatever happened to that malicious little entity you were having problems with? Did you get a chance to use the White Light on it?"

Andrew squirmed uncomfortably in his chair. Somehow it didn't feel right to discuss We-Be with Lana, and he found himself resenting her calling We-Be an "it." Staring into the cup of greenish-brown steaming liquid he held in his hands, he said, "No more problems. It worked just like you said it would."

"Well, I knew it would. Works every time! Evil can never hold its own against the Light of Good."

As though afraid Lana would psychically pick up on the fact that he had lied, Andrew quickly changed the direction of the conversation, pushing himself into the subject he had been dreading bringing up. "Look, Lana, I really do benefit from these pep talks. I need to be around you as much as I can right now. How about letting me stay here for a while, until I get something else going? After all, sleeping in my car wouldn't exactly be great for my prosperity consciousness, now would it?" The words out of his mouth, he bit his lip in nervous anticipation of her reaction.

Lana just stared straight through him for what seemed like an eternity, before stating bluntly, "Oh, I couldn't do that, Andy dear."

Her words hit Andrew in the face like cold water. He had really been counting on her kindness and cooperation, what with all the spare rooms that were scattered throughout the huge house. Panic clutched his stomach, as he desperately tried to think of the right words to cajole her into helping him in his time of need.

"Why not? I can help you out around here. I won't get in the way; you won't even know I'm here. I can clean up, feed the cats, tend your garden. . . ."

"My garden doesn't need tending, and I can feed my own cats." Lana's countenance became rigid, her lips pursed, showing wrinkles that Andrew had never seen before. The tension in the room was thick, and for a few moments all he could hear was the ticking of the countless clocks and the purring of the cat at his feet. He was stunned by her words, and it took him a second or two to find his tongue.

"Lana, I just don't understand. I thought we were friends, and I'm really in a bind."

"Look, Andy, as much as I love you and care about you, I really can't afford to be exposed for very long to your negative vibrations. I've worked long and hard to create an aura of positive energy in my home, and your continued presence here would throw it out of balance. I have to protect my psychic energies; having you here would drain them, and I wouldn't be any good to anyone then. Try not to take it personally, dear," she added, striving to make her voice sound sweet again.

Andrew could tell that no amount of pleading was going to change her mind. "Well, then how about a small loan? A couple of hundred dollars to get me through the week and back on my feet? I could pay you back in a month or two." He winced as he heard himself making the same promise he had made to so many people and never kept. But visions of missing his car payment and having his car towed away flashed through his head. He could almost hear We-Be tallying his latest worry-thought: "That makes fifty, Morgan!"

"I can't in good conscience do that either, Andy."

"Why not? What's two hundred bucks to you? Hell, you made more than that just in the few hours I was waiting for you!"

"That's not the point," Lana said in irritation, as she got up to clear the dishes off the table, banging them down into the sink. "If I were to help you financially at this critical stage in your development, I'd be letting you assign your powers of manifestation to me! You'd be allowing me to form your reality for you, and that would hurt both of us. Remember what I said about suffering:

it's the only way to eventually learn how not to! 'Feed a man a fish, he eats for a day; teach a man to fish, he eats for a lifetime.' It's good for you to see me swimming in my wealth and abundance so you can see what's possible, but it would be bad for me to share it with you."

"Well, would it be asking too much of you to let me at least take a shower before I leave to go God knows where?" Andrew's voice unwittingly relayed the mixture of despair and anger he was feeling over her complete refusal to help him out.

"God does know where. You just have to have faith and remember that you're special and being guided."

"But can I take a shower first?" Andrew was trying hard not to show how furious he was with her. He didn't want to burn any bridges—he didn't have very many bridges left; and at least Lana would still listen to him when he was desperate.

"Oh, I suppose," she begrudgingly acquiesced, and led the way down the hall and up the stairs to one of the bathrooms. Silently, she handed Andrew a towel and wash cloth and laid out a disposable razor. He could tell she was feeling imposed upon, as she closed the door behind her with a little more force than necessary.

Andrew jumped right into the shower, turning the water on full blast. He had never enjoyed a shower as much as this one, and stretched it out as long as he could, groaning with pleasure as the hot water massaged his aching body. The room was lost in steam when he finally stepped out, feeling around for the towel. His hand hit the razor, and he realized that in his eagerness to rid his body of the dirt and grime, he had neglected to shave first. Shaking his head at his own forgetfulness, Andrew rummaged around in the vanity drawer, looking for some shaving cream. Finally giving up the search and cussing under his breath, he grabbed the soap out of the shower and began to lather up his face. He reached up to wipe the steam from the mirror, only to have his hand hit bare plaster. "Damn!" He opened the linen closet, hoping to find a mirror on the inside of the door. No luck. Searching the drawer again, he finally found a lady's compact and opened it up to use it. No mirror. A slight chill crept up his spine. No mirrors? Andrew took a deep breath and shaved as fast as he could, cutting himself twice. Throwing his clothes on, he sprinted down the stairs as he tried hard to erase the subject of mirrors from his mind and not let his imagination get the best of him.

He found Lana in her front study, sitting at her desk, once again appearing completely composed. Behind her hung her assorted credentials, framed in gold: accreditations from various psychic schools and metaphysical institutions; a certified medium's license; and a certificate proclaiming her status as a doctor of divinity.

Smiling at him affectionately, she got up and walked him to the front door. "You'll be fine, just wait and see! Keep practicing your visualization techniques regularly, dear, and don't dwell on the past." Andrew could hear the condescending overtones in her voice, but knew that in her own peculiar way she cared to some degree about what happened to him.

"And remember: feel rich!" Reaching into her pocket, she took out a thin silver chain with something attached to it and pulled it down over his head. The light from the open door caught the object, throwing prisms of dancing color on the walls and ceiling. It was one of the quartz crystals that Lana sold by the handsful to her clients; she insisted they held great healing properties as well as mystical powers of attunement.

"Whenever a bad thought pops into your head, just focus on this crystal and replace the thought immediately with its opposite. The crystal will absorb the negativity and transmute it into positive energy. It will also protect you from evil and harm as long as you have it on."

Andrew studied the crystal and thought snidely, "And it's all yours—a $9.95 value—absolutely free, just for being here today!" But he made himself smile appreciatively as he walked out onto the porch. He was actually glad now that she had refused to let him stay, for he wanted to get away from Lana and her creepy house as soon as possible.

"Oh, and before you go, Andy," she said, following him out, "don't forget that Saturday night is channeling night. I'm going to be having a couple of guest speakers you just have to meet! Peter channels Horzel, one of our space brothers from the Sirius star system, and Krista-Ann channels Celso, an entity who's never been physical. They'll be sharing words of wisdom on the coming Earth changes. Their entities want to warn us of the disasters that are going to befall our planet, and prepare us for survival. You really should try to make it a point to come, for as I've told you before, you have a Uranus-Mercury conjunction in the ninth house of your birth chart, giving you the inborn talent to be a clear channel. You can learn a lot from these two people, and I won't charge you the normal twenty-dollar donation if you don't have it by then. Okay?"

Andrew thought about asking her how anyone could "charge" a donation, but he wasn't sure he wanted to end this friendship just yet. So he simply promised to join her on Saturday, even though he had no way of knowing whether he would be able to keep his promise, or would even want to. Returning her customary farewell hug, he could feel her, as always, taking in a deep breath and holding it for a few seconds, before releasing him. As he drove away from Lana's house, Andrew looked back at the brooding old mansion and suddenly wondered about these required hugs of hers. Catching his reflection in the rear-view mirror, he laughed to himself, playfully pretending that he had it all figured out: Lana didn't suck blood with fangs like the traditional vampire; she drained energy instead, with her loving embraces!

♦   ♦   ♦

It was starting to get late; after-work traffic was beginning to build up at every intersection. Andrew searched the corners of his mind, trying to come up with a quick solution to his homeless state. He found himself driving in circles, and realized he had to decide where he was going and fast, for he needed to conserve every precious drop of gas in his tank.

He had already worn out his welcome everywhere he could think of; he owed money to almost everyone—ten dollars here, fifty dollars there. He never really meant to take advantage of his friends and always had the best intentions of paying them back. But whenever he got his hands on any money, he ended up needing it just to survive.

His mother had moved back north years before, and he didn't even know her phone number. She wouldn't be able to help him anyway; she was probably just as bad off as he was, if not worse. When he had last seen her, she had been in her typical alcoholic stupor, mumbling and feeling sorry for herself. She had slowly degenerated over the years after his father's death, and seemed to care less and less about Andrew. Shortly after his eighteenth birthday, she had taken off in a Winnebago with some drunken retired Marine, and he hadn't heard from her since.

Andrew pulled into a shopping center to park and think out his predicament. Closing his eyes, he leaned back to try to clear away all the thoughts that were spinning uncontrollably in his head. He realized that this type of situation was one that had repeated itself over and over again in his life. He could almost even remember sitting in this same shopping center three years before, feeling the same familiar gut-clutching feelings of despair. But, of course, it didn't matter whether it was the same one or not; it all ran together in his head like one big *déjà vu* nightmare. There had to be some way out of this circle game, some way of ending it once and for all. There just had to be a solution.

In the midst of the myriad thoughts vying for his attention, the tail end of one of We-Be's Space-Time Principles rose up from the depths of his mind, taking the forefront: Accept what you have for now and work from there.

The words made Andrew laugh, and he tried to brush their annoying implications aside. What did he have, anyway? And how could he so gracefully work from nothing and nowhere? But the words wouldn't leave, and instead continued to rustle around in his head. He felt like a helpless victim of circumstances, tossed about like a rag doll in an erratic, uncaring universe. But then, he always felt that way when the going got rough. We-Be had told him that his thoughts were what perpetuated the circle game of frustration and failure that seemed to rule his life, although he didn't want to think about that right now, nor did he have the time to. He just wanted to clear his mind and manifest his way into a better future—immediately.

Andrew leaned the seat back and tried to slip into an altered state, where he could banish all his worries and make the images of his desires dance on his inner eyelids. But, try as he would, he couldn't seem to get focused; the worry-thoughts swirled around creating pictures that dominated his mental atmosphere. Discouraged, he sat back up, running his fingers through his hair. We-Be's words trickled back into his consciousness again, taunting him, challenging him to give them consideration. His stomach growled as a grim reminder of the immediacy of his situation, and he knew he wouldn't get anything solved until he filled it. But how? He was flat broke.

He scanned the storefronts halfheartedly, hoping beyond hope that somehow they would provide an answer. There were no "help wanted" signs visible—and what good would that do, anyway? Cash advances were a thing of the past, or maybe a myth altogether. Suddenly his eyes locked on a store at the very end of the strip with the name "Bob's Used Books" spelled out in huge red letters above it. An idea suddenly popped into Andrew's head and he drove down to check the place out.

Just as he'd hoped, the bookstore showed every sign of being heavily New-Age oriented. The door tinkled behind him as he walked in, and he stood by the register for a minute clearing his throat to try to get someone's attention.

"May I help you?"

Andrew jumped as a stooped little old man appeared, calculator in hand, from between two huge stacks of books.

"Yes, sir. I was wondering if you'd be interested in buying some books."

"What kind of books?" The storekeeper peered at Andrew over his spectacles.

"New Age, mostly. And some money-making manuals—that kind of stuff."

"Well, sure I'm interested, but I have to look at 'em first. I'm about ready to close up shop. Tell you what though, you bring 'em around tomorrow morning and I'll have a look-see."

Andrew's heart fell into the pit of his very empty stomach. "I'm kinda in a jam; can't I get you to look at them now? I'll sell them to you real cheap!"

"Well, I'll tell ya, I only buy cheap—but in good condition!"

"My books are in top condition, and they're right outside in the trunk of my car. How about it? Will you give me a break and let me bring them in? Please?"

The old man scratched his head and thought for a moment. "New Age, you say?"

Andrew took this to mean 'yes,' and dashed out the door to his car. Lugging the boxes of books out of his trunk, he thought how glad he was that he had forgotten to ask Lana to store them for him.

Twenty-five dollars richer and half his books poorer, Andrew left the bookstore half an hour later in search of the nearest burger joint. He could almost hear We-Be congratulating him for thinking of a way out of his immediate predicament all by himself. Now he had a little more to work with, and once he had eaten something he would be in better condition to figure out what to do next. And, amazed as he was at his own feelings, he wasn't even particularly upset over parting with so many of his prized possessions. He had thought he would be; after all, he hadn't just hocked them—he was used to hocking his things on a regular basis—he had sold them. He assured himself that he would buy all the same titles again someday, after he had mastered the methods they prescribed.

Andrew pulled into a fast-food place that was advertising a buy-one-get-one-free burger special. While gulping down his dinner, he thought about how magical it seemed to have accidentally found the bookstore in the right place at the right time, and how good it felt to have solved even a small part of his problem without any help from anyone. As he pondered this, he noticed a man staring at him curiously. His face seemed familiar, but Andrew couldn't place it, and he guessed the man was having the same difficulty. Shrugging it off, Andrew got up to leave, just as the stranger tapped him on the shoulder. "Hey, buddy! Aren't you the guy I smashed into the other day?"

Andrew didn't understand at first what he was talking about, but then it dawned on him: it was the backward driver! He nodded and smiled, not knowing what to say.

"Well, how'd everything work out? Did my insurance company take care of you okay?"

Andrew hadn't really studied the man at the time of the accident, but did now. He was in his early thirties, big and burly with a well-trimmed mustache. Patches of perspiration dotted his sweatsuit, telling Andrew the guy had just finished jogging or working out. He was the epitome of the all-American male.

"Yeah, they sent me a check and I got another car." Andrew could see a look of relief pass over the man's face, telling him that the man was feeling a little guilty. Something inside Andrew switched on and started gears turning. He added: "Or I guess I should say, I made a down payment on another car. They really didn't pay me enough to replace my old one outright."

The backward driver's face fell. "Boy, that sucks! Jeez. Well, you doin' okay besides that?"

Andrew was an old pro at this game. He had been here before. Grinning inwardly, he thought to himself:

"Morgan's Principle Number 1:
Someone else's guilt can prove to be very lucrative,
if you just allow him the freedom to express it."

Like a spider weaving its web, Andrew chose his guilt-enhancing words carefully: "Well, not really; actually it's been all downhill for me ever since the car accident—lost my job, stuff like that. But that's really no fault of yours; you didn't mean to run into me."

The backward driver cringed outwardly. "Jeez . . . I feel real bad about all this. Is there anything I can do?"

Andrew sized up his prey and tried to determine what to aim for. "Naw . . . not unless you know where I can get a lot of money in a hurry."

"Another job, you mean? Hell, I can get you a job, buddy, no sweat!"

A job wasn't necessarily what Andrew had in mind. But he decided to hear him out. He could almost see the guy's brain clicking away under the impetus of guilt.

"As a matter of fact, maybe a great job. You ever do any bartending?"

Andrew's spirits fell. Bartending didn't sound like his ideal job by any means. "I've done a little, here and there in the restaurants I've worked at. But I'm not really a pro."

"Hey, so long as you know something, right? Plus, you know me now! Oh, by the way, the name's Pete."

Slapping Andrew on the back, Pete filled him in on the job he had in mind. As it turned out, Pete was the food and beverage manager at the Ryecroft Country Club, a very elite establishment on the north side of town. Just that day the guy who managed the locker room had quit. The job sounded easy enough. It amounted to serving simple mixed drinks and beer to the male club members and golf pros who hung out in the plush locker room, and taking care of their equipment and various needs. Pete impressed upon Andrew that the position he would be filling was a very prestigious one, coveted by all the other bartenders working there.

"Funny how things work out," Pete said. "I was going to have to shuffle everyone around tomorrow and hire someone to fill another spot. I'll get some flack, I'm sure, for bringing you in and not moving everyone else up a notch, but the hell with 'em." Pete beamed as he felt his guilt being alleviated with each additional facet of the job he described.

Walking out together, Pete told Andrew that as the manager of the locker room, he would be on a weekly salary of three hundred dollars plus tips, which usually were in excess of another three hundred a week. He would have to supply his own uniform—black dress pants, white shirt, black vest, and bow tie. Luckily Andrew already had everything except the tie, which he knew he could buy at any department store.

"I'm handing you this job on a silver platter, kid. It's one of the easiest jobs for that kind of money that I know of. Hell, you don't even have to work up a sweat! Most of the time you can just put your feet up and watch TV. So whatdaya think? Can you start tomorrow?"

Andrew liked the sound of it. "Easy" was right up his alley, he thought; and working in an exclusive country club setting surrounded by opulence would do wonders for his prosperity consciousness. "Sounds good to me! What time do you want me there?"

Pete told him to be there at eight a.m. sharp, and then continued to rattle on, telling Andrew more about the job and the people he would be working with. Grinning from ear to ear, he was obviously pleased with himself and his generosity.

"Well, buddy, I'm glad I ran into ya. Hope this'll make up for screwing your life up so bad!"

Andrew was having an inner war with himself. Normally, he would play this role to the hilt and try to finagle a place to stay out of the deal. But he was afraid to push his luck; this turn of events was already quite a coup all by itself. Besides, he was starting to feel a little guilty himself for taking advantage of this guy who seemed to be genuinely nice. He'd just have to figure out where he could crash until he made some decent tips, which sounded like something that would happen right away.

Pete waved as he drove off, and Andrew climbed into his car to contemplate this unexpected development. What a coincidence! Had he manifested this? When? How? He didn't remember. A nagging little thought in the back of his mind kept telling him he had somehow created this, and yet he hadn't even begun to see it coming. It had taken him completely by surprise. The thought teased his memory, and he remembered We-Be's words: ". . . let the magic flow through you . . . let it surprise you at every turn." Andrew shook his head, dazed by it all. He started up his car and drove off, without the slightest idea where he was going, except to the nearest mall in search of a bow tie.

"I'm really on a roll now!" he said smugly to his empty car. "A little spending money, and now a job that doesn't even sound like work."

Pulling into the mall entrance, he found the best parking spot wide open, as though the Universe had reserved it just for him—like magic. Andrew half skipped, half walked across the parking lot, high on his own manifestive powers. Was he "getting with the rhythm" like We-Be had suggested? He knew he should be concerned about where he was going to sleep for the night, but decided to let the powers-that-be surprise him again. He dropped eight dollars on a bow tie and walked around looking in the store windows, dreaming about what he would buy in a couple of weeks with all the money he was going to earn. It seemed to Andrew that at any moment someone he knew would happen along, just in time to offer him a temporary place to stay. After all, it would certainly be in keeping with the streak of good luck he seemed to be riding.

He killed time playing video games and thought about catching a movie, but the chances of his running into someone in a dark theater seemed slim. He strolled up and down the main aisle for another hour, before starting to worry. Why weren't things panning out? Was the Universe toying with him, keeping him in suspense until the very last minute before surprising him with out-of-the-blue living arrangements?

Ten minutes before the mall's closing time, the familiar feeling of panic began clutching at his insides again, and he went in search of a phone. He couldn't wait around for a miracle to find him; he had to seek it out. So, pulling a handful of change out of his pocket, he started making calls. One after the other, his old friends either told him to drop dead, or hung up in his ear, or both. He even called Amy's number, hoping that she had had a change of heart, but hung up when a male voice answered the phone.

His good mood was rapidly deteriorating as he left the mall and headed for his car. One of the friends he called had given him the old "You-made-your-own-bed-now-you-have-to-lie-in-it" routine. Andrew thought this was quite ironic, since all he had been asking for was a bed, and he didn't give a damn if it was made or not. He was fuming inside. "The hell with magic," he thought. "If it's gonna work at all, why doesn't it work all the way? Why couldn't it have simply given me a bed for the night?"

Clear as a bell, he could hear We-Be's voice ringing in his ears: "Jesus, Morgan! A bed yet? I suppose you want the Universe to tuck you in and sing you a lullaby, too? Give it a break!"

Andrew tried to argue out loud with her, but to no avail. The voice was gone as fast as it had come. Embarrassed, he noticed the driver in traffic beside him staring at him curiously, and realized it looked as though he had been yelling at his steering wheel.

Red-faced, he immediately turned onto a side street to escape the onlooker's prying eyes, and headed for a quiet park on the outskirts of town to sleep for the night. He hadn't been to this park in many years, not since he had hocked his telescope to pay some bill or another. He had spent many a night in his late teens gazing through it at the heavens, amateur astronomer that he had been.

Parking in the open to avoid the night bugs that infested the tree-laden areas, Andrew pulled out his blankets and pillow and made himself a bedroll. He would sleep under the stars and try to recapture the old awe and wonder they had instilled in him as a youth. Setting his alarm clock for six a.m. and placing it on the roof of his car, he sprawled out on the hood in his makeshift bed. He stared straight up to get his bearings, and leaned back, snuggling in for the night. Immediately he recognized the pale yellow "star" that was just rising in the east as the ringed planet, Saturn. Craning his head back as far as he could, he traced the cloud-like band of light that was an arm of the Milky Way. And there was Mars, the planet that had always intrigued him the most, a bright red dot set against the black velvet sky. . . .

Chapter Eight

Terraforming Could be Terrifying

Andrew didn't remember closing his eyes to go to sleep, or drifting off into the dream state, and yet he felt as though he was soaring through the air at the speed of light. He could hear the wind howling in his ears as it rushed past him. Assuming he had finally achieved coming awake in a dream—something he had been trying to do for months—he didn't question the experience and focused his attention on the exhilarating sensation of rushing upward into the night sky.

The view in front of Andrew was a blur of stars, tinted with a hazy swirl of red. He was transfixed by the light show in front of him, coming at him at an unbelievable speed. An object began to take form in the distance, and he closed in on it rapidly. It looked like a large orange-pink grapefruit, with white mold tipping either end. His eyes watered from forgetting to blink, making it temporarily impossible for him to focus on the approaching object, until the view in front of him was filled with it, blocking out anything else. It took his mind some time to comprehend and assimilate what he now saw.

Craters were scattered among vast sand dunes, and Andrew could make out an occasional cloud-topped volcano. What appeared to be dried-up riverbeds etched themselves across the rust-stained surface of—he was sure of it now—the planet of his childhood fantasies: Mars. The bright red dot in the night sky had invited itself into his dreams.

Suddenly, Andrew felt the sensation of descending—not falling, but gradually being lowered closer to the planet's surface through huge wisps of cirrus clouds. It was as though an unknown part of him were in total control, putting him at ease and relieving him of any unnecessary fears. Leveling out, he picked up a little speed and found himself hurtling through a deep, fog-filled canyon. Then he started to climb once again back to ground level at an incredible speed, the view around him melting into a creamy reddish-pink blur. Totally disoriented, he squeezed his eyes shut to try to regain his equilibrium. He began to tumble uncontrollably, and panicking, heard himself screaming out loud for help. As though in answer to his plea, his sense of balance immediately returned and he could see the landscape around him begin to sharpen as his speed decreased. Andrew could dimly make out the ground rushing toward him before he came to a screeching halt, landing feet first in the dusty red soil.

Still dizzy from the tumbling experience, he took a few deep breaths before focusing his eyes and looking around him. Awestruck, he gazed at the mysterious alien landscape. He stood poised on a sloping plain in the middle of a vast expanse of sand and rocks—millions and millions of rocks. Patches of frost and snow were strewn here and there. The distant sun was just rising, its light muted by the heavy mists clinging to the horizon. Over his right shoulder hung Phobos, one of Mars's two tiny moons, looking just like a small, pockmarked potato. Far off, a bright, blue-green star twinkled in the fast-disappearing night sky. It took Andrew a few seconds to realize that the star was his own home planet. The Martian landscape around him became forgotten momentarily as he stood wonder-struck with reverence for the luminous stellar body that was Earth.

Ripping his gaze away from the heavenly spectacle, Andrew once again focused his attention on his immediate environment.

If he hadn't known better, he would have sworn he was standing on the outskirts of Sedona, Arizona before the tourists and developers had claimed it. But there were no trees or cacti in sight, no crystal-clear water running in the river gullies, no desert creatures slithering at his feet. Except for the sound of his own breathing, the entire atmosphere of this barren world was permeated with the sound of silence. Taking all this in, Andrew thought to himself that there was no question about it: this was definitely a dead planet.

"Dead my ass!"

Andrew nearly fell over from the shock of having the heavy silence broken so rudely. He swung around to face We-Be, clad in a space suit and helmet, sitting on top of some sort of strange man-made contraption.

"This planet is no more dead than I am—or than you are, for that matter," We-Be announced as she lifted the sunshield from her face. "Gee, and I thought I was good at picking the settings for our rendezvous; this is the best one yet! You're more creative than I thought, Morgan! Been a long time since I've been to Mars. It's so much fun: three-eighths the gravity of Earth, you know!"

With that, We-Be stood up and leaped to the ground, giggling as she landed in slow motion a few feet from Andrew. He ignored her as he walked around inspecting the large spiderlike object on which she had been sitting. Brushing the dust off the metal surface here and there, he uncovered the corner of an insignia of some sort. With the whisk of his hand he wiped the area clean, revealing the logo of a Viking ship. Trying to confirm his suspicions about this contraption's point of origin, he immediately brushed off another area and exposed enough to furnish him with undeniable proof: a segment of an emblem displaying the Stars and Stripes.

"Figure it out yet?" she asked, taking her helmet off and placing it on a metal rod that jutted out from the ship like an arthritic leg. Shaking her hair out, she grinned impishly as she watched him scowling and rubbing and muttering to himself.

"Of course! I should have recognized it right away. It's one of the Viking landers that came here to look for life back in '76."

"Congratulations! You just answered the One-Billion-Dollar-Question!"

As usual, We-Be was in top form and talking in riddles. Andrew decided not to take the bait, but instead gazed up at the last glimmer of planet Earth as it faded out, overpowered by the Martian sunrise. He wanted to just enjoy his dream creation without any interference from her. But We-Be was becoming stir-crazy; he could hear her behind him humming to herself and shuffling her feet back and forth across the frozen ground. Giving up trying to block out her mounting impatience, he reluctantly tore his eyes away from the pageant of colors being painted in the sky by this seemingly foreign sun, and turned his attention to her. "And what theme, may I be so bold as to inquire, are you supposed to be acting out this time?"

Looking very pleased with herself, she smoothed the tight silver space suit with her hands. "Today I'm a space being here to channel great wisdoms to you, absolutely free of charge!"

"And what solar system are you from, pray tell?"

"What solar system? The Solar System, silly! The name of the star your planet and this planet revolve around is Sol: S-O-L. Nothing irks me more than to hear someone refer to all star systems as solar systems. People need to get their stellar semantics straight. For instance, how would it sound to call all star systems 'sirian systems'? That would be pretty dumb, don't you think?"

Andrew stood there sullen and silent studying the porous rocks at his feet, aware now of the tell-tale signs of a lengthy We-Be lecture.

"Just as dumb as it would be to spend time or money seeking advice from some 'space brother' from a planet revolving around the star Sirius. 'Oh, wise Sirian brother of mine, tell me about the coming Earth changes! Where shall I hide from thy prophesied doom? Should I convert my dollar bills into silver or gold, oh Great Supreme Brother? How much grain should I buy and store away? If I'm very, very good, will thou beameth me up and saveth me from my own destruction and thy growing wrath?' Oh, brother!" Exasperated, We-Be hit her forehead with an open palm.

"Jesus, you're cynical!"

"No I'm not! I'm fed up! Plagues and famine! Earthquakes! Landslides! Tidal waves! Hell, I happen to know for a fact that there aren't even any oceans on any of the planets in the star system this Horzel character is supposed to hail from. How on Earth can he even begin to understand the nature of the tides? You'd be better off asking the entire scientific community to predict the next appearance of a tidal wave, except even it's smart enough not to try to second-guess Mother Nature in that respect."

Andrew refused to look at her, and instead focused on a small red dust devil dancing in slow motion on the desolate plain behind her.

"And as far as Lana's channeled being who's never been physical goes: What's his name? 'Seltzer'? 'Sayso'? No, 'Celso.' That's it. What the hell kind of a name is that, anyway? Sounds like a medicine for hangovers. What does a being who's never been physical need a name for? And I ask you, why does he have a Middle-Eastern accent? And why, on top of that, does he speak in archaic English like he's quoting Shakespeare, while all the time displaying the vocabulary of an illiterate twelve-year-old?"

Though he tried to keep his resistance up, Andrew couldn't help but see the points she was making, especially since he had on occasion wondered about some of them himself. But he decided he would just as soon jump off a Martian cliff before ever letting We-Be know he identified with anything she was espousing. He sat down on one of the smoother boulders, now totally engrossed in witnessing her tirade. She stormed back and forth in front of the Viking lander, like a female version of its namesake, a cloud of fine red sediment rising up around her as though to complement her hair.

"Oh, aren't the pitiful little Earthlings blessed? The Great Celso has graciously lowered his vibrations enough to bestow them with his all-knowingness. Poor little things. There they are, trapped in lowly, dense, untrustworthy, corporeal forms, totally at the mercy of the elements. 'Oh Great God-Thingy, please tell me what to do! How do I rise above my Earthly lot in life? Tell me what to eat and what not to. Tell me how to make love and who to do it with. Tell me who I am and what I'm here for.' Ye Gods, Morgan! There must be a Space-Time Principle for this, but I'm too pissed off to think of it right now. Do you believe the balls this character has? I mean . . . he doesn't even have any balls!"

Andrew burst out laughing, almost falling off his makeshift seat. But We-Be was now oblivious to her audience of one as she continued with her trashmouth soliloquy, her feisty figure elegantly framed by the brilliantly lit vista behind her.

"Never has had. So how's he going to give anyone sexual advice—sex being the very basis of physical existence? What to eat? What does a being who's never been physical know about food, anyway? Manna from Heaven, maybe, but certainly not a staple Earthian diet. Maybe he's just jealous 'cause he can't taste anything and he's cosmically constipated."

Laughing so hard that his jaws ached, Andrew tried to imagine what Lana's face would look like if she were observing this blasphemous display. And thinking of Lana sobered him just enough to make him feel a slight obligation to put in a good word for her channeling friends. "But wait a minute; maybe it's precisely because some of these channeled entities aren't physical or Earth-connected that they can perceive things from a broader perspective. And since they're not bound by time, they can foresee future events. Maybe it doesn't matter that they can't identify with the mechanics of the tides or how to make babies; if they can see into our future and warn us of impending disasters, who are we to condemn them, and why would we want to?"

We-Be simply glared at him and tapped her booted toe on the powdery ground.

" Space-Time Principle Number 33:

Concern yourself with your now and your future will take care of itself.

"Your today was formed by your yesterday," she said solemnly. "Tell me, Morgan, what will your tomorrow bring? It's all up to you, not some doom-and-gloomer from outer space. Do you not, as an individual and en masse, create your own future with your beliefs, thoughts, fears, and expectations? Expectations, Morgan, they're the deciding factor. Do you really think the prophets do you any favors by filling your head with worries about the future? The future is too malleable to be predicted by any one personality—except if that personality can get others to add energy to his manifestation-in-the-making! When enough people believe something to be true, then they create that 'truth' into reality. For nothing yet exists in the future, or rather, everything exists in the future. All possible futures exist right now in an unformed state, and the outcome is literally chosen and molded by mass consciousness day by day. You want peace on Earth? Then believe in it. Live it. Teach it. Bring it into reality. You want tidal waves? Just be afraid of them and spread the word. Prepare for them. Expect them. Build an ark, 'cause you're gonna need it."

Andrew considered what she had said for a moment, impressed with this slant on prophesy. He had thought about individual reality-creation many times, but had never considered the forming of mass reality in this manner before. He had to admit, it made sense.

He could see the muscles in her delicate jaw twitching in agitation as she continued: "Every day more and more twisted fear-beliefs are dreamed up, not only by prophets but by 'experts' of all kinds, and then spewed out into your world, affecting mass reality and making your planet seemingly more deadly and less fun with each passing thought. Experts are stressing that not only should you beware of strangers but of familiar faces as well. Poof! Another pervert!" We-Be paused for a moment to catch her breath, or perhaps to sigh in disgust.

"And you're not just being taught to distrust each other, but also even your own bodies. Diseases, old and new, are on the rampage, according to the experts; and most people feel helpless and hold no faith in the strength and integrity of their bodies to remain healthy. These fears are contagious and are escalating at an ominous rate. This 'plague mentality' is passed on from one person to another, caught not by simply drinking from the same glass or breathing the same air, but by unquestioningly adhering to the same concepts about reality. If you take all the beliefs about death and disaster—from cancer to cataclysm—and lump them into one large, joint manifestation, what do you get? Could it be the 'end of the world' or 'the last days' that have long been prophesied? Think about it, Morgan."

"Cataclysm? Are you saying that man's group mind controls Mother Nature?"

"Not 'controls,' but influences. Your weather forecasters are some of your more obvious prophets, and fine examples of people who can sway mass consciousness with their expert predictions. They bemoan rain, then turn around and bemoan drought. They make their living trying to second-guess the weather, telling you what to look for the next day."

"Well, anyone who doesn't take an umbrella with him after a weather forecaster tells him there's a ninety-nine percent chance of rain is a fool," Andrew said as he gazed speculatively up at the cirrus clouds dancing overhead, wondering off-handedly why it never rained here.

"Ahh, but I bet you've never stopped to think that perhaps the mere act of so many people carrying umbrellas and constantly peering upward, looking for rain clouds, actually encourages the rain. Mass-fulfilled prophesy, Morgan—with a little help from their symbols of expectation and their persistent 'looking for.'

" *Space-Time Principle Number 32:*

If you look for something long and hard enough, you're sure to eventually find it."

Andrew remained silent as he carefully considered her words. "But back to weather forecasters," We-Be continued. "They do much worse than predict rain. For instance, they pass out hurricane charts and tell you to expect the worst hurricane season ever, year after year. Mother Nature doesn't always cooperate with these media-prophets' predictions, but occasionally cooperates with mass consciousness to show it how powerful and influential its thoughts can be. Remember, Morgan, nature is man's mirror.

"And even though man fears Mother Nature and cowers under her occasional demonstrations of power, he tries his damnedest to top her majestic feats, to be more powerful than her. Through his technology, he has managed to unleash power that he has yet to understand, let alone learn how to control. Like a ten-year-old playing in a real chemistry lab, man knows not what he creates—only that it looks pretty when it fizzles and glows and goes 'bang.' Then he turns around and transfers his fears into his creations, and they end up being one more thing for him to fear. Your nuclear technology is directed, like so many other things, against that which man doesn't understand and therefore fears: culture against culture, country against country, brother against brother, bomb against bomb. And Mother Nature takes it all in and, in her infinite patience, attempts to heal the injuries she suffers at the hands of man's foolish little-boy games.

"Man's technological abilities are accelerating at an ever-increasing rate, but, sadly, they have far surpassed his moral maturity. He needs to slow down and take the time to catch up to himself."

Andrew shook his head and smiled grimly. "You really have contempt for us humans, don't you?"

"No, just channeled entities from outer space, weather forecasters, bomb builders, and other assorted doom-and-gloom experts."

"I can't believe how critical you are!"

We-Be crouched down, and scooping up a small patch of snow at her feet, began forming it into a snowball. "I don't mean to be critical, Morgan, though I know sometimes I can really get on a roll. It's just that I want you to become sensitive enough to care about what your species is doing to itself, the other species, and the planet you all share, so that you'll start doing something about it."

"If you're so gung-ho on making changes, why don't you do something yourself?"

"Who says that I'm not? What do you think these talks we have are all about, anyway? It's my way of doing something—through you!" We-Be reared back and threw the snowball straight at Andrew, splattering the powdery stuff all over his chest.

With a look of annoyance, he stood up and brushed the snow off himself, leaving a stain on his shirt that looked like dried blood. "Look, I can't even seem to make changes in my own life, much less in the rest of the world. First things first, if you don't mind."

"Oh, so you think you have to be perfect before you can help make effective change in the world? What if I were to tell you that by involving yourself in broader challenges, you'd broaden your own scope of personal evolution?"

"Be ye therefore perfect, as your Father in Heaven is perfect." Andrew half whispered the words that he recalled from his childhood days in Sunday school.

"Give me a break!

" *Space-Time Principle Number 114:*

Perfection is not only impossible, it is undesirable; for to be perfect would mean to be beyond change, and everything is in a constant state of change.

"Besides, Morgan, perfection would be terribly boring. Still water turns stagnant in no time at all. I don't know about you, but I like a few ripples in my experience. Think about it: there are few things in your life that you considered perfect at one time that you didn't at a later date choose to disregard or re-evaluate. Perfection today will seem flawed tomorrow, for you and your life and your

'Father in Heaven' will be more and different with each passing day and each new experience. And I wish you'd cut out that 'Father in Heaven' crap. Makes me feel like I'm in church or something."

Before Andrew could respond, We-Be continued: "Now, where were we before you derailed me with your perfection kick? Oh yeah . . . man needs to catch up to himself. He needs to let go of his I-me-mine perspective, develop more sensitivity to his environment, and learn to respect and have compassion for everything that co-exists alongside him before proceeding any farther down the path of technological advancement."

"I suppose it was a crime to have ever invented the horseless carriage then?" Andrew said sarcastically. "I mean, Jeez . . . look at all the exhaust fumes they've spewed out in the last hundred years! For that matter, maybe man never should've invented the wheel. Just think, we could all still be on foot, living in caves and hunting with stone spears!" Andrew jumped around, hands hanging down to his knees, giving a rather impressive imitation of an ape. But, forgetting the difference in gravity on this strange planet, he lost his balance and tumbled sideways, landing on his hands and knees on the cold Martian turf.

"I haven't once said technology was wrong, Morgan," We-Be countered, ignoring his antics. "When man first invented the automobile, the idea of polluting his atmosphere was a worry that hadn't yet been realized. Man needs to catch up to himself, though, and recognize when one of his technologies needs a major adjustment. If not, a beneficial technology can evolve into a detrimental one. Everything changes, and even the 'perfect' means of transportation—which the car was once hailed as being—eventually shows its faults.

"Once on the technological wheel, you have to keep up with the momentum, or it begins to work against you. It becomes so big and strong—with everyone depending on it—that it's almost unstoppable. Like the god Jehovah, it becomes all-powerful, depended upon, feared, and yet never questioned. The person who tries to interfere with and stop it is likely to get run over and smashed flat, unless he can gather around him enough others who see the need for technological reform and the need to begin applying the brakes. But those others are usually few; they're the ones who can see past the blind spots created by the I-me-mine perspective."

"I don't know what you mean by that," Andrew challenged. "Everyone sees things from their own perspective; we all gauge life from our own unique viewpoint."

"True, but the scope of that viewpoint is what decides for each person what is important to him and where his sympathies lie. It molds his reactions to all events.

" *Space-Time Principle Number 140:*

Your sense of allegiance to other consciousness is in direct proportion to your understanding of your connection to the whole.

"Right now, various technologies, while providing security or comfort to some, injure or threaten others—human and nonhuman. Every person holds different loyalties that are so much a part of him that they seem inborn. Most people never seek to extend those loyalties past some invisible line they've created or accepted without question. And yet, this line determines their moral maturity, or emotional evolution."

Picking himself up and brushing the dirt from his hands onto the back of his pants, Andrew tried hard to get a handle on her train of thought as she continued: "A young child's psychological perceptions dictate that he is the center of the universe, that nothing is important except his needs and desires. As he grows, those quite natural boundaries of selfishness usually expand to include mother and father, and then later, extended family and friends. In your society, as it is set up, everyone creates their own stopping point, their own boundaries, and constructs their world views accordingly. Everyone chooses their own outlines of identification. Some cannot identify with anything beyond their sense of 'I'; their selfishness prevents them from developing meaningful relationships of any kind. Others are furiously loyal to the family structure, having stretched their boundaries of 'I' to include those closest to them. Still others expand their loyalties to embrace those of the same race or religion, and hold disdain and hatred for anyone with a different skin color or set of beliefs."

We-Be paused in her thoughts and, half walking, half bouncing over to the Viking lander, laid her hand gently on the half-exposed emblem of the American flag. "Then there's the identification with country—patriotism. In polite society, prejudice against different races or religions or sexes is taboo, and yet patriotism is considered a noble trait. Few see patriotism as the form of prejudice that it is—lines drawn by man between countries, lines that originated due to natural geographical boundaries. At one time, before your technology brought about great advances in communication and transportation, such lines of distinction were natural. But once again, man needs to follow up on his technological advances and make the necessary adjustments. Communication and transportation have made all those distinct, individual countries into one world, one people. It's time for mankind's morality to catch up with its technological advancements. The divisions are now not only obsolete and unnecessary, but extremely limiting and dangerous. If allowed to continue, they will actually prevent the next giant technological step in man's evolution from occurring."

"And what might that be?" Andrew asked.

"I don't know. The answer won't begin to form itself until enough people start asking the right questions. Why not get busy and start thinking your questions out?"

"That's what I'm doing! I'm asking you: What could the next giant technological step be?"

"Well, I suppose expanding the boundaries of man's experience to include worlds besides his own."

"'To boldly go where no one has gone before . . .'" Andrew bounded up on top of the Viking in one elegant leap and struck a conqueror's pose.

"Exactly! Except man will have little real success in other-worldly adventures until he has learned how to expand his boundaries of perception to include all Earthly life. Then, and only then, can he truly call himself a representative of Earth. Can you imagine a couple of astronauts landing on a planet circling Alpha Centauri and saying: 'Hi! We're from Cape Canaveral, Florida, U.S. of A.; take us to your leader'?"

"They wouldn't say that! They'd say they were from Earth."

"Yeah, they'd say that at first, Morgan, but they'd follow it up with the planting of their particular country's flag on the highest hill. Am I wrong?"

Andrew knew she wasn't. His mind was brimming over with thoughts of the possibilities of a united-Earth space program. No more competition between the major powers, or any powers, for that matter; no more secret military payloads that detract from the more peaceful goals of space exploration.

As if reading his thoughts, she said: "And the money that's spent on waging war and rebuilding afterwards could be applied to more important matters, such as feeding and sheltering Earth's hungry and homeless, and mending Earth's damaged environment. And, I might add, if your space program is ever to be truly successful, some 'space' will need to be put between it and the military. The expenditure of time, money, and energy on military purposes negates the peaceful exploration of space and prevents the next giant step from being actualized."

Andrew listened to her words intently as he cautiously eased himself down to a sitting position on the slippery surface of the Viking lander.

"Even when man's intent is the peaceful exploration of space, he tends to confuse his true priorities. That metal contraption you're sitting on right now, together with its twin, cost a whopping billion dollars. That billion dollars could just as well have been spent answering a whole lot of important little questions and solving much more pressing problems back home on Earth. And what was so imperative about the mission to this planet that it took precedence over Earthian dilemmas? To detect life on a rusted red planet when so many people haven't even begun to respect the assorted life forms on their own world, not even their own kind. If you ask me, that billion dollars would have been better applied to preserving the countless life forms already on Earth's endangered species list.

" Space-Time Principle Number 161:

Before a beneficial new age of technology
can begin, the age preceding it
must be in good order so that
no adverse residue clings to it.

"A beneficial new age of technology will be made possible because of knowledge gleaned from the old, but the new must not inherit the old's problems. It must start clean if it is to survive and maintain strength and integrity."

"Are you talking about the militarization of space?"

"Yes, but more. For instance, your present technology creates extraordinary amounts of deadly waste, and man can't figure out what to do with it; although he's trying to recycle by using it for such things as fuel for rockets and food irradiators. And, if everything continues as is, space will become the next dumping ground for it. Hell, you're sitting on the beginnings of a space junkyard right now and haven't even thought about it!"

Andrew looked at the Viking lander beneath him with new understanding.

"Space junk! The other Viking that landed here a couple of months after this one is on the other side of the planet up near the north polar region. Already you've got the beginnings of two dumping grounds. And let's not forget the fact that your moon has

113

been considered the logical location for future waste disposal; after all, it's 'dead' too. Besides the assorted lunar bases that will eventually be built there, of what other use could it possibly be?"

Gazing out over the magnificent expanse of colorful rocky terrain, Andrew cringed at the mental image of it becoming a dumping ground for man's cast-off junk.

"Of course, that's just the beginning. The overlapping of the old technology into the new can be seen in other phases of the space industry, such as the powering of spacecraft with nuclear reactors or radioactive materials. The future then inherits the mistakes of the past. For what goes up stays up . . . maybe; but it's more likely to come down sometime, somewhere, to haunt someone. Every gizmo sent up—nuclear powered or otherwise—eventually becomes useless and has to be replaced. The defunct ones will either re-enter Earth's atmosphere due to orbit decay where they will endanger life on the hit-or-miss plan, or they will remain in space, circling the planet as space junk. Eventually, there will be so many satellites and so much metal garbage orbiting Earth that they will form an impenetrable shield of whirling objects and particles, preventing not only those responsible for it, but future generations as well, from ever reaching the stars."

Andrew looked at her skeptically. "Aren't you being just a little extreme? I mean, there's more space between us and the stars than we know what to do with."

"Extreme? Hell, Morgan, not so very long ago that same type of argument was applied to your oceans—many of which are now either polluted or in danger of becoming polluted by man's inconsiderate and thoughtless misuse of them. It's a fact that leaving Earth's atmosphere will eventually be worse than dodging bullets in a combat zone. I don't think that's an extreme prophesy at all. The space junk problem is merely one example of how man can thwart his own future technological progress by carrying the problems of the old into the new. The satellites wouldn't be a problem if people weren't so obsessed with continuing the paranoia created by the 'us versus them' mentality, if governments would quit spying on one another to try to gain the upper hand. It's time to be creative and share all knowledge, rather than maintain the lines between peoples with deadly competition." We-Be's eyes were trained solemnly on the distant horizon in the direction of Earth.

"And what's really sad, Morgan, is that the majority of the people who truly love the idea of space exploration don't allow themselves to be aware of any of this. They're too caught up in the romance of it all to see that their own military is putting a permanent lid on the program, ruining the future expansion of mankind's boundaries by corrupting the new technology with unnecessary greed and competition.

" *Space-Time Principle Number 173:*

Competition is the antithesis of creativity when the competitors forget that they're supposed to be having fun and that winning isn't the goal. "

Andrew's blood ran cold. The disastrous implications of what she had said were beginning to sink in, and he didn't like it at all. He couldn't believe he had been so oblivious to all this before. He began to feel his own invisible boundary lines of loyalty—that he had drawn sometime in the past—starting to slip and slide all over the place.

"Scientists love to say that space exploration is the answer to the world's problems, that the by-products of the industry can be applied to Earthly dilemmas. Gee, come to think of it, the military has always said the same thing: that wartime research and development generates technological advances that otherwise would not occur. But, the truth is, if mankind had not always sunk so much of its time, energy, money, and talent into preparing for war, waging war, and rebuilding afterwards, it would be technologically advanced beyond its present comprehension. But man will never know what heights he could have reached, because he always tries to escape into a new technology before cleaning up the old one, therefore tainting the new.

" Space-Time Principle Number 13:

You cannot run away from
your own creations.
They follow you wherever you go.

"Your creations will only transform any new environments and experiences into disguised versions of themselves. Dealing with Earth's problems should be man's first priority. It's ludicrous for him to venture off into new areas, carrying his trash with him, when he has a vast, unknown frontier on his own planet that he has exploited more often than explored. I'm speaking of the oceans, of course. Their potential resources haven't even begun to be realized and tapped. And the zeal to discover intelligent life on other planets is ironic; there are intelligent species right on planet Earth that man could learn a thing or two from."

"Like the dolphins, right?"

We-Be nodded her head in acknowledgment. "And the whales. But because they aren't humanoid or 'industrious,' there is little interest in developing a form of communication with them. Instead, they're captured and put into fancy aquatic prisons and coerced into doing circus acts for children's amusement."

A vision of Shamu the Killer Whale jumping through a huge hoop materialized in Andrew's mind, and a deep sadness touched the depths of his soul. How could he have never before considered these gentle giants as an intelligent species with rights of their own?

We-Be watched Andrew compassionately out of the corner of her eye. "It's a shame that a few of the people who do recognize the sacredness of all life aren't at the helm of space exploration. But sadly, they're not; and at this point in time those in control show signs of carrying this exploitive, insensitive mentality with them as they venture into space. They lack respect for anything they can't identify with. And although they seem hell-bent on seeking 'new life and new civilizations,' they don't like things that are too alien to them. What they really seek are resources, anything and everything that can benefit the continued advancement of their own kind."

"Okay, so man's not perfect. But I seem to recall someone, not too long ago, saying that I didn't need to be perfect before I did important things in the world. Now you're saying that man in general shouldn't venture out to other worlds until he's flawless! Sounds like a contradiction to me. Let's see you dig up one of your little Space-Time Principles to explain that!" Andrew grinned from ear to ear, thinking he really had her this time.

"Don't need one," We-Be said lightly, her expression showing no sign of confusion. "We're not talking about perfection here, Morgan, we're talking about responsibility and compassion. If you had a chronic compulsion to kick cats, I wouldn't suggest that you go out and volunteer your services at the animal shelter. And I don't suggest that an industry that repeatedly shoots deadly cargoes over people's heads should be allowed to put much energy into discovering life on other worlds." The grin faded from Andrew's face as fast as it had appeared. As usual, she had backed her way out of one of his shakily constructed corners.

"What do you think would happen, Morgan, if these explorers found a civilization in the stage of the pre-Columbian Native American whose land was encrusted with gold and diamonds and uranium? What would happen to that civilization? Would your species be able to resist the temptation of furthering its own ends at the expense of this 'less-evolved' species? Would these innocent inhabitants of 'the new world' end up on reservations with a new god to answer to and their fists full of beads? And, if they weren't humanoid, God forbid they should look like they might taste good!"

Andrew gazed out over the Martian plains stretching as far as the eye could see, and once again was reminded of Arizona. He remembered an Indian reservation he had seen there—the poverty, hunger, and desperation that showed in the eyes of the proud Navajo people who inhabited the area. People, Andrew realized, who were once free and independent; people who were to this day still being treated unjustly and exploited for the minerals their land contains.

"Consider the planet we're standing on right now, Morgan. Earth's planetary scientists are already talking about 'terraforming' it in the not-too-distant future."

"Terraforming? What's that?"

"You know, making Mars hospitable for Earth-standardized life. They have this brilliant idea to seed the carbon dioxide atmosphere of this place with genetically bioengineered bacteria, which will digest the carbon dioxide, thereby creating an oxygen-rich atmosphere. Through the use of giant orbiting space mirrors, they'll focus the sun's rays on the polar ice caps and create free-running water to fill the dry riverbeds once again. This, of course, will prepare the way for the introduction of plant life on the surface; and after that, insects to pollinate, assorted animals—even some laboratory-concocted ones—and, finally, human beings—the new homesteaders staking claim to their own piece of an open frontier."

"So what's wrong with that? I don't see any Indians running around here worrying about being displaced. In fact, I don't see any signs of life at all."

"You don't see, they don't see; that's not the point here. The point is, you shouldn't disrespectfully trash a place and then simply move on to a new one, especially when the one you leave behind is in need of serious attention. And 'what's wrong with that' is that I seriously doubt Mars will be used for much more than mining, anyway. Beneath the rusted surface of this planet lie more precious minerals than man can even imagine. The endeavors of planting forests and farming crops would end up being the furthest thing from the minds of any visitors from Earth once they've discovered that 'there's gold in them thar' hills.' The new territory of Mars could create a pioneering panic unlike anything ever seen before, making the gold rush of 1849 look like a simple Sunday excursion. And this new glut of precious stones and metals would devastate the economy of Earth, not help it. Mars would be a prize that could bring about wars that would wipe out both worlds at the same time. *War of the Worlds*: H.G. Wells had the right title, at least."

Andrew once again looked around at the barren terrain. It sure looked like it could have been a war zone, like a bomb had wiped the face of this world clean many years ago. As if on cue, he could hear an avalanche rumbling in the distance—or was it a volcano? The 'angry red planet,' he mused as he climbed down off the Viking. His curiosity was piqued by what she had said about precious stones and minerals. Picking up a jagged rock, he dug around in the permafrost. Were there really gold and diamonds here?

"All I'm saying, Morgan," We-Be said, as she watched him scratching away at the rusty red surface for Martian gold, "is that man needs to clean up his own backyard before he moves on: feed and shelter his needy, end pollution and stop punching holes in the ozone, make war obsolete, and respect all life forms and each other. Once he's established these basic qualities of awareness and integrity in himself, he can branch out into the universe in an unexploitative manner, carrying these standards with him. Exploration and exploitation are two different things, though Earth's history would be hard put to prove it.

"It's curious, really, that the present course mankind has chosen to follow is slowly devolving Earth back into its primordial state—a world of toxic gases and swamps and deserts. Because of man's decaying, insensitive technologies, Mars may just end up being man's only hope for survival in the end. But then, how do you know this isn't a pattern repeating itself? Maybe your ancient ancestors did the same thing here on Mars millions of years ago: raped this planet for its raw materials, destroyed its atmosphere, and killed off all the other species. Maybe they looked out and saw a bright blue-green star as their only hope and packed their bags for an Earthly adventure, hoping for a new lease on life."

"C'mon, that's crazy! I don't believe that!" Andrew threw the words at her over his shoulder as he wandered off a few yards to prospect another patch of frozen ground.

We-Be trailed closely behind him, responding to his skepticism: "I'm not saying I do either, but it kinda makes you wonder, doesn't it? Maybe everyone has a little green man in their woodpile!"

Andrew never knew when to take her seriously. But before he could figure it out, his hand pulled out something shiny, causing him to lose the thought entirely in his excitement as he polished the object on his shirt sleeve. "No, Morgan, that's not a diamond," We-Be said, as he squinted through it toward the distant sun. "It's a quartz crystal, like the one Lana gave you to ward off evil spirits—which, by the way, she's dead wrong about. The only spirit I've ever met that I could consider being anywhere near 'evil' was compulsively attracted to shiny things."

"Jesus, you sure say the weirdest things sometimes."

"Yeah, well that's why you love me."

"I don't love you, I tolerate you."

"Whatever. Do you have any idea how ironic it is that Lana and her friends are bewailing the end of the world, while at the same time indirectly supporting the strip mining of Earth for the crystals they're so fond of wearing around their necks?"

Andrew could sense that she was about to go off on another tirade and felt himself cringe inwardly. Snatching the crystal from his hand, she held it up before his face, looking upon it with reverence. "They claim to understand the magical properties behind crystals, yet fail to grasp this mineral's real place in the scheme of things. They've never stopped to consider that perhaps crystals have a purpose for being in the ground in the first place. Maybe crystals don't want to get dug up and worn around people's necks. Maybe they don't want to be tortured with the negative thoughts people are told to place inside them by the crystal 'experts.' Maybe they don't want to absorb people's sickly vibrations."

"And maybe trees don't want to get cut down to be made into houses, and maybe tomatoes don't want to get picked and eaten either," Andrew shot back.

"Ahh, but there's a difference between what has to be disrupted for your survival and what is just needlessly interfered with. Once again, it's all part of understanding the give-and-take process of the unity of the whole. Besides, Morgan, any healing or fixing of 'bad vibrations' comes from a person's beliefs and not from any magical amulet or rock."

Guiltily, he gently reburied the crystal in its hole and smoothed it over with rusty dirt. Watching him, We-Be remained quiet, as though talked out for the first time. Finally, Andrew sighed deeply and broke the silence. "I realize that you think I need to know all about the world's problems, but sometimes the things you say really depress me. I was miserable enough about my own life; now I feel even worse. I mean, how can life ever be fun if I'm so aware of all the horrible stuff that goes on? How can I ever solve my own problems if I get all caught up in the world's dramas? It makes me feel like I have a responsibility to do something, but what can I possibly do that would make any difference?" Andrew sank down on the ground as though he suddenly felt very drained.

We-Be, on the other hand, was bouncing around exuberantly, full of energy. "First of all, Morgan, it's perfectly natural to get depressed once your attention has been turned to the undesirable aspects of life. But that doesn't mean you have to become so overwhelmed that life can't be fun anymore.

"Actually, it can be lots of fun to experience the good feelings responsibility can grace you with. So, instead of thinking you have to ignore those quite natural impulses to create change and making yourself pretend that the ugly circumstances that generated them don't really exist, why not pay attention to your impulses and see where they lead you?"

"But I told you, I don't feel like I can make a difference; and just thinking about all the misery in the world makes me miserable!"

"I'm sure it does," We-Be said sympathetically, "but the truth is that you feel miserable because you don't follow your feelings through—the feelings that come from a part of you that deeply understands your connection to the whole. They stir in you the impulse to react, to express your outrage, maybe to fix things somehow. And yet you block this impulse, maybe because you feel that if you allowed yourself to get involved you would end up as miserable as the situation you're concerned with. Or perhaps you believe, like Lana and her cohorts, that by simply sending an unfortunate person 'love and light' or by ignoring his plight completely the situation will simply fix itself."

We-Be's voice took on an affected childlike tone: "'Concentrate on the positive and the negative will simply fade away!' Isn't that what they say? Just send him love and light and bless him with prayers, and then get back to life as usual.

" Space-Time Principle Number 11:

One of the best ways to keep something undesirable in your reality is to try to pretend it isn't there.

"Take world hunger, for instance," We-Be said as she stumbled and almost fell into a small gully. "For the hungry to be fed, someone has to grow and harvest food. You can think very positively about growing an abundant and healthy crop, and if you're smart you'll believe the picking will be fun and easy, and manifest it to be. Plus, through your positive thinking, you can undoubtedly harvest enough to feed everyone. But someone has to get his hands dirty, someone has to plant a few seeds. 'Love and light' alone just don't cut it.

" Space-Time Principle Number 23:

The quickest and most sensible way to achieve physical results is to put forth physical energy."

Andrew cautiously climbed down into the gully to explore it, and, once again, We-Be followed his lead, continuing her thought: "And this also applies to what you said about any action on your part being just a waste of time—after all, what can one person do to make a difference anyway, right? And so you make yourself miserable in a different way. You burden yourself with the subtle, underlying guilt that comes from noninvolvement."

"So what am I supposed to do about the mistreatment of Native Americans, or violations in space, or the strip mining of crystals? Give up my future, don a hair shirt, and carry a picket sign around for the rest of my life? Should I make myself miserable, too, just to avoid feeling guilty?"

"And there we have it, the classic noninvolvementalist escape route, guaranteed to work every time! And that, my dear Morgan, is why such violations continue to exist."

"Okay then, what exactly would you suggest I do?" Andrew had reached the bottom of the ravine and turned around to watch We-Be climb down the last few feet.

"Whatever you can do; it doesn't matter whether you get involved in big ways or little ways, so long as you react to situations that disturb you. If everyone reacted just a little, then no one person would have to carry the weight of the world on his shoulders, or even a picket sign, for very long. The introduction of your emotions to an unpleasant situation is more important in the forming of mass consciousness than you can even imagine. It's mass consciousness asking you directly for your personal feedback, your ballot as a registered member of its ranks. Every time you ignore a violation and don't speak out in some way, it's like casting your vote for the violation to continue. Your acquiescence, apathy, or complacency gives strength to the parties who would continue to do the very things you find distasteful. In other words, when you abstain, you cast a vote for the violator. And it's certainly more productive to react than to keep your mouth shut and just psychically bombard whomever or whatever is being violated with positive thinking or prayers."

In one swift movement, We-Be leaped upward, out of the gully. Andrew tried to do the same, but didn't quite make it, having to cling to the jagged sides and hoist himself the last few harrowing feet to ground level. She appeared unconcerned by his seemingly dangerous predicament and continued talking as she headed back in the direction of the Earthian spacecraft.

"Everyone has abilities and talents, no matter how seemingly insignificant, that they can present to their world. They don't have to be great speakers or leaders, or attend protest rallies and demonstrations. But they can express themselves in whatever way comes naturally, and actually have fun in the process.

"You may never even realize the influence you can have, the lives you can change by actively contributing your opinions to mass consciousness, Morgan." She turned around and walked backward to make sure Andrew was still following her. "For instance, Thoreau was by nature a recluse, a hermit. Yet, he recorded a great deal of his thoughts about the world around him. One essay in particular just happened to strike a chord in a man named Gandhi, who used Thoreau's ideas on nonviolent protest to help change the future of a nation. Not long after that, a young black preacher named King adapted Gandhi's concepts to his own people's struggle for freedom and significantly changed the future of black Americans. These same ideas have continued to resound throughout the world, affecting China, Europe, Russia, South Africa, and other lands far and wide, and will continue to do so.

"Space-Time Principle Number 102:

Though perhaps just a spark,
a good idea, passionately expressed,
can spread like wildfire.

"But it may take more than just a few people to fan the flames." We-Be said these last words softly, winding up her dissertation on involvement and responsibility just as they reached their starting point in the shadow of the Viking lander. As usual, Andrew's head was reeling, and he felt overdosed on her strange, hard-to-dispute brand of philosophy.

Looking at him fondly, she said: "Well! I've really interfered with your Mars excursion, haven't I? Guess I should get going and let you enjoy what's left of it. If I remember correctly there's a fifteen-mile-high volcano the size of the state of Montana somewhere around here, which shouldn't be too hard for me to find. I think I'll go check it out this time around. Be careful on your way back; don't run into any stray satellites!"

Her words yanked him out of his reverie and back into the moment. "I don't think space junk can hurt me in a dream."

"Dream? I wouldn't really call this a dream, although I guess there's only a fine line between dreaming and projecting your consciousness. But I was just kidding. The space junk can't hurt you."

"You mean I'm out of my body?"

"Well of course you are, silly!"

"Wow! I've never done that before!"

"Sure you have . . . every night," We-Be laughed. "You've just never done it consciously before."

Andrew stood there stupefied, mouth hanging open, but We-Be didn't seem to think it was any big deal as she put on her helmet and continued talking matter-of-factly: "One more thing, Morgan. I really didn't like the way you tried to manipulate poor Pete last night. You almost blew it, you know. You didn't need to interfere with your own magic; it was doing just fine on its own. Consider yourself lucky this time, and when you start this job remember to be glad and to try not to 'look for' things to hate about it."

But Andrew's eyes were glued to the area in the sky where the bright blue-green star had been, and he could feel an irresistible tug in that direction. Then with a whoosh! he was instantly catapulted upward, into and through the swirling pink clouds of Mars, homeward bound. Within seconds, Earth loomed in front of him, in all her breathtaking majesty. A loud ringing seemed to be coming from all around him, and, turning around to see where it was coming from, he felt a familiar falling sensation. Instinctively jerking forward as though to brace himself, he squeezed his eyes tightly shut against the inevitable jolt. The ringing was even louder now, and, opening his eyes, he saw the starry sky above Earth disappearing into the first rays of sunlight, the red dot that was Mars still visible.

Stunned and disoriented, Andrew looked around to see his alarm clock on the top of his car, its annoying racket now winding down. The iridescent green numbers on its face announced that it was six a.m., time to start a new chapter in the life of Andrew B. Morgan.

Chapter Nine

Andrew Goes to the Dogs

Andrew had planned ahead by hanging his work clothes from his side mirror to unwrinkle in the night dampness. Draping them carefully across the car seat, he drove to an all-night laundromat that had a decent bathroom with hot water. He had stumbled upon it the year before when he had been in a similar situation. No one would be there this early in the morning, and he could shave and wash up in relative privacy.

He knew he looked pretty sharp in his bow tie and vest, and wondered if any cute girls worked at the club—or better yet, belonged to it. Running imaginary romantic encounters through his head, he drove to a diner that offered a $1.99 breakfast. He was getting a little nervous now, and told himself that it was just first-day jitters. This was one of his best manifestations yet. Nothing could possibly go wrong, not this time.

Andrew breathed a sigh of relief when the guard at the gate had his name on a list and a pass already made out for him. He drove down the winding road, past a perfectly manicured landscape toward the sprawling clubhouse, nestled behind giant weeping willows. He couldn't help but wonder just how much the road alone had cost: close to half a mile of perfectly laid bricks. This place dripped with opulence, and Andrew's stomach knotted with a mixture of excitement and tension.

He wasn't at all sure where he was suppose to park; surely not next to one of the Mercedes or Rolls-Royces or Cadillacs out front. Driving around the back of the building he spotted Pete's MGB, and parked next to it. As he stood there in confusion about what door led to where, a beer delivery truck pulled up and the driver started unloading cases. Andrew followed the man through one of the doors and immediately saw Pete standing there, notepad in hand, counting and checking off the cases of beer.

He looked up and grinned at Andrew. "Glad you made it, buddy! Be with you in a minute."

Andrew looked around the expansive kitchen, already bustling with employees in their assorted black and white uniforms.

"Comin' through!" Andrew jumped back to get out of the way of a pint-sized bus boy carrying a tray of dishes twice his size. A voluptuous blonde waitress making coffee smiled at him coyly, and he could feel a red blush travel from his bow tie to the top of his head. "Hot stuff!" Andrew spun around to get out of the way of another waitress loaded down with plates of steaming food. He backed toward the wall, trying to get out of the path of traffic, and ran right into Pete.

"So, you ready to sling the sauce?"

Andrew looked at him blankly. "Do what?"

"You know, sling the sauce, booze 'em up, make 'em happy!"

"This early in the morning?"

"Buddy, you're gonna have a run on Bloody Marys in a couple of hours that you wouldn't believe, so let's get you situated, okay?"

Pete led the way down a series of halls past the pro shop to the locker room. "Some locker room!" Andrew thought. The carpeting was over an inch thick under oak tables and plush chairs that were set in front of a large window overlooking the first green. Marble lined the walls, and behind the bar were panels of beveled mirrors. He couldn't figure out why it was called a locker room at all, until Pete threw open a door that led to an adjoining room. Rows of solid oak lockers covered one entire wall, opposite the restroom facilities, which were decked out in polished gold fixtures. Still another room led off that one, and Andrew could see an extravagant assortment of exercise equipment, a sauna, and a steam room.

Pete showed him where everything in the locker room was—towels, toiletries, etc., and then led the way back to the bar area. For an hour he ran over the bar procedures and standing etiquette of the club, which amounted to doing whatever was called for to make the members happy.

"Remember, buddy, these Ryecroft guys pay a lot of money for what they get, so treat 'em like royalty, okay? Make 'em like you and they'll take real good care of you. If you get into a jam, just dial my extension and I'll help if I can." Pete jotted down his number on a pad next to the phone.

Andrew watched his new boss saunter off. His head was swimming with all the things Pete had laid out for him, and he wasn't at all sure he would remember everything. What if he blew it?

"Oh yeah, one more thing," Pete said, sticking his head around the corner, "be sure to treat Skip McKenzie especially good, 'cause he's a real stickler for detail—besides the fact that he owns a good chunk of this place. The last guy who had your job forgot that and Skip canned his ass."

Andrew squirmed as apprehension ran up his spine. "Well, how will I recognize him?"

"There ya go," Pete said, pointing to a mural-sized portrait hanging above the bar, "the Skipper himself." And with that, he strode off, back to the kitchen where Andrew wished with all his heart he could be right now.

He tried to gather his wits: towels there, vodka here—olives somewhere . . . where? He could feel sweat trickling down the back of his neck, darkening his shirt. He closed his eyes to center himself and steady his nerves, searching the corners of his mind for words of reassurance.

"Prosperity? You want prosperity? Well, here it is Morgan, in luxurious living color!"

Andrew shook the voice out of his head and said out loud to the empty room, "Why don't you just beat it and leave me alone!"

"What's that, boy?"

Andrew swirled around, mouth agape to face his first customer, standing there with a confused frown on his sunburned face. He quickly took in the man's startling blue eyes, white hair, and stocky boxer build. There was no doubt about it: it was Skip McKenzie in the flesh.

"Nothing, nothing . . ." Andrew's mind raced frantically for a way out of the situation. "There was a fly or something buzzing around and I couldn't find a fly swatter. Guess I just lost my patience. But I killed it, just now."

"Damn exterminators. You pay 'em an arm and a leg and they still can't do their job right." Andrew remembered Pete's directive and shakily mixed up a Bloody Mary for the golf pro without having to be told.

"Good boy! You're gonna do just fine here—not like that smart aleck little shit before you."

Andrew winced, recalling how many times in the past he had been called similar names himself. But this would be different; he was off to a good start, thanks to his ability to think fast on his feet and smooth over a potentially bad scene by fabricating his talking-to-flies-that-weren't-there story.

One by one the members streamed into the locker room, dressed in flamboyant golfing attire, making the room a hodge-podge of plaid and primary colors. Andrew flitted back and forth between making Bloody Marys and making change for the cigarette machine. He plastered a smile on his face and said "sir" more times in one hour than he could remember saying in his entire life. But it paid off: he collected twenty dollars in tips, plus a fifty-dollar bill that Skip had slipped him with a sideways wink. Finally, the room was empty again, and Andrew busied himself putting the place back together. He breathed a deep sigh of relief. He had passed the first test.

The rest of the day went by without a hitch, as Andrew handed out towels, emptied ashtrays, made mixed drinks, and smiled . . . a lot. He was still smiling at quitting time as he patted the one-hundred-dollar wad in his pants pocket. At this rate, he would be on his feet in no time. In fact, he felt as though he thoroughly deserved a motel room for the night. He could hear Lana's words from the past affirming his decision: "If you want to be rich, you have to act rich!"

By the third day, Andrew had the job down pat: from ten to eleven he served the members their Bloody Marys; from eleven to twelve he cleaned up after them; from twelve to four he tended to the needs of the golfers as they straggled in from their rounds—but mostly he kicked back and watched television; from four to six he faced a madhouse, doling out towels and scotch and waters and listening to each member's golf glories and woes.

On this day, as usual, Andrew sat and eavesdropped on the members' conversations spilling across the room. He liked to listen to the varying tales of wealth and abundance and dream of being there himself one day. The Admiral—an old, retired navy doctor who was called the "Rear Admiral" behind his back, due to the fact that he had been a proctologist—was giving his friends the low-down on how to win at the dog track. Andrew's ears perked up; this was something within his means; the dog track was a low investment venture. He casually walked over to empty the ash trays and clear away empty beer bottles.

"It's not a matter of smarts or studying the track records," the Admiral said, as he puffed hard on his Cuban cigar to get it going. "It's just a simple matter of understanding basic physiology. I walk over and study the dogs before each race instead of sitting up in the grandstands fiddling with the program and flirting with the pretty gals."

Skip, who evidently loved to playfully pick on the old man, interjected: "How in the hell is studying the dogs gonna tell you which one's a winner?" The table of golfers guffawed at the question, and the Admiral turned purple with indignation.

"Well, it's real simple, and anybody with half a brain could figure it out." He squinted up his eyes and leaned forward. "You just study those hounds real close and take stock of which one takes a dump. And sure as shit, he'll come out the winner, long shot or no. If more'n one takes a dump, well then, you bet on them, too. Works every time!"

"Old man, you're crazy!" someone said, and the Admiral's companions roared with laughter as they got up to hit the showers.

The Admiral sat there stiffly, highly insulted by his friends' chastising. Andrew walked up to him and gently asked him if he wanted another drink, which the Admiral declined with a wave of his hand. Then, working up his nerve, he asked, "So, does your system really work every time?"

The old gentleman looked up at Andrew with grateful eyes. "Well, not every time . . . but damn near it, damn near it. You tell me, son: How well do you run when you haven't loosened your load?"

"I get it! The lighter you are the faster you are!" Andrew said, only half humoring him.

"There ya go! You're a smart one, aren't cha? Not like those other idiots—all pansy asses, they are."

He helped the Admiral to his feet and saw him to the door. The doorman would call him a taxi, as usual.

Andrew couldn't decide: was the old geezer crazy or brilliant? He was, obviously, an educated man, so he wasn't stupid—though maybe senile. Was this the big break Andrew had been trying to manifest for years? A way to make lots of money without having to work for it? That's what manifestation was, after all . . . wasn't it? He decided he'd check it out that night, as soon as he'd returned to his motel room to change out of the monkey suit.

◆　◆　◆

It was five minutes to post time, and Andrew stood at the fence closely watching the eight greyhounds being led to the starting gate by young men dressed in their dogs' colors. He was fidgety with frustration as he waited for one of the dogs to do its thing and give him a sign. Then it happened: the kennel boy dressed in green stopped and looked down at his number six dog, then turned his head away in bored impatience. Andrew sidled over to verify the reason for the dog's pause in the procession, and almost clapped his hands in excitement when he confirmed what he had been looking for. Almost at a dead run, he charged toward the ticket window to place his bet. "Two dollars to win on number six," he gasped, shoving his money at the ticket girl. He had decided to test the system before laying out any serious cash.

As he walked away from the counter back toward the fence, the warning bell sounded. He had just made the bet on time.

"And therrre goes Swwiffty!" blared the loudspeakers, signifying the start of the first race. Andrew held his breath as the electric rabbit on rails bolted past him, trailed by a flurry of speeding hounds. He watched number six bringing up the rear and shook his head in disgust. "I should have known," he scolded himself. "That's what I get for listening to a senile old proctologist."

The dogs disappeared from his view as they rounded the track. The announcer was babbling off numbers and names faster than Andrew could them sort out in his brain. He heard his dog's name garbled—"Surefire Maybe"— among the rest, and stood at the fence halfheartedly to watch the outcome. The dogs bounded toward the finish line, a rainbow blur of colors. Suddenly, a green streak flew past the others, taking the lead. Andrew thought perhaps his eyes were fooling him, and he craned his ears to hear the announcement of which dog had won. "And the winner by two lengths—Surefire Maybe!" Groans of disappointment and yelps of joy echoed down from the stands behind him as he stood there in shock, a winning ticket in hand.

After fighting the crunch of the crowd to cash in his ticket, Andrew sauntered happily back down to the fence to repeat the process, pocketing his sixteen dollars in winnings. This time, dog number four, displaying red and black, graced him with the peculiar sign of good fortune. And sure enough, true to the Admiral's word, he won—an easy eleven dollars.

Andrew was convinced now that the dump-system really worked, and decided to bet more heavily. However, none of the dogs came through with a sign for him, and he impatiently waited through the third race for the next one. But, once again, the dogs let him down—and again and again. By the last race, Andrew was highly irritated and anxious to win his fortune. He was beginning to feel uncomfortable just standing around drinking beers in the midst of so many frantic people, some seemingly so desperate to win, as though their very lives depended on it. He had studied the program to distract himself and kill time, and was particularly interested in one dog in this final race because of its name: Admiral's Choice. What a coincidence! He decided that if this dog gave him its blessing before the race, he would bet everything he had on it.

The kennel boys led the dogs up to the fence, and Andrew zeroed in on the one in blue: Admiral's Choice, number five. But the dog in front of it elected to do the honors, and Andrew half turned to go when Admiral's Choice caught his eye again by pausing to follow number four's lead. For a second Andrew was confused. Two dogs? Then he remembered the Admiral's solution to this dilemma: bet on both of them. He'd bet a four-five quinella; that way no matter what order the two winning dogs came in, he would clean up. Everything was falling into place—like magic.

He darted to the ticket counter, almost knocking people over in his haste to place his bet on time. Pulling his whole roll of money from his pocket, he quickly counted it and put the entire two hundred dollars on dogs four and five. He had it all figured out: when he won this race, he would have enough money to get an apartment and furnish it to boot.

"And therrre goes Swwiffty!" They were off and running, and sure enough, Andrew's two benefactor dogs were right out front. He watched as long as he could see them clearly, four and five a good three lengths ahead of the pack, neck to neck. He giggled out loud, for he didn't even care which of the two crossed the finish line first. Confident of the outcome, he turned and headed for the ticket counter to get a jump on the lines. Screeches of excitement drifted through the crowd—more pronounced than usual—drowning out the announcer's garbled voice. An instant replay of the race appeared on the TV monitor above his head, and he stopped to watch it, an uneasy feeling in the pit of his stomach. There were his two dogs, tearing toward the finish line, vying for first place. And then for no apparent reason—whammo!—they ran right into each other, knocking one another off their feet. The other dogs scampered over them in a chaotic frenzy, leaving the would-be winners behind, walking in confused circles. The numbers of the winners then flashed on the monitor, verifying what he had just witnessed. Andrew was busted, his dream of an apartment shattered in one swift collision of two clumsy canines.

He drove back to his room in stunned silence, not even turning the radio on. He felt like an idiot. How could he have done such a stupid thing? How could he have ever been so dumb as to believe in the Admiral's system in the first place? He was out every penny of the money he had made so far at the club, and it would be almost a week before he got his first paycheck. The only reason he didn't go into a complete state of panic was because he knew he could live off his tips on a day-to-day basis. He sought consolation by reminding himself that he had only set himself back by three days. But still, he found it hard to sleep that night.

The next day he was hit with more bad luck: the club was closed all day due to a major electrical problem. Crews of electricians swarmed the place, trailing multicolored wires behind them. Andrew was devastated. The old familiar feelings of panic rose up in him, clutching him by the throat. His motel room was paid through the day, but this meant he wouldn't have the money for the following day. And, he would have nothing to eat until then either. He decided to hang around the club with the hope that just maybe it would end up opening for a couple of hours at least, later on. If he showed his face in the kitchen, perhaps someone would offer him breakfast or lunch, thinking he was on the clock.

The kitchen staff was absent, but there was a pot of coffee and a tray of doughnuts set out, Andrew guessed, for the crew of electricians. He chugged down two cups of coffee and pilfered three doughnuts before slipping back out the door. He didn't want to just hang around all day with no excuse for being there, so he wandered off onto the golf course to kill time.

It was really quite beautiful and peaceful walking over the rolling greens. Andrew found a cozy spot well away from anyone's view, under a huge shade tree next to a crystal-clear pond. The picture-perfect environment felt surreal—nature sculpted by man and not really natural at all. Sitting down, he leaned against the tree and closed his eyes.

He ran through his mind's eye the events of the past few days—how everything had seemed to fall into place; that is, until the night before. Why had he been introduced to the Admiral's scheme only to have it backfire in his face? It was as though the Universe was playing dirty tricks on him, tempting him with manifestive tidbits only to snatch them away and leave him worse off than before. Was he being told that gambling was wrong, that it was bad to take chances? What about We-Be's lecture on how the Universe likes surprises? Well, it had surprised him all right! Right into being flat broke again.

"So much for magic being my ace in the hole," he muttered out loud.

"Curious choice of words there. Speaking of holes . . . looks like you've dug yourself another one, huh, Morgan?"

Andrew swung around at the sound of We-Be's voice, just in time to see her sink a twenty-foot putt, the ball disappearing into the hole.

"Course, we're mixing our metaphors a little here, wouldn't you say?" She strode over and leaned down to scoop the ball out of the hole, polishing it on her plaid Bermuda shorts.

Andrew groaned. He really didn't need a lecture from her today. He was miserable enough. "How did you get in here? You don't have a pass!"

"Don't need a pass. I'm not real, remember? Besides, you invited me." She tugged her golf cap down snugly over her red curls.

"I did not!"

"Sure you did; you had some questions, didn't you? Well, who's gonna answer them if I don't?"

Andrew groaned again and put his head between his knees.

"So, magic wasn't your ace in the hole, huh?" We-Be set the ball back down a few feet away and tapped it lightly with her club, sending it whizzing back into the hole.

Andrew ignored her question and her good aim, and stared off into the distance, aware that We-Be was commencing with one of her speeches specifically designed to address his situation.

" Space-Time Principle Number 78:

When you play the odds in the game of life,
always be on the lookout for the joker,
which cannot be cast aside,
for the Universe insists
on playing with a full deck."

"What does that mean? That there's always something out to get me, to do me in when I least expect it?" Andrew looked at her in dismay. "You can't mean that!"

"What do you think 'playing the odds' means in the first place, Morgan? It means playing against others who also want to come out on top. They expect the same blessings from the Universe as you do. So what's the Universe to do? Everybody can't win, you know. Magic isn't a wild card dealt out to just some 'special' people. Everybody's kinda on their own when it comes to playing the odds, for the Universe doesn't play favorites." She daintily retrieved her ball from the hole again and set it down in the turf a good ten feet away.

"Put yourself in the Universe's shoes. Take last night for example: There you were, hoping for your dogs to come in first—trying to beat the system—and behind you a whole crowd of other people were doing the same thing in their own ways with their own systems. Now I ask you: What would you do if you were in the Universe's position? C'mon, Morgan, what are the odds?"

"Okay, I admit it was pretty stupid. I won't be doing that again, that's for sure." As she tapped the ball with her club, Andrew glared at it, psychically trying to make it go off course. Once again it dropped into the hole, unimpeded by his thought-waves.

"What you don't realize is that many times when you try to manifest something, you're playing the same type of odds. If you want that girl or that car or that job, often you're competing with someone else. What makes you think the Universe will decide to favor you over another?"

"Maybe my beliefs will be the deciding factor. After all, beliefs form reality, remember?"

"Yeah, but whose beliefs? What if the other guy's beliefs are as strong as yours? What if he's more qualified or more desperate or more deserving or handsomer?"

"More handsome," he impulsively corrected her.

"Right. Should the Universe give you precedence over the other guy just because you try to manipulate it with your hundred-and-one tried-and-tested visualization techniques?"

"So what are you getting at, We-Be?" Andrew poked at the grass with his toe in agitation.

"What I'm getting at, my dear Morgan, is that there's an exact and undeviating sense of order and rhythm behind the workings of the Universe. Become sensitive to this order and attuned to this rhythm and you'll find you won't ever have to play the odds. You'll find life to be stacked in your favor after all—though maybe differently than you expected."

"Hey, it wasn't that big of a deal that I played a long shot. I didn't hurt anyone except myself, now did I?"

"Well now, that's a different subject entirely, but if you want to get into that, it's fine by me!"

Andrew sighed and settled in for the lecture he knew was coming. At least he had distracted her from her never-miss putting, which had begun to drive him nuts.

"I guess you have to consider exactly what you mean by 'didn't hurt anyone.' As in just people?" We-Be stood there with her hands on her hips, waiting for his response.

"You must be referring to the dogs, right? Well, looks to me like they enjoy chasing that silly mechanical rabbit around in circles. How is that hurting them? Are you going to give me some dumb speech about exploiting dogs now?"

"How can I resist?" she teased him. "Jesus, Morgan, you're so unaware of the reality behind things; how can I hold myself back from rubbing your face in it? Do you have any idea what goes on behind the scenes at those tracks?"

"No, but I'm sure you're going to tell me."

"Doggone right I am!" Andrew flinched at her obvious play on words.

"The only thing that the kennel owners are interested in are winners. Every year, thirty-thousand greyhounds are disposed of because they don't meet up to their owners' expectations. If they're lucky, they're put to sleep immediately, but the rest of them end up living their last days in pure hell. They're sold as test animals to medical research labs that value them because they're considered ideal surgical models. Or, they're sold to veterinarians to be used as living blood banks, for which greyhounds are perfect, since they stand quietly without putting up any fuss while they're being bled. Their veins are tapped regularly for transfusions for the vets' preferred canine patients, who are apparently more worthy of life, especially since they have owners with money in their pockets. Eventually they fall over dead. Thirty thousand healthy dogs a year, Morgan, needlessly destroyed. And all because they don't win, place, or show often enough to remain a necessary part of a three-billion-dollar-a-year gambling industry."

Andrew's expression showed that he felt a little queasy. He hadn't been aware of any of this, and found it hard to believe, though he could tell she wasn't just making it up. Hanging his head, he mumbled, "I didn't know . . . but surely, I'm not responsible for what those dogs are subjected to."

"That's like saying the Romans who attended the games at the Coliseum weren't responsible for the death of the Christians. Spectators are always indirectly responsible for supporting what they watch; they're responsible for checking out the integrity of a sport or whatever before endorsing it with their presence and financing it with their money." We-Be settled down spraddle-legged on the grass across from Andrew.

"And speaking of history," she continued, "did you know the greyhound was revered and used as a holy symbol by the ancient Egyptians? Maybe because they figured out that 'dog' is really 'God' spelled backwards!"

Andrew wondered what the religious right would have to say about that one. But then, this mysterious woman of the ethers would alienate people from almost every school of thought, as far as he could tell.

"Well, for that matter, the Hindus consider the cow to be sacred, don't they?" Andrew countered, squirming around to reposition himself against the tree. "And the Native Americans honored the buffalo, even though they hunted it, if I remember correctly. Probably everything has been thought to be sacred at one time or another."

"Yes, the Native Americans hunted the buffalo while at the same time respecting and honoring it; but they killed only what they required for their sustenance and utilized every part of the slain beast for something necessary to their survival. Within your mainstream society, however, no other species' life is thought to be sacred. The cow, for instance, is often seen as merely foodstuff; its main purpose on Earth being simply to please man's palate."

"Great! Now you're going to tell me that it's wrong to eat meat!"

"That depends on how in touch you are with your own natural guilt, and the circumstances you find yourself in."

"Natural what?"

We-Be smiled good-naturedly. "Natural guilt; what may also be referred to as 'conscience'—a person's deep, intuitive sense of right and wrong. Though it's inborn, natural guilt is often blocked by unquestioned social mandates and may lie dormant until activated by a particular event. When you commit an act that hurts someone or something and later feel miserably guilty over it, this is natural guilt making itself known, teaching you that you never want to repeat the incident, never want to feel that miserable again."

Andrew had a flood of memories of such pangs of conscience wash over him, mingled together in one thirty-second sweep.

"Now understand, Morgan, you can become numbed to natural guilt because of the dictates of your society. Since early childhood you were served meat at least once a day. Somewhere along the line you must have realized what it was you were eating—Clara the Cow or Porky the Pig, your favorite cartoon characters, nestled between the green beans and mashed potatoes. Suddenly, you were probably confused and upset, but your parents made everything all right by teaching you that cows and pigs were made for people to eat, and you had to eat them to grow big and strong. And since your parents seemed so infallible and all-knowing, you believed them, and your natural feelings of guilt were suppressed—as were your parents' feelings before you."

"Well if there's 'natural' guilt, then what is 'unnatural' guilt?" Andrew asked.

"Guilt that ain't natural, silly!" We-Be giggled and threw a handful of dried grass in his hair.

"I'm being serious!" Andrew said, brushing the grass out of his hair in irritation.

We-Be studied him with curiosity for a moment. "Okay then, I'll answer your question seriously. Unnatural guilt is just that—unnatural. It's manufactured through a person's beliefs. Because of this, unnatural guilt can be confused with natural guilt, the line between the two often indistinguishable. Unnatural guilt insists that you respond to a given situation in a certain way, even if it causes you to limit your own experience. This type of guilt usually stems from early childhood conditioning or from beliefs that are blindly accepted as truth through interactions with others. For instance, a woman who stays with an abusive husband is someone who's trapped in her own unnatural guilt. Because of her upbringing, she may believe that the man is the authority, never to be questioned; that he has good reason to be abusive because she isn't perfect or because he works so hard to support her; that she owes it to him to stay no matter what. She feels guilty for not being whatever it is that would make her husband happy. Through our perspective, we can see that her beliefs are faulty and therefore limit her experience, but she can't recognize that her guilt is unnatural because it's formed by those very beliefs that she accepts as truth."

"So, how do I tell the difference between natural and unnatural guilt? How does that abused woman ever realize her guilt is unwarranted? Guilt is guilt, it would seem, when you're experiencing it, right?"

Andrew thought he had her stumped. But We-Be cocked her pretty head, pursed her lips in deep concentration, and as usual, came through:

" Space-Time Principle Number 148:

Unnatural guilt keeps you tied
to a situation, whereas natural guilt
provides you with the opportunity to
release yourself and make necessary changes.

"Unnatural guilt perpetuates itself and offers no solutions. Natural guilt offers a lesson and equips you with the ability to find solutions. Natural guilt allows you the opportunity to alleviate it; it doesn't cling. It strengthens you to face similar situations in the future. Unnatural guilt keeps you forever bound to the past."

"I can understand that. But I don't understand how this all ties into eating meat. I mean, I don't feel guilty at all about eating a steak. Does that mean I'm totally insensitive or something?"

We-Be laughed and shook her head. "No, Morgan, it simply means you've never had to kill your own cow. You're oblivious to that aspect of the situation, therefore any latent natural guilt you may possess hasn't had a chance to surface. So I ask you straight: Could you kill it yourself?"

"Huh?"

"Could you go out into a field, kill a cow, and then eat it?"

This was something Andrew had never really thought about. He had always unmindfully presumed that that was why God made butchers. Frowning, he pulled at a tuft of grass and fell silent, a tinge of long-dormant guilt creeping up from the core of his being, nipping at his conscience.

"Aren't you in some way partially responsible for the death of that animal if you eat a steak that was carved from its body?" We-Be whispered softly, almost apologetically.

" Space-Time Principle Number 143:

If you can't kill it yourself,
you need to question whether
you have any business eating it.

"Conscience is the real issue here, Morgan. If you wouldn't feel guilty killing your own cow—or chicken or fish, for that matter—then you don't have anything to worry about. It's not that you really have to kill it yourself. Just . . . could you?"

"Well, I have to eat something; I have to sustain myself in some way, don't I? So what can I possibly eat that doesn't have consciousness?" Andrew threw his hands up in a gesture of helplessness. "I mean, shouldn't I feel guilty even when I eat a tomato? Doesn't it have consciousness, too? Where do I draw the line?"

"Simple. Your own natural guilt determines your boundaries of conscience. Keep in mind that you don't kill the plant when you eat a tomato. The plant freely offers its fruit for the picking, as its gift to you. If you don't pick it, it rots on the ground. A cow, on the other hand, will run like hell if it knows you want to shoot it between the eyes. Think of it this way: You're a human being, but there are other beings occupying this world, too: cow beings and pig beings and chicken beings and . . ."

"Yeah?" Andrew interrupted. "Well what about lima beings and pinto beings?!"

"Very funny, Morgan. I wonder how funny you'd think it was if a race of giant-sized beings landed on Earth and decided man tasted good. To those beings, consuming human flesh would seem like the natural thing to do—after all, man would be considered by them to be a rung lower on the food chain."

Andrew made a face to disguise the fact that her analogy unnerved him more than a little.

"It all depends on your perspective," We-Be said, getting back to the subject, "on how far you can stretch your conscience to encompass the interconnectedness of all things. Obviously there are humans who will kill their own meat without a second thought, and that's okay for them; they can only follow the patterns established by their particular perspectives on survival. And no one can tell another what is and isn't conscionable to eat, because every person's perspective of right and wrong is different."

"What about people who kill animals just for the fun of it?"

"Without a doubt, that's a violation against those animals. In nature, no animal kills just for the fun of it."

"Oh yeah? Have you ever watched a cat gleefully torture a mouse to death?"

"Not in a while; but understand, it's the inbred nature of that cat to hunt the mouse. It doesn't comprehend that it's torturing the mouse; it just follows its nature."

"So, I guess it isn't wrong then for animals to kill each other, huh?"

"Well, think about it, Morgan: the animals kill their own food; they don't hire hit men to do it for them. Guilt isn't a factor they have to deal with, for just like the cat, instead of reason, they all operate purely on instinct. Guilt is a human-mind mechanism. Once again, if you can kill it yourself, have at it. No one says you have to feel guilty. But if you do feel guilty and choose to ignore it, then you violate yourself, and end up violating your prey in a way animals never do, for that natural guilt was designed to direct you to alternatives."

We-Be paused to listen to a song bird that perched itself on one of the branches hanging over Andrew's head. Smiling, she proceeded with her dissertation: "Everyone has their own personal dietary do's and don'ts and their own perspectives on what forms of life they hold too important, or too intelligent, or too cuddly to kill and eat; and what forms they consider irrelevant enough to utilize as foodstuff. But, most people could stand to expand their perspectives a little and look deeper into their own consciences."

Peering up at the sky, her attention was caught by the song bird as it took flight, swooping gracefully over the hill. "The earthworm is gobbled up by the sparrow, which in turn is swooped down upon by the hawk. In this scenario, most people would feel sorry for the poor sparrow but feel no remorse for the worm. And yet, the earthworm is a god to the consciousness of the soil, which supports all life. For without the worms, there would be no fertile soil to grow the trees that the mighty hawks and sweet sparrows build their nests in. It's all a matter of perspective, Morgan, as is everything. Your perception of reality depends upon the focus you've chosen to view it through. No one perceives his experience in exactly the same way as another, even though everyone shares the same reality."

We-Be crawled over beside Andrew and, lying on her belly, pointed the golf club at the small pond next to them. "Look at the pond, Morgan. What do you see?"

"What?"

"What do you see?"

145

"I see water; what am I supposed to see?"

"Well, how about the fish swimming around just under the surface?"

"Yeah, I see them. So what?"

"And the dozen or so golf balls turned slimy green?"

"Okay. And there's a rock or two and a broken-in-half golf club. So what's the point?"

"Well, that's one perspective of this pond. What else do you see? Can you view it now from another perspective?"

Andrew was confused. "A pond's a pond. How can I see it from another perspective?"

"It's simple, just shift your focus. Look at the surface for a second. See the lily pads? The cattails? The little water bugs scurrying across the surface? Can you see the remnants of the grass you shook from your hair floating there?"

Andrew nodded his head and stared intently at the various things she had pointed out, trying to figure out the great mystery to which she was alluding.

"Now, shift your perspective again. Can you see the reflection of the trees in the water? The clouds and blue sky?"

Andrew switched his focus once more, still unsure of what she was trying to prove.

"Now, while staring at the upside-down mirrored world in front of you, can you still see the fish and the water bugs clearly?"

Andrew tried, but realized after a few attempts that to see any one aspect of the pond's reality clearly, he had to let go of the other.

"See? Even though each perspective is there to behold, they're visually separate from one another. Reality is perceived in such a way from person to person. That's why there are so many diverse views about reality: black, white, and gray; left, right, and straight ahead. They all exist at once and they're all valid."

Andrew peered into the pond, entranced with the shifting of the setting at his will. "Can a person ever get to the point where he can see all the different perspectives of life at once?"

We-Be touched the water with the golf club, creating gentle ripples on its surface, as though trying to demonstrate yet another perspective for him to consider. "Do you think you can ever get to the point where you can see all versions of this pond simultaneously?"

"No . . ."

"You've just answered your own question, Morgan. But you do have the ability to remember as you view through one focus what the other focuses were like, and learn to switch back and forth at will."

"I think I understand what you're getting at. Everyone thinks their beliefs are truth—which they are, for them. Everyone has the right to believe what they want to believe, and every perspective is valid—everything is truth." Andrew let the words he had heard so often from Lana and her cohorts tumble out of his mouth.

"Let's not get carried away here, Morgan. There are many truths that govern your reality, but I wouldn't go so far as to say that everything is truth.

" Space-Time Principle Number 98:

There's such a thing as bullshit.

"And even though it's a fact of life, it still stinks."

"How can you be judgmental like that?" Andrew demanded, bolting straight up and banging his head against the tree. "Who are you to say that other's views are bullshit? They may be bullshit to you, but uniquely perfect for them, so how can you criticize their beliefs?"

"And I suppose that all views are beneficial to their holders? Cut the crap, Morgan. Should someone not have criticized Jim Jones's brand of truth? Did his followers benefit from his unique, 'God-inspired' perspective that they adopted? Hitler thought he had the truth, and he convinced a whole nation of the 'perfection' of his views. Should someone not have criticized him? More than one of your modern-day, self-proclaimed messiahs espouse big-otry against other religions, or against homosexuality, or against anything else that suits their twisted beliefs about the truth. Talk about extra-sensory persuasion!"

As though thoroughly provoked by her own words, We-Be rolled over and jumped to her feet, hands clenched by her sides. "Why do so many basically intelligent people refuse to be practical and discriminating upon hearing such trash? Do they think it somehow makes them 'higher' to pretend to accept everyone's views, no matter how distorted, as valid 'on some level'? Is it somehow enlightened to excuse prejudices and limitations put forth by so-called 'experts' as being simply different perspectives? And why is it when some brave soul dares to challenge the versions of truth pushed on the public by these 'experts,' that person is labeled 'judgmental' and 'limiting'? What's wrong with throwing a little pragmatism and logic into the works?

"Space-Time Principle Number 97:

*It is not genuine wisdom
if it limits you or
unnecessarily hurts another."*

"Wait a minute," Andrew interrupted her. "Aren't you limiting others' freedom of expression by the mere labeling of their wisdoms as limiting? Maybe those people in Jonestown needed to experience that kind of reality for their own reasons. They created it, after all. Maybe it's wrong to interfere with another person's karmic lessons."

We-Be continued with her thought, her tone registering annoy-ance at his interjection: "Maybe if enough people had had enough guts to stand up and challenge the Great Messiah Jones and expose him for what he really was, those naive, impressionable people might have learned some much better lessons—like:

" Space-Time Principle Number 93:

*To follow others is
to leave yourself behind.*

"Forget karma, Morgan. Karma is just a cute little word some people use as a rationalization to keep from making responsible choices.

" Space-Time Principle Number 149:

*'Karma' is simply natural guilt
playing upon itself by repeating itself,
expressing something that was ignored
instead of learned and acted upon.*

"The followers of Jim Jones thought they were seeking the 'truth,' but actually were seeking a sense of belonging. Everything Jones uttered was interpreted through their emotional needs for a secure social structure. Once a great leader type has filled an emotional hole in someone's psyche, any of his own imperfections are ignored or overlooked; for to recognize his faults would mean disturbing the neatly-filled hole and digging up pretended-away, buried insecurities."

"So maybe belonging was everything to them and therefore their way of seeking the truth. How can you be critical of that? How would you feel if someone openly criticized your ideas about truth or your precious Space-Time Principles?" Andrew sneered.

"Hey, have at it. I welcome criticism because it gives me the chance to firm up my views." We-Be seemed to puff herself up as though preparing to do battle. "I'm not afraid of having holes punched in what I know to be true. As far as I'm concerned, once someone makes statements or publishes material for the public, he silently consents to receiving comment, challenge, and criticism. That's the name of the game. Without such an open arena for debate, there would be a handful of unchallenged, self-appointed pseudo-gods displaying what they consider to be the truth while suppressing any important ideas presented by would-be contenders. Face it, Morgan, there just isn't enough healthy criticism and open skepticism these days."

Taking a few deep breaths as though to center herself, she continued: "Shouldn't people question this 'unconditional-acceptance-don't-judge-others' bit? Who sets these unconditionally accepted standards of what is the 'enlightened' way to be, anyway? Can a person really believe in anything until he has torn it apart and put it back together again, adding his own ideas and subtracting any limiting ones he may have found? Credible teachers don't need to be sheltered from any outcries. If they're worth anything at all they should welcome comment, questions, debate, and even criticism."

"Have you ever considered going into politics?"

"And what, limit myself? No thank you!" We-Be shook her head in mock disgust and stood up, brushing off her behind. "Are you trying to change the subject on me? Okay by me; I can talk politics for hours. . . ."

"No, no, never mind; I was just kidding! Jesus!"

"Jesus? Okay . . . that too; wanna talk about him?"

"I gotta get out of here. You're driving me crazy."

"Suit yourself! I guess I've loaded you down with plenty to mull over. Me, I think I'll finish out this round. I'm just three holes away from making a perfect score of eighteen." Grinning, she strode past Andrew nonchalantly and climbed into a golf cart that wasn't there the last time he had looked. Then, waving good-bye, she sputtered away over the hill, disappearing as abruptly as she had come.

Chapter Ten

The Case
of the Lucky
Lizard-Skin Shoes

Andrew just stared at the hill for what seemed like several minutes. He couldn't figure it out: had he been asleep, awake, or somewhere in-between? He looked into the pond, and sure enough, there were the algae-encrusted golf balls and the broken club. Had he unconsciously recorded their existence in his brain before falling asleep? Shaking his head to come to his senses, he got up and headed back to the clubhouse.

Slipping back into the kitchen, he hoped to find a few leftover doughnuts. No such luck. But, fortunately, the place was totally deserted; so, opening one of the walk-in refrigerators, he quickly snatched a loaf of French bread and a hunk of cheese and stuffed them into a paper sack. Sometimes, to Andrew Morgan, the line between manifestation and thievery was very thin.

He had nothing to do except return to his motel room and kill time until the next day. Looking at his gas gauge, he comforted himself with the fact that he had filled his tank on the way to the track the night before. But still, he decided to conserve gas by avoiding traffic and taking a short cut down a series of dirt roads. He had taken this route once or twice before, but this time Andrew saw things he had never paid much attention to previously: like cows—lots of them—with cute little calves scampering around their heels. Following an impulse, he pulled over to the side of the road and got out of the car to watch their antics for a while. After all, he had plenty of time to spare. The calves came right up to the fence, curious about this two-legged creature who was whistling at them. The mother cows followed warily, protective of their young, as he stood there for some time, entranced with these clumsy, big-eyed animals who looked so cuddly. They wouldn't get close enough for him to touch them—just almost.

"Whatcha doin' there, boy?" Andrew jumped at the sound of a man's voice, and spun around to see a grizzled old farmer eyeing him suspiciously.

"Nothing much; just looking at your cows to pass the time. Been a while since I've been in the country."

"Won't be country long; damn city's gettin' closer every day!"

"Know what you mean. Things are changing fast, huh?"

"You bet." Leaning on the fence next to Andrew, the old man fell silent as though listening to progress's steady encroachment.

"So, what are these? Milk cows?"

"Nope. Them's beef. Don't mess around with dairy no more; ain't no profit in it."

Andrew's blood ran cold. This possibility hadn't occurred to him at all for some reason, and he felt stupid that it hadn't. All of a sudden he couldn't bring himself to look at the farmer or his beautiful brown-eyed creatures that were doomed to death. He had to get out of there immediately. Mumbling something incoherent, he turned and walked back to his car, keeping his eyes trained on the ground.

He drove fast, concentrating his vision solely on the road. "My God!" Andrew said out loud to himself, "are those little calves going to end up wedged in-between two sesame seed buns with some pickles, onions, and special sauce slapped on for good measure, only to find themselves at the bottom of my stomach?" He looked at the sack of bread and cheese appreciatively, very glad now that he hadn't filched roast beef instead.

All the way back to his room, We-Be's words ran through his head, always ending up with: "Could you kill it yourself?" He knew he couldn't—now or ever. Somehow he felt as though We-Be had tricked him into taking that back road, set him up for the kill. But he knew that wasn't likely; after all, he formed his own reality, didn't he?

Turning on the television, Andrew sat down on the edge of the bed and tore off hunks of bread and cheese, stuffing them into his mouth. He decided to lose himself in old movies for the rest of the day and night. Not having a *TV Guide*, he switched the channels back and forth, finally catching a movie just beginning: *Attack of the Killer Tomatoes*. His conversation with We-Be about gifts from the tomato plant and her comments about other life forms devouring humans seemed to be ironically twisted together in this movie's plot. Not completely sure that the TV programming wasn't somehow influenced by We-Be herself, he laughed out loud and quickly changed the channel. He had had enough lessons impressed on him for one day.

The next morning, Andrew woke up especially early to avoid the possibility of the motel manager seeing him. He left a note on the dresser explaining that he would pay him for that day's lodging when he got back from work that evening. Besides, if he arrived at work early enough, maybe he could sweet-talk breakfast out of someone in the kitchen.

As it turned out, he didn't have to sweet talk anyone. Pete was already there, and jovially invited him to join him for some steak and eggs. Andrew poured himself a cup of coffee and sat down across from Pete, who was anxious to hear about how things were going in the locker room. He assuaged any fears Pete had by telling him things were great and totally under his control. One of the waitresses plopped the plates down in front of them, and Andrew dug right in. Pete was recounting some movie he had seen the night before about murderous tomatoes that bled ketchup when they were shot. It was as though Pete had been prompted by the Universe. He could hear Pete as though from a great distance, and a chill settled over his body. All his attention was on his fork, which carried the scorched piece of flesh that had once been a living, breathing cow being. The flesh that tasted so good . . .

Trying not to look obvious, Andrew scraped the steak from his fork back onto the plate and quickly switched to the eggs and potatoes. He knew he would never look at meals with the same perspective again.

Pete babbled on, jumping subjects from killer tomatoes to the upcoming golf tournament. He warned Andrew to be on his toes because out-of-town bigwigs would be filtering in daily and hanging out in the locker room. Andrew was bored with the conversation and took his first chance to break away. "Well, I guess I need to go spiff the place up a bit then, don't I?" Taking a last gulp of his coffee, he thanked Pete for the breakfast and the advance warning and headed for his station.

Andrew spent the next couple of hours vacuuming the floors, polishing the furniture, and setting up the bar before being swamped by the army of golfers eager for their Bloody Marys. Performing menial tasks for the rich and powerful wasn't exactly his cup of tea, but the money he was making helped somewhat to soothe his battered ego. Besides, he reminded himself, this job was only temporary, the wealthy atmosphere merely acting as a bridge for his manifestive abilities, helping them to become more finely tuned. The best was yet to come.

The club members drifted off, one by one, leaving only the old Admiral still nursing his bourbon. "Can I get you anything else, sir?" Andrew wanted him to hurry up and leave so he could put his feet up for a while.

"Now that you mention it, there is." The old guy leaned over and fished around in his gym bag. "Shine these shoes up for me real good, would you boy?"

Andrew's mouth fell open. Shine shoes? Was that part of his job description? How low did he have to go? But, without voicing his chagrin, he took the shoes and turned around to walk off.

"Take good care of those shoes, ya hear? They're my lucky shoes."

Sulking, Andrew tore through the cabinets in the back room for five minutes before locating a collection of assorted shoe polishes. The shoes were lizard skin. What the hell color was he supposed to use on them? He dare not mess them up, for they looked terribly expensive. Finally settling on a tin marked "neutral," he proceeded to polish them up carefully.

When he had finished, Andrew walked back out into the barroom and returned the shoes to the Admiral, who was pretty well sloshed by now. The old man didn't even say thanks, let alone proffer a tip, and Andrew retaliated by not helping him to the front lobby. He watched sullenly as the Admiral stumbled and weaved his way out the door.

Andrew only had a few chores to catch up on. Then he could kick back for a couple of hours and watch TV before the crunch started again. Finishing, he breathed a sigh of relief and leaned back in a stool with his feet up on the bar. But his feet barely touched the oak surface before he had to jerk them down again in response to the opening of the door. His heart fell, as it always did when Skip McKenzie and his crew entered the scene. It was unfair; Andrew was supposed to have at least a good four hours to regroup and to fiddle away before having to deal with the demanding needs of the members.

"Hey, Andy, break out a deck of cards. The boys and I are gonna play a little poker. And while you're at it, bring us a round of brewskies!"

Scrambling to get his act together, Andrew put aside his frustration at not getting a break.

"Hey! How about some pretzels over here?" one of the members hollered.

Finally, they were all squared away, and Andrew dared to sit down behind the bar. He knew he had to look as though he were at attention, and so kept his eyes focused in their direction. Bored almost to tears, he started eavesdropping on their conversation and game. He found it hard to believe that anyone could gamble the amounts being bet in this game: thousands of dollars exchanging hands in no time flat, with no remorse. He felt himself resenting these men and their nonchalant attitudes concerning money. They played with more money in an hour than he would see in the next two years.

"So, Harry, I hear your daughter got married last week!"

"Yeah! How come we didn't get invited to the wedding?"

Harry, a burly, dark-complected man in his late forties, didn't look happy. "There wasn't a wedding, that's how come. The little shit eloped. Sent her to the best schools, gave her everything on a silver platter, and what does she go and do? Runs off with a good-for-nothin' bum! The son of a bitch is just after my money, that's all. Well, he's got a long, hard wait ahead of him, I can tell you that!"

The others rumbled their commiserations. "The bum tends bar for a living. Can you imagine? She could've married anyone, and who does she marry? Some no-account fortune hunter who lives from day to day off tips! Jesus! My daughter's living on handouts!" Harry's face was turning purple with rage. "I just can't figure it out. . . ."

Andrew's face was as red as Harry's was purple. He felt as though he couldn't breathe, and wanted to get out of there as fast as he could. But he was trapped. Just then, Skip called for another round of beers, and Andrew had to suffer the indignity of waiting on these men who looked down upon his kind. They didn't even recognize his presence as a human being, but, rather, as a mere provider of a service.

For the rest of the day, Andrew felt violated and insignificant. Even the seventy dollars he made in tips couldn't erase the mounting resentment that coursed through him, giving him a pounding headache. Seventy dollars in tips: just what he needed to pay two days rent on the room, with ten dollars to spare. Those same tips that had made him feel like he was finally getting someplace now made him feel like an indentured servant. Funny thing, too, he mused on his way back to the motel: he had actually begun to believe there was such a thing as magic, like We-Be had said. How could he have been so foolish as to believe the words of a crazy hallucination in the first place?

Andrew started the next day full of hostility. He thought about all the manifestation books he had read that repeatedly insisted that no one was a victim of circumstance; that no one should ever have to suffer needlessly; that the proper use of thought and imagination could easily lift one from hell to heavenly heights. Yet he did feel victimized, as if he were nothing more than a helpless pawn on a big Ryecroft Country Club chessboard. The money was good, and at least this kind of work wasn't anywhere near as hard as all the other jobs he had held . . . but was it worth it? Shouldn't his self-respect come first? If Lana knew what he was experiencing she would surely agree with him, making sure to rub it in, for the millionth time, that she didn't have to work for a living. Skip McKenzie and his friends didn't seem to ever work, either. It looked as though they just played for a living, which was exactly what Andrew felt like he deserved to do. He decided he hated this job, no matter how much money he was making. He was better than this.

The morning's rush was worse than ever since it was the day before the big tournament, and Andrew walked through it with a stony disposition, resenting every "yes, sir" that he had to force from his mouth. Just as the crowd was beginning to thin, the Admiral signaled for him to come to his table where he was sitting with Skip McKenzie and the hated Harry.

"Boy! Are my shoes done yet? I need 'em tomorrow, you know."

Andrew stared at the Admiral in disbelief. "Why, sir . . . I gave you your shoes yesterday before you left, don't you remember?"

The old man stared blankly at Andrew for a second or two before speaking. "Are you telling me I don't remember right? I may be gettin' old, but my brain still works." He struggled angrily to get to his feet. "You tryin' to get away with my shoes, are ya boy?"

"No sir, it's just—"

"Just, my ass! You better get me my shoes right now, on the double!"

Andrew stood his ground. "I can't get your—"

"Now hold on here," Skip interrupted. "I'm sure Andy has simply misplaced the shoes and will find them before the day's over. Isn't that right, Andy?"

Andrew had had it. He was nobody's fall guy. "No, it isn't! I didn't misplace anything. I gave those shoes to him yesterday, plain and simple."

Skip scowled and shook his head, as the Admiral jumped back in: "Those are six-hundred-dollar shoes I handed you, boy; hand-made 'specially for me. You gonna pay me for those shoes?"

Andrew's whole body trembled with rage. Skip was up from the table now, and standing between the Admiral and him. Andrew's eyes fell on Harry, who seemed to be enjoying the whole charade, as he leaned back in his chair, hands cradled behind his head, grinning.

"If Andy doesn't find your shoes, I'm sure he'll be more than happy to compensate you for them. He understands he's responsible for everything that happens in this locker room. He knows the rules." Skip attempted to put his arm around Andrew's shoulder, but Andrew stepped away. He wasn't about to give away over a week's earnings just to placate some rich old coot who was going brittle in the attic.

"I don't know anything about the rules. All I know is—"

"I'll give you till the end of the day to refresh your memory." Skip's steel blue eyes bored straight into Andrew. "You've got some serious thinking to do, son."

Andrew stared into those eyes and hated them. Then he looked into the Admiral's half-coherent eyes swimming in his face and Harry's gloating triumphant ones, and exploded: "I don't need till the end of the day. I'm not paying for anything I know I didn't lose, rules or no rules. I'm outta here—now. I'm history!"

Andrew turned on his heels and headed for the door. He staggered, his vision blurred with angry tears, as Skip McKenzie shouted after him: "You already paid for 'em. Don't bother trying to collect a paycheck come Monday!"

The last thing Andrew heard as he slammed out the door was Harry's sadistic bellows of laughter that echoed after him as he ran down the hall and out to his car.

Chapter Eleven

The Magic of Logic (And Vice Versa)

Instinctively, Andrew drove straight for Lana's house. He wanted someone to tell him he had made the right move and hadn't just screwed up his life again. Lana would agree that it was counterproductive for him to stay at any job that robbed him of his self-esteem. Moral support and someone to help him justify what he had just done was what he needed.

As Andrew pulled into her driveway, he could see Lana out front watering the petunias. He thought it odd to find her outside in the heat of the day, but then realized it was quite cloudy and gloomy—the type of day that suited Lana to a tee. And it suited his mood, too, he had to admit. She looked up from under her large straw hat, raising her eyebrows slightly to acknowledge his presence.

"I had a dream about you," she greeted him, as she walked over to shut off the water. "You were being chased by a big animal of some sort—a slithery reptile, I think. Does that mean anything to you?"

Andrew ran this through his head, thinking of all the slithery reptiles he could, and then asked, "Could it have been a lizard?"

"Why yes, I think it was a lizard, now that you mention it. Did you have the same dream?"

"No, but I did lose my job today because of a stupid pair of lizard-skin golf shoes. Guess you could say they kinda chased me out the door." Once again, he was amazed at her psychic abilities. Lana beamed—as much as she could without too much expression—gave him the inevitable hug, and led the way into her kitchen.

Nursing a cup of herb tea, Andrew gave her the rundown on the events in his life since he had last seen her. "And they expected me to shell out six hundred dollars for a pair of shoes that some taxi driver probably inherited after dropping the old geezer off at his home."

"Look, Andy, how many times do I have to tell you that menial work isn't the answer for you, that a typical job is only a temporary measure to take when you're making a transition from a belief in poverty to one of wealth and abundance?" Her voice held a trace of irritation.

"But this job was set against a backdrop of incredible luxury. I thought for sure that this meant I was on my way to making the transition. Everything seemed like magic!" Andrew let the word escape from his mouth before he could stop it. He hoped it would slip by unnoticed, but Lana was as sharp as ever.

"Magic? All that job was was a sign that something better was on its way, that your manifestive powers were starting to work. If you had been centered firmly within your being, however, the perfect situation would have presented itself to you instead and you wouldn't have taken that particular job."

"But how was I to know that? How am I ever supposed to sort it all out and determine what direction to go in?" Shoulders slumped over the table, Andrew covered his face with his hands in despair.

Lana leaned over and pulled his hands away, making him look her straight in the eye. "A true manifestor learns to manipulate the world around him. He doesn't sit back and allow the world to manipulate him. You're entitled to the luxuries of life; after all, you're a son of God. What's His is yours—if you're adept enough to claim it. But first you must realize your special place in the scheme of things and resist giving in and becoming just one of the herd—one of the herd that you're supposed to love unconditionally, of course, but not overidentify with. That seems to be the lesson your Higher Self is trying to teach you."

Andrew was confused, although comforted by her recognition that he wasn't supposed to stay at the country club job. But now he was back to square one: almost zero dollars in his pocket, no place to crash, and an overdue car payment.

"You have to have faith, Andy, faith in yourself and in your true destiny. Sometimes I get so frustrated with you that I could just scream. You've got so much potential yet you keep throwing it away. You wasted a week in servitude to other people instead of waking up and realizing that this reality is designed to serve you. You just have to learn to make it obey your commands!"

"That's all well and good, Lana, but what's to become of me now? Looks like I've backed myself into another one of my corners. I mean, I have to have a job of some sort—just as a transitional tool, of course—in order to pay my bills and to eat."

Lana studied him intently, then got up and paced the floor, deep in thought for a minute before speaking: "I had another dream that just may have something to do with your situation. It was about a great being who was incarnated here but still in child form. This morning, after I dreamt it, the phone rang and it was a client of mine calling to ask for some advice. It seems she's had a difficult time keeping a nanny for her little boy. Evidently he's a very precocious, rambunctious sort, full of energy that he hasn't yet learned to channel. After I hung up, it occurred to me that perhaps her son is the great god-being I dreamt about! When I thought that, shivers of confirmation ran up and down my spine. Then I was sure of it!"

Andrew couldn't figure out where her train of thought was leading. "So what does that have to do with my situation?"

"Well, funny thing . . . I actually told Mrs. Van Morris that perhaps she should consider hiring a male nanny next time around, that perhaps little Holden needed a stronger influence in his life, someone who could handle his unusually high energy levels."

"Me? A nanny? Are you kidding? Christ, Lana, I'm hyperactive myself! And besides, wouldn't I still be playing the role of the humble servant?"

"But your high energy level would be so compatible with this great little being's! Don't you see? And you wouldn't be acting as a servant if you were watching over a budding avatar! Oh goodness, I'm rushing again!" Lana's shoulders twitched uncontrollably with shivers. "I can tell this is destined to be; that's why you came to me today. It all fits so perfectly! The dream, her phone call, your coming here this morning . . ."

"I don't know. . . ."

"They're very wealthy, Andy! And very generous when it comes to their son. I need to call her right now and tell her about this marvelous turn of events. I told her things would work out!" She strode across the room and down the hall toward her office, leaving a dumbfounded Andrew alone in the kitchen to nervously contemplate this strange twist of fate.

"Well, there you have it!" Lana sailed back into the room a few minutes later, looking quite pleased with herself. "She's expecting you tomorrow morning at eight-thirty. It'll be a wonderful experience, dear Andy! Plus, they'll pay you three hundred and fifty dollars a week, in addition to room and board. And they're hardly ever home, so you'll have the run of the place. All you have to do is entertain little Holden during the day and tuck him in at eight o'clock at night. Just think of it . . . the chance to oversee the development of a god!"

Andrew didn't understand any of what was happening to him, but he decided not to fight it. He'd check it out in the morning and try to remain open-minded until then. But one thing bothered him, and he couldn't resist bringing it up. "I can't see how I manifested this nanny job. It seems to have dropped right into my lap out of nowhere, just like the last one. So what makes this one any different? How do I know I'm not making another mistake?"

Lana made a little clucking sound and shook her head. "Well, of course it's different! You came to me, and now my energies are involved. You should feel privileged, actually, for it's rare that I ever allow my energies to directly intercede in the affairs of others. But it's obvious that in this case I'm merely operating as a mediator for divine forces, helping to manifest something that was meant to be."

Andrew pondered her words as he got up to leave. She followed him to the front door and hugged him good-bye. "Don't forget the channeling sessions tonight. We'll talk more then, okay?"

But Andrew begged off, using preparations for his new job as an excuse. She didn't seem to be annoyed by this or curious about what preparations he could possibly need to make. Lana was still caught up in the cosmic event she had set into motion. "Now you remember: I recommended you to Mrs. Van Morris, so don't disappoint me! I have a reputation to keep, you know."

◆　◆　◆

He knew absolutely nothing about children. Whether this made his projected imaginings of what he was walking into more terrifying or less terrifying than it would actually be was an unknown factor. All Andrew knew was that he didn't have any other choices right now, and the money offered was too hard to pass up. Who knew? Maybe Lana was right and Holden would turn out to be a miniature enlightened being. But somehow he felt quite skeptical about it; it all seemed too far-fetched. Andrew turned it over and over in his mind as he drove back to his room, trying to feel positive about his new nanny job and justified in quitting at the club. Time would tell.

After picking up a pizza and a six-pack of beer, he returned to the motel. He stopped in the office to pay his bill and then resigned himself to another lonely night of television. As he sat on the side of the bed and ate, he could almost feel We-Be lying in wait, ready to pounce on him and give him the inevitable lecture. It was a sure bet, he thought, that she would view his actions this morning differently than Lana had. Sometimes he thought she purposely took the opposing side of any subject, just to get on his nerves. He was going crazy swerving back and forth between Lana's and We-Be's distinctly different philosophies, and right now he didn't want his personal she-demon to pop out of the ethers to screw with his head.

Andrew switched through the channels to find a movie he hadn't seen yet and settled back against the pillows, beer in hand. He decided to stay awake as long as he could, hoping that We-Be would get bored waiting for him to fall asleep and find someone else to pick on. After watching four movies back to back, the only thing he could find besides movies so old that all the actors were already dead was a program by a renowned minister who espoused teachings that seemed to be a cross between Christian and New Age thought. Her topic this particular evening was unconditional love. Even though love was the last thing Andrew wanted to think about now that he and Amy were no longer together, he decided to hear what she had to say. Yawning, he strained to keep his eyes open.

". . . and unconditional love, my friends," the minister cooed, "is what you need to practice. For only by loving each and every person just the way they are can you find everlasting happiness. God loves you unconditionally and wants you to do the same unto others. Simply cast away your cares and woes and learn to love, love, love! And you can show that love in many wonderful ways. One way is by opening your hearts, opening your wallets, and picking up your phone right now to call the number on the screen. . . ."

Her image was suddenly blanked out, followed by the announcement, "We interrupt this program to bring you the following special report." Then, to Andrew's dismay, the picture tube was filled with an all-too-familiar face. He stared at the TV in disbelief: We-Be, decked out in purple choir robe and blonde pixie wig was gazing at him out of the screen, hands clasped in front of her beatifically beaming face.

"Love, love, love! Love is all around you. Take some love and douse yourself with it. Wash your face in it. It's especially good with a cup of coffee or spooned over Rice Crispies. It flows like honey and spends its money. Get a move on it friends; it's a lovely way to start each day! Love, love, love!"

He buried his head in the pillow to try to block her out, but her syrupy-sweet, sing-song voice found its way through the spun-polyester barricade. "Love is the answer, can't you see? So love everyone . . . unconditionally!"

"Are you nuts or something?" Andrew hurled the pillow at the television. "I don't know who you think you are, but you just can't go cutting into a TV show anytime you damn well please!"

"Can't I? Well, you can always get up and change the channel if you want to, Morgan; but then, that wouldn't be very loving of you, now would it? Love, love, love!" We-Be bent down and scooped up a few blooms from the flower-laden stage and threw them toward him, but they bounced off the inside of the screen.

Andrew jumped up and switched the channel, but her image was still there. "I thought you said I could change the channel?" he snarled.

"So, I lied. That's nothing new in the business of TV evangelism, is it?" She stuffed a red curl back up under her wig that had escaped when she bent down, and picked up where she left off. "Love, love, love . . ."

"C'mon, knock it off; I know most of these shows are scams. What do you think I am . . . stupid?" He squirmed uncomfortably at his own words, since he already felt pretty stupid talking to an image on a TV screen.

"No, I don't think you're stupid, Morgan. I realize you aren't going to get out your wallet and send a 'love gift' to some gushy prophet for profit. But I know for a fact that you haven't got a handle on unconditional love, and haven't ever questioned whether there's really even such a thing."

Andrew was speechless for a few seconds before he stuttered, "Really such a thing? I can't believe what I'm hearing! Now you're knocking love of all things. I'm starting to think you really are a she-demon from Hell. Jesus, everyone knows that love is the most powerful force in the universe; and there's nothing you can say to discredit it."

"Actually, I'm not the one who's discrediting it," We-Be fired back. "It's people like that TV evangelist whose show I pre-empted and Lana with her hypocritical huggy-huggy, love-everyone-but-keep-your-distance-and-don't-forget-to-pay-in-cash policy who are ruining the true meaning of the word. They may be able to give beautiful sermons on the virtues of unconditional love, but their flowery words only serve to mask their own smug self-absorption and excessive need to show others how enlightened, advanced, or special they are. And let's not forget the obsession they have with boosting their cash flow."

"If you were the great enlightened being you pretend to be, you wouldn't criticize people like Lana, 'cause you'd know you're supposed to love them just the way they are." Andrew's voice reflected his righteous indignation.

"What does that mean?"

"Huh?"

"What does 'love them just the way they are' mean? Does that mean I have to like them? Approve of them and what they do?"

"Well, sure. That's what unconditional love is all about."

"Where on Earth did you get that idea? Never mind, I guess I just answered my own question."

We-Be strode haughtily to the throne-like chair behind her that was a twin of the evangelist's and sat down before continuing: "Far too many people searching for the 'truth' get caught in the trap of believing that they absolutely have to love everyone, without question, without really understanding what unconditional love is. They believe this because someone 'more enlightened' than they are told them so, or because they're afraid they'll create 'bad karma,' or because they're scared they'll end up going to Hell for all eternity—compliments of their unconditionally loving Father in Heaven!"

"Wait a minute! You can't honestly believe those are the only reasons why people strive to love everyone. What about those people who are really sincere about achieving such a goal and who aren't motivated by fear, greed, or the need to play 'follow the leader'? Those people who seem to naturally identify with others on an emotional level and feel compassion for everyone?"

"Yes, there actually are people with noble intentions when it comes to unconditional love. They're expanding their sense of 'I' to include more, and are learning to feel their connection to the whole." We-Be absent-mindedly picked up the Bible that was laying on the end table beside her and fanned through its pages.

"So unconditional love does exist. I wish you'd make up your mind!" He took a swig of his beer and sat down on the edge of the bed.

"As an ideal, Morgan. But striving for a goal and actually achieving it aren't the same thing—even for those with the best of intentions. It's crucial to understand exactly what you're letting yourself in for when you set such an ideal as your goal."

"Like what?"

"Well, for one thing, you have to be capable of loving the most sinister, vile, malicious, corrupt, depraved, person you can imagine—and then some."

Andrew briefly considered her answer. Then, not sounding at all sure of himself, he said, "I bet there are at least a few enlightened people out there who can love someone like that—they just remain detached and don't allow themselves to get emotionally involved."

"Hold it! Wait a minute! Time out!" We-Be placed the Bible back on the table and made a time-out signal with her hands. "You just finished telling me that unconditional love has to do with identifying with others and feeling compassion for them; now you're saying that it involves detachment and emotional uninvolvement: 'I don't have to get to know you to love you. I don't have to have any feelings for you whatsoever. I just have to say I love you—whatever that means—and make myself believe it.' That's quite a contradiction, wouldn't you say?"

Andrew was trapped and he knew it. He thought about simply unplugging the television, but realized it wouldn't do any good: We-Be would still somehow be broadcasting live and in living color. His mind was a blur, as he desperately tried to justify these two diametrically opposed ways of viewing the same concept which had somehow become part of his world view. But he couldn't, and so just sat there.

"Look, Morgan," she said, smiling at him sympathetically, "why don't you put aside all the stuff you've learned about unconditional love from Lana and her friends at her assorted spiritual workshops and stop for a moment to really examine this thing called love? It may be the most powerful force in the universe, like you said, but what does that really mean? Pretty arcane stuff! But coming down to Earth a bit, we can also say that love is the most intense emotion experienced in physical reality. And since that's where you presently reside, I ask you: can you really feel the same kind of emotional intensity you felt for your mother, your Aunt Martha, or even for that mongrel dog you had when you were a kid, for a whole world of people, the vast majority of whom you'll never even meet and a lot of whom you wouldn't even want to be in the same room with?

"Of course you can't," she added, not giving him a chance to respond. "And you certainly wouldn't feel it for the most detestable person the world had to offer, no matter how powerful a force love is."

"Well, obviously the love you'd feel for an aunt or dog isn't the same thing as unconditional love. I never thought it was." Andrew's voice carried a tinge of annoyance.

We-Be nodded her head, as though expecting him to take this tack. "Love is love, Morgan, and by its nature demands to be expressed. But to express love, you really have to feel it. You could pretend to, which is what a lot of people do, but you'd end up watering down the ideal of unconditional love so much that it wouldn't exactly be an ideal anymore."

As she began to speak, white letters appeared at the bottom of the screen, spelling out her thought:

" Space-Time Principle Number 94:

When embarking on the search for truth,
it's important that you never forget
the point from which to start:
being truthful with yourself.

"If you're truthful with yourself, you'll admit that trying to emotionally embrace the entire human race isn't a very practical goal." Reaching into one of the pockets of her robe, We-Be pulled out a lighter and a cigarette and lit up, an action out of keeping with this latest role she was playing. She took a long drag and blew an unusually large halo-like smoke ring that magically rose to a point directly above her head before fading away.

"A far more attainable goal would be unconditional acceptance of everyone: trying to simply accept them as they are, to recognize their uniqueness as individuals, to understand that their faults and failings are all part of the human condition. But keep in mind that it's just as impractical to pretend you unconditionally accept everyone as it is to pretend you unconditionally love them. Unconditional acceptance means accepting not just others' positive qualities, but their undesirable ones as well. Easier said than done; for trying to convince yourself that you don't want someone to change certain qualities that you dislike—under the guise of acceptance—will, in the long run, only work against you. For those very qualities will eventually create a wear and tear on your so-called 'acceptance,' forcing you to see that you really weren't being honest with yourself. And by pretending to accept someone simply because you think you have to, you're not only fooling yourself, you're negating any chance you have for loving him. Because—this is important, Morgan—until you can admit you don't like someone and zero in on why, you can't begin the process of understanding why he is the way he is, which leads you to accepting and finally, maybe, going on to unconditionally loving him."

"What if I never get to the point where I can like or accept him?" Andrew gulped down the last of his beer, crunched up the can, and tossed it in the trash.

"Then simply accept the fact that you don't like him and take it from there."

"To where?"

"The hell away from him, maybe."

Once again letters appeared at the bottom of the screen in unison with her next words:

" Space-Time Principle Number 133:

The goal might be to love everyone, but that doesn't mean you have to like them.

"The semantics are important here—liking someone is not part of the unconditional love equation. To like someone, you have to approve of him, which is a completely different thing than accepting him. However, you can disapprove of someone yet still accept him—if for nothing else than being a horse's ass."

Andrew was trying hard to assimilate the meaning behind this latest twist in her philosophy as she added, "The whole point of my little 'sermon' wasn't to trash the concept of unconditional love, but simply to help you put it in the proper perspective."

"You certainly have a way of taking everything I've learned, everything that's held sacred by millions of people, turning it upside-down, shaking it out, and magically making it end up sounding so logical," he said, his face registering surprise at his own admission.

"That's because magic and logic go hand in hand, Morgan. Contrary to popular opinion, magic doesn't defy logic but actually makes it possible. Without magic, the ability to be logical would be nonexistent."

"Space-Time Principle Number 75:

Magic creates the space in which logic can show itself."

The words materialized at her feet, and curious as to how We-Be was going to explain how two such opposite concepts could be related, Andrew leaned forward, closer to the set.

"All great logical thought is birthed through inspiration, and inspiration is conceived in the domain of magic. Inspiration brings forth new, profoundly logical concepts that can roll off the tip of your tongue without any conscious awareness on your part about how you formed them. It's magic that allows this to happen. Spontaneous logical thought isn't contrived, and neither is real magic. When you allow them to just be and one doesn't try to defeat the other, they reinforce each other and their diverse attributes become interconnected, which helps them operate at their fullest capacity."

Andrew's bladder felt like it was about to burst, but he was so engrossed in what she was saying that he didn't want to miss a word.

"Take a break, Morgan," she said, as she put out her cigarette in what appeared to be a solid-gold collection plate on the table next to her. "You can hear me fine if you leave the bathroom door open. I won't peek, I promise."

Red-faced, he turned the volume up a notch and relieved himself behind a partially open door as We-Be continued preaching to an empty room.

"There are basically two extreme schools of thought. One states that logic is the ruling factor of the universe, that magic is merely a bunch of hocus-pocus nonsense indulged in by idiots and charlatans. It insists that anything that can't be seen or touched can't possibly exist. The other claims that magic is the only relative factor involved, that logic merely serves to defeat or limit magic at every turn; that magic is only hindered by any thoughts of practicality."

He returned to the foot of the bed and sat down just in time to see We-Be, tiring of the high-backed chair, slide down onto the floor to assume a cross-legged pose.

"Anyone who says that magic isn't practical hasn't recognized the fact that throughout history countless practical inventions have been ushered into physical reality through the very magical medium that he chooses to ignore or belittle. But, if he were to simply let down his hyper-logical prejudices and give magic its due, he could multiply his own creative abilities a hundredfold. And if the person who shuns logic by labeling it 'limiting' were to recognize that without logic magic could become hopelessly confused with fantasy, then he could save himself from disappointment, frustration, and embarrassment when certain spells fall flat."

More words formed beneath her, and We-Be whisked them playfully away.

" Space-Time Principle Number 76:

Logic provides the discipline
so necessary to magic's chaotic nature.

"When magic without the assistance of logic is sifted through some people's beliefs, those people can run amuck, creating delusions in which they can lose themselves. You've seen this before: people misinterpreting magic because they shut the door on the logical side of their nature. They confuse magic with all kinds of preconceived notions and end up believing in a distorted version of reality, creating endless hallucinations around themselves because they've thrown away their good common sense."

Andrew understood most of what she was saying, but still felt puzzled over some things. "Isn't this odd-ball philosophy you're preaching awfully pragmatic to be coming from someone who's not even physical? I mean, I really don't understand how the absence of logic can make magic run amuck. I thought you said that magic works best when I get out of my own way. But isn't throwing logic into the works, in essence, 'getting in my own way'?"

"I didn't say that magic can run amuck, Morgan; I said people can run amuck. A person's beliefs can blow up the magic into an unrealistic fantasy bubble that surrounds him, distorting everything he views through it. With any luck, somewhere along the line a little logic will seep in and deflate that bubble. Practical mysticism—the balance between logic and magic; that's what this 'odd-ball' philosophy that I'm trying to drill into your head amounts to.

"And, as far as getting in your own way is concerned, I wasn't referring to the purely natural presence of your logical mind; I was referring to the manipulative, I-want-it-my-way-and-no-other part of you that demands magic behaves a certain way. True logic doesn't make demands, but instead fine tunes the magic so that it can fully express itself. It keeps you from getting sidetracked or straying too far from your natural Earthly experience. Once again, practical mysticism. Your desire for a Porsche to magically materialize out of thin air is a perfect example of how a person's misconceptions and lack of logic can distort his own magic. Your beliefs do form your experience, but remember, those beliefs must be in absolute accord with the principles that rule your chosen reality in order for them to give you what you want."

Andrew could feel his defenses rising at the mention of his Porsche. Popping open his other beer, he asked belligerently: "How does any of this pertain to what I've just gone through? Sure, at first I thought that the golf course job was evidence of my own magic, but then it got to the point where the only logical thing to do was quit. How is that magic? What, the magic giveth and the magic taketh away? Doesn't sound like the magic is in very good accord with me!"

Getting up and straightening her robe again, We-Be paced back and forth, never taking her eyes from the screen between them. "But it was in accord with you; magic is always in accord with you, in the sense that it inevitably gives you what it thinks you want. Remember, it isn't magic's place to question or judge; it simply listens to your thoughts and responds. Thoughts are powerful things and produce an emotional charge; and when you allow your thoughts and, therefore, your emotions, to run away with themselves, they can suppress your logical perceptions, which in turn can screw up your magic. You decided you hated your job, that you had been placed in a subservient role that you were too good to play. Those are pretty powerful thoughts, Morgan, and they created an emotional charge so strong that you lost all sense of reasoning. You emotionally reacted before you even had time to think things out."

"Think things out? They treated me like an insignificant inferior, a servant who deserved no respect."

"That's just the way you perceived it. So Harry's a jerk who thinks bartenders are low-lifes. He's entitled to his opinion. And the Admiral got flustered because he misplaced his shoes and his ego had to find someone to pin the blame on. So what? Every job has its bad days, every day has its sorrier moments. Of course you were treated like a servant, for in essence that's exactly what you were getting paid to be! That's not to say that it was right for two or three of them to treat you poorly, but you could have gotten past that. You want so desperately to become a great and powerful master of the manifestive arts, but how can you begin to do that when you haven't, as yet, even begun to master adversity?"

"Look," Andrew said defensively, "I was unjustly accused of stealing a pair of shoes, and if I hadn't quit I would have been fired. Or at best, I would have had to pay for them."

"Well, didn't you end up paying for them anyway?" she asked sarcastically as she walked toward a VCR sitting on a table on the far side of the stage.

He couldn't argue with her on that point, but he wasn't about to let her get the best of him, not this time around. "I quit the job because of the principle of the thing."

"Principle of the thing? Here's the principle of the thing:

"*Space-Time Principle Number 36:*

*When you don't appreciate something,
it will more than likely go away.*

"You lost your job because you bitched and moaned it right out of existence. Come to think of it, that's how you made your last car go away: you hated it to death, remember? Don't forget what I said about accepting things as they are for the time being. Your magic was doing just fine until you got in your own way and messed it all up. You allowed your emotions to override your common sense, Morgan. Had you simply kept your temper and tried to reason your way through the situation, you would have experienced a much different outcome."

"Oh, c'mon, how can you possibly know that?"

"It's simple. It's all here on this video tape: Andrew B. Morgan: Events That Might Have Been.'" We-Be picked up a tape from the table and waved it in front of her as the camera from who-knows-where zoomed in for a close-up.

"Where did you get that from?"

"Where else? The Vault of Videos."

"The Vault of what? Is that your twisted way of saying the 'Akashic Records' or something?"

"Akashic Records? I never did like that term. Besides, haven't you ever heard of progress?" Inserting the tape in the machine, she said, "Watch closely. Maybe you'll see a part of yourself that you aren't aware of yet."

And with a flick of a switch, her image on the TV faded out, to be replaced by an image of the country club locker room. Every detail was the same as before, including the Admiral sitting at the table with Skip McKenzie and Harry.

"Boy! Are my shoes done yet? I need 'em tomorrow, you know." Open-mouthed, Andrew watched as his TV image stared at the Admiral in disbelief, the dialogue falling into line with the events of the day.

"Why, sir . . . I gave you your shoes yesterday before you left, don't you remember?"

"Are you telling me I don't remember right? I may be gettin' old, but my brain still works. You tryin' to get away with my shoes, are ya boy?"

"No sir, it's just—"

" 'Just,' my ass! You better get me my shoes right now, on the double!"

"I can't get your—"

And, just like Andrew remembered it, Skip entered the conversation: "Now hold on here. I'm sure Andy has simply misplaced the shoes and will find them before the day's over."

All of a sudden the scene disappeared and was replaced with We-Be's image. "Now watch carefully, Morgan, because the rest of what you'll see is what might have happened had you kept your wits about you and tuned in to the subtle undercurrents in the locker room atmosphere. She pushed the play button on the recorder again and the "Might Have Been" tape resumed playing on Andrew's screen.

"Isn't that right, Andy?" Skip gave him a subtle wink, a wink that Andrew originally hadn't caught in the middle of his rising fury and frustration, but, for some reason, in this version of events was instantly recognized by this other self. He could see the tension lessen in the body of his video counterpart, and noticed that this Andrew was working hard to keep his composure.

"Those are six-hundred-dollar shoes I handed you, boy; handmade 'specially for me. You gonna pay me for those shoes?"

Andrew watched carefully as his TV image stood at the table observing Harry leaning back in his chair, grinning from ear to ear, trying to push his buttons. But the other Andrew simply ignored Harry—hard as it was. Skip stood up from the table, a perfect replay of his earlier action, and said: "If Andy doesn't find your shoes, I'm sure he'll be more than happy to compensate you for them. He understands he's responsible for everything that happens in this locker room. He knows the rules." Skip put his arm around Andrew's shoulder, just like before, and smiled at him. Andrew Two was quiet for a moment as he studied Skip's expression closely. Then, unlike in the real event, Skip winked at him again, with the eye that was turned away from everyone but Andrew. It was a wink of conspiracy, a be-smart-and-follow-my-lead kind of gesture.

"Yes, sir. I'm sure there's a reasonable explanation for what's happened here, and I'll do everything I can to rectify the situation. I'll get on it right away."

"Well, see to it that you do," growled the Admiral as he stormed out of the room. Sober faced, Harry trailed after him, obviously irked that Andrew hadn't been fired on the spot.

"I really did give him his shoes back, Mr. McKenzie. I—"

"I'm sure you did, son; the poor old fella's always losing things these days. You have to understand, he's really having a hard time facing the fact that his memory's deserting him. Real sad. I appreciate you handling the situation like a professional. I like that." Reaching into his pocket, Skip pulled out a wad of money and peeled off a couple of bills. Handing them to Andrew, he said, "You're doing just fine here, Andy. Fine indeed. Now how about getting on the horn and calling that taxi company to see if they can turn up those shoes? Tell them there's a reward."

The video version of the locker-room scenario abruptly cut off and switched back to a close-up of We-Be's face. "So you see, Morgan, there are many ways to deal with situations." She walked back to the chair in the middle of the stage and sat down. "In that version of events, you ended up tracking down the shoes, keeping your job, and feeling good about your ability to control your emotions and therefore your reality."

"Well, what ended up happening in the long run? Did the other me ever get his Porsche? Or, for that matter, does this me ever get one?"

"That's on the tape 'Andrew B. Morgan: Events That May Be.'"

"Can I see some of that?"

"It's not possible."

"Huh? Why not?" Andrew pulled at his face in exasperation.

"All events that 'may be' are formed in your present. Your 'tomorrow' is a blank tape waiting to be filled with the results of your 'today'. Start 'today' watching your thoughts, and remember, you're setting the stage for your 'tomorrow'."

"So I should stay with a job, no matter how much crap I have to take, just to make my 'tomorrow' tolerable?"

"Look, Morgan, you're free to quit a job anytime you want; but when you continually find yourself repeating negative patterns, then you need to sit back and ask yourself how you wound up where you are in the first place. In the future, instead of losing your head and walking off a job all bent out of shape, why not use it as an opportunity to confront some beliefs that have long out-lived their purpose?

" Space-Time Principle Number 10:

An undesirable situation
can become an endless circle game
if you don't straighten out
the bent beliefs that formed it."

Jumping up, We-Be executed a couple of flawless pirouettes and then plopped down at the edge of the stage. Singing the chorus of an old folk song at the top of her lungs, she swung her legs in rhythm with the lyrics: "'Round and 'round and 'round in a circle game . . ."

Andrew rolled his eyes and covered his ears. "Okay . . . I'd say it's time for a commercial break . . . please?"

"So my singing isn't the best in the world. But it's a lot better than that song-and-dance routine Lana's been giving you."

"What do you mean?"

"That bit about a job being just a 'transitional tool.'"

"Well, I don't see that there's anything particularly enlightened about sticking with some menial job. I only take jobs like that in the first place just to get by until I—"

"Yeah, yeah, until you manifest, materialize, and creatively visualize your way into wealth and abundance! Every time you get a job, Morgan, you go into it already resenting it and seeing it as a temporary inconvenience. You've never even considered applying your manifestation theories to the job itself. Talk about a tool! A job is just that—a medium that can provide you with feelings of self-worth, the lack of which is one of your biggest problems in the first place."

Andrew could feel his resentments rising again, as was always the case whenever this subject came up. He listened to her without interrupting, afraid to drag it out longer than necessary. Stuffing a slice of cold pizza in his mouth to help him keep it shut, he swore to himself that he would never be swayed by her opinions about work.

"Whether you realize it or not, Morgan, constantly bumming off other people tears away at your self-esteem and your inherent—though perhaps forgotten—sense of honor. And I find it quite ironic that the very people you mooch from do hold jobs—often jobs they aren't thrilled with—and accept responsibility for themselves. By giving your power to other people in such a manner, you're saying that they're strong while you're weak, and yet you tell yourself that they are wasting their lives away.

" Space-Time Principle Number 67:

Not working for a living isn't dishonorable,
but living off another's energy
while putting out none of your own
sure is."

"Well, there are all kinds of energy. I've never taken anything from anybody without giving thanks to the Universe." Andrew wiped his hands on the tail end of the bedspread before crossing his arms across his chest defensively.

"The Universe isn't looking for thanks; it's looking for you to be a responsible part of the whole."

"If your idea of being responsible means I have to have permanently dirty fingernails and punch a time clock every day, then I guess I'll never be responsible, at least not in your eyes."

" Space-Time Principle Number 64:

You may have to get your hands dirty, but work doesn't have to be a dirty word."

We-Be stood up and brushed off her behind. "Remember, everything in your society is the result of someone's work. The trick is to think of a job that would allow you to express yourself. Zero in on the most perfectible part of yourself and find a job that complements it and helps you to develop it to the utmost. Then it won't feel like work anymore; it will feel like a means to self-fulfillment."

Andrew couldn't contain himself any longer. Gulping down the last bite of pizza, he said: "But lots of people don't have to work for a living. They're born into it, or inherit it, or just manifest it like Lana did."

We-Be laughed. "People who are born into money may have opportunities that others don't, but that works both ways. They never experience the satisfaction of making it to the top on their own. They miss out on the feelings of great achievement that come from carving out their own destiny, chip by chip."

"You really hate money, don't you? It's probably some carry-over from that Zen Buddhist past life of yours or something. Guess you're going to give me the old you-can't-take-it-with-you rap next, huh?" Andrew shook his head and snickered with disdain.

"Well, of course you can't take it with you, silly. And no, I don't hate money, even though I personally have no use for it. Certainly I realize that much more is involved in the experience of being physical than merely obtaining the bare essentials. And I know that in your reality it often takes money to get the things you want. But I need to add here that money—simple paper and coin—was designed purely as a means of exchange in physical reality. At best, it represents appreciation and gratitude that go beyond the physical. Money is confined to the physical, but the expression behind it doesn't need to be. Appreciation and gratitude are usable in any realm of existence and can be taken with you . . . anywhere."

Tired of wearing the wig, We-Be took it off and ran her fingers briskly through her hair to straighten it out. "So it isn't wrong or bad to have money, Morgan; if you want to be a millionaire, go right ahead, you have my blessings. Just don't expect the Universe to drop gold bricks in your lap. But I will tell you this: If you'd spend your time and energy trying to manifest certain attributes in yourself, such as independence and self-respect, then you'd find everything you need at your disposal. And as far as Lana goes . . . she never really told you where her money came from, did she?"

"What do you mean?"

"Do you really believe she materializes hundred dollar bills in the palm of her hand, directly from, what does she call it? 'Universal Thought Substance'?"

Not giving Andrew a chance to answer, she continued: "I guess it's easy to brag about your wealth and abundance when you've been married to two different wealthy men—both over the age of seventy, I might add. Widowed twice and left as the sole beneficiary on each occasion; hell of a manifestation, wouldn't you say? But she never tells anyone the details of her wealth, only that she didn't have to work for it. If she ever did reveal the truth, it would destroy her mystique and tarnish her image in the eyes of her admirers."

Andrew was shocked speechless as her words tumbled through his head, knocking into the idealistic image he had formed of Lana. Lana, a fortune hunter instead of a fortune creator? Was it possible? All his hopes and dreams of manifestation had rested firmly upon the foundation she had laid for him. She had been the model for his beliefs, the example of how to master physical reality. And now this . . .

We-Be looked at Andrew's face, the color slowly fading from it, and felt concerned. "Sorry, Morgan, but it's better that you know the truth. Maybe you'll learn something from all this and even see the humor in it one day. After all, many a good story took much pain in the making."

Acting like she wasn't there anymore, Andrew stood up, staggering a little, and walked around the bed to lie down. Still fully dressed, he crawled in-between the covers, turned his back on the television, and curled up into a ball.

"Goodnight, Morgan," We-Be whispered gently, aware that he couldn't hear her through the blankets pulled up over his ears. "Sleep well. You'll need all the energy you can muster tomorrow when you face the god-child."

And with a snap of her fingers, she turned off the television from the other side.

Chapter Twelve

Damian for a Day

Andrew awoke in the morning feeling very anxious. Not only had he dreamt about We-Be again, but also about Holden the god-child who was shortly to become his charge. He remembered the dream of We-Be in total detail—a typical We-Be dream complete with strange evangelical television props. But the Holden dream had slipped away, leaving just a lingering uneasiness in his psyche.

Andrew loaded up his car and headed for the address Lana had given him. As he drew closer to the Van Morris residence, his eyes felt as though they would pop out of his head. St. Charles Harbour—with the British spelling—wasn't your typical community for the well-to-do. These weren't homes, as Andrew thought of them; these were more like full-blown palaces, sprawled over a three-mile stretch of private beach. He chuckled to himself as he thought what a befitting neighborhood this was for a growing god.

As he pulled up to the Van Morris's front gate, the butterflies in his stomach began to flutter wildly. He announced himself, and the gate opened to allow him passage, without any word of acknowledgment at the other end of the intercom. The house was a wood and glass, three-story rambling affair, covering a good acre of ground. A cocker spaniel romped across the well-trimmed lawn that spread neatly between lush flower beds and perfectly clipped hedges. All in all, it was the epitome of the American dream.

Surprisingly, no butler or maid answered the door. Andrew knew immediately that the woman who greeted him was Mrs. Van Morris. Tall and elegant, in her middle thirties, wearing a floor-length silk get-up, she beamed at him and motioned him in. Inside, the house was like a botanical garden: huge palms and tropical plants surrounded a fountain made in the likeness of the god Neptune. A floor-to-ceiling brass cage held a large assortment of colorful exotic birds whose screeching and squawking completed the atmosphere of a jungle paradise.

"So, you must be Andrew!" Her distinctly Bostonian accent seemed to clash with the decor. "Let me have a good look at you!" Stepping back a foot or two, Mrs. Van Morris opened her eyes wide and stared at him—or almost at him; actually her focus seemed to be at a point directly over his head. Afraid to breathe or blink, Andrew waited in agony for her stamp of approval.

"What marvelous colors! I can see why Lana thinks so highly of you."

Andrew wasn't sure at first what she was referring to, but then realized he was receiving an aura reading.

"Lots of yellow—that shows you're quite intelligent; and there's even a trace of violet, the most spiritual color of all!"

Andrew couldn't hold his motionless pose any longer, and shuffled his feet, looking at his shoes with a new-found interest. His movement broke her fixed gaze and she took him by the arm, leading him past the fountain.

"Of course, there are a couple of holes in your etheric web—nothing a good rebirthing experience can't heal. We'll have to see about that."

She chattered on about his aura and the assorted hues it contained as they walked through the house and across a courtyard into another wing.

"Now, when you meet Mr. Van Morris, be sure not to bring up any of the things we're interested in. He's definitely not metaphysically minded, and ignores all my attempts to educate him." She squeezed Andrew's arm and winked conspiratorially as she knocked on a heavy mahogany door; then she opened it at the sound of a muffled voice behind it.

"Eric, dear, this is the young man I told you about. I knew you'd want to meet him before I take him over to Holden's wing."

A hulking silhouette of a man's figure loomed behind the massive desk, his features lost in the shadows and the glare from the window behind him. Andrew waited politely, but Mr. Van Morris remained silent. Andrew fidgeted with his hands behind his back, not sure whether he should speak first. Still trying to decide, he jumped at the sound of his own knuckles popping and made himself step forward, hand extended.

"Glad to meet you, sir. I want to thank you for this opportunity. . . ."

Andrew's voice cracked as he stared at his new employer. He could just make out Mr. Van Morris's cold, emotionless features in the dim light. The man shook Andrew's hand brusquely across the desk, clearing his throat.

"I'm sure you'll work out just fine. My wife will fill you in on the details. And if you need anything else, ask one of the help."

As he stood there waiting for Mr. Van Morris to say something else, Mrs. Van Morris once again took him by the arm and led him toward the door. He felt thoroughly intimidated by this man, and his mind flashed on We-Be's lecture about keeping his emotions in check. He didn't want to blow this job, too, by developing resentments for yet another discourteous rich person.

Mrs. Van Morris was more subdued after visiting her husband's den. As she led the way through the complex series of courtyards and hallways, she said apologetically: "Eric's a very busy man, Andrew; you'll have to excuse his seeming lack of interest. He loves Holden, of course, but he doesn't have any idea how special his son really is."

Mrs. Van Morris walked Andrew around the rest of the house, introducing him to Janis the maid and Marguerite the cook, before showing him his room.

Next, they entered her son's wing through a large sunny playroom stacked from one side to the other with every toy imaginable. Holden's mother called his name affectionately, and, not getting a response, walked into the adjoining bedroom with Andrew trailing behind. Sound effects of an imaginary war wafted out from under the bed, and Mrs. Van Morris bent down, silk rustling, to get her son's attention.

"You aren't playing army again, are you darling? You know Mummy doesn't approve of that."

The battle sounds stopped, but she received no answer to her question. Getting down on her hands and knees, she peered under the bed-turned-foxhole and cooed: "Your new friend's here to play with you, Holden. Don't you want to come out and meet him?"

A full minute elapsed before a camouflaged helmet slowly emerged from the other side of the bed, followed by two wide raven-colored eyes. The eyes bored straight into Andrew, as though trying to read his very soul. He had never seen eyes like these before, and was slightly taken aback. It was hard to believe that they belonged to a five-year-old. Andrew bent down a little and smiled at his charge. "So, who won?"

"My side, of course. I never lose." Andrew was impressed right away at how intelligent Holden sounded.

"Now, how many times have I told you, dear, that in war no one ever really wins." Mrs. Van Morris scolded her son gently, and looked at Andrew for approval of her teachings.

"Really, Mother, anyone knows that's what war's all about—winning!" Holden rolled his incredible eyes in disgust and shot Andrew a sideways look to affirm his own ability to discern his mother's ignorance.

"Well, come introduce yourself properly, Holden." She grabbed the helmet off his head and combed his shock of black hair with her fingers.

As the child walked around the bed to accept Andrew's outstretched hand, Andrew studied him closely.

"I'm very pleased to make your acquaintance, sir," Holden said politely.

"Just call me Andy. Do you have a nickname, too?"

"No. I'd prefer it if you'd called me 'Holden,' please."

Andrew felt as though he were conversing with a pint-sized college graduate. His eyes locked with Mrs. Van Morris's, and she nodded as though to confirm the secret they shared about her son's true identity. Then, patting Holden on the head, she said: "I have to hurry now to get ready to go to the airport. You know your father detests being late! We won't be home until very late this evening." She walked over to the miniature desk and shuffled through its contents. "Andrew, here are Holden's lesson books. He needs to study them for at least two hours a day. Other than that, you boys have a good time getting to know each other. And here's the number where we can be reached in case of an emergency. If you need anything else, just ask Janis or Cook. You'll be fine, won't you?"

Andrew looked at Holden's smiling angelic face and then nodded, not at all sure that he would be. After all, he thought, how on Earth did one go about babysitting a god-in-the-making?

"C'mon, Holden, you can help me bring in my gear." Andrew was eager to get his stuff out of the car and into his new living quarters.

"No thank you. I'd rather stay here and finish my game, if you don't mind."

Andrew wasn't sure how to handle such polite disobedience, and so, just stood there and watched as Holden disappeared back under his bed. The re-enacted sounds of guns and bombs echoed behind him as he returned downstairs to fetch his belongings.

It was already getting hot outside, and by the time Andrew had carried all his things up the flight of stairs to the bedroom across from Holden's, he had worked up quite a sweat. He needed something cold to drink, but decided to round up Holden first.

Entering the playroom, Andrew was greeted with silence. He tiptoed into the bedroom and peeked under the bed. No Holden.

Concerned, he looked in every nook and cranny of the bedroom and playroom. Still no Holden. Andrew could feel a growing anxiety in the pit of his stomach as he rushed down the stairs to check with Janis and Marguerite to see if Holden was with them. But neither of them had any inkling as to where he might be. Trying to keep calm, Andrew decided to start at one end of the house and work his way to the other in search of the runaway avatar.

After a good fifteen minutes, he made his way back to the front jungle room. As he peered behind the plants in front of the wall of windows, he froze, breath catching in his lungs. He had forgotten all about the Atlantic Ocean in the backyard! Seized by panic, he frantically felt around to see if one of the windows was a sliding glass door opening onto the beach.

"Janis gets very angry when she finds fingerprints on the glass."

Jumping halfway out of his skin, Andrew swirled around to see Holden, dressed in what appeared to be an authentic Indian headdress, face smeared with warpaint, peering at him from behind a giant palm frond.

"Where in God's name have you been? You scared me half to death!"

"Looking for you. Where have you been?" Holden stared at Andrew with a straight, painted face, bow and arrow in hand.

Knees giving way, Andrew sank down on the tile floor, and leaned against the window.

"I do hope you're not tired; I was hoping you'd play cowboys and Indians with me."

Andrew looked at Holden's eager expression, and couldn't help but smile. "Okay, I guess I get to be the cowboy, huh?"

"Obviously. Here, I brought you a gun. It's loaded and ready to go." Holden pulled a cap gun out of his back pocket and bounced over to hand it to Andrew.

"I'll count to ten while you hide, and then I'll come looking for you to kill you with my arrows."

Trying to be a responsible nanny, he looked at the arrows clasped in Holden's hand to verify that they had the proper rubber suction cup tips, which they did. Then, as Holden slowly counted, Andrew scrambled to find a good hiding place.

Just as he had wedged himself between the sofa and a bamboo plant and covered himself with a large floor pillow, he heard Holden yell, "Ready or not, here I come!"

Andrew felt silly, but, even still, a little giddy—like he had felt when he had been a kid playing the same game. He could hear Holden's noisy unIndian-like footsteps as the boy searched every corner of the room, shouting "aha!" each time he thought he had found his prey's hideout. Andrew tried not to breathe or move to give himself away, but then after a while, thought perhaps he should give the kid a break and put out some telltale sign of his whereabouts. Reaching out, he grabbed the base of the bamboo and shook it, rattling the shoots.

"Aha! Gotcha!" Andrew felt the thump as the arrow struck the pillow. Then, carrying the game out as he thought he should, he jumped up and yelled, "Oh no you didn't, Geronimo, you missed!" And grabbing Holden, he threw him on the couch and started tickling him.

"You cheated! You cheated!" Holden screamed. "If you hadn't used a pillow, you'd be dead!"

Holden pulled away from his grip and stormed out of the room. Grumbling under his breath, Andrew started to straighten up after their game before getting back on Holden's trail. Bending over, he picked up the pillow under which he had hidden and gasped in dismay. The arrow was sticking a good two inches into it, rubber tip obviously gone. Pulling the arrow out, he gasped again, horrified. The end of the arrow had been sharpened to a precision fine point, making it a deadly weapon.

Furious, Andrew grabbed the arrow and ran after Holden, who was just making his way into the kitchen.

"Okay, mister, hold it right there!"

Holden turned around, an expression of complete innocence on his paint-streaked features.

Andrew waved the arrow, point down, in Holden's face. "Do you mind explaining this?"

"What do you mean?" His big black eyes peered up at Andrew guilelessly.

"Like where the suction cup went and how the point got to be so sharp?" Andrew tapped the arrow in the palm of his hand and stared at the boy with severity.

"It's simple. I used Father's pencil sharpener. Anyone knows Indians didn't use arrows with rubber tips! They must have used the rubber things to keep the arrows sharp when they weren't using them."

Andrew looked at him in disbelief. Was Holden really that naive, or was the kid actually smart enough to concoct such a story and merely playing him for a sucker?

"Well, you have to give me all of your arrows now. You can't play with them anymore. It was bad to sharpen them like that, and I think you know it! But we'll let it pass this time."

Tears welled up in Holden's eyes as he relinquished the arrows to his new nanny. Andrew's anger melted at the sight of the miniature Indian chief with tears running down his face, cutting trails in the warpaint.

"Tell you what, Holden m'man, let's go down to the beach and you can show me around. How does that sound?"

Holden's tears were instantly replaced by a gleam of excitement in his eyes and a big smile.

"But first, let's get rid of the warpaint. We're beachcombers now, pal."

Andrew scrubbed the boy's face and then they changed into their swimsuits.

"What's a beachcomber?" Holden asked as they walked down the stairs leading to the beach.

"Well, it's someone who scavenges for interesting things along the shore. That's why I brought this bag." Andrew held up a plastic bag he had found in the kitchen. "You can find all kinds of unusual things, like old bottles, neat shells, and wood twisted into weird shapes that look like other things. Sometimes, you can find pieces of old sunken ships or even pirates' treasure, if you're lucky."

Andrew could feel a side of him coming out that he had never experienced before—his paternal side. It made him feel good. Taking Holden's hand, he led the way down to the shoreline, moving slowly so as to not miss spying any objects of interest. "Look at this!" Andrew bent down and picked up a scrap of a fishing net half buried in the sand. "And how about this? I haven't seen one of these in ages!"

"I see them all the time. What's so special about it? What is it, anyway?" Holden scrutinized the white disklike object that Andrew handed him.

"A sand dollar."

"You mean it's money?" Holden asked, eyebrows raised skeptically.

Laughing, Andrew proceeded to teach the boy everything he knew about the sea-urchin-turned-beach-artifact. Then, after collecting a few other objects, including an old wine bottle and a medium-sized conch shell, Andrew began noticing an occasional plastic six-pack holder strewn here and there. As he bent to pick them up, Holden asked why he thought trash was interesting enough to collect.

"Because they kill the animals," Andrew explained. "The birds and turtles get tangled in them and drown."

They both lapsed into silence as they walked along, and Andrew flashed back to the night he had spent on the beach, when he had dreamed of We-Be as the wingless savior of sea gulls.

"C'mon, kid, since we're becoming such good friends, I want to show you something neat." Andrew sprinted down to the water's edge, yelling behind him, "Ever take the time to watch a periwinkle before, Holden?"

"A what?"

"One of these." Andrew started digging around with his toe in the froth-covered sand, unearthing some of the little creatures for Holden to see.

"Oh yeah, those are the things Trevor gathers in a bucket to take home to make into soup."

"Who's Trevor?"

"Our gardener. He's from Jamaica."

Andrew was a little put off by having Holden refer to his chosen symbol as soup during their first philosophical session, but decided to try to enlighten the boy anyway. He bent down and picked up one of the wiggling little creatures and held it in his hand.

"Look closely," Andrew said as he pulled Holden in for a better look. "This little pink fella is a living thing, just like you and me, only he doesn't have to worry about anything at all. His whole life consists of glistening in the sun and playing in the water and sand with his friends and being happy. He simply lays back and gets stroked all day by the actual water in which he lives. All his needs are met, and he doesn't have to do a thing."

"Just like me, right?"

Andrew looked at Holden quizzically, not understanding the comparison at first. "How is it like you?" Andrew said as he crouched down to let the periwinkle go.

"Well, all my needs are met, too, and I never have to do anything I don't want to do. Father hires people to do everything for me."

The boy's tone was surprisingly cocky, and memories of We-Be's talks about responsibility and the importance of self-accomplishment rose up from the depths of Andrew's mind. Here before him was an example of someone who would never have to work for a living; someone who would most likely never be able to identify with normal folk; someone who held the position in life that Andrew had always yearned for. He just stared at Holden and shook his head sadly. At this moment in time he was honestly glad he wasn't so blessed himself, and felt very sorry for this poor little rich boy.

"I wasn't saying anyone does anything for the periwinkle, Holden. I was . . ." Andrew's original philosophical point had been derailed by Holden's comments, and he struggled to get his thoughts back on track. He studied the boy as they continued to stroll down the beach, and decided he had to immediately start teaching this child about responsibility. "I think, m'man, that it's time for you to learn a few things about real life."

Holden crooked his head and silently looked at Andrew through unreadable, narrowed eyes.

Andrew contemplated where he could best begin, and finally decided Holden's first lesson in responsibility would be held in Holden's own bedroom. The toys scattered from one end to the other would serve as the perfect place to start. He would cut the periwinkle lesson short, but not before impressing one final thought on his charge. He leaned down and scooped up a handful of periwinkle-inhabited sand; then, picking one of the shelled creatures out, he released the rest of them back to their playground.

Taking Holden's hand, he placed the periwinkle in the boy's palm and said softly, "I want you to take a minute and try to feel the sacredness of the life in this little critter and realize that he's much more than merely something to put into soup."

At first, Holden cringed and made a face, as though he was holding something repulsive. Andrew backed up a step or two and watched the boy's expression closely. For the first time in years he felt as though he were doing something of importance. This child before him would grow up to be a rich and powerful man one day, and Andrew wanted to make an impression on him now, before it was too late. He, Andrew B. Morgan, would give this future wielder of power a strong foundation built on respect for the world and responsibility for his own actions. He would expand this boy's perspective and teach him to understand the interconnectedness of all things. Suddenly, he realized the impact We-Be's teachings had had on him. As much as he hated to admit it, his personal she-demon had expanded his perspective, and he could feel a new sense of power and purpose.

Holden's body posture seemed to lose its tenseness, and a smile touched his lips. Andrew smiled, too, and mentally patted himself on the back for teaching the boy to commune with nature. Holden glanced up and caught Andrew's look of triumph. Their eyes locked for a split second, and Holden's wisp of a smile turned into a full-fledged grin before he turned his attention back to the tiny shelled being couched in the palm of his hand.

"Squish!" The almost indiscernible sound seemed to block out all the other sounds of the seashore.

Andrew stood, frozen in place, unable to move. Holden turned and looked up at his teacher, grin still fixed on his little face. Slowly, the boy opened his fist, peering at its mutilated contents.

"Yuck!" he squealed in disgust, as he shook his hand instinctively before wiping the remains of the periwinkle on the side of his shorts.

"I can't believe you just did that! What's the matter with you?"

"What's the matter with you? It was just a dumb ol' periwinkle. Trevor kills them by the millions and eats them. What's the big deal?"

Andrew, shocked to the very core by what he had just witnessed, found himself speechless at the boy's callous attitude.

"Why are you staring at me like that?" Holden stared back at him, eyes like lumps of hard coal. "I'm bored. I want to go home now." And, turning on his heels, he headed back up the dunes and onto the stairway home.

Andrew stumbled along a good distance behind Holden, trying hard to sort out what had just happened. It had felt so good teaching the boy to respect life, and he had honestly believed he was getting somewhere. Holden was skipping up the stairs, singing to himself, seemingly oblivious to the devastation he had just wreaked on Andrew's psyche.

"Cook! Is my lunch ready yet?" Holden ran into the house, yelling at the top of his lungs for Marguerite. Andrew slumped down into a lawn chair to try to collect himself and figure out how to best deal with such a strange child.

After a good five minutes or so, he took a few deep breaths and forced himself to go inside to rejoin Holden. He found him perched on a stool at the breakfast bar, stuffing tacos into his mouth as fast as Marguerite could make them. Smiling at Andrew with downcast eyes, she offered him some of the same, but he declined, his appetite killed along with the periwinkle.

Sitting down opposite Holden at the bar, he studied the boy intently. He wasn't sure just how egocentric boys of this age usually were, and therefore hesitated to be too critical of Holden's total self-absorption. Andrew's instincts told him that the best thing he could do for this child would be to follow his original impulse and somehow instill in Holden a sense of responsibility. This kid needed to "get a job," as We-Be would say.

"As soon as you're done eating, kiddo, I want you to go upstairs and clean up your room. It looks like a bomb hit it."

Marguerite glanced up at him, surprise registering on her face. Andrew gave her a stern look, and then returned his attention to Holden's reaction. The boy was calmly ignoring him, picking the tomatoes out of his taco with great concentration.

"Did you hear what I said, Holden?" Andrew leaned back in his chair nonchalantly, not taking his eyes from the boy's face.

"I heard you. But that's a stupid idea; Janis cleans my room every afternoon. It's her job to clean up my messes, not mine."

"Well, from here on out Janis won't be picking up after you anymore. You're gonna learn to take care of yourself, young man, and we'll start with that personal toy store of yours."

Holden stuck out his bottom lip and narrowed his eyes. "I don't like you. I'm going to tell my father to fire you as soon as he gets home. And he'll do it, too!"

"Oh, no, he won't. I'm going to have a talk with your father and explain why I'm doing this. I'm sure he'll understand my point; after all, your father doesn't want you to grow up being irresponsible and helpless."

Holden glared at him, and then, picking up his last taco, smashed it on the bar top, grinding it viciously into the polished surface. Marguerite immediately moved forward, dishcloth in hand, as if used to mopping up after such tantrums. With a new, unquestionable authority, Andrew motioned silently for her to withdraw; and she stopped halfway between the sink and the bar, bewildered by Andrew's stringent tactics with his charge.

Unruffled, Andrew watched Holden until he finally looked up belligerently. Then, maintaining his composure, Andrew said coolly, "Now you get to clean it up."

The next few minutes were spent with Andrew mechanically working Holden's hand, dishcloth clamped forcibly in the boy's fingers, while Holden squeezed his eyes tightly shut and stubbornly tried to stiffen his arm.

Ignoring Marguerite, who was hiding in the pantry, muttering to herself in fear and confusion, Andrew wiped Holden's hands and face and led him from the kitchen.

"Now, that wasn't so bad, was it?" Andrew smiled, as though unperturbed at the boy. Holden remained sullen, and snarled, "I'm not going to pick up anything!"

"Oh, yes, you are. And, when you're done with your bedroom, you can come downstairs and I'll show you how to wash the dog. Now that's a boy's job if there ever was one!"

Holden whirled around, pulling against Andrew's grip, eyes wide with disbelief. "Mother takes Gizelle to the doggie salon for that!"

"Well, we're gonna save Mother some bucks today. Just think how proud of you she'll be," Andrew responded matter-of-factly as he struggled up the last few stairs with his unwilling charge. Then, throwing open the door to Holden's wing, he stood there surveying the turmoil of toys. "Looks like you've got your work cut out for you, huh?"

Holden moved into his playroom, dragging the toes of his shoes in the plush carpet. "Why don't we wash Gizelle first?"

Andrew was elated at this sudden show of interest, but quickly decided not to budge from the original plan of discipline. "As soon as you straighten up your toys, we'll get out the shampoo and figure out what's big enough to wash her in. I'll leave you alone now, so you can get to work. When you're done you can find me out front."

Slowly, Andrew closed the door, catching a last glimpse of Holden as he petulantly pushed around one of his playthings with his foot. He even waited outside for a few minutes, ear pushed against the door, listening for sounds to indicate that Holden was doing his job. It was working, as far as he could tell.

As he walked downstairs, his feet felt lighter than usual, as did his mood. He had remained cool and collected through a difficult situation and had mastered his own emotions, at least so far. He only wished We-Be had been there to see it all . . . or had she been? But then, he still wasn't quite sure she had ever really "been" in the first place.

With a new bounce in his step, he made his way through the house and slipped out a side door. He felt like being away from curious eyes while he mulled over the tack he was taking with Holden. Spying a small wooden building next to the Van Morris's greenhouse, he decided to check it out. The heavy scent of peat moss and fertilizer permeated the air as he cautiously opened the door to the adjoining shed.

"Jesus, it's dark in here!" Andrew remarked out loud to himself, allowing the door to swing closed behind him.

"That depends on where ya eyes have been." A deep, rumbling voice came out of nowhere, and Andrew nearly fell backward into the door.

Peering into the darkness Andrew could see no one at first, and for a moment thought he had conjured up yet another demon from Hell. Then he saw movement, followed by a flash of white teeth grinning at him.

"Who are you?" Andrew wasn't sure he wanted to be isolated in such an out-of-the-way place with whomever this was.

"And maybe it is me who should be askin' ya this question, hmm?"

"I'm Andy—"

"I know who ya are; I see everythin' that goes on here."

Andrew felt a shiver run up his spine and tried to shake it off. "So, you must be the gardener."

"Yes, the gardener—Trevor—at ya service." He walked out from the shadows—a tall bent man in his sixties; skin literally so black it gave off gleams of blue in the sparse rays of light—and opened the door to the greenhouse.

Andrew took a step backward, not yet comfortable in the company of this latest addition to the Van Morris's cast of characters.

"It isn't me ya should fear, mon; it's that little child who will do ya harm!" Trevor said, picking up on Andrew's apprehension.

As Andrew puzzled over the gardener's remark, he studied the man closely. Trevor, dressed in white baggy work clothes, stood there amid the tangle of green plant life trying to straighten his stooped back as though attempting to strike a posture of grandeur. "Why do ya want ta work this job? Ya crazy, ya know that?"

"Well, why do you work here then?"

"The money, it is good. Besides, I leave this place before the sun goes down. That's why ya crazy, mon; ya sleep here!"

"Now wait a minute. I know the kid's a royal pain in the ass, but I don't think he turns into a man-eating monster when the clock strikes midnight. C'mon!"

Trevor rummaged around in a big box on one of the tables, and then, taking a couple of steps toward Andrew, stuck something in his hand.

"What's that?" Andrew asked, peering at what looked like a jumble of dried weeds tied together with a white ribbon, lying in his palm.

"It is protection from The Evil One."

"The 'Evil One'?"

"That little boy, he has a bad spirit in him. He is The Devil."

"Gimme a break!"

"Ya think I lie to ya? I speak the truth. Even the onimals know him. They run from him. Ya watch and ya will see."

Andrew could feel hysterical laughter welling up inside him, and knew he had to get out of there fast. This old man was nuts for sure, as far as he was concerned.

"I'll watch myself," Andrew promised as he backed out of the door, banging his head on a hanging pot.

"You need ta do more than that! Ya need ta watch that boy."

Letting the door slam behind him, Andrew headed back to the house at a dead run, relieved to get away from the strange old Jamaican. He stopped outside the side entrance to catch his breath and center himself. He found himself laughing out loud now as he thought about the bizarre extremes in opinion he had heard regarding Holden. Lana talked about him as though he were the Second Coming, and this demented old man acted like he was something straight out of *The Omen*.

Circling around the outside of the house at a trot, Andrew didn't spot Holden anywhere. "Probably sitting on his bed pouting," he thought; and then, mentally correcting himself for being so negative, he slipped through the side door to head upstairs.

Opening the door to Holden's playroom, he couldn't believe his eyes: the place was spotless. He almost ran into Janis, who was standing in the room, duster in hand, looking very perplexed.

"Did you clean up Holden's mess?" Andrew asked suspiciously.

"No . . . I don't know who did this." Turning wide eyes to Andrew, she asked with anxiety, "They haven't fired me and hired someone else, have they?"

Patting her on the back comfortingly, Andrew turned on his heels and ran down the stairs in search of Holden. Bursting into the kitchen, Andrew yelled to Marguerite, "Have you seen Holden?"

"No, but he came in and stole my dish soap when he thought I wasn't looking. Who knows what he's up to this time, the little devil. He's not my problem, he's all yours!"

Spinning around to backtrack, Andrew once again tore through the house, looking out the windows as he passed by them for the chronically missing child. He instinctively headed for the place he had found Holden the last time, and, sure enough, as he approached the tropical front room, he could hear the boy giggling.

Relieved, Andrew silently watched Holden for a moment to see what he found so amusing. He was kneeling by the fountain, drenched from head to foot, water splashing out onto the tile floor. The ruckus the boy was making drowned out the sound of Andrew's steps as he moved in for a closer look at what Holden was so engrossed in. Suddenly, a slight feeling of dread swept over Andrew as he heard Holden talking in baby-talk to someone or something.

"Just a little while longer and you'll break my record!"

Andrew realized with horror that Holden wasn't just playing in the water, but actually had the dog in the fountain. Obviously, it was Gizelle's thrashing about that was causing the deluge of water that was in the process of flooding the place. Now, standing directly behind Holden, Andrew could see clearly what the boy was doing: he was using all his strength to hold the cocker spaniel under the water—head and all. The dog struggled frantically to reach the surface, to no avail, as Holden tried to submerge the dog deeper still.

"What in the hell are you doing?" Shaking off his momentary shock at what he was witnessing, Andrew made a desperate grab for the dog. Gizelle broke away and bobbed to the surface, wild-eyed, and started swimming in frenzied circles. Pushing Holden aside with fury and disgust, Andrew rescued the tortured beast.

As he stood there with the dripping, violently shaking animal in his arms, Andrew hissed at Holden, "Go get some towels—now!" and headed for the front door.

"I was just—"

"I said now! "

"Okay! But I was just trying to see how long Gizelle could hold her breath under water before I gave her a bath!"

"I swear to God, we're gonna see how long you can hold your breath if you don't get me a goddamn towel!"

"My mother will be very upset when I tell her you cursed at me. She fired one of my other nannies for that," Holden said smugly as he shuffled off in the direction of the bathroom.

Andrew's jaw muscles tightened as he attempted to restrain himself from retorting to Holden's threat. He held onto the squirming, whimpering Gizelle as best he could while he waited on the porch for Holden, who finally showed up, tears brimming in his eyes and towels in hand.

As he dried the dog off, Andrew ignored Holden sitting next to him, who was now cooing to the pet he had tried to drown a few minutes earlier. Turning his back on the boy, he noticed Trevor in the distance, loading dead tree branches into the back of a pickup truck.

The Evil One. Could it be that the old Jamaican was intuitively on to something, through all the superstitious nonsense? He looked warily at Holden out of the corner of his eye. Surely the boy wasn't the Devil incarnate as the gardener had suggested, but perhaps something more along the line of a "bad seed."

As though in tune with Andrew's thoughts, Trevor halted his work and stared across the lawn at them, an imposing silhouette against the sun-blazed sky. Andrew could feel the talisman in his pocket prickling his chest through the cotton material. As he involuntarily touched it, the Jamaican nodded his head—almost an imperceptible gesture from such a distance—and climbed into his truck. Andrew watched the old rusty beater as it sputtered and choked its way down the drive and out the gate. Trevor was gone for the day, in plenty of time to beat the setting of the sun.

A chill crept up Andrew's spine as he turned to confront Holden. Letting go of the dog—who scrambled off toward the back of the house—he cleared his throat to get the boy's attention. Holden looked up at him, different expressions flitting across his face, as though trying to read Andrew's mood before settling on one.

"That was the meanest thing I've ever seen anybody do. How could you have done such a thing?" Andrew felt calmer now, but was still gripped with outrage over the boy's cruelty to the dog.

"I wasn't trying to be mean, Andy, honest! I was just playing with her." Holden wore an expression of innocence that was hard to resist.

"Well, I have a hard time believing that, but I'll give you the benefit of the doubt and let it slide for now. But to tell you the truth, chasing you around has worn me out. I think the best idea is for you to go to your room and stay there for the rest of the day."

Holden looked solemnly at Andrew and didn't comment. Getting up, Andrew grabbed the boy's hand and led him inside the house. "And one other thing: I'm gonna leave the door to my room open, so I'll see you if you try to sneak out again. Got it?"

Jerking his hand out of Andrew's, Holden stomped up the stairs and into his room. As Andrew closed the door to the playroom, he could hear Holden throwing and kicking his toys around, undoing everything he had done earlier.

Sighing, Andrew dragged himself to his room, and, leaving the door standing open as promised, collapsed on the bed. Turning onto his side, he trained his eyes on the open doorway and listened for the fall of footsteps that would tell him Holden was sneaking away again. After ten minutes of staring at the empty hallway, Andrew closed his eyes and tried to center himself. It seemed like months since he had last plugged himself in to the Universe, and he felt a desperate need to do so now. Manifesting wasn't his goal this time; he simply felt the urge to think clearly, or, perhaps, to quit thinking altogether.

But not thinking wasn't so easy. Even the attempt to not think was, in essence, a thought. He couldn't get the scene of the drowning dog and giggling child out of his mind. He had never witnessed anything that seemed so evil, and, in a little boy, yet! How could anyone be that evil at such a young age? He could still feel Trevor's amulet resting against his chest, and somehow this gave him a feeling of security. He pondered these thoughts, though he tried not to think, and drifted off, following the thoughts as they escaped from his waking reality.

◆　◆　◆

"Andrew!"

Andrew bolted out of bed at the sound of the maid's call coming from down the hallway. He cleared his throat frantically to try to make his voice sound even, to dispel any notions she may have that he had fallen asleep on the job. "Yes! What's the problem?"

"Well, it's past dinner time, and you and Holden haven't come down yet!"

"Just freshening up! Be right down." Andrew was panic-stricken. How could he have fallen asleep for so long? Or, more important, what had Holden gotten himself into in the past few hours while he had been dead to the world?

Stuffing his shirt into his pants and grabbing his shoes, Andrew dashed across to Holden's room and threw open the door. The room was dark except for the sparse lighting offered by the two huge arcade games against the wall. Straining his eyes to make them adjust to the sunless room, he caught a slight stirring in the middle of a mound of toys. Andrew switched on the light and blinked at what he saw. The toys were piled up at least four feet high, forming a crazy ring in the middle of the room. He made his way over to the pile of playthings and peered in. In the center of this peculiar fortress sat Holden, legs crossed and arms held tightly to his chest. The boy was swaying back and forth, eyes wide and locked on Andrew's face. Andrew gasped involuntarily, caught off guard by the disquieting expression on the boy's face.

"Okay, Holden, I don't know what you're trying to pull, but enough is enough. I know you're angry with me, but you really brought all this upon yourself. C'mon, it's time to get cleaned up and go down to dinner. You can play with your toys later."

Holden didn't respond and simply continued his swaying routine, dark eyes still laser-beaming Andrew.

Shaken, but trying to give the impression of being in control, Andrew leaned over the towering wall of toys and snatched him by the arm out of his makeshift stronghold. He expected Holden to put up the same resistance he had shown earlier in the day, but, instead, the boy followed Andrew calmly—if somewhat stiffly—to the bathroom to wash up.

Andrew carried on a one-sided conversation as they went downstairs to face a disgruntled cook. Holden's eyes barely left his nanny's face through the entire meal, as Marguerite watched the two of them suspiciously. Andrew felt completely unnerved, and finally fell into an uncomfortable silence. He couldn't believe what a frustrating twist this job was taking, and tried desperately to think of some way to put his and Holden's relationship back on an even keel.

Marguerite poured Andrew a cup of coffee and began gathering up the dishes from the table. Sipping from his cup, he leaned back in his chair and stared out the window, trying to distract himself from Holden's unrelenting gaze. This kid was definitely weird, Andrew decided. He couldn't help but think Holden was much smarter than his five years to be able to dish out the silent treatment in such a cool and calculating manner.

The screeching of Holden's chair on the tile floor brought his thoughts back to the situation at hand. Holden was standing as though at attention, eyes still riveted unyieldingly on his nanny. Andrew tried to smile at the boy and suggested they go up to watch television.

"I'd like to go to bed now, please."

Andrew felt himself shudder as Holden finally broke his vow of silence. The boy's tone, while polite, was like ice.

"So early?" Andrew tried not to let his voice show the relief he felt. The thought of spending an evening with Holden gave him the creeps.

Not responding to Andrew's question, Holden turned on his heels and headed upstairs to his room. He silently refused any help getting into his pajamas and curled up into a little ball in his bed.

Returning to his room, Andrew alternated between reading one of his few remaining manifestation books for the fourth time and tiptoeing in to check on Holden. The god-child-turned-hell-on-wheels slept soundly, not even shifting positions once. Well past midnight, Andrew heard footsteps on the stairs and instinctively knew it was Mrs. Van Morris, home from her trip and coming up to check on her son. Quickly, he reached over and killed the light, not wanting to go through the ordeal of having to speak to her or answer any of her questions.

Chapter Thirteen

In the Realm of the She-Demon

He lay there in the dark, wide awake, wishing he hadn't accidentally taken such a long nap earlier. Slowly, as the clock beside his bed ticked away the minutes-turned-hours, he drifted into semi-sleep. Physical reality seesawed with his dream reality, images of the day's events bouncing around crazily in his head. The Evil One? A bad seed? Damian? Even though he tried not to think about it, Holden haunted his half-formed dreams.

Suddenly assaulted by something that smelled like a combination of smoke and rotten eggs, Andrew's eyes flew open, terrified at what Holden was up to now. Jumping up, he found himself in a cavern of some sort with his head barely clearing the stalactites hanging above, instinctively making him feel like he had to bend over a little to avoid cracking his skull on one of them. The air around him was heavy with the smell of what he now could identify as sulfur, and he could hear rhythmic explosions echoing in the distance in unison with red flashes.

"Hell of a place, huh?" Looking behind him, Andrew could just make out We-Be's figure walking in his direction. "I'd watch my step if I were you," she warned as she drew closer. Looking down, he saw that he was standing on a flat boulder surrounded by pools of steaming lava, his pillow at his feet.

He wasn't caught too off guard; he was growing accustomed to being abruptly jerked into We-Be Land with its bizarre assortment of themes. Better able to see her in the smoke-laden darkness now, Andrew stifled a laugh. "I see you've finally decided to show your true colors."

She was dressed in a full red leotard, complete with a curly tail that had an arrow-shaped end. On her feet were black knee-high boots; her eyes were covered with a cheap black costume mask; her ears two inches longer than usual and pointed. "Well, aren't red and black the colors that traditionally symbolize evil? And isn't evil the topic of the day?"

Andrew shifted his position uncomfortably, wishing he could move about a little without falling into one of the lava pits. "So, you know what I've been going through today, huh?"

"Sure I do. I always have a front row seat when it comes to you."

Andrew cringed, and suddenly felt like his privacy had been violated. He wondered whether she watched him when he got undressed or went to the bathroom, too.

"No, Morgan," she said, tuning in to his thoughts once again. "There's such a thing as common courtesy—better known as the She-Demons' Code of Ethics." She leaned on her pitch fork and smiled at him sweetly.

Relieved, he returned to the subject at hand. "So I suppose this is going to be a crash course on good and evil, right?"

"Good and evil?" We-Be asked, still smiling. "Funny how you can't talk about evil without talking about good, too, huh? I guess that's because they're perceived as being absolute extremes, total opposites that never criss-cross one another."

"Total opposites? Of course they're total opposites! But that's just because everything is in a state of balance. You know that! If there's up, there's down; if there's black, there's white; if there's good, there's got to be evil. That's the way it is, like it or not."

"Interesting that you mention up and down, Morgan. People watch the sun come up in the morning, but is it really rising? Of course not. You know as well as I do that Earth's rotation brings it to a point that gives the inhabitants of any given location the appearance that the sun is rising. It's stationary in respect to your planet; only a ground-based perspective gives the appearance of things rising and setting or moving up and down. Put yourself in outer space and the words 'up' and 'down' lose all meaning.

What she said made Andrew flash back for a split second to his incredible out-of-body excursion to Mars, and he realized that her words carried a lot of truth.

"And black and white may seem to be opposites," she continued, "one, it is said, being the absence of all color and the other containing all color within itself. Yet, ask any artist if he's ever come across black paint so true that it didn't betray a hint of green or purple, or if he's ever been able to make white paint by pouring all the different hues together. It's all theory, Morgan, and doesn't necessarily have anything to do with real-life application.

"And the same goes for what you term good and evil. There's always a little something else intermixed with that evil; and it's hard as hell for all the ingredients in a person's make-up to be so perfect as to be totally pure. Besides that, even though black has been equated with evil and white with good, to some people the opposite may hold true. Likewise, what appears good to one person may appear evil to another, and vice versa. It's all a matter of perspective."

"I think I understand what you're getting at." Andrew crouched down to try to get comfortable and used his sleeve to wipe away the sweat beading on his forehead before continuing: "Sometimes what's considered evil ends up really being good because it serves a definite purpose. Like in the case of a person shooting and killing another person. At some level, the second person wanted to die. While it's obviously evil to kill another person, the guy with the gun is really only fulfilling his victim's unconscious desire for death. Actually, they're friends working out a prearranged agreement. There aren't really any victims."

We-Be responded immediately, her tone more serious. "Oh really? Well, following that line of thought, I guess that means you shouldn't save someone from dying either! What if you saw a little kid drowning in the ocean? Would you rush in and save him, or would you simply turn your head and let him live out his supposed death wish?"

Andrew pondered her question briefly before asking, "Is the kid as evil as Holden?"

"Forget about that brat for now. Think of it this way: he's just a mean old man trapped in a little boy's body. But, I'd be real interested in hearing your answer without any more wise-cracks."

Andrew stared into the lava bubbling at his feet as he thought out his answer. "Well, of course I wouldn't let a little kid drown. But, ultimately, as horrible as it sounds, I probably should; I mean, who am I to interfere with his karmic plans? I don't mean to sound cruel, but the truth is he wouldn't be drowning in the first place if on some other level he didn't know it was his time to go."

"Sometimes it really amazes me just how much you've got to unlearn!" We-Be jerked her mask off and rubbed her eyes in frustration. "How do you know that 'on some other level'—God, I hate that term—your happening along wasn't part of his 'karmic' plans? How do you know that the two of you aren't friends honoring a prearranged agreement, too? Maybe you were sup-posed to save him!" Her expression registered her self-assurance that she had made a good point.

"That's what really annoys me about this 'everyone forms their own reality' concept, Morgan. Although it's true that we're all ultimately responsible for our own realities, it's too often used as an excuse for selfishness and noninvolvement and actually pushes people further away from their understanding of their connection to the whole. 'I'm just going to worry about myself, and the hell with everyone else. You form your reality and I'll form mine . . . that is, until something goes wrong and I need your help!' "

Andrew scowled and shuffled his feet self-consciously. "Look, maybe deciding not to save a drowning kid and shooting someone are two different things."

"I don't think so. You may think it's somehow noble for a person to cooperate with someone else's desire to be victimized, but believe me, it isn't. If that guy with a gun was really a friend, he'd refuse to play the role of the violator and help his buddy figure out what self-destructive beliefs lie at the bottom of his desires.

"You can't justify any violent action by saying that the violator was merely playing a role that the victim 'needed' him to play. And you can't excuse the violator's actions by saying they're a necessary evil intended to offset good. Anyone could use that excuse to justify his evil actions—from a murderer, to a rapist, to a wife beater." We-Be struck a theatrical pose, distant red flashes serving as a dramatic backdrop. "I can just see it: 'Well your Honor, you see . . . the man I shot dead really wanted to be killed—he needed that experience—so I simply played that role for him. He got just what he was asking for, so why punish me?'"

"So what are you getting at?" Andrew asked warily. "That evil isn't necessary? C'mon, anyone knows that you can't appreciate the light without also experiencing the darkness."

"If evil serves any purpose in your world at all, it's to teach mankind responsibility for its own thoughts and actions, since, ultimately, evil represents the misuse of creative energy. And when you speak of good and evil you're speaking about energy, the same energy, differently interpreted and applied."

Sweeping her devil tail to one side, We-Be sat down gracefully on a boulder directly across from Andrew. "Idealistically, man is meant to learn how to be 'good' by experiencing the results of his 'evil' actions and thereby making the necessary adjustments. Notice that I said idealistically, since there are many people who don't learn from their mistakes, especially when they believe their evil actions are good. And remember, beliefs are the foundation of all experience. They determine each person's perspective of what's right and wrong and what's good and evil. You have to understand, Morgan, that the person you would call evil is almost always convinced his beliefs are the truth and, therefore, feels justified in performing his seemingly evil acts.

"So you see, there may be such things as good and evil acts, but there just isn't such a thing as absolute evil or absolute good, personified—or nonpersonified, for that matter. There's no such thing as an absolute villain or a perfect saint—only people whose actions reflect such beliefs. And, along the same line, there isn't a God with a capital G to bless you, or a Devil to make you 'do it.' God and the Devil are simply creative personifications of the qualities and potentials within mass consciousness that are projected outward by people who don't want to accept responsibility for their own actions. Mass consciousness is responsible for creating its own deities and demons, and is most certainly responsible for those men or women who come into power upon the world scene and act out its beliefs and fears."

Andrew felt exhausted from the heat that rose up from the lava pits and he sank down onto his pillow that had somehow transported itself with him into this hellish place. Yet, even with the sulfur invading his nostrils and threatening to render him unconscious, a question sprang into his mind: "Does that mean that we're all ultimately responsible for everything our leaders do? I mean, if they decide to command the army to overrun some little nation and do evil things, does that make me personally responsible?"

We-Be crossed her legs and calmly lit a cigarette. "If you go along with the majority who support such actions, then you're just as responsible for the violations committed by your armies as they are themselves. You can, however, at any time choose to step away and focus your energies in other areas to counteract the energies of the majority. Then, if you choose, you can find others who also desire to divorce themselves from the prevailing social mood. Such minorities can eventually become so intensely focused and well organized as to affect the majority, which is not as cohesive in its beliefs. Understand, most of the majority are unquestioningly following the wishes of their leaders or the demands of society, and, therefore, are not strong in their beliefs. That's why they're able to be swayed by such intensity.

"Space-Time Principle Number 55:

The concentrated energies of the minority override the scattered energies of the majority—every time."

"Seems to me that all wars are presented to the people as being just and necessary. So how can I tell the difference between a just war and an unjust war?" The sporadic explosions from the depths of the caverns behind them lent a graphic atmosphere to Andrew's words.

Taking a deep drag from her cigarette, We-Be responded abstractly, "You could just as well ask how to tell the difference between a liberation and an occupation, or the overthrow of a tyrant and the assassination of a great leader." She stood up and began pacing back and forth, a frown creasing her sweatless brow. "Any country or clan at odds with another is always seen as evil by its adversary. And usually the most deplorable acts committed during war are condoned because the majority of each country's citizens believes they were committed to achieve a greater good for its own kind. And each side believes it's the good guys, regardless of the seemingly evil means it uses to reach the desired end. So who's right and who's wrong? Who's good and who's evil? I guess it all depends on which side you happen to be on at the time—or who wins and writes the history books.

"And the same thing goes for individuals. Good and evil are interpreted through the beliefs with which an individual identifies. A Christian may perceive a Muslim as being evil. A Korean War veteran may think all communists are evil. Some women think all men are evil. Again, it's all a matter of perspective; and yet these beliefs combine to make up the collective views of every group or country.

"Space-Time Principle Number 151:

What you perceive as good and evil is merely your private and mass beliefs objectified. 'Good' is simply the physical expression of the personal or social ideal, and 'evil' is nothing more than the externalization of unacceptable beliefs."

We-Be leaned forward, green eyes eerily reflecting orange from the bubbling inferno at her feet. "If you think about it, Morgan, geographical locations and boundary lines tend to be the reason given for most wars and disputes. Every party thinks it has the greatest claim to a piece of land, or mineral rights, or port access, or anything else it can dream up. Every country on the map was called something else first and occupied by others who thought they belonged there, too. Wasn't your own country occupied by others before the Europeans claimed it as their territory and gave it its name? There's no end to the historical displacement of indigenous peoples and the wholesale slaughter that has taken place over chunks of land. The original deeds have long since been lost in the shuffle. It no longer matters who was right or who was wrong. What matters is what mankind does right now about these situations. It's time to stop warring over unnecessary lines drawn between peoples—on a global and an individual scale—and end such trifling disputes.

"Now, I could go on and on here, but to sum it all up, there just isn't any such thing as absolute good or absolute evil, except for those illusory guidelines man has created in order to define them. Good and evil coexist and it's impossible for them not to cross the line and rub off on each other, if even just a little."

Andrew rolled onto his side, hugging his pillow, silently reflecting on the strange twist this dream woman put on the meanings behind good and evil. But he couldn't help but be distracted by the perspiration soaking his clothes, and his eyes locked on her forehead as he marveled over how cool and dry she had remained throughout their entire conversation. She grinned at him and started to respond to his quizzical expression, but then suddenly froze, the grin abruptly vanishing from her face to be replaced with a look of alarm.

"What's the matter?" Andrew raised himself up on one elbow, aware that her sudden mood change reflected something of utmost seriousness.

"Morgan!" Her voice carried an unmistakable tone of urgency. "Wake up, right now!"

Andrew bolted upright, her command sending shock waves through his body. He was disoriented: the infernal cavern setting was replaced with his bedroom, which was in almost total darkness except for a faint stream of light trickling through a crack in the window blinds. We-Be was nowhere in sight.

Nothing seemed amiss, and yet his nerves still tingled and he could literally feel his hair standing on end. He sat stock-still, hardly daring to breathe, as he waited for his eyes to adjust to the dark. Suddenly, out of the corner of his eye, he saw the quick flash of something shiny catching the beam of light from the outside. He strained his eyes, watching for it to appear again. There it was; a definite reflection of some sort that he could now attach to a subtle rustling sound.

Andrew dove for the lamp next to his bed, and frantically tried to remember how to turn it on. His finger finally found the switch, and the room was flooded with light. Half-blinded, he squinted in the direction of the noise, and could just make out a figure scurrying toward the door. He knew, even before he was able to focus his eyes, that the intruder was Holden.

Andrew leaped out of bed just in time to grab the boy by the pants and pull him back into the room. Holden landed with a "thud!" on the carpet, struggling desperately to break Andrew's grip.

"Hold still! You're not going anywhere until you tell me what you were up to!"

Holden quieted down and rolled over to face Andrew, one hand behind his back. He looked up innocently at his nanny with one wide eye, the other one covered with a black patch. His hair was sticking out in clumps from under a bright red bandanna, and his tattered shirt displayed a skull-and-crossbones.

"Pirate time, I see," Andrew said. "You sure picked a strange hour to plunder my bedroom!" He was relieved to confirm that it really was just Holden playing games, but still felt uneasy and couldn't figure out why.

He studied Holden suspiciously, trying to read through his guileless demeanor. Something was putting him on edge, but what? Then it hit him: the boy had the same expression on his face that he had had while trying to drown the dog.

His attention zeroed in on the hand still hidden behind Holden's back. "Okay, kid, let's have it. What are you hiding?" Andrew glanced up to make sure his wallet was still on the desk.

"Nothing. I just wanted to play pirates with you, but you were sleeping."

"Let me see what you have there, Holden. I'm really tired and I don't have time for your pranks."

Holden's expression turned belligerent, and he squeezed his lips tightly shut in defiance. Andrew heaved a sigh of disgust and jerked the boy's arm out from behind his back, exposing the concealed object.

"Jesus. . . . Andrew's mouth dropped open in horror at what the young pirate's clasped hand held: a large stainless-steel butcher's knife. Gingerly, he pried Holden's fingers apart to release the deadly utensil and then tossed it onto the bed, out of reach.

Andrew stood over him, stunned and unable to utter a single word. Holden's eyes narrowed as he hissed through clenched teeth: "That's my knife, not yours. You better give it back to me!" In a flash, the boy jumped up and made a dive for the bed, scrambling to retrieve the weapon.

This time Andrew caught him by the scruff of the neck and jerked him roughly away from the bed. Dragging him over to the desk, he dropped Holden into the chair and blocked the path between him and the bed. Out of breath and shaking all over, he said firmly, "You're going to stay right here in this chair until you tell me what you were going to do with that knife."

Holden stiffly removed the patch from his eye and dropped it on the floor. As he looked up, his eyes shining with loathing, Andrew could almost swear he could see them shooting out glints of red fire. He instinctively moved back a step, intimidated by the five-year-old's ability to project such hatred.

Holden smiled contemptuously, as though confirming to himself that he was now in control of the situation. Looking at his face, Andrew was aghast that such a little boy could exude such a sinister presence. Then he remembered what We-Be had said about Holden being a mean old man trapped in a little boy's body. Surely, she had been kidding . . . but looking at him now, Andrew wasn't so sure.

Gathering his wits, he stared back at Holden, keeping his eyes steady and his voice even. "I said, tell me what you were doing with that knife!"

Holden didn't break his fixed gaze, but giggled sardonically and leaned forward in his chair. "I wanted to stab you in the eye and watch you bleed!"

Andrew felt his knees buckle under him and his breath catch somewhere in his solar plexus as he heard this bizarre child's explanation and watched him giggling and swinging his feet back and forth. He honestly had no idea whether Holden was serious or just playing with his head. Either way, Andrew decided, the kid had serious problems.

"Okay, that's it. I've had it with you." Andrew pulled him up by the arm and walked him to his bedroom. Without saying a word, he forcibly undressed the would-be pirate and put him to bed. He could hear Holden humming to himself as he closed the door behind him, confirming, in Andrew's mind, the need to lock his bedroom door from here on out—which he did, right after he braced it firmly shut with the desk chair.

Chapter Fourteen

Periwinkle
Pandemonium

Andrew got very little sleep the rest of the night as his mind kept returning to the knife he had secreted in a safe place. Feeling quite cross when his alarm went off at seven o'clock, he dressed and reluctantly walked down the hall to get Holden, only to find he had apparently already gone downstairs.

He found the boy sitting in the kitchen, Marguerite serving him his breakfast. Bracing himself for a continuation of the hateful streak of the night before, Andrew poured himself a cup of coffee and sat down, avoiding any eye contact.

"Thank you very much, Marguerite!" Holden sang out cheerfully, startling Andrew into looking curiously into his face. The little devil-incarnate now seemed to be transformed before his very eyes. He beamed at Andrew happily and slurped down his pancakes. Completely baffled by the change in Holden's behavior, Andrew just smiled back, feeling idiotic.

"Can we go someplace neat today, Andy? Like the zoo? Mother will let you use the car to take me any place I want to go!" He squirmed around in his chair excitedly, seemingly retaining no memory of their conflict of the previous evening.

"Well, let's wait and see. First we have to have a talk with your parents about your attitude yesterday while they were gone."

"What do you mean?" The brightness slowly drained from Holden's face.

"You know what I mean. I'm going to have to tell them about the incident with Gizelle and your escapade last night with the knife. I can't let things like that just slide!" Andrew felt bad, even though he knew Holden deserved to be punished by his parents. This kid was out of control, and obviously needed more help and discipline than he was in the position to give him.

"I don't know what you're talking about!" Holden said indignantly, looking up at Marguerite and shaking his head in mock bewilderment. Marguerite looked at Holden, then at Andrew, and then, mumbling to herself, disappeared into the pantry.

"Look, kid, it's got to be done if you and I are ever going to make a go of this arrangement. I'll be as easy on you as I can, and I'll even give you a chance to visit with your parents before I talk to them about your antics yesterday. Fair enough?" Sulking, Holden slumped over his plate, ignoring Andrew's attempt to reason with him. But Andrew didn't have time to think any further about how to handle the situation, for at that very moment Mr. and Mrs. Van Morris walked in and sat down to join them.

"Good morning, boys!" Mrs. Van Morris chirped, leaning over to plant a wet kiss on her son's forehead. Mr. Van Morris reclined back in his chair, indifferent to everyone at the table, and commenced to read the morning paper. Marguerite bustled into the room to serve them their coffee, and then proceeded to prepare their breakfast.

"So, how have you two been getting along?" Holden's mother looked expectantly from her son's pouting face to Andrew's anxious one.

"Fine, fine," Andrew blurted out. "There are a few rough edges to smooth out, but we can talk about that later."

Mrs. Van Morris seemed oblivious to the implications his words carried, and happily began fussing over her son's uncombed hair. "So, darling, did you get your lessons done while I was away?"

Andrew's heart sank into the pit of his stomach. He had forgotten about making Holden study his lessons amid the turmoil of the day before.

"No. Andrew had me do other things he said were more important." Holden looked up at his mother with big soft eyes.

"Oh?" She looked at Andrew, eyebrows raised in concern. "Such as?"

Andrew tried to find his tongue, but Holden beat him to the punch. "He made me clean up my room and wash Gizelle."

A look of confusion crossed Mrs. Van Morris's face as Andrew cleared his throat to speak. "It's a long story, m'am, but I'm sure you'll understand when I explain it to you later."

"Hmm . . . well, we'll see about that. But he mustn't miss his lessons, you know. He must be properly prepared to start school in August."

"I understand. It won't happen again." Andrew glared at the boy when his mother turned her attention to her breakfast being served by Marguerite.

"So, what else did you boys do yesterday?" Mrs. Van Morris asked, daintily wiping the marmalade from the corner of her mouth.

"Last night we played pirates!" Holden looked across the table at Andrew deviously, making Andrew panic inside, not sure of what was coming next.

"Surely," he thought, "the little brat wouldn't . . ."

"And we used a real knife, too!"

"Now wait just a minute, Holden! Don't you want to tell your mother the truth?"

Mr. Van Morris peered over his paper at Andrew, suddenly interested in the conversation.

"But I am telling the truth, Andy! Whatdaya mean? We played with the knife from the kitchen drawer that you still have in your bedroom. It was fun!"

Andrew grabbed his head and groaned in frustration. This situation was getting pretty sticky. "Look, we need to talk about Holden's imagination. I had to take a knife away from him that he took from the kitchen last night. I had nothing to do with it, except to correct him, and now he's mad at me and trying to get even."

Mrs. Van Morris's face was unreadable, but her usual bubbliness had vanished completely. Mr. Van Morris folded his paper and trained his eyes steadily on Andrew as he sipped his coffee.

"Okay, Holden. Enough's enough. Tell your parents about the other things we did yesterday—without exaggerating or making things up—like our walk on the beach."

Holden looked at his nanny with eyes of ice, a slight smile turning up the corners of his mouth. "Okay, Andy . . . let's see. . . . Well, we walked down to the beach and looked for 'interesting things'."

Andrew breathed a sigh of relief and leaned back in his chair.

"Then Andy told me he had something real special he wanted me to see that he only shared with his very best friends. So he pulled me real close to him and put his periwinkle in my hand."

"His what?" Mr. Van Morris broke his silence and sat up straight in his chair.

"His periwinkle. He said that's not really the right name but a silly name that some people call it."

Andrew was suddenly filled with dread as he saw the direction Holden's account was taking, or, at least the way it was being interpreted. "Now wait—" Andrew was cut off in midstream by Holden's father, who silenced him harshly with a severe look and a sharp wave of his hand.

"His periwinkle? What did it look like, Son?"

Holden's huge eyes made him look like a pitiful Moppet child as he concentrated on his father's question. "Well, it was all pink and kinda yucky, and at first it really grossed me out."

"At first?" Mr. Van Morris looked up at his wife who had recoiled into her chair, knees hugged to her chest in horror.

"Well, Andy told me that it was sacred and liked to be stroked, so I petted it for a little while and tried to like it, honest I did."

Mrs. Van Morris was sobbing now, tears streaming down her face. This was getting entirely out of hand. Frantically, Andrew tried again to explain what this insidiously brilliant child was twisting into such a nasty nightmare.

"Please! You can't believe—"

"Shut up!" Mr. Van Morris's voice sounded murderous, which made Andrew want to run for his life, but, unfortunately, the enraged father was positioned between him and the door.

Mr. Van Morris stood up and set his cup down violently, coffee spilling onto the lace tablecloth. "And then what happened, Son?"

"Well, Andrew ended up getting real mad at me 'cause I squeezed it too hard."

Andrew could tell by Mr. Van Morris's expression that the man would never listen to reason now, and that he was in big trouble. He glanced at Holden's face, which was a study in triumph, the expression completely unnoticed by his parents: one busy turning into a blubbering basket case, the other an avenging madman.

This man who not even five minutes ago had appeared like he couldn't care less about Holden's well-being, now faced Andrew as his son's devoted champion-protector. "I'm going to give you ten minutes to get your things and get the hell out of my house," he threatened, jabbing his finger into Andrew's chest. "If you're not out of my sight and away from my family by then, I'm going to call the police." Fists clenched, Mr. Van Morris moved slightly to one side to allow Andrew passage.

His now ex-employer's words ringing in his ears, rudely reminding him of his last unexpected eviction, Andrew nervously sidled past the enraged hulk of a man and ran up the stairs to his room to gather his belongings. He mechanically threw his things into a bag and started picking up the boxes he hadn't even gotten around to unpacking, to carry them downstairs. As he brought down the last of his things, he could hear Mr. Van Morris's angry words clearly as he yelled at his wife, giving her the I-told-you-so lecture concerning her goofball friends and their irresponsible recommendations. Andrew's heart lurched as he realized he had just burned his bridges, once and for all, with Lana. She would never understand or forgive him—not this time around.

As he opened the front door, he almost ran head-on into Trevor, who had his hand up ready to knock. "Boy, am I glad to see you! How about doing me a big favor and helping me load my stuff into my car so I can get the hell out of here fast? You wouldn't believe what that little bastard did to me! I guess you were right about that kid after all! "

The old Jamaican stood there patiently waiting for Andrew to stop babbling before he matter-of-factly stated: "I can't, mon. Ya don't have a car no more."

"What?" The color drained from Andrew's face.

"Ya car, it is gone. That's what I was comin' to tell ya. Some men, they came and towed it away, see?" Trevor pointed down the long stretch of driveway where Andrew could just see the back of his Toyota, its nose in the air, trailing behind a big blue tow truck.

"My car payment—shit! How did they find me?" Andrew asked no one in particular, sinking down on the porch in total dismay.

"I don't know, my friend. Who knows that ya here?"

It hit him like a slap in the face. The only person who had known his whereabouts was the very same person whose name he had given as a reference at the car lot. Lana—of course! She must have gotten on one of her righteous honesty-is-the-best-policy kicks and turned him in. It was almost like she had psychically foreseen this morning's events and retaliated ahead of time.

"So what ya goin' ta do, mon?"

The door opened behind Andrew, making him jump up and spin around, ready to run. Mr. Van Morris, filling the majority of the door frame, stood there glaring, with Holden peeking out from behind his legs, grinning victoriously from ear to ear. "Your ten minutes are up, pal. I wasn't kidding about calling the police."

Andrew felt tears welling in his eyes as the utter hopelessness of his situation began to sink in. He opened his mouth to speak, but no words came; and he heard himself making little gurgling sounds in his throat.

He winced as he felt a firm hand on his shoulder, and heard Trevor's deep voice fill in the silent gap he had left.

"This boy's car, it is gone. If ya like, I can leave early taday and take him with me, yes?"

Mr. Van Morris looked at Andrew and then at his pile of belongings with disgust. "If you can stand having such a degenerate in your presence for that long, then I'd appreciate it, Trevor. I just want him out of my sight." And with that, he slammed the door in Andrew's face. The last thing Andrew saw before the door closed was one of Holden's malicious dark eyes winking at him.

"I told ya, mon. I warned ya about that little child. I told ya he is The Evil One." Shaking his head, Trevor started picking up boxes, with Andrew following suit in a zombie-like fashion.

"So, where ya goin', my friend?" Andrew could hardly hear the old man's voice above the roar of a busted muffler.

"I don't know—I mean, I don't have anywhere to go. That's why I took this job in the first place." Andrew held his head in his hands, feeling like it was about to fall off from the vibration of the old truck and the migraine headache that had begun to form between his temples.

"Well, I know a place I can take ya to. It's a home for boys in trouble. I am goin' there ta help my friend finish up some last-minute repairs the place needs. I'll only be there for three days, but I think my friend may give ya work for a week, at least." And without waiting for Andrew to shake himself out of his stupor and respond, he headed straight for the place he had in mind, leaving Saint Charles Harbour and the nefarious Evil One behind in a bellowing cloud of black smoke.

Chapter Fifteen

Last Chance Ranch

The sudden ceasing of his body swaying back and forth and the absence of the truck's thundering din in his ears jolted Andrew awake. Rubbing his eyes, he grimaced from the lingering pain in his head as he craned his neck to look outside. The change in scenery surprised him—it was actually hilly and heavy with pines and old hardwood trees. Groaning, he fought with the cranky old door to open it, then stepped outside to stretch.

Trevor was already outside waving to a man walking up the road from a large old country house that seemed to be the main building. Scattered all around were smaller structures that looked like they were meant to be living quarters, making the place reminiscent of a southern plantation. Andrew could imagine this place hadn't changed at all since the mid-eighteen hundreds; in his mind's eye he could see black slaves toting bales of hay from the fields to the weather-beaten barn that still stood, suspended in time.

He leaned against the rusty old beater, trying to get his bearings. He didn't even know where he was, but something told him they had driven quite a distance. Of course, he couldn't be sure since he had slept through the entire trip. Trevor and the man were now talking and looking straight at him. He felt very self-conscious all of a sudden, and completely out of his element. What had he gotten himself into this time?

His Jamaican friend and the stranger—a tall, well-built man in his early fifties—walked over to where Andrew stood, smiles on their faces. "Ondrew, I want ya ta meet my good friend, Mista Campbell."

The man extended his hand, and Andrew shook it cautiously. "Call me Charlie, please. Welcome to Last Chance Ranch, Andy. It's okay if I call you Andy, isn't it?"

Andrew nodded his head to show that that was fine with him, while mentally cringing over the place's name. It felt too personally apropos for comfort.

"So, ol' Trev tells me you're in a bit of a bind and need a job and a place to stay. There's only about a week's worth of work to be done around here, but you're welcome to hire on for the duration. Ever done any remodeling work before?"

Andrew's already low spirits took a nose-dive. He had always been a hopeless case with a hammer in his hand. Besides, he hated doing any kind of manual labor. But, taking stock of his immediate situation, he suppressed his feelings as best he could and answered politely, "No, sir, but I'm a fast learner."

"Well, that's good, but remember, you promised to call me Charlie." Charlie laughed and slapped Andrew on the back, which reverberated through his already pounding head. "Okay, Andy, let's grab your gear and get you settled into Trev's cabin. Don't mind doubling up, do you?" And with that, he picked up two of the heaviest boxes like they were nothing and led the way toward one of the substructures.

Setting down the boxes, Charlie informed them that the kids and bunkhouse counselors would be arriving the next day. Then, after Andrew declined to join them for lunch, Trevor and Charlie left him alone to unpack, informing him that dinner was at seven o'clock sharp. There would be no work today; he would follow Trevor's lead tomorrow and do what he could to appear to be useful around the place.

Andrew was depressed. He felt like a tormented character trapped in a book written by some twisted, sadistic author. Falling into his bunk he lay there wide awake, staring at the ceiling. He dreaded the next week; seven whole days of doing what he hated most in the world: hard physical work. And the worst part of it was that he was sure he wouldn't even come close to making enough money on this short-term job to get out of his long-term predicament.

He was too antsy to lie still, and so got up and paced back and forth across the small cabin, becoming more and more agitated. Last Chance Ranch? What kind of a cruel cosmic joke was that? Then, feeling as if the walls were closing in on him, he went out onto the porch, letting the screen door slam behind him.

Andrew leaned on the railing and gazed out over the landscape in front of him. It was incredibly beautiful, he had to admit, but somehow this fact made him all the more angry inside. In less than three days he had gone from a high-paying job at a fancy country club, to being a nanny living in the lap of luxury, to being a manual laborer in a paradise for delinquents. It had been bad enough being around one little brat kid; now he would be surrounded by dozens. He promised himself to stay clear of them, no matter what, for it terrified him to imagine what kind of job he would end up with next if he blew this one.

He decided to take a walk and investigate this place that was to be his home for the next week. The rolling hills seemed to stretch for miles, and Andrew couldn't determine where the property lines were, since there was no fence. This seemed rather odd, considering this was a home for wayward boys. Maybe that was what his job would entail, he mused: building a fence.

Andrew walked for what seemed like miles, losing himself in the adventure of exploring the unknown countryside. Finally exhausted, he sat down next to a creek that cut a crooked path through the hills and back down to the center of the ranch. The sun was just beginning to disappear behind the tall majestic pines, telling him that it was time to be getting back. As he drew closer to the estate he could hear what he assumed was the dinner bell ringing out from the main house, so he hurried to his cabin to wash up before joining the others.

Charlie and Trevor were already sitting at a large table with another man when Andrew walked in. He could feel his face turn red as they all stopped talking and looked up at him.

"Grab a plate, Andy, and help yourself." Charlie smiled and waved his hand in the direction of a buffet-style table, and then returned easily to his conversation. Trevor kept his eyes on Andrew, concern showing on his features. The other man, who introduced himself as Jones the cook—which Andrew had already guessed from the apron tied around his big belly—didn't seem to take any notice of anything except the heaping plate of food in front of him.

"Now, c'mon Trev. You know the boy's just a spoiled brat. Hell, you've raised five kids of your own! Don't be feeding Andy your superstitious nonsense. God! How can a guy as wise as you are believe such crap?"

"But if ya could just see this boy, see the bad things he does. . . ."

"Bad? You want to see bad? Just stick around awhile, Trev, old buddy. You're gonna see bad times fifty!" Charlie winked at Andrew and said, "Or at least some of them think they're bad!"

"No, thank ya, mon," Trevor answered, in a serious tone. "Ya are my friend and I owe ya a great deal, but I don't need no more troubled young ones ta deal with. One is plenty! I will help ya get this place together and then I must go."

As Andrew sat down next to Trevor, his stomach tightened at the thought of fifty teenage Holdens running around loose. Charlie's laughter echoed through the large dining room, making light of the whole conversation. Andrew had never heard such a laugh before—deep and genuine, and very contagious. He suddenly felt very hungry and voraciously attacked the vegetable stew.

Charlie leaned back in his chair and grinned at him. "So, how good are you at painting?"

"Painting?" Andrew's mind went blank. "Painting what?"

Charlie reached over the table and grabbed Andrew's hand, turning it over, palm up. After studying it for a moment he shook his head and said, "Trev, I'd say this friend of yours is in for some blisters this week in places that've never even seen calluses before." He stood up, coffee cup in hand, and laughing his extraordinary laugh again, walked over to the table for a refill.

Andrew felt his face flush once more, and fought the impulse to sit on his hands to hide them. "Of course I can paint; I've painted lots of times! What's the big deal?"

This time Andrew caught Trevor hiding a chuckle behind his hand, and even the cook looked up, on his way out the door, grinning at Andrew's words.

"Well, Andy, starting tomorrow you'll have a chance to show us your stuff. Coffee?"

Momentarily put off by Charlie's sudden change of subject, it took him a second to respond by nodding his head gratefully. It always made him feel more secure to hold a cup of warm black coffee between his hands, which was exactly what he did for the rest of the evening as he sat back in silence and listened to Trevor and Charlie discuss the state of the world.

At ten o'clock, Andrew's eyelids started feeling heavy and he excused himself from the group to head back to the cabin. The other two men didn't even seem to notice him leave, as they were deep into a conversation about the political situation in some Central American country.

He was glad he had returned before Trevor so he could have a little privacy as he undressed and crawled into bed. His headache still lingered just a little, and his brain was numb from listening to politics for three hours straight. The evening with Trevor and Charlie had almost been as draining as a We-Be dream lecture.

Andrew tossed and turned as he tried to figure out how he had ended up in this strange out-of-the-way place. What the hell was the purpose behind it? What awful sin had he committed to have the Van Morris job turn out so screwed up, anyway? He had done his best to keep his cool; he hadn't bitched and moaned about anything; and he had actually tried to make friends with the kid. So what gave? And now he was stuck out in the middle of nowhere with fifty other maladjusted brats to torture him. He just didn't deserve this. If one Holden was too much to handle, how would he even begin to cope with a whole army of them? Something told him that no matter what his job was supposed to be, these kids would seek him out and do him in.

And who was this guy Charlie? What was his story? He appeared to be more than just a maintenance supervisor; his knowledge of this whole set-up seemed to go much deeper than that. He had talked off and on through dinner as though these kids were something special, and as though helping them were the greatest task on Earth.

Surely We-Be would have the answers he was looking for; and she wouldn't even be able to lecture him about messing the Van Morris job up with his negative thoughts—not this time. But, how could he get in touch with her on purpose? He had never consciously sent out an S.O.S. for her before, and wasn't quite sure how to go about it. Searching his memory, he tried to pick an image of her out of the motley collection of crazy characters she had portrayed since she had first appeared in his dreams. Finally, settling on the angelic guise she had adopted the night he had slept on the beach, he drifted off to sleep.

Chapter Sixteen

The Dimension of the Dumpster Diver

He woke up feeling stiff, his bones aching from the damp night air. Something had alerted him, even in his sleep, to impending trouble. Rolling over on his side in the sand, he scanned the beach for anything unusual, but nothing moved, except for a tiny fiddler crab scurrying across his tar-caked sneaker. Still, his nerves tingled with anxiety about something, and, sitting up, he slumped low to shake out the jacket he had become accustomed to using as a pillow. The rumbling in his belly had turned into a roar in the few hours he had slept, sending waves of pain into his backbone. He fished around in his backpack, looking for anything edible that he might have overlooked earlier. Nothing.

Gazing up at the moon and stars and across the dunes at the lights from the highway, he surmised it wasn't even midnight yet. He had to eat something, though—right now. Usually he waited until the wee hours of the morning to hit the dumpsters behind the strip of restaurants along the beach road. But this night he would just have to take his chances and go foraging early. He would have to remember to be extra careful, extra quiet.

He darted over the dunes and across the highway, ducking into the shadows behind the buildings. This strip was a frequent haunt of his. He had depended on it, off and on, to provide him with food at night and with large crowds to vanish into during the day for over a year now, ever since he had ended up on his own.

Slinking down the alley, he passed by the seafood restaurant's dumpster without stopping. He had been discouraged long ago from pilfering in this particular dumpster when he almost cut his finger off on broken glass. He later found out from another fellow dumpster diver that the management purposely broke up empty beer bottles and scattered the fragments over any discarded food to stop "their kind" from trespassing.

As hungry as he was, he decided not to walk the extra two blocks to his favorite place: Boomer's Bar-B-Q. It wasn't uncommon to find meals of ribs or chicken there that were completely untouched. He never could figure out why they threw out such perfectly good food in the first place, but then, he didn't want to mess things up by questioning his good fortune.

He settled for pizza: in and out, quick and easy. Raising the lid of the dumpster, he eased himself up onto the edge and then dropped noiselessly into its depths. He was sorry he didn't still have his flashlight. He had lost it the week before in his mad panic to escape from a dumpster when one of the employees came out and caught him in it. Tonight he would just have to let his fingers do the deciding. Feeling around in the dark he located a stack of pizza boxes, two of which still felt warm. Just as he grabbed them and slipped them under his arm, his eyes were assaulted by a blinding light. Damn! Frantically, he let the boxes fall as he clawed his way back toward the opening. But, in one split second, he went from light-blindness to being in total blackness, as not only the high-powered flashlight beam but also his opening to freedom disappeared.

He could hear someone yelling and laughing outside the closed dumpster lid. "I got one of 'em, Ralph! Call the cops!"

Hysterically, he tried to force the hatch open, but to no avail. The man outside was hooting and hollering like a victorious hunter who had just bagged his first prey, and drumming on the lid with his fists. It was clear to him that his captor was sitting squarely on his only exit out and wasn't going to budge until the police arrived.

Sinking down on the metal floor, tears rose in his eyes and his empty stomach went into spasms. With any luck, maybe he would die right now and get it over with, for he would surely die if he had to go back to Juvenile Detention. He hated everyone there and they hated him. Maybe he would kill himself this time . . . before one of the creeps there did it for him.

Pain stabbed his ear drums as the rusty metal lid screeched open above his head. He rolled up into a ball in the corner and decided that if they wanted him so bad, they would have to come in after him.

"Okay, scumbag, c'mon out, party's over!"

God, wasn't it amazing, he thought, how all fucking cops were the same; like one big turd that had divided itself into thousands of little pieces of shit?

He looked away from the opening to spare his eyes from the flashlight beam that was seeking him out, and concentrated on the dull reflection of the red and blue flashing lights as they bounced off the inside of the dumpster. He detested those goddamn cop-light colors.

"If I hafta come in after you, you're gonna be real sorry."

So what else was new? When wasn't he sorry? But he could never be as sorry as one of these sorry sacks of shit with a badge. So he'd be sorry again for the millionth time—big deal.

"Give me a boost, Al, I'm goin' in."

Thunk! Crunch! "Damn!"

Ha! He hoped the bastard cop had gotten pizza sauce and mozzarella cheese all over his big fat ass. He heard himself giggling uncontrollably, as though another person were laughing with his mouth. Then he felt himself being jerked up roughly by his arm, and yet he felt no pain, as though that other person inside him were feeling it for him. Maybe he really was dying. . . .

Before he knew it, he was hoisted out of the metal contraption and into the arms of the other officer, who immediately hand-cuffed him before slamming him against the patrol car to be frisked down. His eyes fell on the two employees of the restaurant, standing by the back door, talking in excited whispers.

Proud of yourselves, boys? he thought. Big brave heroes. Go home and tell your bored little bitch wives all about it—how you saved all your customers from the dangerous ol' dumpster diver!

"Hey, Al, I think this is the kid we've been lookin' for." Again he was blinded by the hated flashlight. "Lemme see that picture."

God, had they put his name on the Most-Wanted List, just for going over the wall at J.D.?

"What's your name, kid?"

He loved this part—refusing to talk no matter what. It drove them crazy.

"Yep. I'd say that's him. Says here we're supposed to deliver him to H.R.S. Says this kid's goin' someplace called 'Last Chance Ranch.'"

"Last Chance Ranch? What the hell is that? Sounds like a crock of liberal crap to me!"

"Or some kind of salad dressing!"

Laughing, the cop named Al opened the back door of the patrol car and motioned the dumpster diver in, helping him along with a rough hand on his shoulder.

He could still feel his empty stomach heaving, and he was damn sorry there was nothing in it to throw up all over their stupid car. "Last Chance Ranch?" What did they mean? He could feel himself drifting off, escaping into an exhausted sleep. His last thought before unconsciousness was that anything would be better than going back to J.D.—or so he hoped.

◆　◆　◆

He woke up in agony, a dreadful pain in his arm. Had he slept on it wrong? No, he remembered, that stupid-ass cop had jerked him up by it; probably dislocated his shoulder. The memory of getting busted in the dumpster rushed into his consciousness, and he grimaced and turned over.

But, something was wrong here: where did the back seat of the police car go, and how did he get into this bed? He felt the pillow under his head and the sheets covering him. Straining his eyes in the darkness, he tried to orient himself. Was he back in J.D. after all? If so, why didn't he remember getting out of the car?

His attention was suddenly caught by the sound of someone snoring, and he peered in the direction of the noise. He could barely make out a huddled form across the small room on a bunk, a single bunk. This didn't look like J.D. He sat up and felt the wall behind his head, looking for the standard institutional light fixture. No light, but his hand hit rough wood. A cabin? Whose cabin? Where the hell was he? Was he dreaming? Another snatch of memory popped into his head: "Last Chance Ranch" . . . wasn't that what the cops had said? Was that where he was? And if so, how did he get here without remembering it?

Last Chance Ranch . . . he felt a dull memory of the place—but that was silly; how could he have a memory of a place he hadn't even seen yet? Still, there it was, playing around in his mind: an old dilapidated barn, a black man with a funny accent . . . In fact, he suddenly knew that the sleeping form across the room was the black man with the funny accent. Trevor! Of course!

But of course that was Trevor! What was he thinking? And this was Last Chance Ranch. Why had he thought he hadn't been here before? But . . . his last memory was of falling asleep in the cop car, which meant he couldn't have been here before. Now what did that mean? He grabbed his stomach, expecting to confirm his earlier agony. Somehow he wasn't in pain at all anymore, and he suddenly had a strong memory of eating vegetable stew—he could almost still taste it. He shook his head, trying to rattle all the myriad memories into their proper place.

Trevor . . . and Charlie . . . and vegetable stew—Last Chance Ranch. And kids, lots and lots of kids coming tomorrow; kids with problems that were way beyond his ability to understand. Hell, he couldn't understand kids period, let alone kids with troubles.

"What? Why wouldn't I understand kids? I'm a kid my—"

"What? No I'm not!" He jumped up and shook his head violently this time, then began pacing back and forth, muttering to himself, "I'm Andrew Morgan," over and over again. Finally assured by his own words, he said out loud, "God! What a nightmare!"

But just to make totally sure that he was now awake and still him, he went to the bathroom and looked in the mirror. He had never in his life experienced anything like this before—he had actually forgotten who he was! After drinking a glass of water and looking in the mirror one last time, he returned, still shaken, to his bunk and sat on the side to run the dream through his mind. But first, just to reinforce his sense of identity, he repeated once again with conviction, "I don't know who that other guy was, but I'm Andrew Morgan."

"Yep! Andrew Morgan, Master of Disaster!"

For the first time in a while, Andrew nearly jumped out of his skin over one of We-Be's sudden appearances.

"Why so surprised? You summoned me, didn't you?" Sure enough, she had affected the guise of the angel from the beach. She hovered over by the door, her luminescent glow softly lighting up half the room.

Finding his voice, he stuttered, "You're a little late, don't you think? I just had the most horrible dream of my entire life! Figures the first time I actually ask for you to come help me, you pull a no-show. Instead of We-Be wisdoms—which for some idiotic reason I thought I needed—I get thrown into some god-awful dream reality."

Andrew watched her as she glided gracefully toward him and settled down cross-legged on the end of his bunk. "Don't be so quick to say 'dream reality.' That experience was just as real and valid as the experience you're having right now as Andrew B. Morgan. The odd thing about it was that the memory of it flowed so clearly and smoothly from that life experience into this one. And, by the way, you weren't 'thrown' anywhere against your will."

"Against my will?" Andrew heard himself raising his voice, and cringing, looked over at Trevor's sleeping body. "Of course it was against my will," he whispered. "I programmed myself for a We-Be dream and instead got caught up in somebody else's nightmare. I thought I formed my own reality!"

"No one said that you didn't form your own reality, Morgan." She talked in a normal tone, disregarding his obvious concern about waking Trevor. "But what you don't realize yet is that the part of you that you call 'Andrew' isn't the only part that influences your experience.

> " Space-Time Principle Number 212:
>
> Before you can really understand
> the meaning behind the statement
> 'I form my own reality,'
> you must first understand
> what the word 'I' means,
> for there is more to you
> than meets the 'I.'"

"You mean that was a real experience? And I'm somehow somebody else somewhere else?" Forgetting to whisper, he glanced worriedly at Trevor again.

We-Be grinned and also looked over at Trevor. "You don't have to worry about waking your friend up. He's too deep in his own dreams to be disturbed by us." Then, dismissing Trevor with a wave of her hand, she returned to Andrew's question. "Real, yes! Now you're catching on!"

"I get it! I had a flashback of a past life of mine and that's why it seemed so real!" Andrew actually bounced up and down in his excitement, but suddenly stopped, and looked like a kid who had just had his ice cream taken away. "No . . . wait a minute . . . that can't be! It was happening now; that was a late-model police car I was in! I don't understand. . . ."

"Well, that's good!" We-Be laughed and leaning forward punched his arm good-naturedly.

*"Space-Time Principle Number 91:
The sooner you can admit to yourself that
you don't understand something,
the sooner you can learn it."*

Andrew scowled at her words. "Isn't that kind of negative and limiting? I mean, isn't that like programming myself for stupidity? Seems to me I should affirm that I already know everything and then I'll open myself up to that possibility."

"But if you think you already know everything, then how can you really be open to any new ideas or possibilities? Think about it, Morgan." She scooted across the bunk and leaned against the wall.

"But we're sidetracking, aren't we? Let's get back to that experience of yours that you don't understand."

Andrew shifted around so he could still see her. "It was incredible, We-Be. I was actually him; not me, him—whoever 'him' was. I mean, I felt like me; I was there and everything . . . but I didn't feel at all like me. Do you see? I was somebody else entirely!" He looked at her with a pleading expression. "Do you know who 'he' was? If he wasn't me in a past life, but you insinuate he's somehow me, then who the hell was he?"

"He's you, Morgan. But to understand that, you have to understand what 'you' are. Are you only that which your name is attached to? Only that which you look at in the mirror every morning? Do you stop where your skin does? Where your breath does?" She paused and looked at Andrew with wide, serious eyes.

"First of all, try to grasp the fact that you made you. The individual you know yourself to be is merely one expression of the whole you. And that boy whose drama you experienced firsthand is yet another expression of the whole you. In other words, you are each versions of the same overall you!

"Now, usually an experience like you had tonight is interpreted as being a 'reincarnational drama.' Lucky for you though, it was a contemporary one, and you recognized it as such, which makes what I'm about to say that much easier for you to comprehend. There are no such things as past selves or even future selves; there are only simultaneous selves. Even if another self of yours is living in the seventeenth century, he's experiencing his life simultaneously with yours—right now. I know this is really hard to understand when you're perceiving time in a linear fashion. But from where I sit, it makes perfectly good sense. I can just as easily tune in to the reality of a version of you in ancient Greece, or even one working at an observatory on one of Jupiter's moons one hundred years from now, as I can the reality of the you sitting right here on your bed. And I couldn't do that if they weren't all happening at once."

"Wow! There's a 'me' on one of Jupiter's moons?" Andrew nearly fell off the bed in his excitement. "Which one?"

"Guess you'll have to tune in to that particular experience and see for yourself." We-Be tried to keep a straight face and not laugh at his childlike enthusiasm. "Actually, that self ought to be one of the easiest for you to tune in to, since his experience has already spilled over into yours—and yours into his—from time to time."

"How so?"

"Well, for one thing, like you, he's always held a fascination for the stars. He also was transfixed by the night sky as a child, only he focused in on astronomy so intensely that he made it his main interest in life. And since your little excursion to Mars last week, he's been playing around with the idea of transferring to an observatory there—though he doesn't have the slightest inkling why."

"So we influence each other and don't even know it?" Andrew asked, astonishment registering on his face.

"Some selves more than others. When you end up on like-minded tracks of thought with other selves, this tends to open up certain channels through which feelings or information can subtly pass through."

"Channels? You mean channeling?"

"Well, yes and no. Channeling, as in gaining access to other parts of yourself. You channel other parts of yourself all the time without realizing it. Everyone does, though often people don't realize that the source of these curious and seemingly foreign thoughts or feelings is actually another portion of themselves slipping through. Artists and philosophers call it 'inspiration.' Christians perceive it as 'divine revelation.' And people like your friend Lana interpret it as contacting 'super beings' from the great beyond. But, in all these cases, that extraordinary wisdom or intuition is simply the overlapping of one self onto another."

"This is getting really bizarre," Andrew said, standing up and beginning to pace the floor. "If that kid was another me and he's on his way here, then I'm going to actually see a part of myself face to face! Right?"

"That would seem to be the case. Any ideas on how you're going to handle it?"

"Handle it? Jesus! I honestly don't know what I'll do. I mean, I suppose I should try to help this kid, this other me, whoever he is. Somebody has to help him, 'cause he's really got some big problems, to put it mildly." He stopped his pacing and looked at We-Be blankly for a moment, unable to fully grasp everything that was happening. "I guess I'll try to hunt him down tomorrow and attempt to make friends with him somehow. It's probably a sure bet that he won't know who I am."

"How will you know who he is?"

"Huh?" Andrew scrunched up his forehead in confusion. "Well . . . I . . . he was about sixteen, I think . . . and . . . well . . . he did have on jeans and sneakers—" Stopping short, he hit his head with the palm of his hand dramatically. "Damn! How can I not know what I looked like when I was him?"

We-Be crossed one foot over her knee and calmly lit a cigarette that seemed to magically appear out of nowhere. "Well, if you think about it, Morgan, who really has the inclination to check out what they look like so they'll remember later when they're not themselves anymore, especially when they're busy scrambling just to stay alive?"

Andrew shook his head, her smoking so incongruous with her angelic persona as to make him feel even more bewildered. "But if I was him, I should have known what I looked like!"

"I'm sure if I'd asked you then to describe yourself, you would have been able to, but you're not busy being him anymore. The link to his memory has been cut off."

"Then how am I going to know him when I see him?"

"I guess you're going to have to develop a new approach to 'finding yourself'!"

Andrew rolled his eyes in frustration at her corny play on words. "Why don't you just tell me what his name is? I know you know; you told me you can tune in to any one of my simultaneous selves whenever you want to!"

"So I did, Morgan. But maybe part of the game you started tonight is learning how to solve your own mysteries; like sleuthing for your simultaneous self! Sounds like a great way to distract and entertain yourself while you're here."

"Quit screwing around! Help me out here." Andrew slumped down on the bunk, looking at her with imploring, little-boy eyes.

"Nope, I don't think I will." She met his beseeching expression with an ornery grin. "It'll be fun to watch you figure this one out for yourself. Think of it this way: You have a hell of a lot of kids to sort through, and in the next few days you'll have to consider the possibility that almost any one of them may be the self you're searching for. And, because of this experience, for the rest of your life you'll always have to stop and wonder about your connection to every person you meet.

"Space-Time Principle Number 126:

Whenever you look at another person,
always keep in mind
that you may be looking at yourself
without even knowing it."

We-Be got up and floated over to the table in search of an ashtray. "If you get this principle down pat, you'll realize that when you help others you quite literally may be helping yourself."

Andrew watched her as she stubbed out her cigarette in an old cracked dish and then returned to the foot of the bed. "Okay, if that holds true then would you mind telling me how I helped myself by trying to help Holden? I really did try to help him, you know; and where did it get me? Stranded out here in the middle of nowhere. Hell, if it weren't for you, that kid probably would've gouged my eyes out with a butcher's knife."

"Good thing I interfered with your 'karmic plans' and interceded in your 'prearranged agreement' with the kid, huh?"

"Don't get sarcastic, I'm being serious! Just what exactly was I supposed to gain from that experience? Or, for that matter, what did Holden gain?"

"I don't know."

"What? You don't know? What do you mean, you don't know?"

"Well, I never claimed to be all-knowing, you know."

"You could have fooled me! I can't believe this is happening! You don't know? Here I summon you right out of the ethers to give me a brilliant, profound explanation for the horrible things I've been through since I saw you last, and all you can say is that you don't know?" Andrew threw himself against the wall and glared at her in disbelief.

"Jesus, Morgan, give it a break! Nobody knows everything—especially 'lower astral entities' like me. I could make a few stabs at the answer you're seeking, but then, I could be dead wrong. Suffice it to say that there isn't always an obvious rhyme or reason to everything that happens in life. Sometimes things take a while to figure out; and even when you think you have everything squared away, you may have misinterpreted something, and in the meantime missed an opportunity to find what you were after. Hopefully, everything will make more sense to you as time goes by."

Andrew pulled at his face in exasperation. "Suddenly I seem to have some sort of weird karma with kids—even myself as a kid. It's got to make sense somehow. There had to be a reason for me to draw that experience with my dumpster-diving self into my reality."

"Your reality? It's more like you were in his reality; or maybe you were both somewhere in-between!"

"This is all just too, too strange. She-demons, evil ones, runaway kid-selves, Jovian-moon-astronomer pieces of me . . . how in the world did I manifest this craziness into my life?"

"Maybe you need to flip your perspective around and learn to look both ways for a change.

" Space-Time Principle Number 25:

The manifestation of others into your life isn't a one-sided affair.
The people you draw into your experience also draw you into theirs.

"And if you look at it that way, Morgan, all the craziness may just add up to something in the end—teach you things you never would have learned without it." She got up and stretched her legs and straightened her gown, as though preparing to make her exit.

"Well, maybe things will be clearer tomorrow," Andrew said, trying to project positively. "At least for once I know I purposely drew someone into my experience. I really did manifest you tonight." Then he fell silent for a moment, something still nagging at him. "But . . . wait a minute . . . I'm already awake! You're not supposed to be here in my waking reality; that's against the rules!"

"Well, if you say so," We-Be said with a touch of sarcasm, and then in a flash, instantly transformed herself into a tiny point of brilliant light, just as she had that night on the beach. As she hovered a few inches in front of his face, he could clearly hear her voice inside his head: "Opportunity is all around you, Morgan—at your fingertips, and wisdom is on the tip of your tongue. Start chewing on it!" And with that, the fiery speck zipped around the room a couple of times and then magically flew right through the cabin wall.

For a full minute Andrew stared at the spot where she had disappeared, thrown off, as usual, by her abrupt departure. His mind was brimming over with all the new insights she had given him. Finally, he snuggled down in bed and squeezed his eyes shut, not knowing if he could possibly get back to sleep, or if he were already asleep without knowing it.

Chapter Seventeen

Faded Jeans
&
Scruffy
White Sneakers

Trevor had informed Andrew that he had half an hour before breakfast, and he used up most of it taking a steaming hot shower. He felt a little anxious about his day; he hadn't really ever done much painting at all. Plus, he was trying to figure out the events of the night before. It was all still very vivid in his mind: the dumpster, the incapacitating hunger, the cops . . . and of course We-Be and her eccentric words of wisdom. Had she really appeared to him in his waking state? And was there really another 'him' about to hit the scene?

After dressing, he spent his last five minutes standing on the porch looking out across the huge expanse of lawn between his cabin and the main house. He spotted a woman who looked to be about his own age strolling self-confidently toward the side door leading to the dining hall. This was curious: for some reason he hadn't expected any females to be present at an all-boys' home. Her appearance made his anxiety grow; he could tell she was attractive, but he wasn't in any position right now to meet an interesting member of the opposite sex. A part of him actually hoped she would turn out to be someone's wife or girlfriend.

Finally, not able to postpone it any longer, Andrew gathered his courage and jogged across the common to face the new challenge he had somehow created for himself.

Everyone looked up at him as he walked in. There was only one new addition to the group from the night before, and he had been right: she was attractive, in a tomboyish sort of way.

"Hey, Andy, grab some food and pull up a chair! I want you to meet someone." Charlie grinned at him as though they were already fast friends.

Andrew could feel his face turn red as he nodded and smiled and nervously dished himself up some eggs. As he sat down, his coffee slopping over onto the table, he could feel the girl's eyes on him and his blush deepened.

"Dagny, Andy; Andy, Dagny," Charlie quipped easily between mouthfuls of eggs, his attention darting playfully from one of them to the other. Andrew looked up at her, trying to appear cool and collected, but only managed to turn redder still as his eyes met hers. Her almond-shaped brown eyes gazed steadily back at him as though to say: "I'm opinionated and stubborn and say exactly what I think. I never screw anyone over and I don't put up with anyone screwing with me." He couldn't help but be immediately reminded of We-Be—although there were no physical similarities—and suddenly felt as though he had known this girl for a long time. She seemed to sense his acceptance of her and showed her appreciation by throwing him a crooked impish grin.

"Dagny's our head counselor. Actually, she's probably the best damn shrink I've ever met."

"Charlie, I swear to God I'm going to deck you if you call me that one more time!" Her voice startled Andrew, for it was surprisingly husky for such a petite woman. Dagny playfully shoved Charlie, sending his forkful of potatoes flying.

Laughing, Charlie pulled her long dark ponytail and winked at Andrew. "Sorry, Dag, I forgot." Then, changing his expression to one of mock seriousness, he said to Andrew: "Dagny here has a real hate-on for labels. Pretty weird, wouldn't you say, for a psychologist? She's got this thing for coining names though; and believe you me, she's called me just about every name in the book!"

Dagny narrowed her eyes and glared at Charlie, suppressing a smile. "Not yet I haven't, but give me time!"

"Know what, girl?" Charlie leaned his elbows on the table and studied her affectionately. "I think I'll turn the tables on you and give you a new name. New place, new name—what the hell! What kind of name is 'Dagny,' anyway? Sounds like something you'd munch down on at Coney Island!"

Andrew studied the faces of everyone at the table and realized that this type of bantering was the norm between these two. Evidently they demonstrated their fondness for one another by sparring. Yet, he could tell their relationship was like that of a father-daughter rather than anything romantic. Somehow, this pleased him a great deal and made him feel a little giddy.

"So what do ya think, Trev? What kind of a name should we give our little gal here?"

"Well, she is right, mon. She don't shrink the mind, she mends it."

"You're right!" Charlie leaned over and slapped Trevor on the back conspiratorially. Then, after no more than a split-second's thought, he said, "So, 'Mind-Mender' it is!"

Getting up, Dagny said, "And on that note, I'm leaving your company before I'm tempted to try to mend your mind—seeing as how your psyche is obviously splitting at the seams." She gave Charlie's hair a playful tousle as she stood up and walked past him. "Besides, I've got lots to do before the kids start arriving today." As she gathered up a pile of notebooks and files stacked at the end of the table, she smiled her charming crooked smile at Andrew. "Do yourself a favor, Andy, and don't let Charlie rub off on you too much, or you may just end up needing some mind-mending yourself!"

Charlie chuckled warmly as she flounced out of the room and made her way up the staircase leading to the offices, ponytail bobbing behind her. "Quite a gal, our Dagny, wouldn't you say?" He looked at Andrew with raised eyebrows and then nodded as though silently answering his own question.

"And I think we need ta follow the lead of the lovely lady and get ahselves ta work, hmm, Ondrew?" Trevor took a last swig from his coffee cup and stood up, stretching his old limbs. Andrew cleared away his plate and trailed after him, trying to make his mind stay on the task at hand—figuring out how to use a paint brush—instead of letting his heart run away with fantasies of a cute psychologist with a sexy voice.

He followed Trevor to the utility room where the paint was stored. "Hey, Trevor, what did Charlie mean when he said Dagny 'coins names'?" Andrew guessed it couldn't hurt to find out a little bit about her.

"Ya see, Dagny, she looks inta the heart of a person—especially her kids—and gives them a new name that fits them, or fits what she interprets their ideal self ta be." He handed Andrew a roll of drop cloths and a ladder.

"Like how? I don't get it."

"Well, where she was before—at the mothers' home—she gave the girls nicknames ta help make them feel good about themselves."

"Mothers' home? You mean unwed mothers' home?" Andrew assumed Trevor's exotic way of phrasing things had made the statement come out a little wrong.

"Mon, ya better not let Charlie or Dagny hear ya say that!" Loaded down with paint cans and equipment, the old man shook his head and frowned in seriousness as he headed for the stairs. "Charlie says, 'Who says a lady gotta be wed ta be a good mother? She just gotta be stable.' Or, as Dagny puts it, 'Unwed sure as hell don't mean unfit.' "

"So, Charlie and Dagny have worked together before?" Andrew was concerned that he may be showing just a little too much interest, but Trevor didn't seem to notice, and was more than happy to fill him in on Dagny's and Charlie's history.

"Oh, yes. They are old friends. Charlie gave her a job before she was even outta college. He knew her father very well, you see, before she even came inta the world."

"Is Charlie a psychologist, too?"

"No, no, he's just a guy who likes ta do nice things for people. Charlie and Dagny's father were in Vietnam tagether. They made big plans ta devote their lives ta savin' the downtrodden of the world when they got back, and ta put an end ta the sufferin' of the innocent. But her father, he was killed right before he was due ta come home. So, you see, Dagny is like a daughter ta Charlie. And Charlie swore ta make his life reflect her father's and his vision."

"Jesus! That sounds like a movie or something!" Andrew was so absorbed in what Trevor was saying, he almost ran into the wall with the ladder.

"So, does Charlie work for the state, or what?"

"Oh no, this is all privately funded. Both homes have a rich benefactor—thank the powers that be! Have ya ever been inside a state-run institution for kids, mon?" Andrew's thoughts instantly flashed on his 'other self's' fear of having to return to J.D. "In an indirect sort of way, you might say."

Trevor looked at him curiously as they walked up the stairs to the office they were scheduled to paint. It was on the other side of the building from Dagny's office, which made Andrew breathe a sigh of relief. He sure didn't need her watching him try to figure out how to paint; he was nervous enough.

They spread out the drop cloths and Trevor patiently demonstrated what Andrew's job would be for the day. It entailed rolling paint onto the walls, which looked easy enough. Trevor handed the roller over, and stood back for a second or two to observe his new helper at work. Then, apparently satisfied that Andrew had the hang of it, he picked up his paint brush and started painting baseboards.

After a while, Andrew felt a little more reassured that he would be able to pull off presenting himself as having painting experience. Trevor seemed to disappear into his own little world, totally oblivious to any conversation Andrew tried to start. At first, Andrew was a little offended, but soon realized that the old Jamaican was tranced out or something. So Andrew just continued to do what he had been shown, overlapping strokes—vertically then horizontally—being very careful not to leave any thin spots or ridges.

After a couple of hours of strict silence, Andrew started a conversation with himself. "So, Andy old buddy, how's the painting business?" "Well, I must say, it's rather tedious, if you know what I mean. Kinda lonely, too, and awfully messy." "Worse than being a nanny?" "No, no, nothing could be worse than that!"

Caught up in the silliness of creating his own dialogue, Andrew was so startled he almost dropped his paint roller when Trevor walked over and laid his hand on his shoulder.

"My, but ya do talk ta yaself a lot, don't ya, mon?"

"Huh?" Andrew was mortified when he realized how ridiculous he must have looked carrying on his one-man conversation. "Just fooling around to pass the time, I guess."

"So, I suppose ya were just foolin' around ta pass the time last night in ya sleep too, hmm?"

"What do you mean?"

"Ya kept me awake half the night talkin' to yaself in ya sleep."

"That's crazy! I don't talk to myself in my sleep!"

"Maybe not ta yaself, but ta somebody for sure. The girl of ya dreams, maybe?" Trevor grinned largely, his old face creasing into a million fine lines. "And who might be this We-Be?"

Andrew was struck dumb. So, Trevor had heard his half of his conversation with We-Be. That meant for sure that it had just been a dream after all. A part of him was very disappointed over this realization, but another part—his more pragmatic side—was not surprised.

He didn't want to think about it right now with Trevor gawking at him with questioning eyes. And so, he purposely and quickly turned the subject around. "Me? What about you? You don't talk to me at all when you're working, let alone to yourself! Hell, you don't even remember I'm here!"

Trevor laughed a deep velvety laugh that echoed pleasantly off the walls of the empty room. "Well, ya see, my friend, I have a different understandin' of work than most people. I get outta the way of normal old thinkin' and get inta the moment. I become the work and it becomes me. Sometimes I don't know where I end and the paint brush begins."

"But, what if you don't like the work you have to do?"

"The way I see it is this: When I use all my time puttin' my mind inta my work, how can I find the time ta think about how bad I may have it? And then, just like magic, time becomes my friend and she don't nag and worry me like she does most people."

Andrew was taken aback by his words. This crusty old sage sounded like he had been taking lessons from We-Be, too, in a rather offbeat sort of way.

"But, we must be gettin' back ta our work now and finish this room before time slips all away and leaves us standin' still just talkin' ta ourselves in the dark."

Andrew spent the next two hours trying to become one with his paint roller. But try as he might, he couldn't seem to ignore the paint splattering white speckles down on his face and hair, or the aching muscles in his shoulders and neck. Plus, he couldn't get a couple of things out of his mind that were vying for his attention: namely his "other self" and Dagny. Possibly the two of them were even together right now. He wished more than anything that he could observe the kids as they arrived, for he was sure he would be able to tell which one was "him." Faded jeans and scruffy white sneakers—it couldn't be too difficult.

Trevor, mentally absent again since their merging-mind-with-work conversation, seemed to have a natural dinner bell in his head; for at exactly twelve o'clock he snapped back to reality with the statement, "Lunch time!" He carefully wrapped his brush in an old rag and showed Andrew how to soak his roller down with paint to temporarily keep it from drying out, just as the dinner bell sounded for real.

Andrew didn't join Trevor for lunch and instead elected to grab a sandwich and some juice and sit alone under a tree. He wanted to observe the arrival of any of the boys who might be his simultaneous self.

He didn't have to wait long before an official-looking van pulled into the entrance and stopped before the main house. Andrew craned his head to get a good look at the boys as they piled out and stood around, shuffling their feet nervously. There were three of them. One was a very chubby boy of about fourteen; and even though he did have on the required garb, Andrew knew this boy could never have maneuvered himself so catlike in and out of dumpsters. The second boy was physically about what Andrew was looking for, but he was wearing cut-offs and flip-flops. And the third one was definitely out because he was African American. Andrew could remember quite distinctly that the hands of his other self had been the same color as his known self's hands. This was a good sign, Andrew told himself; the odds were slimming down nicely.

"Hi ya, mind if we join you?" Andrew knew whose voice it was before he turned around to look.

"No, not at all!" he said quickly, self-consciously wiping mustard from his mouth.

Dagny plopped down across from him, and two gangly young men sat down a little farther away, looking awkward and edgy.

Andrew was uncomfortably aware of the paint freckles covering his face and arms, and could feel himself blushing under them.

"So, how's it going?" He heard how stilted his own voice sounded, and cringed.

"Great so far! We're the welcoming committee. Oh! Let me introduce you: Andy, this is Taylor and Benny."

Andrew studied the boys as they nodded their heads at him and warily studied him back. The one closest to him, Taylor, was thin and very tall for his age—maybe six foot two—blonde, blue-eyed, and pimple-faced. And, he had on exactly the right shoes and pants. "Candidate number one," Andrew thought, feeling his stomach flutter with excitement.

Benny was rather nondescript: brown hair and eyes, average height and weight. And, surprisingly enough, he also had on the anticipated apparel.

It was almost too much for Andrew to handle all at the same time. He could smell Dagny's hair even though he was a good five feet from her, and this distracted him from his initial scrutiny of the boys. Neither Taylor nor Benny showed even a trace of acknowledgment of a connection with him, and he had no feelings of familiarity with them, either. Maybe it wasn't going to be so easy after all. . . .

"So, Taylor," Andrew forced himself to speak, "Where do you come from?"

"J.D.," the boy answered bluntly, looking Andrew squarely in the eyes for a reaction.

"Uh . . . that's not what I meant. I meant what part of the state." Andrew felt himself squirming under the intensity of his stare.

"I know what you meant."

Andrew glanced at Dagny instinctively for help, but her eyes were trained on Taylor, like an animal tuning in to an oncoming storm.

Clearing his throat, he turned to Benny and shakily asked the same question.

"Down south, near the beach," the boy responded, less belligerently than his cohort, but lacking much in tone that could be considered friendly.

Andrew's pulse quickened slightly. So far both of them—as churlish as they seemed to be—were passing with flying colors. He wanted to question them further, but couldn't figure out how to without appearing nosy or pushy. Above all, he didn't want to alienate Dagny by interfering in her mind-mending affairs.

"Well, guys, guess we ought to go greet the newcomers!" Dagny got up and brushed the grass from the seat of her pants. "Catch you later, Andy."

The two young men reluctantly stood up to follow her as she headed in the direction of the main house. Andrew's heart fell; he assumed he had just blown it by showing his clumsiness at communicating with kids.

But, a few yards away, Dagny turned around and hollered back at him, "We're having our first pow-wow after dinner tonight; wanna join us?"

Mutely, Andrew just nodded his head up and down, his disposition immediately boosted. He watched as they walked off, Dagny jauntily leading the dispirited duo by a good ten feet.

He saw Trevor's lank figure standing in the doorway and knew it must be time to resume work. As he got up to go, yet another official-looking vehicle—a car this time—pulled into the entrance. He walked slowly back to join Trevor, keeping his eyes trained on the occupants of the car as they emerged. This time only one kid got out . . . wearing faded jeans and scruffy white sneakers.

Throughout the rest of the work day, Andrew created scenarios in his head about what it would be like to actually meet and interact with a simultaneous self. He was pleasantly surprised when Trevor announced that it was quitting time, for time had actually flown by, though he knew he hadn't done as Trevor had suggested and become one with his work. To the contrary, Andrew mused, he seemed to have left his body behind on automatic pilot and freed his mind to go play. Same general outcome, maybe—achieving freedom from tedium—only he seemed to have arrived at it differently.

In any case, he was glad the day was over and rushed back to the cabin to shower for dinner. He wasn't quite sure what Dagny had meant by a "pow-wow," but he assumed she would tell him more about it over their meal.

Chapter Eighteen

Pow-Wow Psychology

"Okay guys, listen up!" Charlie hollered above the thunderous din in the dining hall, trying to pull everyone together. The number of kids had grown considerably through the day; it looked like the whole lot of fifty teenagers was now present.

Andrew could see Dagny across the room, totally absorbed in the boys sitting at her table. He had chickened out and refrained from joining her for dinner as he had planned, and had instead sat down next to Trevor at the far side of the room. He was glad now, for the crowded table seemed overwhelming. He would catch up with her later by accepting her pow-wow invitation. Maybe things would be calmer by then.

Charlie put his fingers to his mouth and let out a shrill whistle, which caught everyone's attention. "Thank you! Now, I'm sure you've all gotten acquainted with your bunkhouse counselors and know your sleeping arrangements. I'd like to introduce myself. I'm Charlie Campbell, and I kinda run things around here, off and on. Over there"—he gestured toward Dagny—"is Dagny Alvarez, head counselor."

Somebody let out a loud wolf whistle, and the rest of the crowd laughed in appreciation. Dagny smiled, taking it in stride.

Charlie was unruffled by the outburst, too. "Yeah, she's a looker all right, but I wouldn't try to tangle with her if I were you.

A coral snake may be little and pretty, but if you mess with it and make it mad—watch out! Best keep your distance, boys."

Half the room blushed and laughed nervously. The sense of hostility toward authority had increased measurably in the atmosphere when Charlie's took the floor. And yet, this first push at riling him had fallen flat and gotten only a wisecrack in response. Many of the boys looked bewildered, their eyes darting from Charlie to each other and back to Charlie.

"I'm not up here to talk at you—just to introduce myself and make a couple of things clear. First, this isn't J.D. It's probably the best place many of you have ever been. You're here because you need a chance to get out of the garbage heap fate dumped you in. But, understand one thing: this place isn't called 'Last Chance Ranch' for nothing. For most of you, it is your last chance. If you blow it, you're back in J.D., or on the streets, or worse.

"Second, we're all friends here, or that's what we're shooting for. If you have any problems, I want you to know you can come and talk to me about anything—and I mean anything. And if I'm not around, then talk to Dagny or your bunkhouse counselor. You're going to find that everyone who works here is completely different from what you're accustomed to. As of today, you're out of the system. Just follow the few rules and don't be afraid to voice your feelings. And that starts right now—any questions?"

"So, where's the swimming pool and satellite dish?" a scrawny kid with a crew-cut sitting at Dagny's table quipped, pushing against this new authority figure to test how far he would budge.

Charlie smiled. "Well, they just aren't in the budget . . . yet. Tell you what though: why don't you and I put our heads together and work on it? From the looks of some of your files, a few of you have been real creative in coming up with ways to generate extra cash!"

The African-American kid who arrived earlier spoke up: "Yeah, like we could grow some great pot on a place like this!" The room resounded with hoots and hollers.

"Well, I'll tell ya, I can't say as I have any strong opinions against growing pot, or even smoking it for that matter, but the folks that let me run this place sure do. And if I gotta play by the rules, so do you. No way around it, fellas. What we're after here is just too important to jeopardize for a little high."

"I get it; it's the old 'get high on life' rap. What a joke!" Andrew couldn't see the face behind the cynical voice.

"Only if your life's a joke, kiddo. I don't think it's a joke at all, but I can't blame you for your resentment. Must be pretty hard to be high on life when you're down in the gutter, huh?" Charlie's face was a study of an odd mixture of compassion and sternness.

Most of the boys stared into their plates solemnly, each reflecting on his own past miseries. Dagny and the five bunkhouse counselors looked as though they were holding their breath, but there were no more dissenting voices from the crowd.

After announcing the pow-wow, Charlie dished himself up a plate of food and sat down next to Trevor at their table.

"Ya confusin' the hell outta of them, ya know that?" Trevor looked at his friend quizzically.

"Only way to get their attention." Charlie attacked his plate like he hadn't eaten in a week, the confrontational episode he had just been through not affecting his appetite in the least. Then between mouthfuls, he asked, "So, Andy, you going to the pow-wow?"

"Sure, but what is it exactly?"

"Well, a real pow-wow is an ancient Native American ritual in which different tribes gather to celebrate, trade their wares, and share their customs. In our case, it's more like group therapy with a little music tossed in for good measure. Usually pretty effective, but we'll have to wait and see how it works on this bunch."

"Sounds interesting. Guess I'll see you there."

Andrew could see Dagny getting up and then leading her troops out the door—a parade of faded jeans and scruffy white sneakers. His shoulders were burning from the unaccustomed exercise and he decided rest up before the evening's event. So, excusing himself, he headed to his cabin to catch a few "z's."

Luckily he had set his alarm, for when he heard it buzzing it was all he could do to sit up and turn it off. Every muscle in his body ached, and he groaned as he stood up to get dressed. It was almost dark outside and there was a chill in the air—unusual for this time of year.

As he stepped out onto the porch, he could see Trevor in the distance over by the barn, piling up old branches. He felt a wave of guilt: he should have been helping the old man instead of sleeping. Sprinting stiffly across the common, he grabbed up a tree limb and dragged it over toward Trevor, a sheepish grin of apology on his face.

"So, Ondrew, how good are ya at startin' fires, hmm?"

"Well, I wasn't a very good Boy Scout, if that tells you anything."

The old Jamaican huffed and puffed as they toted the last of the firewood to the pile. Then he straightened up—an act that looked rather painful—and briefly studied Andrew with piercing eyes before saying in a soft, mysterious way, "Well, maybe I will teach ya a little about the secret of startin' fires, then."

Andrew felt as though he was about to be privy to an ancient mystical ritual of some sort. He found himself holding his breath as he squatted down next to Trevor to watch his handiwork.

"First, ya will notice, I have put the twigs and dried leaves under the bigger branches. This is where the fire must begin." Andrew watched intently as Trevor used a stick to stir the kindling in a curious circular manner, swaying ever so slightly in rhythm with the motion of his hand. He expected the old man to break out chanting at any moment.

"Then, ya honor the sun that has slipped below the horizon for the night, askin' it ta bestow ya with the necessary powers." He shook the stick three times over his shoulder, due west.

Andrew glanced in that direction toward the last, barely discernible rays of the sun for a moment, before looking back at Trevor's magic-at-work. His eyes widened in surprise; fire was already beginning to crackle among the leaves, a winding trail of smoke climbing into the night sky.

"How'd you do that so fast?" Andrew asked, frustrated that he had missed the most important part of the ritual.

"T'was easy, my friend. We have been blessed; the Spirit of Fire has chosen ta express itself for us swiftly tanight." The Jamaican almost blended into the backdrop of the darkening sky.

"Yeah, but how?"

"How else, mon?" Trevor pulled something out of his jacket pocket and waved it in front of Andrew's face. "With a very important talisman in the fire ritual." Eyes wide, Andrew leaned forward expectantly. "A trusty Bic lighter! A modern convenience, yes, but truly an inspiration from the great Fire Spirit himself!"

Andrew could feel his face redden, imperceptible in the enveloping darkness, as Trevor's rich laughter bellowed out in all directions. The fire was beginning to blaze, and reflected wildly in the old prankster's eyes, making him look for all the world like a fire spirit in the flesh—a cackling, mischievous devil straight from the bowels of Hell. This character was as weird as We-Be ever was, and then some.

"Jesus, Trevor! That was pretty rotten." The unholy laughter faded down, and for a split second Andrew wondered if his tone of voice had offended the corner-cutting fire maker. He picked up a stick and poked at the flames, waiting for Trevor to say something, before finally craning his head around and adding: "But I have to admit, you got me good! You really had me going there for a minute."

No response.

"Trevor?" Still no response. Andrew suddenly realized he had been talking to thin air; Trevor was nowhere to be found. A shiver ran up his spine: Had the Jamaican ever really been there in the first place? But that was silly; Trevor was a real person, not a dream creature like We-Be.

He didn't have any more time to think about it, for at that moment hordes of kids descended upon him, followed by Dagny, Charlie, and the other counselors.

"Nice fire, Andy. Your making?" The fire danced off Dagny's raven hair, hanging loosely around her delicate oval face.

"Actually, it's a blessing from the great Fire Spirit."

"Whaaat?"

"Never mind," Andrew chuckled. "Guess you kinda had to be there."

With a quizzical raising of her eyebrows, Dagny shrugged her shoulders good naturedly.

Charlie slapped him on the back and sat down on the ground, Andrew following suit. They both watched as Dagny and the bunkhouse counselors scurried about rounding up the boys and getting them all settled down for the pow-wow.

"Anybody here play an instrument or sing a little?" Charlie asked, scanning the circle of fire-lit faces. His question was met with silence.

"C'mon, guys, I know somebody here has fooled around with a guitar or something." There was a slight mumble from someone in the crowd. "What's that?" Charlie turned his attention in the direction of the barely discernible response.

"I said, I used to play the guitar."

Andrew could have picked him out of a crowd, for this kid looked like a future rock star. He was tall and handsome, with long, sandy-colored hair tied back in a ponytail. He had a distinctive, self-assured air about him that set him apart from the others.

"That is," the boy continued, "until my old man went on one of his rampages and tossed it out our third-story window. It landed on top of a Yellow Cab. Probably the biggest tip that jerk got all night."

The circle of boys laughed harder than the story was funny, and Andrew instinctively knew that most of them identified with the boy's situation to some degree.

"Well, we're on ground level tonight. Want to give it another go?"

"Hey, you're a real funny guy! Do you see a cab comin' up the drive, returning my strings?"

"No . . . but I may just know where there's a spare set of 'em lying around. Interested?"

The boy's eyes lit up, and then went shaded and doubtful. "You serious, or just screwin' with my head?"

"Well, why don't you go and see?" Charlie pulled some keys from his pocket and pitched them over to the guitarless musician. "The big key'll let you into the storage room. It's just sitting in there, waiting for you to claim it and tune it up." Charlie dug around in his pocket again and pulled out a harmonica, polishing it on the tail of his flannel shirt. "Hurry back and you can give this one-man band some back-up."

The boy looked at Charlie with a mixture of suspicion and excitement as he got up and ambled off in the direction of the main house, the first sweet, wailing sounds of the harmonica following after him.

For a while everyone just sat and listened to Charlie's music. One at a time, Andrew could see the tenseness leaving the faces and postures of the boys as they mellowed out and began to feel comfortable in their surroundings. All except one.

"So what the hell are we out here for, anyway? Mosquito bait?" Dagny turned calmly toward the disgruntled boy. "That's what the fire's for. Mosquitoes don't like the smoke."

"Well, I don't like you. And this pow-wow shit sucks."

Andrew could see the kid's face clearly in the firelight. He was about sixteen, with long dark hair hanging to one side covering his left eye, an earring dangling from his exposed ear.

"I know what you're up to!" he hissed, jumping up and grinding his cigarette into the ground with the heel of his scruffy white sneaker. "You shrinks are all alike; you wanna brainwash us into being good little robots that you can control, that won't give you any trouble. Screw this; I'm goin' to watch TV." And with that, he stomped off, Charlie's blues tune swinging easily into an upbeat tempo in time with the boy's feet, which covered up the uncomfortable silence among the rest of the boys.

One of the bunkhouse counselors sprang to his feet to go after his charge. But Dagny leaned over and grabbed him by the pant's leg. He looked back at her in surprise, but she just shook her head and motioned for him to sit back down. Then she whispered something in his ear and he whispered back, before she cleared her throat to speak. As if on cue, Charlie's music faded off until all that could be heard was the popping of the fire and the cry of a lone whippoorwill in the distance.

"Okay, so Sam isn't happy with our little pow-wow. Anybody want to comment on his comments?"

"Well, it's obvious to me that if he's so afraid of becoming a mindless robot or of being unconsciously manipulated by power-mongers, the worst thing he could possibly do to his psyche is watch television!"

Andrew was astonished by this intellectual-sounding statement made by a very cultured young voice.

"And who might you be?" Dagny peered into the darkness to see a slight, bespectacled, redheaded youth sitting apart from the rest.

"Allan."

"You sound like you know what you're talking about, Allan. A TV hater, huh? So, what do you do with yourself if you don't watch TV?"

The boy hung his head and looked like he was very sorry he had ever opened his mouth. "Lots of things."

"Like what?"

"Like reading and writing."

"Oh? What do you like to read and write?"

He looked around at the other boys nervously, heaved a deep sigh, and then said in a resigned voice, "Poetry, mostly."

Hoots and hollers greeted his admission, but he didn't look at all surprised, as though he were used to this kind of response from his peers.

"Okay, can it everybody! Jesus! Can't a fella be a little different around here?" Dagny shook her head in disgust.

Everyone's attention was distracted from her question by the sudden reappearance of Charlie's young accompanist, guitar in hand. With a smile touching the corner of his lips, he tossed the keys back to Charlie and sat down cross-legged away from everyone else, near Allan.

One of the boys picked up the subject of Allan again. "Only wimps write poetry!"

"What do you think about that, Strings?" Dagny looked straight at the guitar player.

"Who, me?"

Charlie chuckled and said: "Uh oh! It's starting already! 'Strings,' huh? Well, Strings it is! Consider yourself honored, m'boy, to be the first one christened by our fair Dagny!"

"Strings?" The boy asked again.

Dagny nodded her head matter-of-factly, and Charlie added: "And from now on that name will stick to you like glue; Dagny's names always do. So, you'd better get used to it!"

Dagny ignored Charlie's words and repeated her original question she had aimed at Strings. "What do you think; are poets wimps?"

Strings cocked his head, thinking about it, while strumming the guitar softly and tuning up. "If we didn't have poets, we wouldn't have songwriters to write great lyrics. That'd be real bad. But I guess some poets are wimps, I dunno."

"Ever write any songs, Allan?" Dagny returned her attention to the poet, now slouched over with his knees drawn to his chest as though trying to disappear.

"No . . . but it's a thought; maybe I'll give it a try someday. Actually I never thought about it before; but then again, I never knew a musician before. And my stepfather would probably have burned his money before he spent it on a musical instrument for me!"

"Why's that?" Andrew was impressed with how Dagny pursued each turn in the conversation.

"Ever heard the saying, 'beaten like a redheaded stepchild'? Well, that's me. I got beat for everything and nothing. He hated me for not playing football, for making straight A's, for not having a sexy blonde girlfriend. I was everything he detested."

"How about you; ever written any lyrics?" She shifted her attention back to Strings.

"Naw, hell, I can't write nothin'! 'Cept music. I can make up tunes all day long."

"Sounds like the two of you should put your heads together!"

The two boys studied each other as though sizing each other up.

"So, Strings, are you a redheaded stepchild, too?" Dagny seemed to divert the subject again on purpose.

"Naw, he's my real father, I'm sorry to say. What a prick!"

"Why? Because he didn't want you playing your guitar?"

"Among other things. He'd have been happy if I'd just sat in my room quietly all day, pretending like I was dead or something. The biggest thrill of his life was when he had me carted off to J.D. He just didn't want me to live at all. But of course, he got to live! I mean, my ol' man was at Woodstock, ya know? Hell, he tells stories about screwing Janis Joplin! What a hypocrite!"

The tension in the air was released with his outburst, the rest of the boys laughing or interjecting statements of commiseration.

"Hey!" Allan hollered. "That's a catchy title for a song, don't you think? 'My Ol' Man Screwed Janis Joplin!'"

The boys cracked up over this, and two or three of them—including Strings—threw him looks of real admiration. Allan turned red, embarrassed at his boldness, but beaming with pride. Andrew could bet that this was the first time in this kid's entire life that he had ever gained a positive reaction from his peers.

The rest of the evening went smoothly. Strings and Charlie blended their music beautifully, as though they had been playing together forever. Strings sang the songs he knew and Charlie sang the ones Strings didn't. None of the other boys shared much about themselves, but Andrew guessed they would in time, now that Allan and Strings had set things in motion. Around midnight, Dagny stood up, brushed off her behind, and announced that it was time to turn in.

Protests from a few of the boys told Andrew that the evening had been somewhat successful. He suddenly felt very sorry for Sam, the boy who preferred television.

Strings and Allan had had their heads together during breaks in the music—about a future songwriting partnership, Andrew guessed. As the two of them stood up and began to walk off together, still deep in conversation, Dagny called after them: "Hey, Strings! Let me know how Lord Byron there works out, okay?"

Another boy named. Andrew could see the pattern now: as each boy opened up, Dagny rewarded him with a name that suited him and made him feel special. Quite a gimmick!

He held back, waiting for Dagny to finish talking to one of the counselors. Never had he been this impressed with the way someone handled a situation before, and he wanted to compliment her. Charlie walked by him and punched him playfully on the arm. "Don't stay up too late, fella. Trevor'll have you up and painting at the crack of dawn!"

Dagny joined him and they walked back together. As he gently took her arm to help her over the uneven ground, he could feel her body was alive with excitement. She was exhilarated over her first night's accomplishments, it was plain to see. Accepting his compliment with a big grin of appreciation, she squeezed his arm affectionately and then lapsed into a reflective silence. At the middle of the common they said goodnight, and he watched as she almost danced toward her cabin.

Andrew felt exhilarated, too, and not sleepy at all. He sat down on the porch of his cabin to reflect on the evening's events. Running images of the different boys through his mind, he tried to mentally home in on which one was his dumpster-diving self. He found himself continually returning to one in particular: Strings. As far as he was concerned, the guitar player was definitely the most promising of all. After all, hadn't he mentioned being in J.D.? He sure looked like he could slip in and out of dumpsters easily enough. Plus, he was very thin—like he hadn't eaten very well for quite a while. His trash mouth certainly corresponded with that of the boy he had temporarily experienced being. And, to top it all off, he was tan—like he had been hanging around a beach. You didn't get a tan like that wasting away in J.D.

Andrew was jerked out of his mental detective work by a movement he picked up out of the corner of his eye. Leaning forward, he peered into the blackness to try to make out who or what it was. The scant moonlight glimmered off a figure creeping stealthily toward the main road, a knapsack slung over his shoulder. Andrew instinctively knew who it was: Sam, the pow-wow drop-out. He reacted immediately by yelling out the boy's name. At the sound of Andrew's voice, the boy broke into a run, and without thinking Andrew dashed off the porch to pursue him. Sam let out a gasp of shock as Andrew tackled him to the ground. Fists flailing, he struggled to get away, but Andrew pinned him down and held him there. He wasn't much of a challenge, for Andrew had a good thirty pounds on him.

"Get off me, man! What the fuck do you think you're doin'?" Even though the boy's voice was strained and faint from having the wind knocked out of him, he was able to relay his deep hostility.

"What do you think you're doing? What are you doing prowling around in the middle of the night?" He and Sam both knew that his question was stupid, that it was obvious what he had been doing.

"I'm splittin', that's what! This place is freaking me out! It really sucks!" He arched his back and slammed himself against the ground in a futile attempt to break loose.

"C'mon, this place is a paradise compared with some of the places you've probably been. What's with you? Why don't you lighten up and give it a try? You've only been here one day, for Crissakes!"

"And that's enough for me. I'm history."

Andrew could just see in the faint, fractured moonlight the stubborn determination carved into the line of the boy's jaw. "Well, I'm not going to let you up until you promise to at least come up on my porch and discuss it rationally for a while."

Sam struggled belligerently under Andrew's grip.

"Look, I hate this. I don't want to be here bullying you anymore than you want me to be. You're just lucky I caught you instead of some cop, or else you'd be on your way to J.D. So settle down and promise, okay?"

Sam stopped fighting and fell silent, lying there motionless for a full minute. Then, letting out a sigh of disgust, he grumbled, "Okay, I promise."

Andrew slowly loosened his grip on him, making sure that he wasn't planning to go back on his word. Then, offering the boy an outstretched hand, he helped him to his feet and ushered him to the cabin porch, ready to tackle him again if he made one wrong move.

They sat on the bench, side by side, Andrew waiting for him to say the first word. Finally, the silence seemed to get the best of the runaway. "I just can't stay here; you don't understand." He hung his head, his long dark hair hiding his face from Andrew.

"What's to understand?" Andrew wasn't at all sure how to handle this. He knew he was certainly no Dagny when it came to mind-mending, but then, Dagny wasn't around.

"Everything . . . nothing . . . I dunno. Why do you care, anyway? You're not even a counselor!"

It only took Andrew a second to think out his response before he took a deep breath and dove in, pride aside. "You're right! I'm a nobody. In fact, two days ago I was broke, jobless, carless, and homeless. But, somehow I managed to find my way here; and I have to admit, I'm not at all sure how that happened or where I'm going to be a week from now—maybe on the street, or worse. Believe it or not, I identify more with you guys than I do the counselors here. But, the truth is, this place is a godsend for me right now, and I actually like the people running it. And you know what? You would too if you just gave them half a chance. Hell, I'd give anything to be your age again and belong here." Andrew realized he really meant what he had said, and felt his eyes moistening.

Sam raised his head and looked Andrew straight in the eye for the first time. "How come you were in such a bad situation in the first place?" The tone of his voice had become noticeably less belligerent.

"If I told you, you wouldn't believe it. But leave it to say, I've been in and out of bad situations since I was your age."

"That gives me a lot to look forward to."

"My point exactly! I never had a Dagny or a Charlie or a Last Chance Ranch. These people really want to help you get on your feet so you don't end up like me." Andrew inwardly cringed with the self-denigrating admission.

"But, I just can't stay here!"

"For God's sake, why not?"

Sam fell silent again except for the nervous tapping of his foot on the porch floor. Andrew bit his tongue, trying hard not to get frustrated or be too pushy. He would wait the boy out.

It seemed like an eternity before Sam spoke again: "Look, man, I got a real problem, and you just wouldn't understand, okay?" There was a hint of tears in the boy's wide, dark eyes.

"It doesn't hurt to try me. I may just surprise you and help you think of a solution; you never know. You know what they say about two heads being better than one!"

Sam lowered his head again and mumbled, "They're gonna make me go to school on Monday."

"So what? Hell, I hated school, too, but it's just something you grit your teeth against and get through as quick and easy as you can."

"But I can't get through it."

"Why?"

"'Cause I can't read, dammit!" Sam jumped up and looked like he was going to take flight again.

Andrew restrained himself, hoping beyond hope that the boy would stay and see their conversation through. He did, and Andrew breathed a sigh of relief.

"Well, that's a pretty big problem, all right. And you're right, I don't understand. How come you never learned how to read?"

"'Cause no one ever taught me, that's how come!" Sam paced nervously back and forth across the porch, the built-up rage apparent in his jerky movements. "We moved around a lot when I was a little kid: my parents were fruit tramps."

He noticed a puzzled look on Andrew's face. "I mean, they traveled around picking fruit for a living. Anyway, by the time I got to go to a real school, the teachers expected me to already know how to read. So I just pretended and played along as best I could. Then when I became a teenager they stuck me in the retarded kids' class, and I knew I didn't belong there. So, I just quit going altogether."

Andrew was shocked and sickened by Sam's story. How could such a thing have happened to such an obviously bright kid? He was overwhelmed with compassion for this boy who had somehow fallen through a crack in society. "Wow! That's awful! No wonder you're scared to go to school!"

"I'm not scared of nothin', man; I just don't want to go through the embarrassment of being called stupid' again." Sam stopped pacing and leaned stiffly against the porch rail, gazing off into the distance.

"Okay. No problem. . . ." Andrew's mind was racing, desperately trying to think of a solution to Sam's dilemma. "Look, I don't know how long I'm going to be here, but I'll make you a deal. If you promise not to split, I'll spend all my off time teaching you how to read. No one has to know what we're doing; I won't tell anyone. We'll hang out wherever everyone else isn't. And I promise that you'll at least learn the basics before Monday. How's that sound?"

"Why would you do that for me?" Sam turned around and stared at Andrew in disbelief.

"Because I want to, that's all. Maybe you can return the favor someday."

There was a barely perceptible glimmer of hope in the boy's eyes. "Can I really learn very much in just five days?"

"I think so. No, I know so. You're a smart kid; I can tell that. You're going to catch on real fast." Andrew got up and walked over to Sam. "Meet me right here after dinner tomorrow, okay? I'll scrounge up some books right after work."

Sam nodded his head numbly and looked at Andrew for the first time without the self-protective, arrogant façade.

"Okay, enough said." Andrew pushed him playfully. "Now sneak yourself back to your bunkhouse—and whatever you do, don't get caught!" At that moment, they heard a noise from inside the cabin. Andrew froze, and Sam took off like a shot, immediately disappearing into the night.

Andrew crept inside, half expecting to see Trevor awake and waiting to give him the low-down about getting enough sleep on a work night. But, quite to the contrary, he appeared to be sound asleep. The old man would be fresh and ready to get back to their chore of painting as soon as the sun peeked over the horizon. Andrew wasn't worried about the job anymore, and felt like he had the ability and energy to do just about anything. Now he understood what Dagny had felt earlier. He was giddy with excitement over his apparently successful interaction with Sam. Nevertheless, the episode had exhausted him, and he fell asleep as soon as his head hit the pillow.

Chapter Nineteen

The Wall of Amnesia

Andrew rubbed his eyes, trying to figure out where he was. He should have known: another We-Be dream. Dressed in a paint-splattered smock and floppy painter's hat, she was standing before a huge wall that stretched as far as the eye could see in either direction. Humming, she was painting over graffiti on the wall with an appalling fluorescent yellow paint. She turned around and smiled brightly at Andrew, but immediately resumed her task.

"What on Earth are you doing?" Andrew stepped back to try to get a broader view of the monstrous structure.

"Nothing . . . on Earth. Welcome to the Wall of Amnesia—slightly vandalized, as usual. Damn lower astral entities!"

"Whaaat?"

"See these doors painted here?" Andrew looked and saw painted renditions of every kind of door imaginable scattered among the graffiti. Slapping at one of the doors with her brush, she went on: "The dummies try to create an entrance to the other side, not realizing that all they have to do is let go of their Earthly obsessions and they'd immediately end up there."

"The other side? What's on the other side? And why's it called the 'Wall of Amnesia,' anyway?"

"See, you don't remember! That's because you passed through it on your way to physical reality. It's purpose is to make you forget what's on the other side, so naturally you did!"

"Oh, I've heard of that. Only I've heard it called the 'Veil of Forgetfulness'."

"Same difference. Only it'd be hard as hell to paint a veil."

We-Be rummaged around among her paint things, searching for something. "Damn!" she muttered, and then, to Andrew's surprise, she walked right through the painted doorway closest to her and disappeared for a few seconds, reappearing with a paint roller in her hand.

"I thought those doors weren't real!"

"Well, they aren't."

With curiousity, he eyed the doorway through which she had walked. Then, as she turned her back on him and busied herself pouring paint into a tray, he took a deep breath and bravely tried to walk through it himself. Thunk! He rubbed his nose that he had just smashed into the wall, feeling like an idiot, or, more exactly, like the coyote in the Roadrunner cartoon.

"Here, hold this," We-Be said, handing him the bucket of paint and bending down to move her dropcloth over. Gingerly, Andrew took the can, trying not to get paint on his hands. Never had he seen a color of paint this ugly before. He studied the can closely, looking for its color name, and then laughed as he read the name out loud, "ACME PAINT: Squished-Bug Yellow."

"Lower astral entities hate Squished-Bug Yellow," We-Be commented matter-of-factly.

Andrew decided to let her crazy comment pass. "So, why did I have to go through the wall before becoming physical? Just what is it on the other side that's so important that I have to forget it?"

"The rest of you."

"The rest of me?"

"Yep. You'd go nuts if you were aware of all the other parts of yourself and their experiences at once."

"Like my Jovian moon self, you mean?" Andrew's eyes lit up with a spark of comprehension, although he wasn't quite sure where she was headed with her train of thought.

"Yep." She grabbed the can of paint back from him, and commenced to paint out another block of graffiti.

"But how can he be on the other side if he's on one of Jupiter's moons?"

"He's not on the other side, but your memory of being him is."

"So, what if I want to get in touch with that memory?" Andrew was feeling frustrated with the growing complexity of her words, and slumped against a part of the wall where she had not yet painted.

"First things first. You don't need to be dwelling on his life right now. Obviously, you have enough to deal with just being Andrew B. Morgan. That's a much more important itinerary, and trying to remember and follow it should be your main concern."

"Itinerary? Are you saying that I already have my life all planned out but that I left the schedule on the other side?"

"Well, I guess you could put it that way." She made a funny scrunched-up face as she forced some paint into a crack with the edge of the roller. "But, like any good itinerary, even though the destination may stay the same, there are lots of different ways of getting there. And it goes without saying that some routes are preferable to others."

"What does that mean?" He took a few steps farther down the wall as she worked toward him.

"What that means, Morgan, is that before entering physical reality you selected an ideal pattern that you knew, if followed, would lead you to experiences and realizations you needed to enhance your overall world view. So you made your travel plans, you might say, got all your papers in order, and stepped through the Wall of Amnesia and into the world of space and time. And you forgot your destination just so you could enjoy the wonder of each day's events as they happened."

"Well that doesn't make any sense." Andrew shook his head in confusion. "What's the purpose of forgetting everything I came here to do? Seems to me it would be a whole lot simpler to have my memory intact and just get on with it."

"Ah, but then where would the sense of adventure be? The challenge, the excitement is in the experience itself!" We-Be turned to him with a big grin, exuberantly flinging her arms high and wide, momentarily giving up her preoccupation with her monumental clean-up job.

Andrew ducked the paint that flew off her roller. "Wait a minute . . . you told me not too long ago that the future couldn't be mapped out ahead of time. What you're telling me now is a complete contradiction to that." Andrew smugly plopped down on her work stool, curious to see how We-Be-turned-wall-painter would get out of this one.

"No it's not, Morgan. Like I said, you have an ideal pattern that you wish to follow; I didn't say the pattern was cast in stone. You're always free to go in whatever direction you choose.

> " Space-Time Principle Number 41:
>
> Everyone has an ideal destination
> planned out in advance, but no one
> is predestined to have to arrive there."

"But you said that some routes are better than others. How does anyone ever know which is the best route to take in order to reach his destination?"

"Magic."

"Magic?" He thought for sure she had exhausted that subject by now.

"Yep, back to that again. Get in touch with your own magic, Morgan, and you'll automatically find yourself heading in the right direction."

"Yeah, give up my free will, don't try to manifest anything at all into my life," Andrew said sarcastically, We-Be striking a still-raw nerve.

"No, you have it all wrong! It isn't that you have to give yourself over to some magical all-knowing something-or-other in the great beyond. You do have free will. It's just that it's to your benefit to let your magic guide you toward the best way to use that free will. You have the power to choose to either keep to your original itinerary or to head in another direction entirely."

We-Be set the roller back in the tray and wiped the repugnant yellow paint from her hands on the back of her smock. Then, picking up the paint brush again, she continued: "And I don't mean to imply that by choosing a different route you're bound to end up on the road to destruction. For all roads lead somewhere; more often than not, back to the original itinerary. The idea is to try to become aware enough to realize when you're heading down a dead-end street, though even a dead-end street forces you to retrace your steps and try again. Remember what I said about magic working best when you get out of your own way."

She paused in her painting and looked at Andrew intently. "Everything in your life is a manifestation, the result of your beliefs. And your beliefs are your tools of manifestation, your personal magic-makers."

"Then I sure must have lousy beliefs, because my manifestions always seem to get screwed up. I might as well face the fact that I'll never be a Master of Manifestation." He leaned his elbows on his knees and sighed dramatically. "I guess I really am just a Master of Disaster after all."

"Only because your priorities have been screwed up and you're such an extremist; with you it's all or nothing. Hand me that rag, will you?"

"What do you mean?"

"The rag, yo-yo brain, laying right there beside you."

"No, that's not what I meant. What do you mean by 'extremist'?" Andrew said, tossing her the rag, a little harder than called for.

"Oh . . . well . . . when you try to manifest, you're trying to fool yourself into believing things are radically different than they are. You expect immediate and drastic results with a snap of your fingers, a couple of quick affirmations, and a little bit of visualization. But not only have your priorities been bollixed up, your approach has been as well. From now on, why not take one step at a time and give yourself goals that are slightly more believable and realistically attainable?"

"You mean by starting with something simple?"

"Right! Instead of trying to manifest a new Porsche, a plush apartment, and the girl of your dreams, all in one fell swoop, why not zero in on something that seems really feasible to you? Course, what's feasible to you may not be to someone else, and vice versa; it all boils down to what is truly believable to you at any given time. And the reason you should start with creating something simple at first is because once you have, you'll begin to develop a sense of accomplishment that can help you as you go on to manifest more complex, important things.

"Let me paint you a picture of what I'm talking about. . . ." She leaned down and picked up a glass jar and sat down on the drop cloth next to her yellow paint. Then she opened up another can filled with red paint. Taking a spoon, she ladled out a little of the red into the jar.

"Okay, let's say we wish this red paint would become yellow. Now, I don't know about you, Morgan, but I'm too realistic to really believe that the red paint is going to instantaneously transform itself into a totally different color just because we wish it to. But . . ." She picked up another spoon and ladled some yellow paint into the same jar with the red and stirred it, ". . . if we add a little yellow, the paint becomes red-orange; not the desired color, but different than it was. If we were to leave it as it is for a period of time, we would forget exactly what the original hue looked like. Then . . ." Once again she poured some yellow into the jar and mixed it up, ". . . more of the desired color is added. Now we have orange-red. And, as before, in time we could adjust to this slightly different color."

She continued the process of mixing the yellow into the red, step by step, until she reached orange. "Now, we couldn't envision yellow coming directly out of red, since they have no relationship to each other; it was too drastic for our minds to comprehend. But the orange created by the adding of yellow, a little at a time, now makes our goal more believable. Because, even though we can still see the red in the new color that has been brought into being, we can also see a strong hint of yellow—our objective. All we have to do is continue adding yellow, bit by bit, taking the time to adjust to each new stage. After a certain point, the orange will begin to appear closer to yellow than to red. We are gradually diluting the red down to the point of insignificance. Now our confidence in what we're doing can really take off. We can actually see the yellow paint. A teaspoon of red doesn't stand much of a chance in a whole jar of yellow, Morgan. It will always still be there—just as your memories of what you were trying to change in your life will be—but it is now powerless in the presence of our attained goal: the yellow paint."

We-Be grinned up at Andrew, obviously proud of her color-theory analogy. And, as he grinned back, he realized with surprise that he understood what she had been driving at because of it.

"We-Be, the Prophet of Paint!" he joked, picking up the jar and peering into it, as if looking for a trace of the original red. Seemingly satisfied that the red had completely vanished, he said: "So, my chronic pattern of losing jobs, cars, and girlfriends can eventually end up like the red paint. I just have to buckle down and focus on something I know I'm capable of achieving first. Then, eventually, one at a time, I can manifest all the other things that I want."

She got up and closed the lid tightly on the red paint by standing on it and rocking back and forth. "Understand something, Morgan . . . ." she said on a more serious note, "I'm not trying to teach you how to manifest your Porsche, one hubcap at a time. I'm not trying to teach you how to manifest physical objects, for the manifestation process isn't meant to be used merely as a way to get things.

"Space-Time Principle Number 28:

The true objective of manifestation
is to strive for quality of self
rather than for a quantity of things.
Attaining the first will ultimately
lead you to the other—that is,
if you're still interested."

Andrew sat up straight, an expression of annoyance crossing his face. "If I'm still interested? Do you expect me to believe that once I develop certain qualities in myself I won't want anything but the bare essentials in life?"

We-Be calmly picked up the roller and returned to her chore. "That's not what I expect at all. All I'm saying is that as you become more and more aligned with your original itinerary and begin to understand the things that are truly important to you to accomplish in this lifetime, the more your perspective on the manifestation process will change. You'll have less and less desire to direct your energies toward trying to create material objects or toward making things happen, for you'll begin to realize that the process itself may actually be a limitation."

"Look, I don't care how enlightened I become, I'm not about to stop wanting 'things' in my life." Andrew stood up, becoming too agitated to sit still.

"You're still not getting it, Morgan. I'm not saying that material things shouldn't be a part of your life, or even that they're hindrances toward the fulfillment of your original plans. What I am saying is that the more you develop an understanding of what really makes you feel good about yourself, the closer you'll come to being in sync with your original itinerary. No 'thing,' all by itself, could ever make you feel as good as that."

She paused in her work and looked at Andrew over her shoulder. "In other words, you gotta get rhythm. Who could ask for anything more?"

"This doesn't mean that you won't have possessions, only that your happiness won't depend on having them. Then you can be free enough to truly enjoy those things you do have, because you'll know that even if you lost them all tomorrow you've still got rhythm and are right where you're supposed to be!"

She stood poised, alert to Andrew's reaction to her words, as she continued: "Periwinkles aren't the only things that are able to keep time with the Universe, Morgan." Andrew reflected back to the night on the beach when he first heard this strange concept. "If you remember clearly, you wondered why any consciousness would ever want to be a periwinkle, while at the same time asking yourself why your life couldn't be just as simple. Funny how sometimes the smallest things can teach us our biggest lessons. To put it all in a nutshell, or perhaps I should say seashell: The less complex your life, the more meaningful it can become. Simplicity creates space for things you've never even dreamed of."

"But how do I know where the cut-off point is between living simply and living complexly?" Andrew looked at her suspiciously through half-closed eyes.

"Space-Time Principle Number 38:

Live as simply as you can without feeling like you're depriving yourself.

"And before you ask me how you know when you're depriving yourself, all I can tell you is that it's entirely a matter of individual perspective—coupled with the art of being truly honest with yourself. When you're in touch with your innate sense of rhythm, your own fulfillment will always be important, but never at the expense of anything or anyone else. When you're dancing with the Universe, you're linked to the whole and aware that you're an integral part of that whole.

"There's only so much to go around, only so many natural resources and so on. Any imbalance that you see in your world is due to a lack of respect for the energy exchange we've already talked about, a lack of respect that's caused by people not following the Universe's lead. So when I say live as simply as you can, I'm stating an all-encompassing principle that affects all aspects of Earthly existence, from the overflowing landfills, to the extinction of other species, to starving children in Africa."

Plopping her paint roller in the tray, she turned around and leaned against the wall, sliding down to a sitting position. "Let's lighten up and take a break, shall we?" Then, pulling her cigarettes out of one of her pockets, she patted the rest of her pockets looking for something. Finally locating what she was after, she smiled impishly and said, "Where would I be without my trusty Bic lighter?" before lighting up and inhaling deeply.

Overwhelmed by all the new concepts she had talked about, Andrew stared blankly at the lighter in her hand, thrown off track for a moment by the abrupt reminder of the fire-starting episode. "Something told me that you and Trevor are in cahoots. You are, aren't you?"

We-Be laughed and wiped her forehead, leaving a streak of yellow paint dangerously close to a red curl of hair that had escaped from her hat. "No, Morgan, we're not in cahoots; I just like to screw with your head. But he's a pretty wise old fella and you ought to pay attention to some of the things he says."

"Yeah, he's a great guy, but he's only going to be around another day or so."

"Well, maybe you'll run into him again in the future. We'll see. . . ."

"Hell, I don't see how that's possible," Andrew said, scowling. "I don't even know where I'm going to be next week—probably living on the beach, eating out of dumpsters."

"Why not just try to adjust to where you are and quit painting yourself into corners with pessimistic projections?"

"Right now it's all I can do to adjust to painting corners, period!" He rubbed his shoulders and groaned in overdramatic agony.

"You'd be surprised, Morgan, at what you're actually accomplishing by doing the work you're doing, and doing it well. The application of your energies to such a task can create a subtle understanding between you and the physical medium in which you live. It can offer you and it the opportunity to develop mutual respect. Then, when you need something, you're more likely to be graced by materiality than you would be if you hadn't paid it a little 'homage' now and again, so to speak. The use of the body in working with material things creates a type of conduit between you and them. To put it simply, physical actions are a great means of manifestation.

" Space-Time Principle Number 60:

Your body is a generator.
Use it for something other than
just an object to hang clothes on."

"I'll try to remember that tomorrow when I start running out of steam and have paint splattering in my eyes."

"You seemed to do okay today, and I'm sure tomorrow will be a little easier," she reassured him. "Maybe you can spend the time thinking out the lesson plan for your new student."

Andrew had temporarily forgotten about his promise to Sam, and now could feel a knot developing in his stomach. Could he really pull it off? Could he really teach this kid enough to help him out in just five days? How could he possibly concentrate on Sam's problems when he had problems of his own?

Reading his mind again, We-Be said:

" Space-Time Principle Number 124:

Sometimes your problems have
a way of solving themselves
when you redirect your energy and
focus it in other directions."

"What's that supposed to mean?"

"Why not wait and see? My shift's almost over; I gotta split. Besides, it's almost time for you to be awakened by your partner, the human alarm clock, so you can go pull your own shift."

She quickly gathered up her things as Andrew stood there and watched her, trying to think of anything else he needed to ask. Then, just as he formed a question in his head, she stepped through one of the doors and vanished into the other side.

Chapter Twenty

Sam
I Am

"Other side of what?" Trevor asked, shaking Andrew and looking at him with amusement as he rousted him from bed.

Damn! He had been talking out loud to We-Be in his sleep again. If this kept up, Trevor was going to think he was crazy. Andrew shrugged his shoulders to dismiss his cabinmate's question and reached over to turn the alarm clock off before it rang. As usual, the old man had beaten the clock.

Andrew was quieter than normal during breakfast and for the first few hours on the job. He and Trevor seemed to have switched places, for Trevor wasn't his usual laid-back self. He was working at double-speed—undoubtedly because he would be leaving the next day and wanted to finish everything he was there to do.

At lunch time Trevor wandered off to find Charlie, and Andrew grabbed a sandwich and headed for his shaded lunch spot that he had staked out the day before. Once again, Dagny joined him, plopping down next to him on the ground; this time minus the kids.

He was beginning to feel a little more comfortable around her but still had to force himself not to fidget nervously. "So, where are your troops?"

"Eating. They don't need me to do that." She cocked her head and studied him with her sparkling almond eyes.

Andrew hoped his face wasn't turning red again, and blurted out the first thing that came into his mind to try to shift her attention. "I've never heard the name Dagny before. Does it have some special significance?"

"Oh, that's a long story! You sure you're up for that?"

"Well, I've got about thirty minutes. That long enough?"

"For a synopsis, maybe!" She laughed her throaty laugh and threw her ponytail to one side.

"You see, my mother was a hardcore Ayn Rand freak. Ever hear of a novel called *Atlas Shrugged*?"

Andrew looked at her blankly and shook his head. "I don't read much fiction."

"Well, ol' Ayn wrote it, and my mother read it when she was pregnant with me. A whole philosophy built up around Rand's books—especially that one—in the fifties and sixties. Anyway, the heroine in *Atlas Shrugged* was named Dagny. Weird name, huh?"

Andrew wasn't sure how to respond to her question and just smiled uncomfortably.

"Dagny, like many of Rand's characters, was out to save the world—or at least part of it—from mediocrity," she continued, hugging her knees to her chest. "She tied up with a guy named John Galt, who dropped out of society and formed a hidden community of people who strove for excellence. The world around them was going to pot because of greed, ineptness and laziness, and this small band of high achievers couldn't deal with it anymore. They figured the outside world would eventually collapse, so they prepared themselves by developing the qualities and abilities that they foresaw would be sorely needed to rebuild a shattered world."

"Seems like a pretty neat character to be named after."

Dagny smiled at Andrew appreciatively. "Yeah, but the trouble with the Randian philosophy is that it comes off as being rather Darwinian; you know: survival of the fittest. It doesn't have much good to say about the weaker of our species. Those who can, do; those who can't, die." She shook her head sadly. "And somewhere along the line I realized that there's a whole side of humanity that just doesn't fit comfortably into ol' Ayn's capitalistic scheme of the way things should be. I admire her ability to inspire people to reach for excellence, but people have to be given a little help to do that sometimes."

"And that's what you try to do with these kids?"

"You betcha. Each and every one of them can excel at something. They just have to figure out what."

"Like Strings and his musical abilities?"

"And Lord Byron and his writing, too. But those two were easy; they've already pretty well discovered the talents they possess all by themselves. All they need is a little nudge to push them in the right direction. A kid like our belligerent Sam, now, that's a real challenge."

Andrew thought about the secret he shared with Sam and his promise to him. He felt a luscious warmth inside that he had never felt before, and realized that Dagny must feel it all the time. "So, it must be quite a rush when you can look at some kid and know that you single-handedly saved him from self-destruction and directed him down the path of self-fulfillment instead."

"Absolutely! It's about the best high I can think of; and pretty addictive too—this do-gooder stuff. Everyone always thinks working a job like mine is some sort of great sacrifice, a miserable task that only some masochistic martyr would take on. But, in my case anyway, they couldn't be further from the truth. Certainly you must identify with what I'm saying to some degree; after all, you've worked with kids, too."

Andrew looked at her in total bewilderment. What in God's name was she talking about?

"But, then again, Trevor did say the little boy you took care of was a royal monster. It's a real drag when you don't get anywhere with them, huh? I have to hand it to you though; I don't think I could handle being a watch dog for some rich brat."

Andrew suddenly understood what was happening. Trevor had assumed that he was a professional "Uncle Charlie" by trade and must have told Dagny this. Quickly, he tried to cover his brief confusion so as to maintain her illusion of who he was. "I can say one thing for sure: after working for the Van Morrises, I don't think I can ever face a kid under twelve again. God, what a nightmare!"

Andrew swallowed hard and felt his fingernails digging into the palms of his hands. He hadn't really lied . . . more like just allowed her to believe in Trevor's false assumption. He had to admit, he liked the idea of her thinking the two of them had something in common. But he was uncomfortable and afraid she would ask more questions, and so quickly switched back to the original subject.

"So, in a sense I guess you're living up to your name—believing in excellence like the fictional Dagny, I mean."

"I suppose you could say that, but I'm far from being your typical Randian."

"Well, maybe I should read one of her books."

"I think there's a copy of *Atlas Shrugged* in the book room."

Will coincidences never cease? Andrew wondered to himself. He now had his excuse to hunt up some books for his sessions with Sam, without having to explain to anyone what he was up to.

"Well, it's time to round up my kids and practice what I preach." Dagny stood up and stretched her legs.

"Catch you later," Andrew said as nonchalantly as he could, watching her walk gracefully back to the dining room.

His mind was full of thoughts about this delightfully odd young woman as he walked back to join Trevor, who was already busy at work.

"Am I late?"

"No, mon, I am early. I need ta finish this so I can leave in the mornin'."

Once again, they worked in silence. Andrew was beginning to feel more and more like a real painter as the hours slipped by. And he was even learning to like what he was doing: letting his mind play while his body worked.

Before he knew it, he heard Trevor say: "Okay, Ondrew. That's it. Let's pack it up."

Andrew was relieved. He had been afraid that they would end up working later than usual and screw up his plans to hunt down books for his tutoring session with Sam.

As he helped Trevor put away all the paint supplies, the old Jamaican regained his normal personality and started conversing again. He teased Andrew about Dagny for a couple of minutes and then kidded him again about talking in his sleep. "I'll probably catch ya at it again tonight, since I won't be in until late, and I'm sure ya will already be asleep and busy in ya dreams. Charlie and I are goin' out on the town ta talk about old times—even though there isn't much of a town ta go out on!" His velvety laughter bounced off the walls of the empty room.

This was great news to Andrew. He had been a little concerned about where Sam's first lesson would take place, especially since he promised that the boy's inability to read would be kept between themselves with no prying eyes. Now he and Sam could spend the evening studying in the privacy of Andrew's cabin. After leaving Trevor, he wandered into the book room and rummaged through the shelves, looking for the most elementary books he could find. He gathered up four of them, borrowed a notebook and a couple of pens from the desk, and headed to his quarters to shower and change clothes for dinner.

Now his attention was singularly targeted on the task of teaching the boy. He recalled techniques he himself had been taught as a child, and his mind raced with ideas and plans of attack. He would eat as quickly as he could so as to slip off and meet his student at the cabin as planned. Andrew wanted to be sure to be there before Sam to make sure the boy didn't think he had been stood up.

Luckily, Dagny wasn't there yet, for the last thing he needed tonight was a distraction. He gulped down his food, knowing that she would undoubtedly walk in at any minute. He spied Sam across the hall, sitting off by himself, detached from the camaraderie that seemed to be developing among the other boys. Sam looked directly at him with a sober, unreadable expression, and Andrew smiled and nodded to assure him their game plan was still on.

As he got up to leave, he noticed Trevor and Charlie looking at him in a curious manner, talking softly between themselves. It made him uncomfortable, wondering what they were saying, but he shrugged it off and made his attention return to his evening's agenda.

His stomach was doing flip-flops as he paced back and forth on the porch, waiting for Sam to appear. What if he failed and let this kid down? How would he ever live with himself? How much could be accomplished in just five evenings? If there really was such a thing as magic, Andrew mused, he would certainly need it now.

"Looks to me like you're expecting somebody. Thought we were gonna keep a low profile!"

Andrew jumped at the voice that seemed to come from nowhere. "Sam?"

"You're expecting someone else, maybe?" The bushes beside the porch rustled, giving away his whereabouts.

"Well, let's go inside and hit the books, okay?" Andrew held his voice steady, trying not to let any of his self-doubt show. He walked to the door and held it open invitingly. Sam slipped out of the bushes, up the steps, and through the door almost faster than the eye could see.

"Don't happen to have any smokes on you, do you?" Sam sat down gingerly on the foot of Trevor's bed.

"Sorry, that's one habit I never developed." Too bad We-Be wasn't around, Andrew thought; Sam could bum one from her.

"Okay, I got some books. I think the best thing to do is dive right in." He picked out the most basic of the books—*Green Eggs and Ham*, a Dr. Seuss story—and sat down next to Sam on the bed. He was a little worried that the boy would be insulted by the childish subject matter, but Sam showed no signs of it. To the contrary, he seemed pleased that the book's main character was named Sam. Andrew was relieved to discover that his student already knew the alphabet and recognized a few simple words from sight memory. As they read the book out loud, Andrew referred back to the copy of the alphabet he had printed on the pad, phonetically sounding out each letter and stating any rules that applied. Sam dropped into an intense concentration, absorbing everything Andrew threw at him with amazing speed. They kept at it for hours, not even stopping for a break. Finally, Andrew looked at the clock, surprised that it was well past midnight and Sam's curfew.

As he said goodnight to Sam at the door, he was impressed by the boy's demeanor. His standing smart-aleck attitude was replaced by an aura of seriousness and deep commitment. Andrew offered him the book they had used that evening, not expecting him to take it. But Sam surprised Andrew by eagerly accepting it and stuffing it inside his shirt. This was good: if Sam spent time during the day brushing up on their studies of the previous night, his learning would be accelerated.

Thoughts of Sam and their project drifted gently through Andrew's mind as he curled up in bed. Once again he felt a warm, glowing feeling inside and fell quickly into a deep, uneventful sleep.

Chapter Twenty-One

Pride
&
Potholes

The first order of business for the day was trailing after Trevor as the old man instructed Andrew on all the tasks he was to complete for the rest of the week. Trevor's truck was already loaded with his gear, and he was eager to get on the road. Andrew found it humorous that his ex-cabinmate looked a little hung over, and couldn't resist jabbing at him about it.

"Looks like you had a slight run-in with some pretty mean 'spirits' last night, huh?"

"Don't ya know it, mon! I have this great weakness for Margaritas, ya see. But I rationalize my fondness for them by imaginin' they help ta preserve this old bag of bones." He laughed and then moaned, grabbing his head.

Andrew had prepared for this moment ahead of time. Pulling a discarded aftershave bottle filled with water from his jacket pocket, he handed it to Trevor.

"What's this?"

"This be holy water, mon," Andrew said in his best Jamaican dialect, "ta ward off The Evil One. I owe ya this much for savin' me from his murderous clutches."

In his frazzled state of mind, Trevor couldn't figure out for a second if Andrew was kidding or not, but then realized his friend was retaliating for the Fire Spirit routine he had pulled. He played along though, peering into the bottle curiously.

"And what is it I'm supposed ta do with this holy water?"

"Well, you throw it on The Evil One, of course," Andrew answered, falling back into his natural accent. "And then you step back and watch him sizzle and pop!"

Trevor's rich laugh was a little weaker than usual, and once again he grabbed his head.

"What's the matter Trev, ol' pal; can't hold your liquor?" Charlie walked up behind them and playfully threw his arms around both of their shoulders.

The Jamaican scowled at his drinking buddy. "And what are ya so cheerful about, hmm? Ya drank two ta my every one. I'm surprised ta even see ya up and about!"

"That's because I know the antidote to tying one on: a big glass of water and two aspirin before turning in! How's that for heap big magic?"

Andrew walked a short distance away and pretended to be absorbed in watching the kids walking to the dining hall in order to give the two old friends a couple of minutes to say their good-byes. Then waving, he watched the rusty old beater as it choked and sputtered its way down the driveway.

Even though he had known Trevor less than a week, he would miss him. With his departure, Andrew could feel the worries and fears of his own impending last day on the job surfacing. What in the hell was he going to do when he left here?

He walked down to the dining room with Charlie, trying to drive the worry-thoughts from his head. He didn't want to "worry for" anything ever again, and so decided to distract himself by starting a conversation.

"How come there isn't a fence around this place?"

"Why would we want a fence?" Charlie raised his eyebrows as though genuinely surprised by Andrew's question.

"Well, to keep the kids from taking off."

"I can't say as I've ever met a boy who couldn't climb a fence."

"Maybe just as a psychological intimidation or something?" Andrew was starting to feel like an idiot for asking the question in the first place.

"Lemme tell ya, Andy, about an old dog I once had." Charlie slowed his pace as his concentration shifted to the story he was about to tell. "I lived in the city with that old dog and kept her in a fenced yard. Well, every chance she got she'd take off. She'd sail right over that fence, because she was one big, long-legged mutt. So, I bought a taller fence to put a crimp in her style. But that didn't stop her. She started digging holes and going right under it. That old dog almost drove me crazy."

"So what happened?"

"I moved to the country where there wasn't a fence. She prowled around for a week or so, checking out the neighboring land, but before too long, she laid down on the porch and stayed there, happy as could be, till the day she died. See what I'm getting at?"

Andrew did, but Charlie was on a roll and stayed on the subject of fences. "Only other use for a fence I can think of is to keep people out. But then again, that's the surest way there is to invite someone in to cause trouble. Makes him wonder what it is that's so important that you have to protect it or hide it from him. And you have to admit, both sides of a fence are the same. It's as easy to climb in from the outside as it is to climb out from the inside." Smiling to himself, Andrew realized he would never look at fences in quite the same way again. Charlie whistled a catchy little tune, seemingly without a care in the world, and picked up his pace again in the direction of breakfast.

They were late. Almost everyone had already finished and gone, except for a few hangers-out. Lord Byron and Strings were sitting at a back table, Strings strumming away while Byron looked on like an attentive mentor. Andrew guessed they were working the kinks out of their first joint project. He could hear String's voice, warm and pleasantly rough, carrying the lyrics softly across the room:

Anyone who touches
the wings of a butterfly
has surely never flown himself.
Angels fly, so why can't I?
Because you touched
the wings of a butterfly
You must always be a passerby.

Pretty deep, Andrew thought, the memory flitting through his head of a butterfly he had, as a child, caught and fatally injured by merely touching its wings. The accompanying tune really seemed to capture the feeling of a wounded angelic creature, too. Andrew made a bet with himself: If these two kept it up, they were going places.

"Good, huh?" Charlie sat down next to him with a heaping plate of eggs and potatoes, beaming in the direction of the song-writing duo.

"Yep. I'd say they're a winning team, all right. Ever catch a butterfly?"

"Sure! Everybody has." He stuffed a forkful of eggs in his mouth, eyes still glued on the two boys. "But, the thing is, most of us only do it once and then we learn. It isn't a real violation if you kill something out of ignorance, you know."

Andrew looked at Charlie curiously, thinking that his last sentence sounded suspiciously like a Space-Time Principle. But, he was being silly of course; first he had suspected Trevor of having We-Be connections and now he was wondering about Charlie.

"Where do two kids from such lousy backgrounds get such talent?" Andrew asked, not really expecting an answer.

"Funny thing . . . so many talented people come from bad home situations or the wrong side of the tracks," Charlie replied, not missing a beat. "I think hardship sometimes breeds a strong personality and therefore an exceptional brand of creativity; that's all I can figure out. They have to turn inward and entertain themselves more than some kid from a *Father-Knows-Best* family structure. Maybe total contentment deprives one of challenge and ends up breeding mediocrity." He wiped his mouth on his napkin and then added with a chuckle, "Makes sense when I hear myself say it, anyway."

Andrew wanted to say that he himself was living proof that there were holes in Charlie's theory, or at least that it wasn't an iron-clad rule. But then, he reminded himself, he hadn't been lucky enough at age sixteen to have a Dagny pulling for him and goading him to discover his true abilities. Plus, if his suspicions about Strings being his "other self" were right, maybe the boy was expressing enough talent for the both of them.

He finished eating in silence, listening to Strings and Lord Byron practicing their song. Then, as Andrew stood up to excuse himself, Charlie said: "By the way, here's a list of boys who signed up for extra chores to earn some spending money. Pick one of 'em to help you the rest of the week." He handed Andrew a crumbled piece of yellow lined paper with about twenty names scrawled on it.

Andrew's eyes raced down the list, looking for String's name. He had been hoping to spend some time with the boy, and here was his opportunity. But, his name wasn't there—probably too busy making music, Andrew guessed. Surprisingly enough, though, Sam's name was on the list; and he realized that he would have to pick him to boost the boy's confidence in himself and their relationship. Besides, the two of them could utilize the additional time to work on their reading project, if just during breaks.

Charlie's face didn't register any surprise when Andrew indicated his choice, although Andrew could swear he detected a slight knowing smile touch the corners of his boss's lips. "I'll round Sam up and send him out to find you," Charlie said briskly, also getting up to leave.

Andrew headed for the storage room to gather up the tools and equipment he would need. He was done with painting. For the next three days he would be making repairs on the long driveway: filling potholes and ruts with a shovel. It would be backbreaking work, but at least he couldn't screw it up. It was just the kind of job he would be comfortable with now that Trevor was gone.

As he lugged out the wheelbarrow and puzzled over which kind of shovel was suitable for the job, he spied Sam walking across the yard toward him. The boy joined him and wordlessly grabbed two shovels without having to ponder over which one did what, and dropped them into the wheelbarrow. Then, waiting for Andrew to lead the way, Sam maneuvered the wheelbarrow easily down the drive to their starting place.

"Looks like you know what you're doing!" Andrew commented as he watched Sam pick up a shovel and dig right in.

"Sure I do. I told you I was raised by two people who made their living—such as it was—out of the dirt."

"I take it it's not exactly what you want to do the rest of your life."

"Not hardly!"

"Any ideas about what you do want to do?"

"Well, it probably sounds dumb, but what I really want to be is a body man."

"You mean like a weight lifter?"

Sam laughed—the first real laughter he had heard from the boy. "No, man, like cars, you know? Take a dented-up body and make it as smooth and pretty as the day it came out of the factory." Sam frowned and planted his shovel deep into the sand at the side of the drive. "I had a job once, learning to do that, but somehow somebody found out I was a runaway and I had to disappear fast." What a sad case this kid was! Andrew couldn't understand how working on cars could be Sam's dream, for it sounded like the worst sort of drudgery to him. To each his own, he thought, and listened politely as the boy, seeming to come alive, rambled on and on for the next hour about car bodies and chrome and paint. At least, Andrew consoled himself, if he failed to teach the boy to be completely literate, it shouldn't wreck the kid's dream. In fact, he realized he could use Sam's aspirations to be just a "body man" as a rationalization for not working so hard to teach the boy to read. But he doggedly stayed with the program as the week progressed, doing book work with Sam at night and playing spelling-bee games with him while they worked during the day. First, Andrew would spell words and Sam would try to figure out what they were, then Andrew would give Sam a word and let him try to spell it. He was astounded at how fast his student was learning.

On Saturday, he and Sam finished the driveway repairs just as the sun was setting behind the pine ridge. His muscles ached only slightly now; he felt stronger and more agile than he had the week before. Andrew had to admit to himself that after his stay at Last Chance Ranch he was likely to end up being in the best shape of his life. Even now his mind seemed clearer and his senses keener than ever. As he stood there in the middle of the driveway with Sam, viewing their handiwork, he caught himself feeling something he had rarely felt before: a sense of real accomplishment.

"Feels good, huh?" Sam looked at Andrew and grinned, brushing his hair away from his perspiring brow.

Andrew wondered if the boy had read his mind. "Yeah, I was just thinking how work doesn't always have to be a dirty word."

"Wow! Pretty deep! But I can relate, man. It's fun to see the finished product. You shoulda been around when I helped restore a '57 Chevy back to cherry. Now that was a real high!"

Andrew shook his head and laughed good-naturedly as they loaded the tools in the wheelbarrow and carted them off to the shed. He realized he was beginning to understand how Sam could find fulfillment in seemingly mundane work. In fact, the more he thought about it, the more he wished he could keep his job here indefinitely. It may not afford him his stacked-to-the-ceiling stereo system or his shiny new Porsche, but it did guarantee him three square meals a day, the opportunity to feel good about himself, and a chance to get to know a cute psychologist. And there were other things—like Charlie. Andrew was becoming sincerely fond of him, and was actually beginning to think of him as the type of father he wished he'd had. And, from the opposite end, he had developed some pretty strong paternal feelings for his sidekick Sam during the days they had shoveled dirt together.

He had to do something fast, because as of Monday—just two days away—his stint as a temporary helper would be over. He had to figure out a way to persuade Charlie that he could be a permanent asset to Last Chance Ranch. But how?

Andrew's mind searched desperately for a solution as he ate dinner alone and returned to his cabin to meet Sam for the nightly tutorial. Later, after seeing Sam off and preparing for bed, his thoughts kept returning to the conversation he had had with Dagny regarding his supposed experience as a professional nanny. Obviously, the actual experience he had had as Holden's keeper wasn't worthy of one line on a résumé. If he decided to play Dagny's misconception to the hilt, he would end up telling real lies; not just letting a false assumption ride. Somehow, the thought of lying to Charlie made him feel uncomfortable and guilty as hell. But . . . it might just work. He couldn't figure out what was the best course of action to take. Maybe he should simply trust the Universe and see where it would lead him. But, then again, hadn't he trusted it a million times before, only to be led astray? In the end, he decided to throw his fate into the arms of the Universe, at least for the night, and sleep on it.

Chapter Twenty-Two

Present Perplexities
&
Future Memories

Actually Andrew felt very peaceful as he lay there, listening to the frogs and crickets outside his window. He could feel his body relaxing completely as he let go of his worries, every muscle succumbing to oncoming slumber.

And yet, his mind had never been more alert. With amazement, he realized he could hear himself snoring and breathing the deep rhythmical breathing of sleep. It was a curious paradox: his body was unconscious yet his mind wasn't.

Suddenly, there was a brilliant flash of light all around him, driving right through his closed eyelids. It hit him with full force, as if he had been struck by a painless bolt of lightning. Andrew could feel himself gasping in surprise, yet his physical form continued to sleep right through it. Then, as the light subsided, a strange sensation began to creep through his immobilized body, gradually building in intensity. The feeling was wonderful—like miniature orgasms being triggered simultaneously in every one of his cells. The sensation continued to expand, magnifying and blending into an overall feeling of ultimate ecstasy.

But it was too much to handle; it felt too good and was too intense. Finally, Andrew struggled against it, trying to break from its pleasurable but unbearable hold. Suddenly, like a rubber band snapping back on itself, he could feel himself hurtling out of his body, as if there were a part of his consciousness with a built-in safety mechanism that knew exactly what to do in such a situation. Then he planed out and gracefully glided away.

Andrew turned around to look back at his sleeping form, but for some reason it wasn't visible any longer. Instead, everywhere he looked, in any direction, all he could see was infinite blackness. As he peered into it, an endless assortment of stars, galaxies, and nebulae began to slowly appear, becoming three-dimensional before his very eyes. It was almost as if their dazzling, brilliant forms were bleeding through some rich, velvety cosmic tapestry. The awesome spectacle before him was surpassed only by the overwhelming feeling of intelligence and benevolent power now emanating from what only a second or two earlier had seemed to be cold and empty. Andrew knew this was the force that had jolted him out of his body in the first place, but now, disconnected from it, he felt a different sensation, a profound feeling of security in the presence of this awesome power source.

He hung there, suspended in mid-air, eyes wide with wonder. In the midst of the incredible cosmic dance before him, a solitary point of fiery light flashed by him and then seemed to explode behind his back. As he swung around to look at it, he heard a familiar voice.

"You've always wanted to plug in to the Universe, Morgan. How'd it feel?"

"Pretty heavy-duty. I had to unplug myself before I blew a fuse. It's incredible though, to just observe it. Is this really 'The Universe?'"

"As you're able to perceive it, Morgan." The stellar backdrop complemented her loose, flaming red hair, though her jeans and T-shirt were rather incongruous with this strange setting.

"So," she said, gazing at him with wide, innocent eyes, "I take it the first topic of the evening is honesty, huh?"

Andrew felt his face redden as he realized We-Be was aware of his latest quandary.

"Wanna talk about it?"

"You talk, I'll listen," he said, avoiding her eyes by focusing on a particularly glamorous spiral galaxy behind her.

"Suits me!" She seemed to be standing firmly on something that wasn't there. Looking down at his own feet, he realized he was doing the same thing: standing on solid nothingness.

"For starters, Morgan, don't ever allow someone else to define honesty for you; and, of course, that means even me! You decide what's right and what's wrong, and what's to be told and what's to be withheld."

"But doesn't honesty mean always telling the truth?"

"What if you think that the truth will be harmful to another person, maybe even yourself? Don't you feel the impulse to withhold it?"

"Well, yeah, but how do I know when honesty will hurt someone or help him?" Andrew scrunched up his forehead in honest perplexity.

"I guess you have to fall back on your integrity; for the bottom line, Morgan, is that that is the only true guideline you have. Some people insist that the only way to maintain integrity is by always telling the truth. But what if your integrity dictates not hurting another? If that's the case, then somewhere along the line you may have to fabricate a lie or withhold the truth to keep your integrity.

" Space-Time Principle Number 95:

Sometimes stretching or omitting the truth is more honorable than being honest. It is important, however, to make sure your motives are honorable.

"You need to question yourself when you avoid the truth, and be careful that you're not just avoiding conflict or confrontation. Make sure you're not using sparing someone's feelings as an excuse for not asserting yourself. In certain instances, perhaps more emphasis should be placed on feelings, on striving to be kind. Often, that's what people need more than anything—more than brute honesty."

Some sort of glowing dustlike substance began forming around We-Be, and Andrew was so entranced by the sight that he had to force himself back to their conversation.

"This is all great stuff, but to be totally honest with you, I just don't think it really applies to my immediate situation. I can't figure out whether to build on Dagny's misconception of my past nanny experience or to straighten it out and tell the truth."

"Well, are you prepared to deal with any repercussions that may result if you lie and the truth eventually surfaces anyway? By withholding the truth or fabricating a falsehood, you're accepting responsibility for any bruised feelings or problems that may result. And, in the long run, there's the possibility that your decision may end up working against you and tearing away at not only others' respect for you but also your own integrity."

"Now I'm really confused," he said burying his face in his hands.

"Quit trying to pull your face off!" We-Be laughed at his obvious frustration. "Look, Morgan, just do what feels right at the time. Your definition of honesty can alter itself to give you freedom of choice in dealing with yourself and others. Be flexible and don't get caught up in rigid patterns of right and wrong. Anytime you find yourself about to tell a lie or to hold back the truth, step back for a second and ask yourself why. Make sure it's for a worthy reason and not just an excuse to avoid facing reality."

"Reality?" Andrew giggled half hysterically. "I'm not exactly sure what that is anymore."

"I know." We-Be looked at him sympathetically. "I've really messed with your head these past few weeks, haven't I?"

He laughed again and said jokingly, "You, mess with my head? Never!"

"Well," she said defensively, "it has been for your own good, you know! And besides, you asked for it, remember?"

Andrew glared at her with one eye closed for a dramatic effect.

"It may make you feel better to know that I'm moving on. I won't be popping into your life to haunt and harass you anymore."

A wave of shock ran through Andrew's "body." "What? What do you mean?"

"I mean I'm splitting, booking up, exiting stage left."

"But why?" Andrew felt panicked and suddenly realized just how much she had grown on him.

Reading his mind again for the umpteenth time, she said: "I haven't grown on you, Morgan, I've grown through you. And now I'm off to discover other parts and pieces of myself. I think you're well on your way to discovering who Andrew Morgan is; and after that you'll discover more, too. You don't need me anymore. Besides, I don't think you'll be running into as much trouble as you used to, and so I'd be bored to death hanging around waiting to bail you out."

"Does that mean I'll never see you again?"

"Who knows? I have no idea from one minute to the next where I'm going or where I'll end up!"

"But I want you to stay here!"

"How do you know I was ever really here in the first place? Perhaps I have yet to appear. And, for that matter, who am 'I,' anyway?"

"You're We-Be, of course."

"I never told you my name was We-Be. That's a label you put on me. All I ever said was, 'I am, you are, and we be.'"

"Don't think I haven't figured out what you meant by that!" Andrew said, still stubbornly attempting to not let her get the best of him. "I've been playing around with the idea for a while now that you're my Higher Self. That's who you are, right?" Andrew beamed at her, proud of his deduction.

"Me? Your Higher Self? That's a hoot!" Reaching into her pocket, she pulled out a cigarette and lit it, its orange point blending into the starry background. "There's no such thing, Morgan."

"No such thing? Everyone has a Higher Self!"

"Oh, I see. So I guess that makes you my Lower Self then, doesn't it?"

Andrew frowned in confusion. He didn't like the sound of that at all.

We-Be grinned at him, having known what his reaction to her words would be. "This is one of the last important points I want to make. I don't want you to remember me as some 'higher'—if slightly weird—being, floating around in the ethers, whispering words of wisdom in your ear.

" Space-Time Principle Number 215:

When striving to understand
the relationship between selfhood
and any other- 'hood',
resist thinking vertically
and try to think horizontally.

"There may be other selves that are wiser than you, or older than you, or bigger than you, but not better than you—and certainly not higher. If you're thinking horizontally, then you're never looking down at anyone or up at him either—just straight in the eye."

"I'm lost. Why don't you just come right out and tell me who you really are—in terms I can understand?"

She looked at him mischievously and then said: "Watch closely, Morgan. This is the 'me' that you call 'We-Be'." He stared at her uncomprehendingly.

She snapped her fingers loudly and her image quickly shrunk to the point of light she often used when arriving or departing. Her voice echoed out of nowhere, "Now I'm without form, only a bright speck to designate my presence."

The light zipped around his head a couple of times and then, responding to another loud snap, instantly transformed into a radiant mass of multicolored something or other—Andrew had no idea what. "Now I'm something you have yet to comprehend." As she spoke, the mass pulsated in accord with her voice. Rubbing his eyes that watered from the brilliance of her strange new form, he heard the snap again and looked up.

"And now I'm something you're very familiar with." He stepped back, blinking in disbelief. What he saw now was a perfect replica of himself, right down to the fading scar on his forehead. He stood there smiling idiotically at himself, and his Self smiled back.

"You're me?"

"Futuristically speaking, I guess you could say that—if you want to stretch things a little. I am what you will be, more or less."

"So, you're a future me?"

"Well, sort of."

Andrew plopped down, too dumbfounded to question what he was sitting on. She snapped her fingers one more time and became the We-Be he had become accustomed to. His mind raced—something wasn't jiving here. Then he remembered.

"Wait a minute! I thought you said there were no such things as past or future selves—only simultaneous selves! So, how can you be my future self?"

We-Be grinned largely. She felt tremendously proud of him at this minute in non-time. "It all depends on where you're standing, Morgan. In physical reality you're governed by space and time. Things are solid and finite. When you're out of it—as you are now—the same rules don't apply. Case in point: What are you sitting on right now?"

Andrew looked down and saw nothing but an endless stretch of stars. For a moment he became disoriented and couldn't remember which way was up—but then, what was "up?"

"In physical reality there's always an up and down, a left and right, a higher and lower. But in my reality, those terms are irrelevant. And the same goes for 'time.'"

"I don't understand how that can be. There's always a yesterday and a tomorrow."

"Ahh, but which one comes first? Which one affects the other most strongly? Maybe the present is just a point of intersection between the past and the future. Maybe if the past and future didn't exist simultaneously, pushing against one another, there would be no present. You know, if you stopped and thought about it right now, I bet you could remember a future memory as clearly as you can remember a past one! But then again, that future memory can be altered by a past or present event, just as a past memory can be altered by a present or future one."

Andrew was completely baffled, his mind a jumble of fantastic concepts that he would need time to sort out and comprehend. Funny, he thought, that he needed time to sort out "time."

"So, will you miss me a little bit?" We-Be asked in a teasing voice, abruptly changing the subject.

Andrew pulled himself out of his reverie and looked at her seriously, ignoring her flippant tone. "Just a little," he managed to say, and he turned his head to the side so that she couldn't see the tears welling up in his eyes.

"You'll be fine. Just remember to keep your mysticism practical and to practice the principles I've given you. Play around with them until they fit the holes in your head!"

He could hear her musical laughter as he inconspicuously wiped away the tears and turned around to smile at her smart-aleck comment. Then, through clenched teeth he said, "I want you to know that I'm actually glad now that you materialized yourself in the back seat of my car." Andrew could feel his face turning red. "I realize that most people aren't lucky enough to have a 'We-Be' pop into their lives to give them weird wisdoms and help point them in the right direction."

"No, but they might have a Morgan!"

Her words caught him off-guard, and he fell silent to consider them.

She watched him quietly for a minute or two, her expression showing that she really thought he would be okay from here on out—maybe with a few rough spots to smooth out along the way.

Then, walking over to him, she leaned over and put her hand on his shoulder. "It's been great fun, Andy. Stay out of trouble, huh?"

She playfully messed up his hair and once again transformed herself in to the firefly-like pinpoint of light. He stuttered, trying to think of something to say to hold her there, but she was already spinning in orbit around him, leaving trails of light that made it look as though he were encased in an etheric cocoon.

As she finally screamed off into the starry distance, something suddenly occurred to him and he called after her: "Hey! You called me 'Andy'!" But this time, she didn't return for an encore.

He looked around him overwhelmed with emotion and by the cosmic light-show that was her departure. He brooded over the things she had said and thought about the future memories she had told him he could have if he wanted to. He strained his mind, trying to see a time in the future when he would see We-Be again, but got nothing.

Andrew stood up, suddenly not interested at all in the stellar scene around him. He was beginning to feel rejected and abandoned, and yet knew he was being silly. He had his own life, and didn't need some crazy she-demon from Hell telling him what to do. He had more important things to worry about—like Sam and his reading lessons. He was worried sick that the boy would fail at his first day of school, and therefore fail in life, period.

His mind was still reeling, and he sat down again on solid space to clear his head. But, all of a sudden, he realized how ridiculous he was being. Why on Earth should he be worrying? He distinctly remembered Sam getting off the bus, a jubilant smile plastered on his usually taciturn face. He clearly recalled the boy proudly reporting to him the success of the day—how he had read out loud in class and no one had snickered or made smart comments. In fact, the girl sitting next to him had sneaked looks at him through the rest of the class. Everyone had treated him like a regular guy.

What? What was he thinking? Sam hadn't even gone to school yet; how could he be recalling such an event? But, he didn't have time to ponder it, for with a sudden loud "snap!" out of nowhere, he found himself back in his bunk, awakening to the sound of the alarm clock.

Chapter Twenty-Three

A Man with Principles

As Andrew picked at his breakfast, he tried to make his mounting feelings of apprehension about having to leave Last Chance Ranch disappear. He scanned the crowded room for Charlie. It was better to face it head-on, first thing this morning, and get it over with. Doomsday was just a day away.

We-Be was gone, maybe for good. It hadn't really sunk in yet, but he was already feeling depressed. He tried to keep his mind on his immediate problem of securing a job and a place to live, while at the same time remembering to not worry things into reality. He had to find Charlie fast before he drove himself nuts.

"Mornin', Andy." Andrew nearly choked on his coffee as Charlie came up behind him and greeted him with the usual slap on the back.

"Mornin' yourself! I was looking for you."

"Yeah? Well I was looking for you, too. Need to talk to you about a couple of things and pay you your wages." Charlie pulled out a chair and sat down next to Andrew, handing him a wad of bills.

Andrew's chest pounded wildly. Was Charlie going to dismiss him before he even had the chance to plead his case? He took the money without counting it, trying to appear composed. "Okay, what's up?"

"Your stint here is up tomorrow, right?"

"Guess so." Andrew swallowed hard.

"How'd you like to stay on awhile, help me out around here?"

Andrew's heart leaped into his throat; he couldn't believe how easy this was turning out to be. "Uh . . . sure! In fact, that's what I wanted to talk to you about. You think there are enough chores around here to keep me busy?"

"Well, maybe not enough chores, but there are plenty of other things you could do around this place. I was thinking about making you a combination bunkhouse counselor, kid fetcher, and all-round good guy."

Andrew's spirits soared, then immediately fell again. He realized that he was back to the subject he had been dreading facing: whether to be honest about his experience with kids. It was obvious Charlie assumed he was more qualified than he really was. He made his decision on the spot, without even thinking about it.

"Listen, Charlie, I think there's something I need to clear up here. I know Trevor thought I had real experience working with kids, but he was mistaken. The job that I met him on was the first one I ever had that entailed being responsible for a kid. And I blew it, big time." Andrew looked down morosely at his untouched plate of food, waiting for Charlie to withdraw the offer.

"That isn't why I'm offering you the job! I couldn't care less about your past experience. What interests me is what I've seen you do around here—like spending all your spare time tutoring Sam. Hell, boy, you need to get paid to do stuff like that!" Charlie looked at him with dancing eyes, perfectly aware that Andrew had thought his secret sessions with Sam were just that—a secret.

Andrew stared at Charlie in amazement. "How did you know about that?"

"There isn't much that goes on around here that I don't know about—'specially when Trevor's here. He sees and hears everything—even stuff that isn't really there!" He leaned back in his chair and laughed, his fondness for Trevor showing in his expression. "Pretty ridiculous to think you could have a wrestling match and a late-night counseling session right outside Trevor's window and not have that old wizard know about it!"

Andrew was speechless. He thought he had been so slick, keeping his agreement with Sam under wraps. "You won't say anything to Sam—"

"Of course not! Nobody knows but Trevor and me; not even Dagny. So, what do you say? Do we have a deal?" Not waiting for Andrew to answer, he continued: "Pays pretty good, but you'll have to give up your private cabin and tolerate living with a bunch of crazy kids. Sam'll be one of 'em. Also, you'll be in charge of chauffeuring the boys back and forth for things like doctors' appointments and football practice. There's the van out back you can use when you have to haul around a lot of kids. Of course, it gets lousy gas mileage and Jones the cook uses it a lot; you'll have to let him know when you need it."

Pulling a ring of keys from his pocket, he removed his spare set of van keys and handed them to Andrew. Then, cocking his head in thought, he said: "Tell you what. There's an old car of mine out in the barn I've been meaning to whip into shape for a long time, but I just never seem to get around to it. You can spruce it up if you want to, to use for most stuff." Drumming his fingers on the table, he studied Andrew intently for a moment before adding: "In fact, you fix 'er, you can have 'er! Ran fine last time I drove it—a few months ago. Looks like hell, though—but a car's a car, right?"

"Right!" Andrew agreed quickly, his head racing to keep up with everything Charlie was throwing at him. A car? That was beyond his wildest expectations. All he had asked the Universe for was to keep his job—nothing fancy. But it looked like he was getting far more than he had wished for; he wouldn't even be filling holes or slinging around a paint brush anymore.

"So, when can I look at it?" He hoped he wasn't appearing overeager.

"Anytime—door's open." Charlie pulled out his keys again and fumbled through them, looking for the one to the car. The expression on his face as he handed over the key told Andrew that he felt good about his decision.

Andrew could hardly contain himself. He wanted to jump up and run down to the barn right away. But, he was committed to spending the day hitting the books with Sam. Looking across the dining room, he saw the boy sitting patiently, waiting for Charlie's and his conversation to break up. Maybe he could drag Sam along with him to look at the car first.

Taking a last swig of his coffee, Charlie stood up to leave. "I'll have to split my time between here and the mothers' home for a while, so I'll probably become pretty dependent on you. Go ahead and move your stuff over to Bunkhouse C today, okay? I need you to be there tonight since the other fella is leaving this morning. Sam'll show you your quarters."

Andrew nodded his head up and down, smiling from ear to ear. He watched Charlie saunter out the door and then motioned nonchalantly to Sam to follow him. The boy caught up with him as he walked across the common.

"What are we doin'?" Sam seemed on edge, and Andrew knew he was starting to get the jitters about his first day at school.

"I just got hired on full-time, kiddo! And got a car to boot! C'mon, let's check out my new wheels." Sam silently fell in beside Andrew, and the two of them headed for the barn.

The door creaked on its hinges as Andrew struggled to open it. It was dark inside and the place was in a jumble. Sam pulled the other door open to shed more light on the interior. There, in the middle of the hay-strewn structure, was a tarped object that could only be an automobile. Andrew attacked it immediately, yanking on the ropes that tied the tarp down. Then Sam helped him lift the heavy canvas off the car.

"Is this your car?"

Andrew found himself speechless once again. Surely, it wasn't. But, quickly scanning the rest of the place, he determined this was the only car in it. Still, he wasn't sure he could trust his eyes.

"It's a Porsche 944, man! This car's worth some bucks. Looks like a '79. Must not have a motor in it, huh?" Sam instinctively ran his hands up and down the body of the car, admiring it as though it were a beautiful woman. "She's not too bad—a few dents and dings." He continued to walk around the car, inspecting it like a pro. "Chrome looks good; just needs to be buffed. Only reason it looks like shit is 'cause the paint's so bad. That ain't no big deal; after all, you got me around to help you, right?"

Andrew shook himself out of an immobilized stupor and, opening the car door, slid behind the seat. The interior wasn't great, but it wasn't that bad either. Shakily, he inserted the key and turned it, holding his breath. It groaned a couple of times as it cranked, and then caught, roaring strongly.

"Holy Hell, man! It actually runs!" Sam reached in the door and pulled the hood latch, then ran around and threw open the hood. "The engine looks pretty clean. Boy, you're one lucky son of a bitch!" Sam was literally jumping up and down in his excitement.

The two of them inspected the car for another half an hour, with Andrew all the while trying to figure out how in the world this could possibly be happening to him. A Porsche? What had he done right for a change? He wasn't at all sure that perhaps he wasn't still dreaming. Could this all be a big We-Be joke?

Finally, he and Sam begrudgingly quit fussing over the dream machine and walked back to Andrew's cabin to pack and move his things. There wasn't much to move, and they had him squared away in no time. Andrew's new quarters wouldn't be that bad; not as spacious as the other, but at least he still had his own bedroom and bathroom.

When they returned to the old cabin to tidy it up a bit, Sam sank down on the bed and looked around, a confused frown creasing his brow. Andrew silently observed him from the bathroom, curious as to what the boy was thinking so hard about.

"Worrying about school?"

Andrew's voice jerked him back to awareness, and Sam laughed, slightly embarrassed. "Huh? Uh . . . no. . . ." He stared at Andrew intensely for a second as if sizing him up. Then, seeming to decide it was okay to say whatever he had on his mind, he said guardedly, "This probably sounds whacko, but . . . it's just that I've always felt like somehow I've been here before."

"You mean Last Chance Ranch?"

"No, not that . . . I mean this room. I think I dreamt about it the night before I was brought here."

Andrew froze, but steadied his voice before speaking: "What was the dream about?"

"I don't remember, exactly. It's just a feeling, you know? Like I remember trying to figure out where I was, and I thought I was in J.D., but it was this cabin instead. Except that when I woke up, I was in the cop car and not here. Pretty weird, huh?"

Andrew reminded himself to breathe. Was it possible? It must be! Sam was unknowingly telling him that he was the simultaneous self Andrew had been on the lookout for. But he intuitively knew that he couldn't reveal to Sam his insight into the boy's "dream" experience. It would be too much for the boy to handle, especially since Andrew was still in the process of trying to deal with it himself.

"Not so weird. I've had all kinds of weird dream experiences myself," Andrew forced himself to say. "We'll sit down and philosophize about that kind of stuff sometime, okay?"

Sam looked comfortable with Andrew's reaction, and getting up, grabbed his books and followed Andrew out of the cabin.

In the face of this new revelation, it took all the discipline Andrew could muster to keep his mind focused on the task at hand: using these last precious hours to help Sam cram for his first day at school. Without any discussion or forethought, the two of them headed for the barn with its one sixty-watt bulb and the privacy it offered. Then, with their backs securely leaning on Andrew's new prized possession, they cracked the books again.

By dinner time, Andrew felt mentally exhausted, yet more exhilarated than he had been in months. Leaving Sam to study a little longer, he dragged himself happily to the chow hall to feed the growling stomach that he had forgotten to fill since breakfast. Dagny waved at him from the table where she was sitting with six or seven boys, and his heart lurched. He joined her, feeling a little better than usual about being in her presence. Now he was a full-fledged member of the staff and not just some drifter doing odd jobs.

"So, Charlie tells me you've signed on for the duration!" Her almond eyes sparkled, and Andrew could swear that the news greatly pleased her. Was it just his imagination?

"Yep! Figured I'd stick around for a while." Gathering up all the courage he could, he added, "I think I like it here." He looked straight into her marvelous eyes for a whole second without flinching or turning red. Now it was her turn to blush, and she did a good job of it as she dropped her eyes and smiled.

"There's another pow-wow planned for tomorrow night to give the kids a chance to share their experiences from their first day at school. Going to join us again?"

Well, if she had to change the subject, at least she did it by inviting him somewhere, Andrew thought, glowing inside. He wouldn't miss it for anything, and he told her so. For once, Dagny seemed short on words and floundered around for something to say. She was saved by a skinny kid who rushed up, breathless, to show her something.

"Look, Dagny! A *Latrodectus mactans*!" He shoved a jelly jar in her face. Startled, she instinctively drew back from the jar. "A what-who?"

Sighing as though humoring her, he grinned and said, "A black widow spider. See the red hourglass on its belly?" He held the jar high so she could see it from below.

Dagny flinched slightly, but tried to look interested. "Good going, Bugsy. Just make sure it doesn't get loose, okay?"

The wisp of a boy scurried off, holding the trapped arachnid in front of him like a trophy.

"Bugsy?" Andrew asked, laughing at Dagny's latest name creation.

"If the name fits . . ." Dagny laughed back, shaking her head and making a face. "Besides, it's a whole lot easier to say than 'Utsumi the Entomologist'!"

Andrew caught a glimpse of Sam slipping out of the dining room, plate in hand, obviously heading back to the barn to resume his studying. So, pulling himself away, he followed after his student to run him through his lessons one more time before lights-out. Now that he was a bunkhouse counselor, he had to be there to make sure all the boys, especially Sam, turned in early enough to get a good night's sleep. Which Andrew did: he and Sam were in their beds by eleven o'clock, though he could sense Sam anxiously tossing and turning throughout the night.

As the last boy climbed on the school bus, Andrew squinted to catch a glimpse of Sam sitting in the back seat. His student had been exceptionally quiet over breakfast in the middle of the ruckus created by his bunkmates, and Andrew could tell he was running and rerunning all the lessons silently through his head. Long after the bus disappeared over the hill, kicking up a trail of white dust in its wake, Andrew found it hard to get his thoughts off Sam and back to the ranch where they belonged. Looking down at his hands, he realized he had clenched his fists so tightly by his sides that he now had cramps in his wrists and fingernail dents in his palms.

"Calm down, don't worry!" he repeated to himself like a mantra as he flexed his hands and walked back to Bunkhouse C. But it was a hard thing to do. He knew deep down inside that this first day of school was a major turning point in the boy's life. If Sam failed today, he would always think of himself as a failure; but, if he succeeded, his whole life would be different from here on out. And now Andrew felt his responsibility for the boy's future tremendously magnified, for he knew, without a doubt, that Sam was his dumpster-diver self. They were related in a way that was deeper and more binding than even brothers could ever be.

Andrew resisted the impulse to spend the morning admiring his new car, and instead wiled away the time puttering around the bunkhouse, sweeping the floor and straightening things that weren't really out of place. He felt a strong impulse to be responsible to his new role. So far, the job as bunkhouse counselor was going smoothly. However, he couldn't help but think it was just beginner's luck. The boys had been almost too well-behaved the night before; surely ten troubled teens would eventually decide to put him through the ropes.

The sound of the lunch bell interrupted his latest worry-thought before it had a chance to take hold, and he strolled down to the dining hall to seek some company and pleasant distraction.

It was strange to see the place so deserted. The lack of noise was a little unnerving, and he almost jumped for joy when Charlie strolled in, breaking the silence by whistling some old rock 'n' roll tune.

"Hey, Andy, how goes it?" Charlie slopped some spaghetti on his plate and sat down across from his newest employee.

"Pretty good. I'm a little anxious about Sam's first day at school, I guess. Other than that, life couldn't be better!"

Charlie grinned at him with a mouthful of pasta, and raised his Coke bottle in a toast.

Andrew raised his bottle in return and cleared his throat nervously. "I don't even know how to begin to thank you for giving me that car; I still can't believe it. A Porsche! Are you really sure you want to do that?"

"It's already done. Besides, I wouldn't have done it if I hadn't wanted to. I've always felt like it's some kind of a sin against humanity to not use things and just let them waste away when there's someone else who can use those things and appreciate them. I seem to get things when I need them, so when I don't need them anymore I pass them on. Know what I mean?"

As usual, Charlie's logic sounded simplistically brilliant. Andrew tried hard to think of something equally profound to say. "I guess what goes around really does come around, huh?"

"Well now, that depends." Charlie leaned back in his chair and struck a relaxed pose. "I've heard tell that if you could throw a boomerang far and hard enough, it would circle the planet and come back to hit you in the back of the head. But the way I see it, whoever invented that theory didn't take a few things into consideration: like skyscrapers, tall trees—"

"Or mountains," Andrew finished for him.

"Exactly! Obstacles of all sorts that we don't see coming. Sometimes the nicest people end up thwarted at every turn."

Charlie briefly reflected on his own words before continuing: "Take the classic old cleaning lady who barely ekes out a living, for instance. She puts her kid through college, constantly gives and gives to other people, the whole time never thinking about herself. And yet, as kind and generous as she is, she never gets anything in return. Her boomerang never comes back."

Andrew leaned back in his chair also, unconsciously emulating his philosophizing boss. "Maybe that's because she's too busy scrubbing other people's floors. Maybe when her boomerang comes back it wings right over her bent head, without her even noticing it."

Charlie nodded his head and stared at Andrew appreciatively. He could tell he was going to enjoy having this young man around to match wits with.

"So, Andy, taking this old-cleaning-lady analogy a little further—why do you really think she doesn't get her 'just due'?"

Andrew thought for a moment, tapping his chin with his index finger. "Well, seems to me that she must have some kind of a mental block, or a poor self-image or something, that keeps her from thinking she's worthy enough to receive any good in return. So the good that would normally come back to her is deflected, and her life continues in a state of imbalance—heavy on the giving side of her nature—as she constantly tosses a boomerang into the air that never finds its way back into her hands."

"Think that applies to the other side of the coin, too? What about the fella who never gives and always demands? Suppose he's got his neck craned high, always on the lookout for everyone else's stray boomerangs?"

Charlie's questions made Andrew flash back on the "energy exchange" that We-Be had talked about in the beginning. He paused to think for a couple of seconds before responding: "I imagine that fella's life is imbalanced, too—though probably not in the same way as the cleaning lady's. Surely such abuses will eventually cause disturbances in other areas of his life, like his marriage or health or something."

"Interesting . . ." Charlie mused. "I guess whatever area a person focuses intently on is the area he'll find himself engrossed in—whether he thinks he wants to be there or not."

"And whether he likes it or not, he becomes very proficient at keeping his energy focused in that area."

"Perhaps at the expense of other areas."

Charlie and Andrew looked at each other in mutual surprise at how well they quite naturally think-tanked together. As Charlie stood up to leave he said: "We'll have to get together and do this again real soon. Maybe we can figure out how to save all the poor old cleaning ladies in the world from their own goodness."

Charlie closed the door behind him, leaving Andrew alone once again to try to avoid his worry-thoughts about Sam. Finally he couldn't resist peeking at his Porsche any longer; after all, he rationalized, it would help him get thoughts of the boy out of his head. Andrew had spent years dreaming about such a car, and now it had somehow found its way into his reality. It wasn't exactly the shiny red, right-off-the-showroom-floor model that he had anticipated, but he wasn't complaining. With any luck, Sam was as good as he claimed to be at doing body work. Funny how everything seemed to be coming together—just like magic.

As he sat in the driver's seat letting his imagination run free, his anxiety about Sam was temporarily replaced by visions of what his car would look like after it had been restored, and with thoughts about seeing Dagny at the pow-wow. He became so successfully absorbed in these pleasantries that he almost forgot the time. Checking his watch, Andrew was startled to realize the school bus was due any minute. He scrambled out of the car and dashed toward the main road, just in time to see the kids piling off the bus.

Standing on tiptoe, he tried to spot Sam among the throng of excited teenagers coming toward him. There he was, almost skipping down the hill, grinning from ear to ear. Every muscle in Andrew's body seemed to relax at once at the sight of the boy's face, making his knees threaten to buckle. "Sam!" He raised his hand high to get the boy's attention.

Sam trotted over to him, actually throwing a friendly smile at a couple of the other kids on his way. He clearly was feeling proud of himself. Suddenly, a strong sense of *déjà vu* hit Andrew. He had dreamt about this, hadn't he?

"You look pretty pleased with yourself!" he said under his breath, as Sam stood to one side while Andrew greeted some of the other boys from Bunkhouse C.

The two of them trailed after the others, dropping back far enough to be able to talk in private. As Sam proudly reported his success of the day, Andrew felt more and more waves of eerie familiarity wash over him. ". . . I even read out loud in class, and no one laughed at me or cracked off. I only mispronounced one word, and some of the kids did worse than me! And get this: This hot looking blonde babe sitting on my left couldn't keep her eyes off me. No shit!"

Obviously everyone had treated him like a regular guy. Andrew was ecstatic for Sam, and awed by the realization that he had known all this even before the boy had told him. As he listened to Sam jabber on, more animated than he had ever seen his student before, it suddenly occurred to him that he was experiencing first hand what We-Be had called a "future memory," catching up to itself in time.

"By the way, I got homework."

"You mean you have homework."

"Yeah, that's right. So, you gonna help me?"

"Only if you really need me. Do it early, okay? I want to go to the pow-wow tonight."

"Me too. It might be fun!"

Andrew was amazed at the complete change in the boy's attitude—and all because he had learned to read. He pondered this as they approached the bunkhouse.

"So, you proud of me, man?"

"You betcha. Not everyone has the determination to pull off what you did."

"Yeah! I really did something great, huh? It used to seem so impossible! Hey, wait a minute . . . how'd I do it, anyway?"

Andrew answered the boy without even thinking:

" *Space-Time Principle Number 18:*

To change a set pattern in your life,
you must first change your mind set.
Set your mind firmly on your desired goal
and allow the new pattern
to begin settling in."

"Space-Time Principle number what? What's a Space-Time Principle?"

Andrew heard Sam's question and heard his own words ringing in his head. What on Earth was going on? What was he doing anyway, reciting one of We-Be's Space-Time Principles so matter-of-factly? Then he stopped dead in his tracks, Sam staring at him curiously. What was happening here? We-Be had never given him that particular principle. And yet, he knew beyond a shadow of a doubt that it was, in fact, a valid principle. How could this be?

Andrew looked sideways at the boy, who was obviously confused by his strange behavior. Then, trying to smooth everything over as gracefully as possible, he answered: "Oh, just one of a bunch of little wisdoms that can help you understand life and make it through it in one piece. A good friend taught me some of them."

But apparently not all of them, he thought to himself, still perplexed over how he had pulled a new principle out of thin air.

Sam just shrugged his shoulders and returned to relishing his great achievement, Andrew's impromptu principle flying right over his head. It was enough for the boy to know he had done it; he didn't have to understand the whys and wherefores, at least not right now. He was well on his way, and would make it through life with much better odds than he had had a week ago.

♦   ♦   ♦

Andrew kept his eye on each of his boys, making sure they all did their homework and chores before dinner and the pow-wow. A couple of them kicked up a little fuss at first, but buckled under when they realized their new counselor would bar them from the night's festivities if they didn't cooperate. By dinner time they had all taken care of their responsibilities, and Andrew cut them loose to enjoy the rest of the evening.

Dinner was hectic with so many boys to concentrate on, and Andrew didn't even have a chance to think about seeing Dagny at the pow-wow. When the time came, however, he felt the old familiar giddiness returning.

He sought her out by the bonfire where she was sitting, bundled up in an old Indian blanket. Strings was happily strumming away on the outskirts of the circle as the rest of the boys talked freely about their assorted experiences at school. Andrew sat down quietly, trying not to interrupt Dagny's concentration on their dialogue.

"Hi!" Dagny whispered, the crooked smile touching the corner of her lips, her eyes still trained on the group.

Andrew reached over and squeezed her hand softly rather than answering her. He could sense her pulse quicken, and smiled to himself. This had turned out to be a fine day, indeed; maybe the best he could remember ever experiencing.

Charlie's booming voice jarred Andrew from his reverie, his silhouette looming large, obliterating Andrew's view of the fire. "Andy, m'boy! I have to take off tonight for the mothers' home to solve some minor crises that've developed."

He motioned for Andrew to follow him. They walked a few paces from the circle and Charlie rehashed all the things that would be expected of him. "Be sure to ask Dagny for help if there's anything you think you can't handle. I'm sure things'll run so smoothly you won't even know I'm gone. Right, pal?"

Andrew puffed up his chest and acted like he wasn't intimidated by his new responsibilities at all. His stomach was doing loops, but he surely didn't want his boss to know it. Deep down inside he knew he would do just fine.

Returning to the bonfire, Charlie consulted with Dagny briefly; then, slapping Andrew on the back, strode off into the darkness toward his car.

"That guy's a real enigma to me," Andrew sighed.

"How so?"

"Well, he does so much! One day he seems like a foreman, then the next day he seems like the head honcho. What exactly is his position around here, anyway?"

Dagny threw her head back and laughed, ponytail flying. "I thought you knew! He's the founder of both places—the man behind the vision."

"You mean he pays for all this stuff himself?"

She laughed again. "This and a whole lot more that you don't even know about. He's loaded—a millionaire a dozen times over."

Andrew was dumbfounded. He would never have guessed by the way Charlie acted and dressed: his down-to-Earth personality; his time-worn flannel shirts and shabby, beat-up boots. He supposed, in hindsight, that the gift of the car should have given him a clue. But, he must have been too absorbed with expecting gifts directly from the Universe to notice where his manifestations were actually coming from. Everything comes from somewhere, he remembered We-Be saying; and he realized he was truly recognizing that principle in action.

He thought about this latest revelation off and on throughout the evening, and ran other things We-Be had taught him through his head. She had been right: he could sense that he really would be okay from here on out; he was where he was supposed to be. The Porsche didn't even matter that much anymore—not that he wouldn't enjoy it. Even if it hadn't appeared in his life, he would still feel as contented as he did right now. We-Be had been one smart lady. He wondered if he'd ever see her again. . . .

"Andy?" He snapped back to his immediate surroundings at the sound of Dagny's voice.

"Yeah?"

"Nothing. I just wondered where you'd drifted off to." The expression on her face was so sweet it made him melt inside.

Andrew realized many of the boys had wandered back to their bunkhouses, leaving just a handful of kids crouched around the dwindling fire. He tried to get We-Be and Dagny out of his mind long enough to pay some attention to the hodgepodge of youthful conversations going on around him:

"Can I borrow your sweatshirt tomorrow?"

"Math's easy, man; just think about money. . . ."

"Did you see her legs?"

"Check it out, a firefly!"

Alerted, Andrew sat up straight and strained his eyes to see the tiny point of light zipping around a stand of trees behind the group of boys, whose conversation continued:

"You mean a *Photuris pennsylvanica*."

"Huh?"

"A *Photuris pennsylvanica*—a nocturnal beetle with light-pro-ducing organs."

"Oh no, Bugsy's at it again!" Dagny giggled and leaned her head on Andrew's shoulder.

"Hey, Dagny, quick!" Bugsy appeared in front of them in a flash, hand extended toward Dagny's coffee mug. "Can I borrow your cup? I don't have one of those in my collection yet and I need something to catch it in!"

As Dagny moved to give the budding entomologist her mug, Andrew's hand darted out and caught her wrist.

"Bugsy, you lay one finger on that firefly and I'll stick you in a cup to see how you like it!" Andrew made the statement lightly as though he were clowning around, yet somehow, at the same time, his words seemed to carry great authority.

Dagny and Bugsy froze, confusion registering on their faces.

"Didn't anyone ever tell you that fireflies are sacred?" His intentness over an insect caused the two of them to continue to stare at him in bewilderment.

Getting up, he helped Dagny to her feet and secured her coffee mug in his jacket pocket. "It's a long story, guys. Maybe I'll tell it to you someday." Throwing his arm around Bugsy's shoulder, he walked with the counselor and her charge toward the main house, his focus locked on the tiny luminescent speck that was busy spinning magical circles of light in the starry sky.

About the Author

Jan Longwell-Smiley is a graphic designer and editor in Central Florida. For the past eight years she has been the editor of *Just Peace*, Florida's peace, justice, and environmental newspaper.

Her essays, short stories, and articles have appeared in numerous newspapers and magazines. She writes on a variety of topics, ranging from Native American rights to the nuclearization of space.

As president of the Florida Coalition for Peace and Justice, one of the largest and oldest progressive groups in the country, and as a founding member of Voices for Justice, a social justice action network, she is well-known throughout the state as a spokesperson and grassroots organizer.

THE MOLE AND THE OWL
A Romantic Fable about Braving the Wide World for Love
Charles Duffie

A romantic fable involving a mole transformed by the love of an owl. When the owl mysteriously disappears, the mole overcomes his timid nature and goes in search of his lost love. He enters a world of wolves and eagles, of new dangers and ancient joy, a world where he discovers that life is wider than he ever knew and love is a journey that never ends.

The author is well versed in classic children's literature, and is an accomplished storyteller and illustrator. His vision and dedication to his craft are evident throughout the work. Duffie's poignant message of love, faith, and undying devotion will be treasured as a classic by young and old alike. Readable on a variety of levels, as a fairytale, as a modern fable, and as a purely enjoyable love story. For those we love, a lesson and love story as old as the world, true as the wind, and brighter than the sun.

7 x 9¼, hardcover with jacket, Full color illustrations, 120 pages, 1-57174-082-1, $18.95

NAKED INTO THE NIGHT
Monty Joynes

Upon examining his life, Winn Conover, successful businessman and pillar of his community, discovers that "something was missing. It was not material. . .it was something inside." Investigating further, he learns that he is much more than the maddening clutter of his life. Finding that sacred self within but unable to maintain its presence, he walks out of his suburban home one night naked, stripped of his old identity. Thus begins a spiritual odyssey that takes him across the country working as a casual laborer, eating and sleeping in truck stops, sharing his wisdom with his new friends. In Santa Fe, living among the pueblo Indians, he becomes "Anglo Who Became Chief Old Woman's Son." But, before he can claim his new identity, he must return to his family and allow them to release him.

5½ x 8½ trade paper, 256 pages, ISBN 1-57174-055-4, $11.95

LOST IN LAS VEGAS
Monty Joynes

In *Naked into the Night*, Winn Conover leaves his suburban home and family to begin a new life among the Native Americans of the Southwest. In the second book of Joynes' trilogy, *Lost in Las Vegas*,

Conover, now called "Anglo" by the people of the tribe, is tasked by tribal elders to go to Las Vegas and retrieve a prodigal son. Like himself before his spiritual awakening, White Wing is lost in a world of mediocrity and physical vice. Anglo gradually gains White Wing's respect, but ultimately, it is a shared vision quest which reveals the path home to both Anglo and White Wing. Masterful and compelling fiction from one of the best Visionary Fiction writers of our day. Look for the the third book in the series, *Save The Lost Seed*, in 1999.

5¼ x 8¼ trade paper, 304 pages, ISBN 1-57174-089-9, $12.95

SOUL SWORD
The Way and Mind of a Warrior
Vernon Kitabu Turner

As a young black man from the South, the author studied martial arts for self-protection and became a legendary black belt and sensei. Then, studying and mastering Zen meditative practices, he discovered the missing heart of modern martial arts: the understanding that technique must "arise effortlessly out of emptiness, out of no-knowledge." In his art he found the center where "the techniques I performed in fact were performing me." In *Soul Sword*, Turner develops this insight into a unique spiritual practice, replete with exercises for stilling the mind amidst the turmoil of modern life and releasing ourselves to the point where "the action and the actor [are] a seamless thread."

"Vernon Turner's writings are poignantly beautiful." — Gwendolyn Brooks

5 x 8, trade paper, 144 pages, ISBN 1-57174-039-2, $9.95

THE MT. PELÉE REDEMPTION
Stephen Hawley Martin

In 1995, the author met Claire, who told him an amazing story. This is the story of Claire, her father, his lover, and the volcano.

When her father suddenly falls ill with no explicable cause, leaving Claire with only cryptic information about "50 years ago, seven o'clock, eighth of May," she begins to follow the clues to her father's mysterious illness. She quickly finds herself in the Caribbean, where perilous adventures await. There, Claire undergoes a ritual that allows her to re-live the events that took place 50 years before on the island of Martinique. This amazing journey, both within and outside her physical body, gives her the answers she needs to help her father, and learn more about herself and life here on Earth.

A thoroughly charming and entertaining page-turner, *The Mt. Pelée Redemption* represents the best that Visionary Fiction has to offer: a story that seamlessly balances insight with adventure, and inner- exploration with life in the real world, the here and now.

5½ x 8½ trade paper, 224 pages, ISBN 1-57174-116-X, $12.95

Hampton Roads Publishing Company

. . . for the evolving human spirit

Hampton Roads Publishing Company
publishes books on a variety of subjects including
metaphysics, health, complementary medicine,
visionary fiction, and other related topics.

For a copy of our latest catalog,
call toll-free, 800-766-8009,
or send your name and address to:

Hampton Roads Publishing Company
134 Burgess Lane
Charlottesville, VA 22902
e-mail: hrpc@hrpub.com
www.hrpub.com